carrying Battlescars

ReproBate saga Book IX

By: S.L. Kotar and J.E. Gessler

Ahead of the Press
St. Louis, MO

carRying
Battlescars

the ReproBate saga
Book IX

S.L. KOTAR & J.E. GESSLER

Library of Congress Cataloguing-in-Publication Data

carrying Battlescars   ReproBate saga Book IX   /
S.L. Kotar and J.E. Gessler

ISBN   KINDLE   978-1-945594-47-2   (ebook)
ISBN   PAPERBACK   978-1-945594-48-9

Ahead of The Press Publishing
St. Louis, Missouri

SUMMARY OF THE REPROBBATE SAGA BOOKS

The ReproBate saga
Book I

Beneath the Rose

Daring. Resourceful. Devil-may-care. Moody. Superstitious. Gambler. Confederate blockade-runner. Captain Rudy Blake was many things to many people, but there as one descriptive word upon which they all agreed. Reprobate.
Captain Blake not only reveled in the nickname, he had the audacity to name his ship after himself. *The Reprobate*. Not a smoke-belching steamer but a swift, sleek four-massed schooner capable of out running the Federal gunboats and slipping behind those dangerous, ponderous vessels to deliver what the wealthy citizens of the Confederacy most sought: luxuries

A man who swore allegiance to no cause but his own, in the opening months of 1863 Blake confronts a Union squadron blocking his entrance into Charleston harbor. Cunningly outfoxing Admiral Meechum's flagship, he discovers a prize greater than the Union gunboats in the officer's quarters — a female passenger named Miss Rose Theodore. Not only does she admit to being the admiral's mistress. she divulges the combination to his safe where Rudy finds Meechum's Master's papers, a horde of cash and the naval plans for the spring campaign. More significantly, Rose reveals a plot hatched between Meechum and Jefferson Davis whereby the president of the Confederacy has traded Blake's itinerary in exchange for the delivery of heavy field ordnance. The deal was consummated, she deduces, because Davis was unable to trust the South's most successful gun-runner because he refused to take the oath of allegiance to the CSA.

The Yankee prostitute and the Southern mercenary form an unusual partnership that leads them to Richmond and near fatal adventures

The ReproBate saga
Book II
skull and cRossBones

Escaping Civil War-torn Richmond, Captain Rudy Blake and Rose Theodore, the newest member of the blockage-runner *Reprobate,* sail for England. During the voyage Rudy and Rose's relationship deepen as he has the opportunity of teaching her shipcraft, armament and the nuances of sailing. Working together to thwart a  plot by the notorious Captain Janey, the pair begin a "conquest" of Victorian England that includes establishing Rose as his chandler, the purchase of the Blake House and a foray into high society where a spirited drinking contest proves one's mettle over the other.

The ReproBate saga
Book III

Redefining Bastions

Leaving Rose Theodore behind in England to serve as his chandler, Captain Rudy Blake returns to war-torn Richmond. Ordering his crew to wait for him aboard his blockage-running ship Reprobate, he travels to Atlanta where he intends to oversee to his wartime enterprises. During the long and uncomfortable train ride, he falls asleep and is transported back in time to relive his experiences of a year ago. In 1862, Atlanta is a rawboned city desiring to become the center of the Confederacy's manufacturing and transportation. Already

having established himself as a speculator and silent partner in numerous operations, Rudy wheels and deals but finds he has met his match when he challenges the gods. They set out to beat their favorite plaything at his own game, with tragic consequences for the man who believes he has no heart.

The ReproBate saga
Book IV
thickeR than Blood

Rudy and Rose are separated by an ocean and
the even wider gulf of the ever-pressing War
Between the States but are never far from each
other's thoughts.

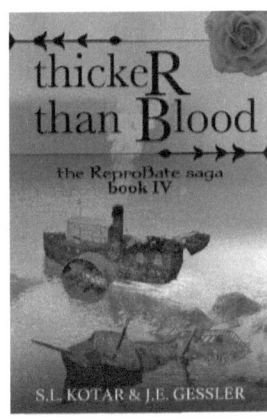

During his absence, Rose has successfully
established herself as Rudy's chancellor, using
the Blake House just outside London as her
"port" of operations. She has procured war
materiel beyond even her wildest dreams and
anxiously awaits Rudy's return, only too well
aware of the danger he faces bringing his
schooner through the Union blockade at Wilmington.

The *Reprobate's* arrival into Liverpool harbor immeasurably relieves her
concern for his safety and marks the beginning of another whirlwind set of
new and unexpected adventures. His familiarity with the Continent has
them hobnobbing with London's high society, walking hand-in-hand
through the streets of Paris and meeting and paying homage to a Jamaican
witch. In an unexpected turn of events, Rudy fulfils his promise to share a
storm at sea by bringing Rose with him on his return to the Confederate
States. With her help, he and the crew evade the costal blockade of five
Union warships and participate in the celebrations that ensue with the
Reprobate's successful arrival into Wilmington.

With his reputation as a scoundrel and reprobate alerting the unfriendly
Rebel authorities to keep an eye on the pair, they encounter both known
and unforeseen dangers before returning to England in what they both
realize will be one of his last voyages before she is compelled to sell his
ships. With the realization the War is drawing to a close, they must also
face the fact his obligation is to bring Elspeth back with him to England – a
task neither anticipate with anything but dread.

The ReproBate saga
Book V
prioR Battles

After running the Federal blockade and returning to England, Rudy and Rose have three days to spend together before he is compelled to return across the Atlantic. To use that time together in a meaningful way, Rose requests Rudy tell her of his youth. Beginning with the tragic circumstances leading to his expulsion from VMI, his return to Charleston and subsequent disinheritance, he then details for her, in words so vivid she experiences his adventures alongside him, his voyage to San Francisco and foray into the gold fields as a '49er.

The flashback, seen through the perspective of the innocent youth, carries them through hope and expectation, misery and failure; a sea voyage and the birth of San Francisco; a friend, many enemies and a life-and-death struggle that leaves Rudy scarred, both physically and mentally, for life. Yet, in the telling of it to his soulmate, Rudy's love for Rose deepens and that gives him the courage to face a very uncertain future when he returns to Southern soil and the raging Civil War.

The ReproBate saga
Book VI

Requited Blasphemy

Reluctantly keeping his promise to sell his fleet of blockade-running vessels when he sensed the War was drawing to a close, Captain Rudy Blake returns to the States in order to fulfill one other obligation: bring Elspeth out of Charleston and deliver her safely to England. As Rose Theodore predicted, the young child-bride refuses to go unless accompanied by her parents. Obstinate that he will not bring the slave trader, Rudy offers her an ultimatum: come with me or stay behind. Unable to make up her mind, he departs for Atlanta where he intends to wait out the waning months before writing her off forever and seeing to his own escape.

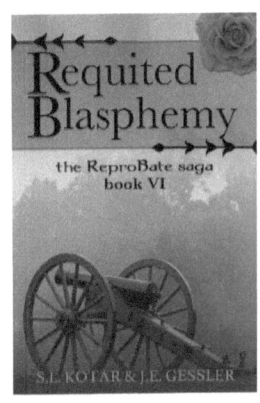

Intent on having the gunrunner save herself and her husband as well as her daughter, Mrs. Odanagh and her family arrive in Atlanta, where she sends Elspeth to Ruth's bachelor rooms, hoping to manipulate his feelings into serving her wishes. She nearly succeeds but as the months pass it becomes obvious they have waited too long: the Federal Army is on the doorstep of Atlanta and it is now too late to escape.

As the enemy enters the city environs, Rudy's loyalty turn to the Blake Brigade. Helping his black "crew" save victims of their church bombing, he discovers his favorite, Cottonball, critically injured. Rising his life to procure a horse and wagon, he takes the boy to a spiritual healer and then departs the burning city, certain, now, of only one thing: he must go to war and die

The ReproBate saga
Book VII
the waR Between

Atlanta has fallen and Rudy Blake has left the city, penniless and without hope. Following in the footsteps of the ragtag Confederate Army, he comes upon an officer and makes the startling announcement he wishes to join up. Proving his prowess with a rifle, he signs his name on the enlistment form and is assigned to the sharpshooters. Here, Private Blake gets his first taste of what war really means: deprivation, fear, loss, death and a despair deeper than any he has ever experienced.

After a particularly dispiriting encounter with Federal forces, he is overheard commenting on the lack of artillery support and after being questioned about his background to discover he had training in the long arm at the Virginia Military Institute, is transferred to the artillery.

Although his desire for death remains paramount in his mind, the friendship of the youthful officer in charge of Battery B, Lieutenant Benjamin Montgomery, and the companionship of the other men compel him to fight, if not for his own life, then for theirs. Instructing them in tactics and the proper care of the equipment, he soon has Battery B the best trained and most accurate company in the Army of Tennessee. None of this matters, however, until he's tasted battle and put his courage to the test. This comes soon enough, with devastating losses that decimate both the Rebel forces and the artillery corps. That he survives these encounters while so many did not confuses him to the point he considers the fact he may be losing his mind.

Broken in body and spirit, Rudy, Benjamin and Battery B are reassigned and are compelled to make a horrendous trek across a bitter winter landscape to arrive in time for spring campaigning against an enemy they have no prayer of stopping, much less defeating. Without prospects of hope, and little more chance of staying alive, the artillerists of Battery B wait out the end of the terrible and tragic War Between the States.

The ReproBate saga
Book VIII
To Richmond or Bust

People called it the Civil War, but it was decidedly uncivil. Newspaper reporters styled it, "The War of Brother against Brother," but the wounds cut far deeper than that. Southerners referred to the years 1861-1865 as "The War of Northern Aggression." It was "Mr. Lincoln's War," "the War over Slavery," "the War to save the Union." It was everything, in fact, but, "The War to End all Wars."

Rudy Blake went to war to die but he did not die. Instead, he suffered through one soul-shattering defeat after another, until his private world shrunk to nothing but marching to hell, fighting senseless battles, protecting the vanguard of Hardee's decimated Corps and suffering personal torments that nearly destroyed both his body and his mind.

After the final degradation of surrender at Durham Station, Rudy has one resolution in mind: get to Richmond where he hopes to make one positive outcome before fulfilling the prophesy he made to himself after the fall of Atlanta. He must find some way to grant Benjamin Montgomery's wish to "give back" and make amends for what he had committed during "the Late Unpleasantness." To do so, these two starving and beaten men must subjugate themselves to yet another humiliation: the attainment of a pardon, before attempting to establish any sense of normalcy in their beleaguered lives.

Hardly recognizable to his old friend Mae Williams of the Weeping Willow Saloon, Rudy makes arrangements for his friend and then prepares himself for the greatest and perhaps the most perilous journey of his life: across the Atlantic to England and Rose Theodore.

Table of Contents

DEDICATION

carrying Battlescars

the ReproBate Saga Book IX

This book is dedicated to those who selflessly work at Wild Bird Rehabilitation in St. Louis, Missouri. Through their tireless efforts, the love they exude for these tiny patients and the efforts they put into saving precious lives, many a songbird (and pigeons, too) are released back into the wild, having recovered from grievous injuries. You are my friends, my fellow volunteers, and the miracle workers who do God's work. Bless you all.

SLK

And JEG, always

CHAPTER 1

It was June 1, 1865, and he was as dead as his past could make him. As cold and stiff as "Stonewall Jackson." As worthless as the hopes and prayers of one million Southerners. As silent as the Rebel yell.

Leaving behind the three spires of Richmond that marked both the approaches to the former capital of the Confederacy and the roads leading away from it, Rudy Blake pulled his coat closer around him and did not look back. The War was over, and he had played his part: captain, infamous gunrunner, factory owner, arms and munitions manufacturer, president of the Southern Central Railroad and finally, for the last, most grueling eight months of the conflict, a private in the Army of Tennessee. It had not been his war, yet his life had been inextricably interwoven into it. Now it was over, and there was no going back.

The times, they were a'changin' and he more than anyone.

Rudy was sick, tired and discouraged. There were no more rules: at least, none any citizen dwelling "below the Dardanelles" of the Mason-Dixon Line understood. The Old Order had died as inglorious a death as the Cause they had struggled to sustain. There were no longer any terms to dictate. Like everything else, those expectations had perished upon the crosses of defeat.

Unconditional surrender. Lee had capitulated at Appomattox Court House and Johnston at Durham Station. The Civil War had drawn to a bitter termination, and with it, the *Book of the Dead* had closed, numbering 600,000 new additions to its honor roll. The names not therein inscribed in blood and pus and splintered bone went home. All but Rudy Blake. He had no home.

Once, he had claimed by dint of association, a magnificent rice plantation along the Ashley River, renowned for the brilliant array of flowers lining the approaches to the mansion. That, and the three story townhouse in Charleston that boasted the finest silver tea service in all the Carolinas.

Once, there existed a mighty clipper ship named *Reprobate*, where her captain could climb the mast and view the world in miniature. Part of what he saw was a warehouse along the waterfront with curtains on the windows. In an bachelor suite in the Atlanta Hotel, there was a room where a man with money could overlook the vastness of his empire. There was even a Sporting Palace in that soon-to-be capital city of Georgia with a piano and a proprietress which might be said to belong to him.

But these were homes of the past. Flowering Tree had been burned to the ground by General Sherman, the intricate irrigation ditches and lovingly-arranged horticultural monuments trampled and destroyed. The townhouse had been, or would be, lost to back taxes by the new Federal authorities, its ancestral heirlooms stolen and scattered to sundry Northern states.

The warehouse, the one piece of property to which he bore legitimate claim, had likely suffered the fate of so many other waterfront buildings, bombarded or torched by either friend or foe, its curtains ripped asunder like so many flags of battle. The ship, sleekest, fastest and most feared of any which braved the Union blockade, boasted a new owner, some fool who thought his luck and the War would last forever.

The suite in Atlanta had undoubtedly been gutted, desecrated and given over to the Provost Marshal, for uses only the United States Congress could guess. The whorehouse, whether or not it still retained its former owner, undoubtedly served as the partying ground for a hoard of conquering Yankees.

There was not one single place, South or North, that Rudy Blake could claim, or be claimed by. He had no home. The War was over, and he was homeless.

He was homeless, yet he was going home. Not to Charleston, where he had been disinherited and rejected; not back to the sea, for he had sold his ship, betrayed her into the hands of another, greedier owner, more foolhardy than he; not to Atlanta, where he had committed the most grievous sin a man could ever perpetrate upon himself.

Rudy was going home to England, to a place where roses grew; where a new set of curtains adorned the windows of a house called "Blake."

Rudy Blake was as dead as his past, and now he needed life. He was going home to Rose "Bud" Theodore. To his best second self.

It was a four hour trip from Richmond to City Point, where he would be able to take a small river boat to Norfolk. The carriage ride was bumpy and uncomfortable, each jolt sending waves of pain through his emaciated frame. Other passengers aboard the horse-drawn conveyance pushed and shoved him away from the glassless windows, staring with dull fascination at the earthworks constructed as both a first and last line of defense against an invading army.

These held no interest to Rudy, however, and he finally sacrificed his position against the wall to free himself from the curious. He had seen war first-hand; had helped erect earthworks very similar to those they now passed, hiding behind and charging over those better constructed by the enemy. He had pulled blue and grey bodies and bits of arms and legs from underneath those blown-out walls, burying those faceless, nameless, lifeless men who had depended on such ineffective barriers to stop the bullets and the cannon balls.

What piqued his curiosity were the scant acres of newly sown crops. Indian corn grew, but none of the stalks were over three feet tall. Other tracts held wheat, desultory and untended. Nowhere did he see men in those fields; no wagons traversed the rutted, dirt roads, no gangs of laborers sawed trees, plowed earth or supervised others do the dirty work for them.

With a little imagination, he could believe a great hand had emerged from the clouds and scooped up all the inhabitants. The countryside was as deserted as if word had just arrived that General Grant was marching on Richmond, destroying everything under his feet.

And then he remembered. That word *had* come and the devastation it wrought was still being felt. Property titles were in flux, slaves had been freed and too many men had perished.

Robert E. Lee had dallied too long before surrendering. With defeat inevitable, he had malingered, prolonging the agony, not only for the present, but destroying the future, as well. His battle-weary troops should already have been home, getting in the spring planting, herding cattle into greening pastures, supervising the lambing, repairing the chicken coops. Instead, these farmer-soldiers had been kept in starvation, rotting their hearts and their bodies out on the battlefields of Virginia.

It was Lee who held the reins, and Rudy blamed him exclusively. Lee, son of the self-proclaimed Revolutionary War hero Light Horse Harry Lee, had wanted power, and they had given it to him. By 1865 he had been the commander-in-chief of all Confederate armies, the last, great hope of the Confederacy. Having just passed through the great winter of discontent, the freezing months of 1776 all over again, it was time to rally the discouraged, to thunder out in a theatrical, well-rehearsed voice, "God for

Harry, England, and Saint George!" It was time to imitate the action of the tiger: the great *American* tiger.

Lee's place in history was in his ability to win. There was no place for losers in the gilded pages of textbooks; the prayers of his men, the beseeching of the widows and their orphans to end the conflict fell on deaf ears. Henry V had won and he became king; George Washington had won and he became president. If Lee won, he would have his choice of either; if he lost, he would be no more than a footnote, buried between the dusty covers of an unread tome on military blunders.

Students at West Point, where he had so conspicuously graduated so many years before, would not speak his name with reverence; they would not compare his tactics with the great generals of the past; nor would they revere him, emulate him. No one wished to emulate a general, whose interior lines and thousand miles of coast gave him the historical tactical advantage.

The War should have ended in 1863, but it had not. Lee dragged the conflict into Pennsylvania, forever altering a defensive struggle into one of aggression, discovering to his cost, that the lessons so well learned on the battlefields of Europe did not apply to America. Without "Stonewall" Jackson's lightning strike-and-run, superior numbers had prevailed, condemning the South to defeat.

Rudy remembered the glory days of '61, when the fire-eaters had bragged and boasted, saluting the mettle of the cavalier while sipping their mint juleps underneath spreading, ancestral trees. He recalled the Southern youths, wealthy, educated, spoiling for a fight, eyes bright with imagined triumphs. He remembered how they scorned him; how he was not willingly received.

In April, 1861 when President Abraham Lincoln issued his famous call for 10,000 men to defend the Union, Rudy Blake had been thirty-three years old. He was reasonably wealthy, established, and set in his ways. He had survived horrendous challenges, suffered irreparable hurts. He was, he fancied, a man alone: a man without a country, without a friend, without a family.

This isolation was by choice, and he reveled in the idea of war. Not, as so many others did, for the opportunity to shower himself with glory. Rudy had no need of the good opinion of others. He had learned early in life that the one, true, outstanding virtue a man could achieve was wealth. Let others fight for heroism, or States Rights. Let them go to War over slavery, or to preserve a way of life. Those were issues which did not concern him.

He would fight in a peripheral sense – neither on the battlefield, nor the stately halls of Congress – Union or Confederate. Rudy's war was not about color: he did not favor white over black, grey above blue. His "war," the only contest which truly mattered, was waged as a competition. His fight was against those who would steal his chances for success.

He fought against fellow gunrunners, businessmen, railroaders, schemers and those confidence men who would prevent him from fulfilling his one, all abiding dream: to be the richest man on earth. Only when he had achieved that exulted status would he be satisfied; only then could he stand upon the pinnacle of power and piss on the world.

There was no god greater than money, no king on earth capable of sustaining his God-given authority without it. No poor man, no matter how bright or intuitive, was worth a plugged nickel without backing. Money was the root of all good, the comfort and security of any age, the beginning and the end. It was A to Zed, the power and the glory.

What was an emperor without an exchequer? What good a president who oversaw a country lacking the means of controlling it? How effective a general without the wherewithal to pay his troops? How existed a captain without a ship? What worth love without the ability to buy affection? All were false who denied the power of money.

God's servants collected their tithe from the faithful. Governments taxed their subjects. Officers promised rewards to the brave. Ship captains were more effective when offering huge bonuses to their crews. The penniless lover was scorned in favor of the wealthy suitor.

Rudy had smelled the scourge of war long before his brethren; he had heard it whispered upon the wind, sensed the restless urgings of the masses, read between the lines of the pacifists. Without the least shred of faith in compromise or debate, he had correctly interpreted the signs in the eyes and hearts of men and prepared himself. While others vacillated, prayed, delayed and denied, Rudy Blake schemed.

While there was undoubtedly money to be made as a contractor or a supplier in the North, the real profit would come from the South. Consequently, he assessed the areas of greatest need, coldly calculated how he could fulfill them, then bided his time. When war came, he was ready.

Offering his services, if not his loyalty, to the Confederacy, this native son became their greatest hero: the man who shone, not on the battlefield, but on the High Seas. Without shedding one single drop of Union red, he defeated the Federal Navy with cunning, ingenuity and the blessings of Neptune, himself.

What those patriots who looked to him as their savior failed to realize, however, was that "Blake the Snake," was not working for them, but in a perverted sense, against them. He understood, where they did not, the greatest victories would come by supplying cigars, French brandy and custom fowling pieces to the aristocracy.

If was, after all, another confirmation of Rudy's religion. Just as he believed "money made the man," so too did his fellow Southerners, those great plantation owners, slave masters, warmongers, beacons of learning and bearers of family heritage. They were the ones who bankrolled the Confederacy.

Deprived of their silk shirts and brocaded vests, they would withhold support from the Cause, no matter how closely allied they might be to its politics. Captain Blake did not risk his life bringing in medicine for the wounded, uniforms, shoes, muskets or tinned goods for the soldiers. He smuggled through champaign, whalebone stays, parasols and the latest European fashions.

That was where the profit lay, and ironically, the false belief a way of life could be preserved.

Before the ink had dried on the declaration of secession, the final paragraphs of the Articles of Confederation drafted, the first puffs of gunpowder dissipated over Fort Sumter, Captain Rudy Blake was ready. With Confederate contracts in one pocket and a hundred thousand requests for luxury items in the other, he had put his ship to sail.

The early days of war were easy. They were child's play to a schemer, a scalawag – a *scamp* - such as he, for he had not yet achieved his greatest accolade: *reprobate*.

That was for the future – a future which was now his past. In one of the great ironies of war, he had achieved all that he desired, only to throw it away by one simple, rash act. After the fall of Atlanta, he had enlisted as a common soldier.

There was no rhyme or reason for his willful abandonment of common sense. Rose Theodore could have explained, for she, in her great wisdom, had foreseen such an eventuality. But Rose had not been there; she was four thousand miles away, praying to her God and his gods on Olympus to preserve his life.

That was all she dared ask, and at that, she requested a great deal, for any rebel man, boy or beast caught up in the final, agonized months of unrelenting bloodshed was a prime candidate for a shallow grave.

She knew, without being told, there would be no victories for her star-crossed lover; no parades, no claiming a hard-contested field, no Thanks from Congress. He promised her he would return to England and safety and he had lied. Not willingly, for he would not, could not have believed such a fate awaited him. He had laughed and vowed, with the sincerity of an innocent, he would return within two months.

It is not my War, Rose and I have no stake in it. I have no duty to any but myself.

Those were his words, but not his heart. Even if he had not seen as much, she had, for she knew him better than he knew himself. Whether it was the capture of Charleston Harbor, the fall of Atlanta, or an event so inconsequential it was not worthy of note in the Yankee newspapers she read with the intensity of one possessed, she felt instinctively he would be touched.

Gone for a soldier was what she had been told. *I heard Rudy enlisted. Can you fathom that?*

Yes, she had thought. I can "fathom" that. Why he went was beyond the comprehension of his crew, released to her charge, but not to the woman who served as his chandler, bookkeeper and ostensive wife. He had "gone" because beneath the hard exterior, he bled as copiously as any sentient man. He was a Southerner and the North was destroying his land. He was a gentleman and the Union was raping his people.

It was to Rose Theodore that Rudy Blake was returning. That he was not the man he had been was a secret he thought to hide and she already knew.

CHAPTER 2

Rudy did not remember reaching City Point, nor did he recall booking passage on the small, dilapidated river boat which would take him to Norfolk. It was with considerable surprise and consternation he discovered himself leaving the boat and stepping ashore in the city which self-proclaimed itself the "hotbed" of secession.

Taking his luggage, consisting of a small, hand-held carpet bag, Rudy alit after the bulk of passengers had departed. He had neither the strength nor the desire to fight a mad rush. Nor was there any point. One thing soldiering had taught him: "hurry up and wait" was a constant of life. The harder people scrambled to get ahead, the longer they waited to be pushed back.

Norfolk was far busier than the waterside at Richmond. To Rudy's confused, numbed brain, the pace was dizzying. Incoming Northerners, eager for their slice of the pie, shouted orders for their trunks to be removed. Outgoing, sullen Southerners, seeking passage to New York or Boston to beg an extension of their outstanding, pre-war loans, hunched their shoulders, casting dark looks, universally ignored.

Black-skinned boys and pale-eyed whites hawked lard-fried pies, lemonade and seasonal fruit, but behind their wails were darker, more menacing sounds. Inextricably intertwined within the pitch and hue of their cries were menacing noises that defied comprehensible articulation. It was a type of anger, a rebellion of spirit, rather than body; a restlessness four years of war had not quenched.

Dirty, rag-clad Caucasians, whose expressions betrayed open discontent, wandered the wharves, with nothing more productive to do than wish ill will on their fellow human beings. Their underlying animosity, not merely toward the freed Negro, but for their lot in life, bode no good for any who happened to run afoul of their disfavor. They were spoiling for a fight, and did not care who they accosted. Bloodshed had become a way of life: one they had not chosen, but now stained their souls.

If one war had terminated, another was just beginning. This conflict was the back alley sort, silent, furtive, insidious. Instead of toting the heavy, nearly useless muskets of their enlistment, the new weapons of choice were knives and rocks. Rather than maintain a semblance of military discipline, these "troops" were each an army of one, with no greater aspiration than day-to-day survival.

The world owed them a living, and take it they would, by theft, robbery and murder. Vagabonds without law, these guerrillas of the Lost Cause looked to the likes of John Mosby and Nathan Bedford Forrest for inspiration. Those wayward soldiers became the true heroes of defeat; men who knew how to loot and plunder for their own especial gain, the "grey ghosts" who slipped in and out without being seen, leaving a score of slit throats as a token of their esteem.

There were Yankees enough for these men to find sport, but it was not just the conquering soldiers they abhorred. The world had become their enemy, and no white planter, Southern woman, or former nigger-landowner was their friend. They wanted what they could not have; craved what they had never possessed. Armed conflict had given them a taste of something just out of their reach. Now, that brass ring had been snatched away and they were determined to go after it.

Rudy counted over one hundred of this group before abandoning the attempt as hopeless. He could only pray his formidable height and flushed brow would scare them away, for were they to discover the true weakness of his flesh, he would be consumed by their insatiable wrath in an instant.

"Hotel! Hotel! Ride ya all ta da hotel!" a boy of indeterminate color bellowed at the departing passengers. He might have been part African, or he may simply have wallowed in filth so long his true complexion no longer showed through "Virginia's bloody soil." Whatever his origins, he was ignored. That did not stop his repetitions, however, and Rudy was finally forced to drop his bag and place his hands over his ears to block out the incessant noise.

Long after the child had finally secured a client and dragged him away to "hotel!" the words ran through his brain, until he thought he would go mad. *Hotel! Hotel! Ride ya all ta da Hotel!* The noise, the confusion, the utter preponderance of ill will; the thoughts of countless men all directed with vicious intent upon the other, was enough to sap whatever strength he had.

He wished he had taken Benjamin, the boy lieutenant adopted from the ranks of the defeated, with him. With Benjamin by his side, he would have been able to block out the hatreds festering in the air, going about his business with a semblance of normalcy. Concentrating on the boy's incessant chatter, taking amusement, if not delight, in listening to him discourse on the various foodstuffs, would have forced him to maintain a semblance of sanity. Buying him a penny pie and observing how the juice run from his eager lips would have elicited a smile from the former private's humorless lips.

Should have, could have... but had not.

Rudy had not dared bring Benjamin this far, and as he stood on the jetty, letting himself be pushed and bumped by others on a hurry to go nowhere, he understood why. It was a shameful revelation that came to Rudy Blake and he fought the urge to cry. He was a broken man. The Great War, the War which had not been his War, had broken him, snapped his spirit, sapped his life's force. There was so little left in him, that if Benjamin had come this far, he would never have sent him away. He would have used him as a crutch, leaned on him, drew the boy's life away as surely as these hawkers and pawners of humanity were doing to him now.

He knew his own needs were so great he would have killed the boy, reminding him of stories heard in childhood, tales told by the fires of the Negro huts. It was not of their own histories they talked of an evening; of the massively waving trees, the sweltering heat that warped a man's vision as he stared into the distance, nor even of the roar of giant, fearsome beasts of their native soil. They spoke of Indian lore, told the Red-Man's tales, as though they shared some common bond that only they could see.

"Wen deys a chil' bo'ne, deys don't let none ob dem ol' folks gits near it," he vividly recalled in his minds ear. "Dey says dat durin' sleep, da ol' folks steals da life from dat chil', until in da mornin' dey ain't no life in dat young'un. Da ol', dey don' wanna stay ol', an so dey takes da life.' Onlest the young is wad dey tak's da life from, so da ol' kin be young agin."

As a child, Rudy had never understood the fable; he had never seen an old person become "young" again, after stealing the "youth" of a baby. He knew his Mammy was old – at least, older than he – yet, when curled under her arm and gently rocked to sleep, he never doubted he would wake the same boy, and see her as the same woman.

As a man, Rudy understood the story far better. He comprehended the wisdom of the warning. What the Indian tale did not make clear – or perhaps Rudy saw it in a different light than intended – was that this transfer of life's rejuvenating energies was a willing one. It was not a theft, but a gift. Had he clung to Benjamin, the boy would have willingly given his life to Rudy; would have sacrificed his youth, his future, for his friend. That Rudy could not allow.

He made the decision to leave Benjamin in Richmond knowing he needed him; fully cognizant the trip to England would tax his strength, perhaps beyond endurance. There was a very real possibility he would die before reaching that sacred shore. With Benjamin beside him, he was sure he could make it. Benjamin would remind him to eat, force him to exercise; would entertain him with his youthful observations, keep his mind active by constant questions.

Yet Rudy knew that by the time they reached London he would be the strong one and Benjamin the weak. He would transform into a vampire, a selfish, evil being that sucked life from a healthy body, infusing it into his own. He had seen such signs in Richmond, and they had frightened him.

That was the reason he left Benjamin. It had been one of the hardest, most selfless gestures he had ever committed, and as Rudy stood helplessly on the wharf at Norfolk, he did not regret his action. He also realized that time would come, for his strength was nearly gone, his resolve of mind wavering, and the fear of death was upon him.

He must make it to England. He must find Rose. She was waiting for him. It was her life he sought to save his own. Rose was not an innocent boy who looked to him as a father, a brother, a worldly savior. Rose was his equal, his love. They shared the same soul. She could save him without sacrificing herself. At least, that was his ill-formed, amorphous hope.

Within her protective arms he would lie and get well. If he did not, they would perish together. Rather than seeming selfish, to Rudy's feverish brain, the idea seemed fitting. With Rose at his side, he would not fear death.

A group of men looking for a ship's captain brushed past Rudy, nearly trampling him underfoot. He staggered from the passing blows of their heedless shoulders, nearly tripped on the slippery, rotting garbage thrown on the wharf, then lost grip on his carpetbag. It fell to the hollow, wooded flooring with a thud. Bending down to retrieve it, the act seemed to require more energy than he possessed. Not even sure he needed it, he debated leaving it where it was, rather than try and pick it up. But he was afraid if he abandoned it, someone would come running after him, shouting his omission to the skies. This dread of being singled out and reprimanded outweighed his fatigue. Stooping down without bending his knees, Rudy grasped the handle, curling his fingers tightly around the leather. Savagely warning himself he must not let go again, he shuffled away, wondering how in the world he was ever going to book passage to New York.

Rudy knew Norfolk well. In better times, it had been a city of wealth and some beauty. Even during the early years of the War it had prospered as a thriving port, boasting its importance to the Confederacy. Men had money and burned with hot-blooded patriotism. With a Southern victory, they stood a chance of becoming immensely wealthy, of having their city become the gateway to Europe. No longer would the new country look to Northern harbors as the only seafaring centers. The CSA would be a new nation, and all the rules rewritten. Rich plantation owners, tourists traveling for pleasure, businessmen selling rice, cotton, sorghum and turpentine would gather here to arrange transportation. And the folk of Norfolk would provide it, establishing a link between Virginia and the world. These were heady thoughts and they had died a painful death.

Norfolk had fallen on hard times far quicker than any politician or speculator could have foreseen. The Union blockade targeted Richmond with an intensity so unflagging the entire Virginian coast was laid to ruin. Wharves went untended, entranceways to harbors were either artificially blockaded with the wrecks of derelicts, or unintentionally filled by the splintered hulls of unfortunate blockade runners.

International commerce never materialized and the conditions so favorable in April, 1861, were nought but a puff of smoke in the aftermath of defeat. When revitalized and returned to a semblance of its former glory, the city and the profits would belong to Yankee businessmen. Such were the fruits of victory and the agonies of defeat.

Hanging onto his carpetbag for dear life, as though it contained his very essence, rather than a change of linen and his shaving kit, Rudy slowly staggered inland. He must locate a ticket office and secure passage to New York. That much was clear. What was not as apparent, however, were the directions. Somewhere between Richmond and Norfolk he had lost his ability to read. Ashamed to ask, yet compelled by the urgency of his predicament, he stopped a number of loiters along the docks. Either they did not know where to direct him, or did not understand his garbled question, for none gave him the answer he sought.

"I want to book passage to New York; can you tell me where the ticket office is?" he asked a passing, well-dressed man on the hope one of his class would take pity on his plight. When he received nothing but a scowl for his trouble, Rudy could only suppose his sentence was inarticulate, for the stranger pushed him aside as so much flotsam.

Too confused to be angry, he tried again, hailing a youth still dressed in Confederate grey. "Ticket office?" he plaintively inquired. The soldier eyed him with contempt, then shrugged and backed away with a snarl.

"Whatever you got, brother, I don't want no part of it."

Misguidedly, Rudy had presumed the "War of Brother Against Brother" was over.

Spinning nearly in a circle, the former artilleryman found himself precariously close to the edge of the wharf. A sudden attack of vertigo nearly caused him to lose his balance and fall into the dark, vacuumous waters. Arms flailing, Rudy staggered backwards, colliding into a portly gentleman smoking a cigar. The contact caused the man to drop his smoke and he accosted Rudy with righteous indignation.

"Excuse yourself, sir!" he roared. "I am Colonel Grammercy and I demand an apology!"

Rudy shuddered. He had had enough military titles to last him a lifetime and did not understand why these defeated officers would not give up their claim to a rank they no longer possessed. More strangely, he noted that a passing Union officer did not bother to turn his head at the portly man's assertion.

Rudy would have supposed the first thing these victorious soldiers would have stripped from the returning Rebels would be their spurious titles. That appeared not to be the case, for nearly every uniform sprouted the gold chicken gut of majors, colonels or generals. Speaking to himself, for he was the only company interested in his opinions, Rudy dryly observed it was not surprising the South had lost the War, for all the troops were officers and thus non-combatants.

"If only 'Old Blue Light' were here," he pursued, delighted to have found a subject upon which he could dwell with some authority. "He'd clear up this mess in a moment. No fancy dress uniforms and peacock feathers for him." Clearing his throat, he imitated the singular general. "'Off the streets with you, for I shall have useful, rather than decorative officers in my army!'"

He laughed, an hysterical gushing forth of bitterness, but it was the first humorous idea he had felt within him in days. Clutching inwardly the vision of the tall, lean Jackson, attired in his old blue Federal uniform and signature kepi, hustling all the cocks off the streets, he found forward movement easier.

In his altered state of mind, his "insult" to Colonel Grammercy had been forgotten, but not by that esteemed officer.

"You!" he roared, pointing a finger in Rudy's chest. "I demand an apology!"

With a tongue sharper than his present sense, and the image of Mighty Stonewall at Harper's Ferry beside him, his reply was preordained.

"Never heard of you. Which army did you fight for?"

A moment before he could not make himself understood when inquiring of the ticket office, but his retort here rang true with the skill of a marksman.

"I do not take kindly to such slurs upon my honor, sir!" the officer screamed. "Defend yourself – if you're able. If not, then I shall kill you where you stand."

"A noble and honorable threat, sir," Rudy replied, a sharp, peculiar ringing in his ears drowning out the sudden buzz of background noise. "No doubt killing an unarmed man will be a suitable adjunct to your family escutcheon."

"You, sir, are no gentleman!" the highly offended gentleman declared, spitting by Rudy's feet. Whatever self-restraint he had evaporated. Reaching into the reserves of his energy, Rudy gave a Rebel roar and propelled himself forward, fingers straining for the man's fleshy neck.

"He's going to murder him!" someone in the crowd shouted. Men pressed closer, eager to witness the deed. Some waved their hats, others took up the cry until it repeated over and over, temporarily deadening the ringing in Rudy's ears.

Grateful for the reprieve, he clutched at the pulsating veins with maniacal power. This stimulated the gathering. A pistol discharged. Yells mutated into shrieks.

Kill. Kill. Kill.

The *Give him to us!* out of his past became *Kill him for us!* He had denied a similar mob once before. He would not do so a second time.

Kill. Kill. Kill.

Arms wrestled him away; a fist was pushed into his spine. His hat was knocked off. Rudy's nervous distemper increased. It was no longer a peacock he was strangling but Charles Blake, who had thrown down his newly won hat in the dust after discovering the note his disinherited son had affixed to it.

"Die! Die! Die!"

"Leave go!"

"Go to hell!"

"That's where you're going if you don't leave go!" A meaningless threat. Rudy was already there. "It's off to prison if you don't let loose."

Prison. The magic word. Elmira. The Federal prison pen off New York City; Point Lookout. With a wail of the damned, Rudy Blake, no longer the auctioneer of hats and champagne, but a man afraid of his own shadowy past, let his arms drop uselessly to his side. The Federal soldier, his own face red from exertion, shoved him into the crowd. Men steadied him; another handed him his hat as they jeered the accuser from the abbreviated field of honor.

When the blue-clad officer looked for him, Rudy was gone, swallowed up in the surly, grinding mass of humanity. With a curse at the "God-forsaken Rebs," he moved away, his duty done.

Confused to be the center of attention, the defender of the faith tried one last time.

"Ticket office?"

"Over there," a fellow in tatters directed him, tipping his battered kepi, the brim of which was nearly severed from the cap.

"Thank you, sir." Rudy acknowledged the respect, hurrying away from the scene, uncertain what he had done to achieve such regard.

In the scheme of things, it was just one more inexplicable incident in a long life of question marks.

CHAPTER 3

Using his sudden rage to propel forward, Rudy asked again for the ticket office. This time his words must have been enunciated more clearly, for he received an immediate answer. Following the instructions, he located the booth in a corner of the wharf. Several customers were ahead of him, their loud harangue over prices and departure dates reigniting the nervous energy in his body.

Irrationally frightened that his shaking hands would betray him for some sort of criminal or worse, a man without a pardon, Rudy made a point of going through his bag, ostensibly checking for passage money. Rearranging his shirts and undergarments several times, he slowly worked his way to the head of the line without incident.

"What'll it be?" the clerk demanded, jutting his jaw forward in an aggressive manner, indicating his expectation of trouble.

"One first class passage to New York, if you please."

The ticket-taker's eyebrows furrowed. Politeness was not the order of the day. Rather than assuage his suspicions, it only increased them. Eying the well-dressed man with contempt, he picked absently at a pimple on his chin.

"Lemme see your papers," he demanded, lading his voice with the authority of an underling who supposes everyone beneath contempt.

A drop of perspiration rolled down Rudy's face, momentarily pooling at the tip of his nose, so that it appeared he were either crying or ill-bred. Inexplicably, Rudy's consternation caused him to laugh. It was a cutting, cruel sound; one no gentleman could tolerate.

But Rudy Blake was no gentleman, and he could not afford a scene. Nor did he possess the requisite written permission to travel outside Richmond. In his haste to depart the city, he had forgotten that salient detail. With a flash of lucidity and a reliance on his well-cherished principle, *gold is king,* he extracted his billfold. Making a show of displaying his wealth, he withdrew a one hundred bill.

"I beg your pardon," he began, smiling weakly. "I have nothing smaller. Does this cover the fare?"

His obvious lack of composure raised warning flags in the clerk's mind, but exactly along the lines Rudy hoped. Gone was the threat of denial, replaced by a lust for a quick profit. Reaching out and taking the bill, he slid a ticket across the counter.

"Exactly right," he declared. "Ship don't leave till tomorrow. Have a pleasant voyage."

Face reddening with shame, although his ploy had worked, the traveler accepted the ticket, tipped his hat and departed. Gone were the days when he would have laughed at his cleverness. Now, he was only relieved to have survived the incident.

The time, scrawled in nearly illegible ink on the paper, read ten o'clock. Just as it had thirteen years before when he was ran from San Francisco, he was left with the dilemma of killing nearly twenty-four hours before departure.

Seeking a hotel room for the night was his sole option. Fearing a repetition of the maniacal screaming, "Hotel! Hotel!" over and over again, he chose not to return to the wharf where he might have obtained some transportation. Instead, he opted to walk half a mile, taking lodgings in a small seaman's home kept by an old sailor who had lost a leg "to a great whale," or so he said.

The room was squalid and claustrophobic. Initials of men, long ago lost to storm, disease or whales, had been scrawled across the walls, or carved into the dilapidated furniture, so that the cramped confines more closely resembled a cemetery than temporary sleeping quarters. Shunning the four walls least they close in on him and smother his already frail body, Rudy left his bag on the bed and went outside.

Fresh air only exacerbated a ringing in his ears. Fearful, lest the condition become chronic, Rudy shuffled into a nearby cafe and bought a plateful of beans and sausage, two bottles of beer and a paper bag containing a handful of berries. Juice had stained through, leaving him with the impression of blood soaking through a bandage.

The connection did nothing to sharpen his appetite. He knew he should eat, had the awareness that the ringing in his head was more from hunger than disease, yet after he had purchased his dinner, Rudy could not bring himself to touch it. Abandoning it undisturbed, he returned to his coffin-like quarters, more depressed than he could easily account for.

The mattress proved lumpy, damp and too short for him by a foot. Curling into a ball, he clutched the carpetbag, wrapping his arms around the lifeless luggage in the hope his twisted mind would somehow believe it were Rose and that thought bring with it blessed repose.

In that, he was mistaken. Sleep did not come easily. Petting the carpetbag with affection, he rose and crossed to the window, lowering the ragged shade. Dimness did not induce sleep. Lying down again did no more than sharpen his senses, so that every outside noise tolled like bells mourning the dead.

Concentrate, he willed his fervid brain. *Relax. The journey from Richmond has tired me. Sleep.*

It was an errant expectation. While his limbs felt heavy and leaden, the mental discharges going on inside his head made sleep impossible. Whenever he closed his eyes, images of intense color forced him to wave a hand across his face to dispel them.

Crimson red: Relly's blood. Butternut yellow, stained with dark patches of sweat: Grainger's uniform. Soulless white, the shade of dead men's eyes. Yankee blue uniforms, buzzing around his head like a swarm of angry bees. Pitch black, the yawning mouth of Hades, waiting to absorb all those careless enough to misstep through its ever-open portal.

Rising after ten minutes, Rudy paced his jail-sized apartment, back and forth like a dead man swinging from the gallows. He felt imprisoned, yet had no strength, and less desire to go out. He knew no one in Norfolk – at least no acquaintances he cared to renew. Worse, there existed the very real fear of being recognized as the daring, devil-may-care blockade runner he had been for so many years. If his true identity were made known to the Federal authorities, he would be imprisoned, for his pardon had been obtained under false pretenses.

The name, rank and army affiliation on the document was correct, but only as far as it went. It listed him as Rudy Blake, private, Army of Tennessee, serving from the fall of Atlanta until the surrender. That much was true. What he had been before those days, however, disqualified him from a reprieve. State politicians, ranking officers and gunrunners were all forbidden pardons. Unlike the lowly men in ranks, they were sought for "high crimes and misdemeanors." If properly identified and captured, he stood the very real chance of being tried and convicted for committing atrocities of war.

To delay his journey meant death. Incarceration, interrogation, a court appearance, sentencing and inevitable imprisonment would destroy his mind as well as his body. As it was, the sand was pit-patting in the hourglass. Two days to New York, then two weeks on the sea was all the time he had left, what he had prepared himself to endure. One day, one second longer, and he would shatter like fine crystal at the pitch of a high note.

Sleep. I must sleep. Kill time.

Before time killed him.

Wrapping his fingers around a gold coin, he made his way downstairs, ordering a boy to purchase a bottle of whisky. The child did so, returning with a half-filled bottle of murky rum. He did not have to bother advising the messenger to keep the change, for none was forthcoming.

With a sour taste in his mouth and a bitter disappointment at being cheated yet another time, he painfully made his way back up the rickety steps, taking one at a time, least he slip and spill what had cost him so much to obtain.

Uncorking the bottle, he brought it to his lips, hand shaking like a drunk's. The taste was so repugnant, he spit it out, spewing miniscule bits of poison over the room in poor imitation of the great whale which had taken the leg of the miserable desk clerk.

Bitterly disappointed, he threw the bottle across the room, taking grim satisfaction in the fact the glass shattered into a million chards. Let the next man who occupied this chamber cut his feet on the glass. It was nothing to him. Gone was his former sentience. All that mattered was reaching England.

Rose was in England. Rose would save him.

He could not even explain why being "saved" was of such paramount importance.

Rose would *release* him. That sounded better. "Saved" was best left for the blessed. "Release" was the most a reprobate could expect.

He resumed pacing, taking care to avoid the broken glass. After completing a landlocked "around the horn" journey, his calves ached, his head hurt and the bitterness in his mouth made him want to rip his tongue out. Deeming that impractical rather than impossible, he settled for a drink of brackish water from a pitcher too long unemptied.

The contents appeared to have benefited from the drowning of innumerable insects, however, for after finishing off the liquid, Rudy finally felt as though sleep would come. Lowering himself gingerly on the bed, he tried lying on his back, knowing beforehand that no one ever willingly put their face into a hotel pillow. When his hemorrhoids screamed in complaint from the pressure, he rolled onto his left side.

With his cheek against the rough, erratically stripped fabric of the pillow, his eyelids fluttered closed. Rest would not be that easy, however, for contact with the pillow directed his concentration once again on the ringing in his ear. Reversing positions had the same effect, forcing him to sit on the bed, feet planted firmly into the dust on the floor.

That position served no better. Too tied to shuffle downstairs and too restless to sleep standing, were that even remotely possible, Rudy rose to his feet and slithered to the window. In desperate need to divert his attention, he managed to pull up the shade without having it come crashing down on his head.

With wry self-congratulations, he stared outward. The home in which he had taken refuge lay just outside the city, making it a passing point between river and settlement. Wagons, loaded with incoming freight, worked their way with tedious regularity toward warehouses situated just beyond his sight. Better paying passengers rode carriages, hired at the wharf.

Most of the men were Yankees, bearing the unmistakable stench of prosperity. Their hair was well slicked, with the scent, he imagined, of bay rum emanating from their bodies as though their ultimate destination lay in one of the many upper class brothels of Richmond, which, he mused, it probably was. Their clothes, wrinkled from sea travel, were tailored and fashionable.

These travelers bore the countenances of snake-oil confidence men. They were men to whom the Late War meant only lists of faceless names, battles fought at unknown creeks, speeches given in honor of those careless enough to have died for a cause they, themselves had taken no part in.

They were the first great influx of opportunists: a contingent Rudy had once fancied membership in. These men who worshipped the Golden Calf: entrepreneurs from New York, Philadelphia, Boston, Washington. Men who understood business, coming to the war-torn South to "rebuild civilization."

Their numbers comprised merchants, bankers, railroad operators, speculators, cotton factor officers, hucksters and inventors. In their midst he identified also the soldiers, soldier's wives, soldier's sweethearts, soldiers mistresses. Before him stretched the Land of Occupation, and make no mistake about it, Virginia was Union country. The Federals had won the War and had come to claim their prize.

Twelve months ago he had been one of them; linked, not by nationality, but the common thread of greed. Had his plans gone according to schedule, he would have passed the waning months in England, returning to his native soil a smug, wealthy misanthrope. Amidst the broken and penniless, he would have snatched up plantations for back taxes and rebuilt railroad lines, charging exorbitant prices to ferry cotton and tobacco to market. The owner of factories, shipping lines and financial institutions, he would have watched from his balcony as the flower of Southern aristocracy – the former slave-holders, rice planters, cotton growers, educators and cavaliers – came begging for a handout.

Four years of attrition had stripped away the vast stores of cash crops; gone were the hopes and dreams of political independence. George Washington was dead and no one had resurrected to take his place. Destroyed were the young, the vital, the fathers of growing families. What remained of the indigenous population were starving, ill-fed cripples, woman and children dressed in rags.

He had anticipated such an outcome, envisioned the aftermath, salivated over the investment opportunities. Here were pickings for a prince. A man with money could buy and trade in souls, as once these same soulless beggars bought and sold his Mammy.

But those dreams belonged to another Rudy Blake, not the one who stood at the window of a down-and-out seaman's hotel. Financially, everything was in place for him to achieve his goals. In his European bank accounts were uncounted millions, more than enough to establish himself as a visionary of the New Order. With a wave of his hand, he could purchase the entire city of Norfolk; with bribery be could become governor of Virginia.

Rudy had never intended to go to war. He had planned and schemed and calculated for this very moment and now that it was upon him, he was mentally unprepared to intervene for evil or good. He had no spirit to spit upon these people; had not even the strength to turn his head away.

He wanted to stand upon his high balcony and crow; he wanted to shout "I told you so!" and lord it over them. He wanted to buy their lands, ruin their businesses, become their god. Yet a poor deity he would be, for he could not even raise his head. God had punished him for his thoughts, his wicked hopes, his merciless desires. But he was not through with God just yet.

Nor could the contrary be ruled out. God was not through with him.

Rudy saw the mob coming long before he heard the sound of their vile oaths, the tramp of their feet, the orders they shouted. From his solitary position by the window he observed the waning daylight reflect off the guns they carried, for in this city of defeated secession, no white man went unarmed. He knew their minds as if gifted with second sight and moved his head with a sickening dread to determine the object of their hate.

A handful of Negroes had gathered at a diminutive, plank-board church. The service recently concluded, they had stepped outside to speak on secular matters: whisper fears, to share a bag of seed, discuss the fate of family long separated. None bore a weapon.

Having the advantage of closer proximity, they had heard the white men coming. Forming a circle, women and children inside, they faced their attackers with the grim knowledge that blood would be spilled.

Several wild shots rang out, reverberating against the quiet setting of the sun. Bits of wood, splintered off the shanty, exploded over the Negroes. A baby cried. Even in innocence it understood injustice.

Men's voices, heavily laden with the dialects of half a dozen Southern states, shouted curses, threats.

"Break it up, you black bastards! Ain't no congragatin' allowed!"

"There's the river. Jump in it and swim north where the nigger-lovers is!"

"Ain't no god gonna listen to yer prayers!"

It was an ugly scene, a clash of blacks and whites, of former slaves and masters, of those trying to live, and those trying to relive. It was an unequal contest of gun against stone, and the man at the window did nothing. There was nothing he could do. He watched as a spectator viewing a poorly scripted play, neither cheering nor rooting for either side, for he was separate from the actors.

His place was in the gallery. Although he had "paid" his penny for a standing room ticket, his presence was superfluous. The actors would perform the drama and it would unfold whether or not he was in the audience.

The dirty, mean, low-spirited whites came after the dark, embittered, angry-spirited blacks. More shots were fired, stones were thrown and blows exchanged. This was the new War, the birth of another battle unleased in the aftermath of the old, the death and rebirth of Southern civilization that cherished legend over life. A new and different world was being created here. Not the kind Rudy had envisioned himself shaping, but a deeper, more insidious type that permeated the blood-stained soil.

In this War there were no generals, no glorious nicknames, no immortalized creeks, no consecrated graveyards. This was the legacy of Lincoln's death, of the Continental Congress's inability to see beyond their own time; of the Bill of Rights that did as much to deny as it did to guarantee. This was the Battleground of Forever After

CHAPTER 4

It was after midnight when the last of the combatants were dragged away and the facade of peace once again settled over the courtyard where one solitary man stood watch. Rudy Blake was the sentinel, the guard, the prodigal son for whom no one slaughtered the fatted calf.

He was the man who thought he knew all the answers, long before the questions were asked. In that, he had erred, and in making that mistake, he had tainted everything he touched. Rather than be a knight in shining armor, he was the Wandering Jew: the orphan cast out, the stray turned loose, the unburied body whose soul was destined to roam the earth; the civilian turned soldier, fated never to have his name written either in the *Book of the Dead,* nor in the *Book of the Living.* His God had abandoned him, and he rejected mankind into which he had been born.

Once upon a time he would have run from his perch, using hot words of sedition as his weapon against the marauding attackers. Not so very long ago, he had intervened at the whipping of a black man, preventing the worthy citizens of Atlanta from dispensing white man's justice. Then, again, he had testified in a court of law, admitting a crime he did not commit, thus freeing an innocent soul of the heinous crime of preaching the Good Word.

For that, he had been accorded the highest honor a colorless man could receive: he had been made one of God's chil'ren. But the miraculous gift of wings had not come with that blessing, and in his landlocked state, he had not raised a hand in defense of his brothers.

Guilt lay heavy on him and he maintained his hollow post at the window for hours, seeing neither the night sky nor the dawn of day. It was only the sea breezes blowing through the glassless portal which finally roused him. With senses dulled from a weariness of having seen too much of Dr. Pangloss' best of all possible worlds, he gathered up his unopened carpetbag and made his way slowly back to sea.

He was sick and he was growing sicker. Time pressed upon him, yet his feet would not obey his urge to hurry. Without volition his eyes closed, causing him to walk into the side of a building. Mumbling an apology, for he feared even the recriminations of inanimate objects, he righted his course, only to repeat the same mistake again.

This time, he tipped his hat, slurring out "I'm drunk," in the hope whatever transgressions he committed would be attributed to drink. Fifteen minutes later, his feet gave out, causing him to fall upon his luggage in lieu of a seat. Flies settled on him and he did not have the strength to whisk them away.

A boy passed, selling newspapers. In order to give himself an excuse to tarrying in the roadway, he bought a paper and spread it on his knees. The words blurred in front of his eyes and it required extraordinary concentration to focus.

"Riot" ran the headline and beneath it, a vivid, if inaccurate depiction of the unequal contest of the evening before filled the front page. More an editorial than any attempt at a factual account, the author decried the "new rules" which "allowed the black man to walk free." Beneath a sketch depicting a mountain of dead white men, a Negro standing atop, arm raised in victory, ran the caption: The Devil's Law.

A list of citizens who had purportedly died in the fight ran down the side. Mr. Frank Thomas, of "this city." Mr. Ralph Johnson, the same. Mr. Robert Crane, of Richmond. Mr. Todd Smythe of Atlanta, Georgia. Mr. William Beatty of Martinsburg, Virginia.

Rudy's lips curled in derision. Not only had the War been lost, but so, too, had Martinsburg. It was no longer Virginia, but West Virginia. Like Appomattox, Rudy supposed the editor had never heard of the Pierpont government.

The names of the former slaves were not chronicled, giving the impression none had died or been injured. While Rudy seriously doubted any "citizens" from Virginia, Georgia or West Virginia had perished, he was equally certain half a dozen "non citizens" of "the same" had perished. Their loss, apparently, was unimportant.

A side bar, written by the *nom de plume* of "Justice," included an interview with "the Union officer in charge of keeping the peace." The unnamed major was quoted as saying, "Both sides were warned against further violence. Retaliation will not be tolerated and will be treated harshly." Negroes were advised "not to be out after dark and not to carry weapons which might incite altercations."

Tossing aside the paper which had grown unaccountably heavy, Rudy staggered to his feet, wavered in the windless morning, then raised a weary hand at a passing wagon. The driver paused, squinting at him with the same expression he might have used to judge rotting vegetables.

"Where to?"

Rudy was unprepared to speak. His lips moved but no words issued forth. He could not remember why he was out and where he was going. Memories of the room so recently vacated returned, waves washing over the head of a drowning man.

Sleep. He needed sleep. As the idea formed in his mind, it became so utterly compelling that he quivered from the intensity of it. He would rest for a day or two, eat and regain his powers of locomotion. That was what he needed.

It was with the greatest effort of self-will that he chose not to obey those yearnings. Time was his enemy, not his friend. Time only asked for more time. To stop his journey now was death. And so Rudy wrapped his arms around his chest and whispered, "To the wharf." Clambering onto the flatbed, he closed his eyes and clamped his teeth shut before he changed his mind.

He must go on: he *must* go forward. Retreat was no longer an option. He had promised... he had promised Rose he would return to England. He had sworn an oath. Already, he would be late arriving. Tardy, by nearly one year.

"To the pier; where the boats sail."

For a man who denied the fact he was a gentleman, his sacred word of honor was what kept him alive and moving.

Your life is precious to me. You must swear you will do nothing which will unnecessarily endanger it.

Rose understood when she made him take that vow, the key word being "unnecessarily."

The journey was tedious and silent. Not until they reached the water did the driver speak again.

"Which boat?"

Rudy had not thought to look. Fumbling for his ticket, he thrust it toward the man, hoping he could read. For his trouble, he had it shoved back in his face.

"This is as fer as I go. One dollar fer the transport."

For once, Rudy did not have the heart to say thank you. Paying his fare, he slipped off, then wandered toward a line forming on the dock. The nondescript sailor checking tickets did not rebuff him passage, so he crept up the unsteady plank, not really caring whether he had chosen the correct vessel or not.

Although an hour late, he barely made the ship, for the moment he set foot aboard, the whistle rang and the plank removed. With a belch of steam, the siderails quivered, the engines groaned and land receded.

While he had paid for a cabin below decks, the idea of retiring there now seemed cowardly. The sea had always meant life to him. If he were to regain his powers of animation, the deck was where he would find it.

The sailing ships of his past, however, had given way to steam and he had forgotten. The *Reprobate,* with her sleek lines and quite movement, was as archaic as he. The *Major Thomas* was a reconstituted freight vessel, had served the previous four years either as a blockader or transporting supplies. The ill-tended machinery deep within her bowels labored mightily, blanketing the deck with the foul-smelling residue of coal.

In a moment his white gloves were soiled black, while his skin took on the complexion of an undusted statue. Coughing into his hand, then finding his mouth full of phlegm, Rudy pushed his way through the overcrowded deck, barely managing to make it to the side before another fit of hacking seized him. After spitting, it was with considerable difficulty that he regained his breath.

"I saw you had a yellow ticket, too," a passenger observed, attempting to make conversation. "When I attempted to checked my berth, I was informed there were none available and that I was fortunate to have obtained standing room. No doubt, sir, you discovered the same. It is a disgrace."

"Yes," Rudy agreed, for the sake of appearing polite. "A disgrace. You should demand your money back."

The stranger would have pursued the subject, but a closer scrutiny of his companion's unshaven face, sunken eyes and dark, unhealthy circles below the sockets changed his mind. Mumbling a good-bye, he pretended to recognize a friend in the crowd and maneuvered away, leaving the man with the consumptive cough alone.

Others, frightened by the jut of Rudy's jaw which seemed to threaten violence to any who dared approach, kept their distance, effectively isolating him. Understanding, truly, that he was a scourge, Rudy made no attempt to solicit any conversation. Standing with his face to the wind, he was assailed by snatches of dialogue between other men, however, and used the opportunity to divert his bleak thoughts.

"... redress from the government. The local authorities won't listen to my complaints. It's a sin, that's what it is, the way our grievances are being ignored."

"They refused me a pardon on the grounds I 'aided and abetted' the former Confederacy. I did no more than the next man. I was just a businessman, trying to make an honest living."

"I heard the interest rates from the Bank of New York are better than any we're being offered here. It's a shame, I say, how our own people are bleeding us dry. Imagine – eight percent, and that with collateral required to back up any future seed purchases."

"... damned blacks won't work and even if they would, there's the Federal 'overseer' making 'em sign contracts. Pay 'em every week and they're drunk and worthless for two days after. I'm going on to Boston to sign on the damn Irish. No one cares about contracts for them!"

All these passengers traveled with the expectation of success, and even with dulled senses, Rudy marveled at their audacity. Had the War no effect on them? Were they unafraid of rejection? It seemed none of them were, and all the arrogance he had despised in their race before the conflict reared its ugly head and stirred his passions.

Could he have been that wrong? In the aftermath of defeat were they still the same bloated, self-important men they had been? Had hunger, deprivation and the death of countless thousands meant nothing to them? Did a declaration of peace mean a resumption of pompous superiority? If that were true, then he had made a grievous misjudgment. This was, then, the best of all possible worlds. At least for those of the ruling class.

With a heart heavier than his depressed spirits, Rudy left the deck, seeking refuge in the passenger's mess. Unlike his earlier travels aboard a "tourist ship," the fare provided was exactly as advertised. Fresh fruit, milk and cream, coffee, freshly baked bread and numerous varieties of meat and fish were set out, buffet style. The smells all turned his stomach, and he found he had lost his appetite. Repulsing the impulse to stuff food in his mouth he returned topside with a sick and nauseous stomach.

Rationalization filled his swirling mind. His teeth hurt. It was hard for him to chew. And when he did eat, his intestines rumbled. When passing stool, his hemorrhoids bled. Already sore, he did not wish to further exacerbate the problem.

He would dine upon reaching New York. After securing himself passage on an eastbound boat, he would take a hotel room, bathe privately and order meals delivered. In a day or two, his strength would return, enabling him to endure the two-week voyage. Such were the best laid plans of mice and men.

"Blanket, sir?" a voice inquired. Rudy ignored it, for like so many others, which he mistakenly believed addressed to him, the query was always for another. This time, the question was followed up by a gentle tap on the shoulder. Hoisting his eyelids open, he stared at the sailor. "You look like you're shivering. Thought a blanket would ward away the chill."

His first impulse was to refuse, for he seldom remembered being cold at sea. Taking stock of his situation, he discovered, to his consternation, he was shaking like a leaf. Accepting the woolen blanket with gratitude, he allowed the youth to wrap it around his shoulders. While he sustained no immediate relief from his tremors, the kindness of the unsolicited act spread a warmth through his emaciated body.

Too late, he thought to offer a monetary reward for when he looked up, the boy was gone. Feebly waving his hand, he attempted to summon him back.

"Steward! Steward."

Several travelers turned their heads in his direction, staring lustily at the bill he offered, but the steward did not return. Bitterly disappointed, Rudy spent the better part of an hour making his way around the deck in search of the crewman dispensing blankets, but found no one who had seen him.

This lack of success added to his muddled consciousness. Returning to the bow, shoulders hunched against the cutting wind, a second shivering fit came upon him. His teeth chattered so badly the noise became unendurable. Placing pressure on his jaw hurt his swollen gums, so he attempted a two-hand maneuver, placing one hand beneath his chin and the other atop his head.

Not only did he feel foolish, but the taut, pinched skin around his facial bones brought to his mind the image of a skull. Without much imagination he envisioned it totally stripped bare of flesh and bleaching white on a deserted South American beach. With his stomach in knots, pictures floated before his eyes. The beach transformed into a pirate's treasure chest, full to overflowing with doubloons and jeweled trinkets. The skull was now skewered on a pole, dug into the ground as a warning to others against trespass.

Without eyeballs, the most prominent feature of the death's head was the teeth, appearing overlarge and grotesque. Running his tongue across those still in his mouth, it lingered over the two gaping holes in the otherwise perfect set and he wondered if those prominent omissions would aid one of his crew in identifying the skull as his.

But no, he bitterly reminded himself, they were not aware he had lost a second tooth: not D'Artagnan, or Jack or Canary. He had seen none of them since going to war. They were unaware of his dysentery and the sticky chalk mixture he had concocted to ease his watery discharges. Coming upon the treasure chest, they would discard his skull without a second thought, having eyes only for the gold.

They had learned their lessons well, those boys of the *Gemini* and the *Reprobate.* He had taught them, never considering his own fate might one day be in their hands. They would not even think to bury it. Without his skull, his spirit would wander the earth, seeking to put together what Man's inhumanity to Man had ripped asunder.

Legends from his childhood assailed his sanity, increasing the tremors.

Dey ain't no rest for dems dat los' dere head, boy. Da spirit be restless, an' cain't find no peace till da body been put back t'gether. Gabriel's horn will blow fer all da odders, but not dat one, chil'. He'll wander da grabe yards foreber an' eber after, an' neber find salbation.

"No!" Rudy screamed, startling a flock of birds which had settled over the water for the night. "No!"

Staring angrily at the avians, Rudy cursed their needless flight. He meant them no harm. He should not have blamed them but he did.

"I am not your enemy."

His words had no effect and the departing birds soon disappeared, reminding him again that he was not one of God's children, for he had no wings. Dropping his head to his breast, he wept bitterly, then snuffled away the tears and steadied himself against the railing.

"I am growing delirious." The idea was horrific. If he arrived in New York raving and out of his mind, he would never get to London. The authorities would lock him up, put him in a room and throw away the key. He would become a virtual prisoner, a "mental case," a man gone mad. The warders would take away his clothes, steal his money, ignore his pleas. He would die alone among strangers, imprisoned in a room without windows, without ever having another sight at sea or sky.

After exhaling his last breath, they would throw his body in some unmarked grave in Potter's Field and that would be the end. Rose would never find him, never place coins on his eyes. He would have no coin for the ferryman.

In desperation, he slapped his face, taking advantage of the stinging pain to clear his head. Using the reprieve if afforded, he retired to the head, where he washed his face and shaved his cheeks. Appearance was everything. If he looked rich and well groomed, someone would save him for the reward they thought might accompany his safe return. He must look presentable. The alternative was indignity and falling into the hands of robbers. Once beaten and penniless, he was at the mercy of strangers.

No one would help. He understood the ways of the world well. He had sold his soul for wealth and must now face the consequences. He must protect himself. That was Blake's Law.

CHAPTER 5

The *Major Thomas* docked in New York after a trip of exactly two and a half days, and Rudy left the ship, carpetbag in hand, having never tasted a bite of food, nor passed a drink of water to his lips. He had arrived in neutral territory, having passed beyond the grasp of provost marshals and those who would question his identity. The next step must be to take a suite of rooms and regroup.

"They're barbarians. All of them. Barbarians."

Startled to be so addressed, Rudy glanced to his right. A well-dressed woman, small boy in tow, stood beside him, a large bonnet shading her eyes from the setting sun, preventing him from penetrating beneath for a clue as to her actual meaning. Mistaking his puzzled expression for a belief he had not heard her, the lady repeated herself, fortunately adding the requisite word to the puzzle.

"Those Southerners; they're all barbarians. I had planned on joining my husband in Richmond," she continued, "but after arriving in that city, I discovered, to my immense surprise, it was unsafe for women and children."

Rudy supposed she had disembarked with him, although he did not remember having seen her aboard. Caught between questioning her motive in speaking and offering his services to help her find a carriage, he merely tipped his hat. Taking his gesture as tacit agreement, she fanned her face with a lace handkerchief

"The Virginia capital is in shambles. I imagine you saw it, too?" He nodded, tongue cleaving to the roof of his mouth. "Buildings with walls blown out. Cannon balls cluttering weed-infested plots of land. No gardens for my son to play in. How, may I ask, am I supposed to raise a child under those conditions?"

Rudy shook his head. He could not imagine how.

"My husband is an officer. He's there to keep the peace. Let them all kill each other, I say. At first, I thought we could rehabilitate those Southerners, but now I fully understand we cannot. You agree with me, sir.?"

While posed as a question, he clearly comprehended the interrogative was a statement with which no Northern gentleman of breeding could disagree. A sad smile flirted across his pinched features, for even he could deduce she had mistaken him for a Yankee. The more pertinent question then became, should he be flattered or insulted?

"I agree with you as much as might be expected," he tried, performing a short bow. Withdrawing from her close proximity, the woman started, as though snakes had issued from his mouth. Clearly his unmistakable Southern dialect had given him away.

"How dare you deceive me like that, sir!" she exclaimed in indignation. "You are no Northerner! I took you for a businessman."

"I plead innocent to your first charge and guilty to the second," he declared, hailing a hackney coach, then offering his hand as she unceremoniously shoved her small child inside. "Allow me to apologize for your misconception by paying your fare."

Removing a coin from his purse, Rudy paid the driver, then stood back as the vehicle lurched away, nearly having his toes rolled over in the driver's haste. He wondered if the hurry was from fear he would retract his offer, or from the thought he might insist on joining her. He shrugged and decided he did not care.

Waving a brief salutation, he clutched his carpetbag closer, then scanned the wharf for another carriage. As a welcome to New York, the encounter was no better or worse than he expected.

The heat was sweltering. It had been years since Rudy had spent any time in the North, and he had forgotten how oppressive and humid the weather could be. Born and bred in Charleston, he had grown up around large bodies of water and the cooling breezes that came off them. In New York, he was as close to the Atlantic as the shoreline allowed, yet the climate was radically different. The air seemed heavier, more difficult to breathe, while the dampness penetrated his clothes, making his shirt stick to his damp skin, while wilting and shrinking his heavily starched shirt collar.

Wiping his brow with a monogrammed linen newly purchased in Richmond, he decided he was comfortable nowhere but at sea. Only there, with the constantly shifting breezes, the rapid temperature changes, the opportunity to sail from snow and sleet into tropical storms was his fiery temperament assuaged.

Discovering it was too late to purchase a ticket for London that evening, he hired a private transport, ordering he be taken to the Osage Hotel. While not the most grand, it was an establishment he was familiar with, catering primarily to men in the seafaring trade. At such a hotel, there was no likelihood he would run into the woman and her child.

Paying in advance for a suite of rooms, he allowed the porter to carry his humble carpetbag up the winding marble and polished wood staircase, while he followed more slowly. At the door he accepted the key, tipped the boy, who addressed him with a nearly incomprehensible Irish brogue, then left orders for an early breakfast and a barber be sent to him rooms no later than nine o'clock the following morning.

Head swimming from exertion, as well as from lack of nourishment, Rudy wearily lowered himself down onto the wide, double mattress. He was in the "Grand Marquis Suite," or some similar-sounding name he had not quite caught. The motif was English, however, making him think he had gotten the intent, if not the name correct.

Lace curtains adorned the windows, while a fleur-de-lis was woven into the bedspread. Four gas lamps, suspended from the walls, were designed to look like sconces. In all, the space lacked only a suit of armor to represent a fine old manor house. The entire appearance was strangely out of place in New York, giving him an odd sensation of disquietude.

Sitting up, he rubbed his eyes, then rested his head on his chin, forcing himself to concentrate. Time blurred and he could not remember how long he had been traveling. Had it been asea two days, or two weeks, or two months? Was he in New York, or England, or some foreign country?

Suspiciously staring around himself, he realized in horror that he could not trust his own senses. Perhaps he had inadvertently booked passage to Canada, or gone the other way, and now found himself in a British hotel along the Gulf Coast.

So unsure of himself that he began to doubt his sanity, Rudy paced around the spacious rooms, trying desperately to discover some familiar object, a New York newspaper, or a former occupant's local business card to reassure him he was in fact, where he ought to be.

Finding nothing to satisfy his nervous mind, Rudy wandered to the window and drew back the frilly, fairly clean and ironed curtain. If not inside, surely outside there would be a street corner, a sign, a business he could recall to memory. If only he could be sure, then sleep would come.

Otherwise, he knew he would pace the floor for hours, finding no solace for his weary, frightened thoughts.

He was six flights up, and as was his custom, had rooms which faced the street. Below him was a teeming metropolis filled with people in motion. That, at least, convinced him he was not in Richmond, for the scene was a far cry from the ruined, rotting, stinking passageways of that Southern city.

"New York," he whispered to himself. "I am in New York. Concentrate. What do I know about New York City?"

He knew much about Manhattan, yet his concentration was focused on the recent, not the distant past.

Draft riots. Street fighting. Lincoln's call for conscription. General malcontent. People standing in line for handouts. But as Rudy stood by the open window, he saw no signs of conflict. All was peaceful. Well-dressed gentleman walked with a purpose, or gathered on street corners to discuss interest rates and business opportunities. Women in long dresses tarried by shop windows, or issued orders for white-skinned servants to mind the children.

Boys with flyers promoted the latest plays. Small carts, laden with ice or fresh fish or hot pastries made their way down overcrowded streets. Children, hoping to earn a penny, scooped offal off the sidewalks or shooed away packs of stray dogs from the paths of important people.

"New York."

The relief was palpable, but not refreshing.

He was in New York but what he had read in the newspapers of the Bloody Conflict had been a lie. A scurrilous fabrication, written by dishonorable journalists. War had not come to this Northern city. There were no gutted buildings, no streets fallen into disrepair, no parks strewn with cannon balls. No hordes of homeless orphans, no begging soldiers. No sleeveless uniforms; no remnants of men, hobbling on crutches.

With his heart throbbing in his throat, Rudy Blake stared at the scene below, eyes unblinking, mouth agape. Perspiration rolled from his brow, past his eyes and down his cheeks. The muscles in his jaw quivered, making his chin tremble.

"Oh, dear God."

In his innocence, for indeed, there was no other word for it, he had believed war had been a two-sided blade, slashing its merciless edges across the wide panorama of Northern and Southern landscape, effecting civilians and soldiers of both nations.

Hunger. Deprivation. Long, unending lists of causalities tacked upon the front of post offices. Unemployment. Factories shuttered, wharves emptied, the sky a perpetual leaden grey of mourning. The wail of brides, the sobs of toddlers calling the name of "Papa" to strangers; the unrequited weeping of parents, the howls of abandoned family pets. The picket fences town down for firewood; the winter crops stolen, the fields un-furrowed, the hogs scattered, the chickens slaughtered.

The ravished countryside; the rape of a population, which would bear only poisoned fruit for generations to come.

Withering inside from a bitterness so overwhelming Rudy was compelled to lean against the solid foundation of the wall, his head sank with unrequited resignation. Four years of intractable slaughter, bloodshed and misery and New York City remained unscathed. It might have been 1859 instead of 1865 and this defeated survivor of Franklin and Nashville bore his scars alone.

"No."

But "no" was not the answer. Nor was it in any way, sharp or form, comprehensible to these untouched victors. Here, it was spring and hope scented the air with the bouquet of new, vibrant life. Rather than a population of blood-soaked ghosts, New York teemed with the spontaneous generation of optimism. Life was not beginning anew from the cold ashes of wanton destruction, it was striding forward with the unscathed attitude of "business as usual."

His throat constricted and he choked, then began coughing until it seemed he would expel his intestines.

In with the new, out with the old.

He was the "old," and the people below him the "new."

The world, as he knew it, had survived. Only he, deep inside, had perished.

Regaining his breath, he sagged against the sill, transfixed by horror. Had this been his contribution? To preserve a way of life for the Yankee aristocracy?

Once, he had thought so.

The devastation of reality was upon him and Rudy Blake discovered he was a Southerner.

Only Rose Theodore, the native New Yorker turned chandler for the erstwhile pirate- without-a-cause, would have understood.

"Rose." He spoke to her as though she were beside him. "Do you see?"

"Yes, Rudy. I see."

His voice was thick, heavy with sadness, dulled by the incomprehensible.

"Where is the aftermath of war?"

"You left it behind. In Atlanta and Richmond and on the battlefields."

Which was not exactly true, for she comprehended, far greater than he, Rudy carried it inside him, and would, until his final moments upon earth. For him, Durham Station was not an end to conflict, but only a slow, agonizing continuation of battles yet to be fought.

"These people never saw it," he whispered, his words carrying gently over the three thousand miles separating them.

"Yes, my beloved. It passed them by."

"How could that be?"

Pressing closer to the window, its pane of glass polished and marvelously intact through forty-eight months of armed conflict, his exhalations fogged the spectacle of the triumphant march toward prosperity.

Without the keenness of eyesight, he heard and she heard the conversations from below, as though they were actually together standing amongst the victorious crowds.

"... retribution for their heinous acts. Congress will levy taxes; make them pay for the damage."

"... never let them back to the Senate and House. We'll put our own men in power. Good Republicans. They'll follow our laws, march to our tunes."

Yankee Doodle Dandy.

When Johnny Comes Marching Home Again.

A way down south in Dixie.

Look away, look away, look away Dixie Land.

"To the victors go the spoils."

Their tones of voices were laced with passion, dripping with a desire for retribution they neither understood nor cared to worry themselves over. Their vengeance was intellectual rather than emotional; their desire for redress over supposed transgressions financial.

The War Between the States was as distant to the East Coast as those in Britain: further, even for there, the suffering had been real and not imagined. Without King Cotton, textile manufactures had closed factories, laid off workers. The carriers bringing imports inland from the docks had gone without work for years. The seamstresses, designers, weavers were all unemployed. Queen Victoria's hatred of slavery had nearly undid centuries of prosperity, leaving scars which would take decades to heal.

The distinctions did not stop there. Expatriates throughout Europe were eager for news. Weeks behind newspaper reports, they eagerly gathered on shore, hailing every ship from home with a passion hard to find across the Mason-Dixon Line. Beyond the confines of Washington, Rudy doubted one out of ten men knew the name of a single battlefield.

The fact of the matter was, they did not have to know, and he should have been the last to condemn them for their indifference. Before the fall of Atlanta he had been one of them. Profit had been his middle name. The fortunes he made had come at the expense of those who need not inquire the price of a cotton shirt, or how many lives had paid for imported wine.

With a twitch and a sigh, he turned away from the window, trudging, the way a defeated soldier turned his back on yet another lost contest. Once, he had glided across a room, head held back, eyes defiant, with the jaunty air of one who knew the world was his oyster. He did not see the difference. He did not have to. In less than one year, the looking glass and joined the ranks of the victorious, casting him aside as surely as the dead at Bull Run or Sharpsburg.

Slumping down into an upholstered chair of crushed red fabric, his head spun with myriad thoughts, all crowding for ascendancy. Confusion was not new to him, but defeat was. Always before, opportunity had knocked. When expelled from Charleston, he had fled the law and his father's wrath to California. Failure to discover gold had opened a new avenue of land speculation and shady deals. Gambling in New Orleans had been lucrative; gunrunning along the coast of South America dangerous and profitable. Owning railroads and Southern factories had supplemented the wealth obtained by skirting the Union blockade.

Were he to collect his monies in one bank, there was no man who could outbid him on a deal. Without knowing his exact worth, it was no matter to proclaim himself the wealthiest man of his acquaintance.

Why, then, was he so depressed? Why did he care whether the Northerners were indifferent to the havoc they had wrought? Why did he identify with the downtrodden, rather than the empire-makers?

Why was he so weak? What had happened to his zest for life? When had he changed sides? Who was he? Where was the Rudy Blake who did not give a damn for anyone but himself?

Crushed by the inexplicable, Rudy sobbed gently to himself. Something had happened, the world had changed. He no longer understood it. For a man who once believed he could divine the deepest, darkest secrets lurking inside the souls of men, he had now only a half-formed awareness. Where he had once plotted to further these same men's destruction, adding to their miseries, humbling their spirits while raising his own, he had no more than revulsion.

The watchword "evil" had become twisted, thereby altering his perception of "good" into an unknown quantity. Gold, once his standard of attainment, had lost its personal value, leaving him destitute. Freedom became imprisonment, hues lost intensity, suns set and tides waned.

The world was upside down and Rudy Blake found himself standing on his head.

Had his celebrated wit not deserted him, he might have likened himself to the court jester.

Poe's Hop Frog.

He was no longer a man but a midget, dwarfed by a war that had not been his war, brought low by the fickleness of Fate and the hands of the gods.

Rudy did not retire to the double bed that night, but curled fitfully in the chair, twisting and turning in the throes between wakefulness and sleep. He might have derived a modicum of comfort from the soft mattress and ample pillows, but the very luxury of it scared him off.

Irrationally, he believed if he were to lie down and dream, the demons of his subconscious would trap him there, arms and legs pinioned to the bedclothes. Caught between nightmare and reality, neither dead nor alive, he would spend the rest of eternity in a rented room, separated from both sides by a veil of impenetrable mist.

He was roused from lethargy at nine o'clock by the arrival of the barber. Summoning what strength he still possessed, Rudy barely made it to the door and drew back the lock before falling heavily into the arms of the stranger. Righting his customer with a cheery "Good morning," the tonsorialist guided him back toward the chair he had so recently escaped.

"A little too much celebrating last night, sir?" he continued, taking the noxious smell of Rudy's breath for the aftereffects of too much drink. "A pot of black coffee and a hot towel over your face will chase away the demons."

Only half listening, the customer reacted sharply to the barber's last word, grabbing his wrist with startling strength.

"Why did you say that?" he demanded, fearful least the hobgoblins of his nocturnal wanderings had permeated his room with tangible shapes. Carefully prying away his hand, the man refused to abandon his good humor.

"I've seen many with hangovers in my day, and yours, I wager, is a classic. You'll feel better once you're shaved and presentable. Never known it to fail."

"No," Rudy halfheartedly agreed, grasping at the flimsy straw the explanation offered. "It won't fail."

Scrutinizing the patron, the barber waved a hand in front of his face, then just as casually, flipped up the long, flowing locks behind his neck. "A haircut, too, if I say so myself."

Without bothering for a reply, he waved a white sheet in front of Rudy, prefatory to covering his chest from stray hairs he intended to clip away. Immediately frightened by the similarity to a winding cloth, he fought it away, then realized his mistake and abruptly dropped his hands.

"No need to bother," he apologized, slurring the words in an effort to hide his misconception. "I intend on bathing afterwards."

If the man thought the explanation odd he did not say so, but his expression darkened.

"Very well. A shave and a haircut it is." With his instruments prepared, he abandoned his earlier idea of a hot towel to soften the whiskers, merely lathering Rudy's face from an already dampened mug. "How are you wearing your sidebars? To the end of your ear? And what about chin hair? A well-trimmed beard would suit you. It's the fashion these days; quite military and —"

"I am not a soldier," Rudy snapped. "The war is over. I want a clean chin and leave the mustache."

Clucking his tongue at the abandonment of fashion, the barber did as directed, but left the hair over the lip too long to suit. Only after repeated warnings did he trim it to satisfaction, before starting on his head.

"Not too short. Just even if off."

"Then you'll need another hair cut in a week," he predicted, sharpening his scissors with his honing strap. "Or else you'll look like a wild man."

"A pirate," came the gritted response, to which he readily agreed before noting the absolute sincerity behind the assertion.

"A pirate's not a very welcome fellow in these parts," came the warning, given as he scrutinized the man beneath his two-bladed weapon. "Especially not one with a Southern accent."

Reading the barber's thoughts, Rudy backed down with what he hoped was an embarrassed smile. "I'm going to sea. With a lady. She imagines I'm a bit of a swashbuckler. I would hate to disillusion her."

Only partially pacified, the hair-trimmer completed his task, offering a looking glass as an afterthought. Inspecting the job without dwelling on his features, Rudy pushed it aside.

"Very well," he declared.

While the barber replaced the tools of his trade, Rudy removed several bills of large denomination from his red Moroccan pocketbook and handed them to the startled man.

"I want you to book passage for me on the first outbound ship for Liverpool. A private compartment," he added, dreading the thought of company. "The best they have... no matter the cost. The sooner the ship sails, the better. Return to me immediately and I will double your fee," he added, fearful the barber would accept the commission but not do as bidden.

Pocketing the money, the man was almost to the door when he was stopped by a harsh warning. "Leave your bag here. You may retrieve it when I have the ticket in hand."

Clearly annoyed, he set down the black leather tote, then shifted his weight from one leg to the other.

"One ticket, or two?" he asked, recalling his customer's recent assertion he was sailing in company with a lady.

Realizing his mistake, but too late to rectify it, Rudy waved him away with a curt, "One," hoping to God the barber would keep whatever suspicions he had to himself. If he went to the port authorities, describing "an odd man with money in a hurry to depart New York," he could be delayed indefinitely while his wartime activities were investigated.

It would not take much to discover he was Captain Blake of the *Reprobate.* Unthinkingly, he had registered in his own name. While he had not anticipated that to ring bells with an illiterate desk clerk, any naval officer would surely identify him as a wanted man. "Rudy Blake" was as known to them as "Jefferson Davis." Given the opportunity to capture the infamous pirate, he could expect fifty armed soldiers at his door within the hour.

Swallowing bitter gall, he paced his room, berating himself for his carelessness. Every footfall in the hall, each screech of a wagon's wheels from the street below set his nerves jangling, until he felt ready to jump out of is skin.

Summoning a boy from the hall, he ordered breakfast and a bottle of rum, then left the tray untouched. He would be fed well enough before they hanged him.

Retrieving a handgun from his carpetbag, Rudy fondled it, judging the heft, staring through the barrel to gauge its accuracy. He could not take down fifty, but he would not go without a fight. That much life and no more remained to him.

He had wound and rewound his watch half a dozen times, cursing God, heaven and a vast assortment of demons before the knock came. With legs bowed at the knees, he answered it, weapon behind his back. Great was his relief to see only the barber.

Pushing him aside, he scanned the hall, searching for the rest. It was empty. His reprieve, for the moment, had been a hard-fought battle.

"You're to sail aboard the *Southern Cross,*" the courier announced, officiously handing across the ticket. "It sails in three days; that is the best I could do."

Wiping a copious amount of perspiration from his forehead, Rudy accepted the ticket, checked it briefly to confirm the fact, then nodded, suddenly overcome with gratitude. The man had not betrayed him; money had worked its magic charm.

"As it was in the beginning," he mumbled, discretely slipping the pistol into his pocket. Money was, still, the root of all good. He had had his doubts.

"What was that?"

Shaking from the relief which only a faithless man could experience at the miracle of the Resurrection, Rudy shook his head, then pressed more money into the outstretched hand. At his feet, he kicked the bag.

"Take it."

Nodding his own appreciation, the barber retrieved his goods and disappeared, grateful to have escaped unscathed.

Had he seen the gun, his prayers would have been the equal of the traveler's.

CHAPTER 6

Three days. The wait seemed an eternity. Doubts assailed him. Had the barber lied? Were there others ships departing sooner? Had he wiggled and wormed his way through ticket lines, determining the cheapest fare, rather than the quickest departure?

Counting the money in his billfold, Rudy could not determine how much he had given the man. One hundred dollars? Five hundred? There was no price on the ticket so he had no way of knowing its actual value. The barber had been gone hours before his return. What if the *Southern Cross* were a scow, without proper accommodations for gentlemen? What if he were thrown into a hold, a converted cattle pen, with hundreds of other deceived passengers?

He should have gone himself. There was no way to justify his cowardice. Weakness was not an excuse. He had not gone because of bodily ills. The truth was as blatant as the scars on his face. He had sent a messenger because he was afraid to go himself.

Afraid. The very word held within it the power of self-destruction. He had never been afraid of anything in his life and now he trembled like a babe. The slightest noise made him jump; the idea of eating filled him with revulsion. Even the act of undressing presented a nearly insurmountable obstacle. His hands shook like those of a drunk. His mind was in a whirl.

"I am sick and ought to see a doctor."

The statement echoed off the walls, reverberating through his brain until he was forced to physically shove them back. "Go away. Leave me alone."

How could a man order himself away? He was talking in riddles. He was losing his mind.

"I am not afraid."

Ghosts filled his suite, crowding around, pushing and shoving their way toward the chair in which he held court. Former shaves from his father's plantation. He recognized them from childhood memories, attempted to address them, but his tongue clove to the roof of his mouth.

"So, dis da way da young massa done ended up," one remarked, wiping his hands on a linen towel, as though the sight of Charles Blake's progeny soiled his otherwise clean hands. "Yuh's a bad seed, Massa Blake. Eberyone said yuh'd come to no good. Ah guess dey right."

"No!" Rudy protested, shielding his eyes with the back of his arm. "I have come to good."

"What yuh done dat makes yuh say so, little massa?"

"I have money," he cried, frantically searching for his wallet to prove his assertion. If only he could make the slave see he had achieved vast wealth, the man would alter his opinion.

His efforts were in vain.

"What good money in dis worl', boy? Money's only good if yuh spend it on good. Yuh hoard it like a miser; yuh gonna build yuhrse'f a castle an' spit on dem what done yuh wrong. Is dat good, or is dat bad? Who yuh he'pped wid day money? No one but yuhrse'f. Dat's bad."

"I'll help you," he pleaded, offering a fistful of bills toward the haint. "Here. Take it."

"Ah got no use o' dat," scorned the black man, stepping back as another pushed his way forward.

"Waterbucket!" Rudy screamed, identifying the shimmering, half translucent figure from his months in the gold fields. "Pete! It's me; Rudy. Help me. Please." Tears dribbled down his cheeks. Running the back of his hand over his nose, he sniffed then wiped the dampness on his trousers. Pete shook his head in disappointment.

"You know'd I was raised a gentleman, boy." He began slowly, speaking with his peculiar twang of Philadelphia snobbery and hide tanner's dialect. "I cain't stand no bad manners."

"I'm sorry," Rudy apologized, searching frantically for a handkerchief.

"You've let yourself get low, youngster. Lower'n a dog."

"I made money, Pete. Not sifting for gold, but you knew that," he suddenly accused, rising into a half-standing position, fists clenched in impotent suffering. "You knew I wouldn't. You left me there to die."

"Didn't know if you'd live or die," Pete Pheeters, otherwise known as "Waterbucket," demurred, stroking his grizzled chin. "But I tolt you, didn't I? Tolt you I had to go up to them mountains alone. I heard the call. Weren't no place to be draggin' a boy wid a chip on his shoulder."

"Did you find it? Did you discover the Mother Lode?"

Pete laughed, rolling his head back in eerie, soundless mirth. His teeth, crooked and blackened, became the dominant feature of his face, obscuring all but the flash of his watery blue eyes.

"Found it an' them some, child. Dug out gold chunks as big as yer head. More gold than me and Lucy could ever hope to carry out."

"I looked for you – asked for you," Rudy sobbed. "Went to the assay offices. Checked for you name in the newspapers. I never found it."

"That's 'cause you wasn't lookin' in the right places." Pete took out his pipe and began to puff away. Curls of grey smoke settled over his head in the form of a tarnished halo. "We never came down from that mountain. Never saw no need. We had that gold, Lucy an' me. That's all a man needs, boy. He don't require no civil-i-zation."

"But you said –"

"Talkin' big, I was," Pete declared, slowly dissolving into a cloud of amorphous, netherworld substance. "Never really planned on buildin' that big house on the hill. Weren't no need. Built me a palace o' gold, right up there on that mountain. Come an' see us sometime," he added, winking grotesquely as he disappeared. "Fer a visit. But I cain't let you stay. You wasn't my boy, Rudy Blake. You wasn't nothin' to me but a boy-in-passin'. I had my own boy, you recall. Don't you?"

"Pete! Pete! Come back. I want to be your boy; I want you to be my father!"

But Waterbucket was gone, returned to Lucy, the donkey, and the mountains where he had found the Mother Lode and never returned.

"He's gone, Mister River Boat," David, otherwise known as John Paul Jones observed, slipping up to the foot of the chair. "He's dead. Just like your Mammy is dead. Remember, one time, Rudy, I tried to make you say 'She's dead,' and you couldn't? It was a quirk of yours. You always were superstitions, weren't you?"

"John Paul," Rudy gasped, throat constricting in horror. "How is it... you're here?"

"Here? Here, where? Here in New York? Or here, among the living?"

Rudy had no answer. His shoulders sagged and he retreated further into the crushed red cushion.

"I followed you. I tried to save you."

"Did you, now? That was very out of character. But you know how much I enjoy characters. They make such good copy. Those articles I wrote on you – 'Mister River Boat'. I made a tidy sum on them; very popular. And you know my one abiding tenet – money is the root of all good."

"No," Rudy protested, waving a hand in front of his face. "You never said that. *I* said that! You never believed it. You hated money!"

"Did I? Perhaps I've forgotten," John Paul mused, holding a pen to the light and inspecting its sharp point. "I never finished your biography, did I? *The Adventures of a Modern-Day Pirate.* Do you still have my copy – the one I started? Where is it? I'd like to see it. Give it to me. I want it back."

Searching his memory, Rudy gasped, then let his hands fall uselessly to his sides.

"Rose has it. I left it with Rose."

John Paul frowned. "Rose? I know no Rose." Then, suspiciously, "Will she take good care of it? I left it for you, you know. I wanted you to read it. Did you?"

"No," came the choked denial. "I never did. What did it say?"

"Oh, I chronicled all your exploits," John Paul smirked. "Not exactly in the manner you might have wished. I never saw your life as romantic. You were a rogue and a scoundrel. A cheat and a liar. I thought I saw some good in you, Rudy, but I was wrong."

"Don't say that. Please."

"You looked at life with a chip on your shoulder. You swore that no one would ever bring you low, again, and look where that philosophy has brought you. To this." Using his pen as a wand, David, the former correspondent for the New Orleans *Echo,* swung it around the room. "You have no home; no friends. What good is all that money you amassed? Has it saved you? Or will all go to pay for a golden headstone over your grave?"

"I'm not going to die! I will live."

"Really?" David arched an eyebrow. "What are you now? You're closer to us than you are to the living. You're the walking dead, Mister River Boat. Everyone you know has... gone beyond." He smiled at his poetic language. "Not exactly journalistic jargon, is it? But it suits my purpose. Language, too, is a weapon, Rudy. One you often used to cut a man off at the knees. That gave us something in common."

"We had nothing in common!" Rudy screamed, rising unsteadily to his feet. "Get out, all of you! Leave me alone."

John Paul was nonplused. "Alone to do what? To wither away and perish in an anonymous hotel room? You're afraid to go out among the living. What happened to the man I knew – the one with the 'devil may care' attitude? Nothing frightened you then, Rudy, and now you're afraid of your own shadow."

He began to laugh. Behind him, all the ghosts from Rudy's past took up the cue, so that the room filled with boisterous glee. Unable to prevent the insidious noise from penetrating his ears, the one living man began a systematic extinction, waving his arms through the substance-less bodies. One by one they disappeared until he was finally alone.

Finally, truly alone.

A man without a past.

A man, David might have remarked, had he lingered, *without a future.*

Gasping from the exertion, Rudy ran to the windows. Drawing back the shade, he opened the sill, shooing out the wispy remnants of lingering smoke. Not satisfied, he went from window to window, opening them all, so there could be no doubt he had exorcised each and every ghost. Only when he was certain they had disappeared did he lean forward, allowing the unlived wall to support his quivering frame.

"I am alive. I will live."

Below him, the city was afire with the activity of night. Gas lights lit the street, illuminating the carriages merrily transporting ladies and gentlemen to plays or taverns. Working women crowded around the shadows, pulling back the edges of their skirts, or baring a shoulder as a prospective man walked past. Horses whinnied; the sounds of horse hooves clip-clopping on the cobblestones, the muffled laughter and the snatches of conversation which drowned out the voices of yesterday.

"I am alive."

It seemed a hollow assertion. Sweating profusely, Rudy loosened his damp collar, then unfastened it at the neck. With the limp band hanging from his hand, he began a slow circumference of the suite, not stopping until he had touched the four points of the compass.

Three days. He had three days to kill before leaving New York.

"Is that what one does? Kill time?"

It was a line from a play, or perhaps he had read it somewhere in a novel or a short story. He had three days to kill, before time killed him.

At the moment, he questioned the outcome.

"If I were a betting man –"

"Shut up!" he ordered, uncertain whether he were addressing himself ,or if David had snuck back in for the last word. "I am a betting man and a better one than you."

Which was true, finally eliciting a wan smile. What had David called him? Mister River Boat. When he had refused to allow his name in print, the scribe had chosen the first *nom de plume* which came to mind. Rudy had been a riverboat gambler, then, and the pseudonym seemed appropriate. "Mister" was undeniable, pertaining to both the upper and lower echelons of society, without conferring the hated appellation, "gentleman." "River Boat" not only applied to the gambler's trade, it also reflected his initials, R.B.

River Boat.

Rudy Blake.

Rose Bud.

I am alive became I am not alone. Rose exists. She is waiting for me; standing on the pier in Liverpool at this very moment, perhaps, watching the ships come in. I promised her I would do nothing to imperil my life. Dying in a hotel room would run counter to my pledge. She expects me to fight. She placed no stipulation on the method of my survival. Storms, war, accidents, sickness, haints, the ramblings of a diseased mind: none are allowed to take me off. That is the pact we made.

He had three days to kill before setting sail for England.

Three days, and then neither hell nor high water would keep him from her.

After that, his life was in her hands.

Then it would be she who paid the piper.

Changing his shirt, then applying a fresh collar, he slipped his hands through his jacket, smoothing out the wrinkles as best he could. In his former lives, he had been a man about town. One more incarnation of playing that role should not tip the scales out of balance.

He did not add that as a cat, he was perilously close to the number nine.

Waving away the attentions of the doorman, Rudy departed the hotel, determined to make a night of it. Once, that would have meant gambling but he had neither the dexterity nor sharpness of mind to handle a game of chance.

At other times in his life, he might have been attracted to one of the women on the street, or possessed in his pocket the address of an exclusive men's club, where the opportunities were equally prevalent but the circumstances infinitely more pleasing. This night, however, as all the other nights for as long as he could remember, he had no desire for intimacy.

Although having eaten nothing since leaving Richmond four days before, Rudy's stomach felt full and bloated. Eschewing the various restaurants and the fine meal he might have obtained, he hurried past the commingling odors of roast beef, fried chicken and fresh fish.

Not even the thought of a sweet roll and a cup of pungent coffee, whitened by cream and sweetened by cane sugar whetted his palate. He would eat, he decided, *when he got to England.*

Numerous saloons and drinking parlors beckoned, where a man could lose himself for three days and nights, but that was not his intent. If insensibility had been the goal, he could have achieved that alone and at considerably less expense in the "Grand Marquis."

He was alive, he was in New York City, and he had money to burn. Without poker, intercourse, meat or drink, he considered what other options presented themselves.

Finding himself standing by a hitching rail, his hand went instinctively toward the horse tied there, first rubbing its nose, then familiarly scratching behind its ears. As the animal responded to his attentions by placing its velvety-soft lips against his hand, a nearly overwhelming desire to ride filled his consciousness. The last time he had ridden was during the War, racing through a checkpoint at top speed. The remembrance came back to him and as though he were actually astride a fiery beast, he removed his hat to feel the wind whip through his hair.

So palpable was the experience he did not see the man come up behind him.

"You want something, mister?"

Startled by the words, he did a double take, quickly withdrawing his offending hand, then replacing his hat with a slight bow.

"You've a beautiful animal. I was just thinking... I had one like him, once. I beg your pardon."

Quickly shrinking from further contact, least it turn unpleasant, he hurried away, bitterly chastising himself for the wanton act of touching another's property.

I am not a horseman, he reminded himself, hanging his head in shame. *Riding is for others, not for me.*

Deprived of that opportunity, he sadly turned his steps toward a playhouse, advertising "A comedy in three acts," starring "Madame FlutterBy" and "Messieurs LoDuca." Paying his tuppence, he entered the darkened theatre, depositing his overcoat at the door.

His arrival was late, for the crowd was just filtering back from intermission. Joining them, he hesitated at the rear, debating whether to sit in front, which offered a better view, or to take a seat near the back. Fearing a seizure of claustrophobia, he searched for an aisle seat, finally discovering one on the left, three rows from where he stood. Drawing nervously on his white gloves, he gently settled in to await the curtain.

The farce was well attended, the room nearly two-thirds full when the patrons, returning from a stretch of their legs and a nip of something from a silver flask, returned to their seats. A ripple of applause rolled through the auditorium as Madame FlutterBy made her appearance.

The star of the performance had hardly been adequately depicted by the outside advertisements. Rather than the corpulent, buxom queen, attired in a gown of jeweled finery, this actress was thin, ungainly tall and dressed in a French soldier's costume. Her opening lines, poorly delivered in English, implied that her character was masquerading as a man. She had apparently joined the service, he deduced, to search for a lost love.

The dialogue was coarse and unevenly executed, leaving the audience to laugh when they supposed a joke was meant to be amusing. Playing off whatever response they got, the actors ad-libbed freely, all of the men's lines meant to underscore their stupidity at not recognizing a woman in trousers. Waving her ridiculously tall hat, decorated with half a dozen ostrich plumes, the "corporal" wiggled what the actress had supplemented into her brazier, eliciting loud catcalls from the mixed audience of men and women.

Discovering there was little plot to follow, Rudy's mind wandered. Counting six men in the rafters directing lantern light toward the stage, he then directed his attention toward the right wing, where he distinctly made out the director. This man, wearing a cap and a flowing cape, used the folds of cloth and occasionally a curt hand gesture to manipulate the players. He was apparently not well pleased with their deviation from the script, for his hissed repetition of the proper lines reached Rudy's ears with clarity.

He had almost lost himself in the drama unfolding behind the comedy when he felt a tickling sensation at the back of his neck. Reaching with as must discretion as possible, he scratched the itch, then started to remove his hand when the crawling sensation migrated down his back.

A cold chill descended over him, causing him to hold his breath. *I'm deceiving myself,* he thought. *My clothes are new. I have recently bathed. It cannot be a gray-back.*

The logic of his assertion proved to be his undoing. Instantly, he felt the unmistakable presence of ten or twenty more bugs crawling beneath his clothes. His entire body began to itch as they bit their way across his torso.

I'm making it up, he cried piteously, desperately scanning the floor for a trail of offending insects. There are no grey-backs in New York. I am not a soldier; I am at a theatre. *They cannot get me here. I left them behind on the uniform and those damned, rotting corpses.*

But indeed they could, if his senses correctly identified the old, sickeningly familiar feel of lice infesting his skin. Soon, they crept into his hair, burrowing so deep inside his scalp a trickle of blood emerged by his hairline.

No! This cannot be happening.

"I am a soldier no longer!"

His tortured exclamation drew immediate attention toward him. At first, the theatre goers thought he was joining the frolic on the stage, but his stricken countenance quickly revealed the sincerity of his cry. A low, rolling murmur began toward the front, working its way back.

"Cottonmouth," a man to his left identified, shooting him a look of hatred. "We don't want your damn kind here. Go back South where you belong."

"I'm not... I'm not a soldier," Rudy repeated, removing his hat and madly scratching his head. "Don't you see? The theatre is filled with lice."

His expression was enough to cause two rows of patrons to stand and move uncomfortably to more distant seats. The director, of whom he had so lately taken a fancy, pantomimed angry gestures with his cape, then inched his way toward the apron, pointing an angry finger at he who had so disrupted his production.

"Get rid of him!"

Before the attendants could carry out his demand, Rudy stood, turned helplessly in a circle, then found himself roughly grabbed from behind as a patron beside him growled, "I paid good money to enjoy this comedy and I don't want you interrupting the performance."

"I'm sorry; I'm so sorry –"

"Take your mother fucking Southern ass out of here," he continued, lowering his voice to express his ungentlemanly sentiment.

"Yes. Of course. I'm –"

The rest of Rudy's sentence was lost as the man placed a large hand over his mouth, dragged him into the aisle and shoved him forward. Losing his balance, Rudy crawled up the sloping walkway on hands and knees until he reached the back. Still itching frantically, he staggered to his feet, swayed a moment as a searing bolt of vertigo struck him, then raced out, a silent scream on bloodless lips.

No one made a move to stop him, which was just as well, for they would have found themselves with a tiger on their hands. Rudy's intent would not have been violence, but his insane scratching would have been interpreted as such, and the combatants would have drawn the attention of the authorities.

As it was, he was left free to escape, a round of thunderous applause for the brave Northerner who had chased him, ringing in his ears.

On his way, the hat check man attempted to toss him his overcoat, then wisely withheld it as Rudy screamed. Plunging outside, he raced away into an alley, only then ripping his jacket and shirt open, giving him access to the insects. Digging his fingernails deep into his flesh, he tore away at the lice, hissing and cursing vile oaths to the Confederate gods which had passed along their curse from war to peacetime.

"Get them off me! Get them off me," he wailed, throwing himself against the brick wall and rubbing raw his skin. Still not satisfied, he rolled in the dirt, covering himself with mud and debris, all in a mad attempt to rid himself from "grey-backs."

Sobbing like a child, he finally slumped down, melting into the earth like green pus from an infected wound. His body was on fire, but finally, mercifully, the itching stopped. With his head between his legs, he caught his jagged breath, then stumbled away, nearly dropping from exhaustion as he struck a gas lamp pole. With the light overhead swaying unsteadily, he inspected his arms, then his chest and finally his legs, frantically searching for the remnants of squashed bugs.

Nothing. Not one sign of lice. There had been no lice. It had all been in his imagination.

Wiping tears of agony from his eyes, he staggered away, having successfully killed one night, if not a legion of crawling insects.

CHAPTER 7

He did not dare go out again. Without a reasonable explanation for what had happened to him at the theatre, he feared a repetition. If he happened to be in a library, dining hall, dance salon, gaming parlor or even our riding, when attacked by a legion of hobgoblin grey-backs, he did not think he could control himself.

Lice. There was only one way a man of culture and breeding could be exposed to "vermin" and that was on the battlefield. While Northern boys were not immune to the insidious "camp followers," his accent would betray him. Taken to a physician, his head would be shaved, his clothes burned and his sanity, if not his freedom, jeopardized.

There were people he knew in New York; silent business partners, men with whom he had dealings in the past. Any would have opened their doors to him. Not from friendship, but rather, from the absolute certainty he had made good his promise to squeeze every penny from the multiple opportunities presented by a wartime economy.

A man with money was not to be scorned, no matter where his place of origin.

Most of these partners assumed the liberty of addressing him on a first name basis. Between 1858 and 1860, the period he had devoted to acquainting himself with the major cities of the eastern seaboard, any number of wealthy Northerners had wined and dined him in their own homes, introducing their wives and children with a simplicity bespeaking the rare acknowledgment of his Southern heritage. True to form, for at one time he had been an actor better than any on stage, Rudy Blake had played the gentleman, ingratiating himself with those he would later use as a banker, associate or confidant.

For a fee, or a share of a factory, or, even possibly, out of pity, any one of them might have taken him to a private sanatorium for treatment, checking him in under an assumed name. There, under the care of a well-paid physician, he might have recovered his strength, put behind him the lingering effects of dysentery, scurvy and talking ghosts.

Might have. That was the key which locked his door, planting his feet on the matching red carpet of his Grand Marquis suite.

He could not take the chance. In his ravings, doctors were no more honorable than bankers. It would be a matter of small consequence to obtain the numbers of his bank accounts, have him sign away stocks, bonds and lands. Worse, while they might tolerate his illness, none of them could understand it. War, to them, was what they had read in the newspapers. Terrible, regrettable and over. Whatever lingering aftereffects a man experienced were expected to pass with the Articles of Capitulation.

Anything beyond that was an indication of moral weakness.

There were others, of the more tender sex, who would also have opened more than their doors to him. Those he eschewed as well, albeit for different reasons. There was only one with whom he sought companionship; one who would judge with her heart, rather than her mind. It was to Rose he must hurry, and time was running out.

One day, twelve hours to kill.

Again he ordered food, this time making an attempt to eat. The milk curdled in his mouth and the beef was indigestible.

"Send a message to Rose. Tell her I'm coming."

It was a plan and he attacked it as though he were a general and the outcome of his private war depended upon its so simple completion.

Dear Rose. I am alive. That would reassure her at the outset. *I am coming.* She would prepare the fatted calf. *I am ill.* Time to prepare the potions and elixirs only she knew how to make. *Arriving on the "Southern Cross" in two weeks' time.* She would meet him on the dock. *Have the books ready for an audit.* That would bring a smile to her lips. She might even laugh.

Something he had not done for a century. A lifetime. An eternity.

Two weeks' time. It would take that long for a letter to reach her. In all probability, he would arrive before the missive. He laughed. One "century" closed and another began.

He did not write the letter, thus failing as a general.

He would have been the last to disagree.

Twenty-two hours and seventeen minutes to kill.

Ordering a newspaper, Rudy amused himself by reading the editorials. Andrew Johnson was loved. Andrew Johnson was hated. No one knew what the hell to make of Andrew Johnson.

"Influx of Negroes Expected for the Winter. Who Will Feed Them?"

"Opportunities for Men with Money in the southern states." Small "s's."

"Women's Charity League Collecting Money for the Unfortunates." Now, who were they?

"Top Dollar Paid for Cotton." The king was dead. Long live the king.

Advertisements for laborers, dock work, sailors. "Ships departing Immediately." He had read such adverts before. "Top Wages. Good Working Conditions." The same old lies.

As much as things changed, they stayed the same.

"The *Southern Cross* departing for Liverpool. Berths available for Gentlemen and Ladies."

It was not until he saw the words in print that the irony registered. The *Southern Cross*. That was the ship he was to sail on.

Southern Cross.

Upon his chest he wore two scars, intersecting in the form of a cross. He was a Southerner.

Southern cross.

"Oh, my dear God." He had played into the hands of the gods. He had gone to war to die and he had not died. Against all odds he had survived and now that he wanted to live, he was to set sail on the *Southern Cross*. The ship was to be his tomb.

There was no other way to interpret the fact. He had challenged the Olympians once and lost, yet they were not through with him. The farce was not played out. Only his death would bring down the curtain on the play he had set in motion three years ago.

"Rose," he cried, the newspaper falling from his insensate hands. "Rose. I am coming.... Too late."

Two hours to kill and he had better hurry. Time and tide waited for no man.

"All aboard! All aboard!"

Rudy's head buzzed with the noise and confusion of the seaside pier. To complicate matters, the irritating ringing in his ears, which had begun in Norfolk, returned, making speech difficult, if not impossible to comprehend.

"All aboardddddd!"

Something was amiss. "All aboard" was the expression used by conductors, summoning passengers to step up to a train. Never, in his life, had he heard anyone yell "all aboard" at a shipyard.

"The *Southern Cross,*" he tried, raising his voice in the hope of being heard over the din. "Is this the *Southern Cross?*"

"Up there," a surely man replied, spittle flying from his tobacco-encrusted lips. Rudy did not bother looking in the direction indicated, for "up there" was not an option. It was "right in front of you, mate," "half a mile to starboard an' move yer ass if you expect to catch it," or "Pier 27," or 67 or 127. But not "up there."

"Up there" was not where he wanted to go. Aboard the *Southern Cross* or via any other conveyance.

"Excuse me," he tried again, this time to a carrier dressed in overalls and wearing a mutilated kepi, the brim of which had been lost, to gauge from its owner's face, sometime between the Revolution and the War of 1812. "I'm to depart this morning on the *Southern Cross.* Can you tell me, please, where she is berthed?"

"Never heard of 'er," he replied in a nasal twang, hurrying away to points unknown.

"Wait a minute! Just a moment," Rudy called, waving his hand in the air. "Come back. I have a ticket."

But the carrier was gone, disappeared into the swarming mob. With a wail of helpless abandon, Rudy attempted to reconfirm the name of his ship by reading the ticket. His eyes crossed, blurring the words.

Perhaps he had gotten it wrong, misremembered. What exactly had the barber said? *Southern Sky? Southern Constellation? Northern Cross?*

Christ on the Cross?

"Somebody, help me, please!"

Waving his ticket over his head, Rudy stood shock still while the ebb and flow of humanity circled round him, as though he were an impediment, a sand bar or a craggy rock, jutting out below the shore line.

He was about to add, "I have money," then bit his tongue. That was an advertisement for a mugging.

"I am a war veteran," he tried, instead. "First and Second Bull Run." His mind worked feverishly on the names of other battles; Northern appellations. "The Seven Days Battles," and then, miserably, "George McClellan."

"Right this way, sir," a voice behind him offered as an arm was placed through his. "Let me show you."

The stranger led him to a boarding ramp, twenty feet from where he had been standing. Gently prying the paper from his fingers, he offered the limp ticket for inspection. With it was approved with a cursory, "Git aboard. Yer late," the fellow guided Rudy upward, settling him by the rail.

"You're in Cabin 19A, sir. Can you remember that? 19A," he kindly repeated, then hailed a porter. "I'll see your luggage is stowed below."

"19A," Rudy replied, desperately attempting to commit the number to memory.

"That's right, sir. Will you be all right here?"

"The *Southern Cross?* Going to England?"

"That's right. In two weeks and not a day longer, you'll be home, sir," the youth whispered, flashing an unexpected grin.

"Home.... How did you know... I was going home?"

Tipping his cap, the boy in a red and blue stripped shirt widened his smile. "Your accent, sir. Thought I recognized it as English. That's right, isn't it?"

"Yes," Rudy agreed, dumbfounded.

"Over there, I expect it's all right to say 'Manassas.'" He winked and took a backwards step. "But I wouldn't go bragging I fought under George McClellan," he added, waving a farewell. "I served under him an' I wouldn't recommend it."

"You know," Rudy gasped, furiously attempting to reconcile the former soldier's words with his actions. "And yet you helped me when no one else would."

"Maybe what I know better'n them is that the War's over, sir. Ain't we done enough killin'? Live and let live is what I say."

"Here. Wait. Let me pay you for your trouble."

Brushing aside the pocketbook which he could have taken with no one the wiser, the boy leapt back upon shore, leaving one former Southern soldier greatly perplexed.

He would have to remember to tell Rose. She would explain it to him.

"19A. Manassas," he whispered. And then, with all the reverence he could muster, "I'm going home."

She would like the story about how he had sounded English. It would make her laugh.

And then there was the part about the man calling "All aboard!" and one hundred thousand conductor's caps....

When Rudy regained his awareness, the *Southern Cross* had left port and was chugging eastward. A stiff wind blew in his face, which was red and raw from exposure. Putting a hand to his cheek, Rudy realized with a shock he must have been standing at the railing for hours for the elements to have that effect on his skin.

Hours. Where had the time gone?

Hours or days? Or weeks? Scanning the horizon, he searched for land, hoping against hope the journey was nearing its conclusion. No land in sight.

"Fool," he remarked. "Damned fool. We've only just rounded the Horn. The coast of California is months away."

He was twenty-one years old again and on his way to San Francisco. The War, which was not his War, had never been fought. Drummer boys who would perish at Second Manassas were not even born.

The gold fields and chunks of precious metal as large as his head were yet to be discovered.

Four score and ten dolphins romped the waters in innocent play.

"Where am I?"

"In your cabin, Mr. Blake. I've just brought your dinner."

"Cabin?" Rudy cried, bringing a hand to his face. His flesh was hot to the touch. "I have no cabin. I sleep on deck... in the huts."

"19A, sir. Call it a 'suite,' if you like," the waiter added derisively. "There's none that sleep on deck but the likes of me. Shall I open the bottle of wine for you?"

"Wine?"

"What you ordered for dinner. Bread and cheese and wine. I've just delivered it."

"I... ordered?" He had no memory of having ordered anything, nor could he remember how he came to be in his "suite." "Tell me, please," he began, then bit his tongue, clamping down so hard tears welled in his eyes. Weakness, he remembered, was a sin. It also invited the waiter and his associates – the porters, stewards and cabin boys – to rob him blind.

In order to survive two more weeks, he would have to take care. Let the staff think him eccentric, but not ill. In this dog-eat-dog world, he could not blame them for thievery. On the other hand, he could wish their light fingers practiced on those who could better afford to lose their pocket change and pocket linens.

"Yes. Uncork the wine and let it sit, then slice the cheese. Very thin."

Obeying his orders, the waiter retired, but not before clumsily ascertaining where Rudy kept his billfold. The act almost brought a smile to the owner's face, and as the man retreated, he dared one act of bravado.

"A moment." Getting to his feet, he walked deliberately toward the door, hands gesticulating in tempo to his words. "In the mornings, I shall require fresh brewed coffee – the first cup from the pot. Also, warm bread and butter and jam, if you have it. For lunch, a steaming mug of tea. For dinner, cream soup or broth, cheese and bread. As long as there is milk aboard, I shall require a full glass with each meal. And sugar. A small bowlful should be adequate."

Patting him familiarly, Rudy continued in a hushed undertone. "Always be certain I have an open bottle of red wine – the best you have – that reserved for the captain's table, if you can get it. For your services, I shall reward you well. Come yourself, knocking on the door three times."

He demonstrated, rapping twice in rapid succession, then once, half beat after.

"You have a pass key; use it. Let yourself in, set the table and depart. Do not bore me with idle chatter. If you must speak, tell me of the weather, the sailing conditions and the time we make. Whether or not you think me asleep, I wish to be informed of the date, date of the week and estimated time of arrival. Is that clear?"

"Yes, sir."

Extracting a twenty dollar bill from his wallet, Rudy tore it, giving the smaller portion to his new man servant.

"At the completion of the voyage, you will come to my cabin and pack my bags, seeing that you overlook nothing. When I am safely on shore, I shall give you the other half of that money."

"Yes, sir!"

"What is your name?"

"Roberto."

"Very well, Roberto," Rudy concluded, stroking him on the arm and upper body the way old men said good-bye to favored grandsons. "We have an understanding."

With a tip of his cap, the waiter disappeared. Rudy began a meticulous countdown, leaning against the shuttered door for support. Ten, fifteen, twenty, twenty-five seconds before a gentle double knock, followed by a pause and a third tap reached his ears. Nodding wisely, he spoke through the thin wood.

"Use your pass key, Roberto."

A pause, longer this time than the one separating knocks.

"I can't, sir."

Disengaging the lock, Rudy pulled back the hinged partition. One look at Roberto's face assured him he had made his point. Indicating the youth hold out his hand, Rudy placed into it the pass key, three watches, one farmer's coin purse, a pearl necklace and matching pair of ear bobs. His own timepiece he discretely held back, clipping it onto his gold chain, then slipping it into his vest.

"Just so we understand one another, Roberto. I tolerate no dishonesty from my cohorts. Not that I damn you for trying," he added conspiratorially, "but practice on others, not me. Or I will see the captain keelhauls you in front of the crew, and I exchange my twenty dollar bill in England for a new one, without ever paying you your tip for services rendered."

Ashamed and frightened, Roberto took the pilfered items, dropping only the key in his trousers.

"An honest misunderstanding, sir," he began, but Rudy stopped his with a look which could have pierced lead.

"Between us, let us have no more misunderstandings."

"You won't say anything – to the captain? About these other things?"

"Who am I to say you don't have a penchant for timepieces... and earrings. We start anew."

"Yes, sir. Thank you, sir."

Roberto saluted a second time, this act one of authority and respect. Rudy acknowledged him with a slight nod, then closed the door behind him. With a sigh of resignation, he wavered back toward the table, barely managing to fall into the chair before the madly spinning room got the better of his equilibrium.

In better days, pickpocketing the raw youth would have been child's play, a game to pass the time, rather than the challenge it now presented to his sick and weakened frame. Yet it had been a gamble he had to take, for if he had let the waiter steal his own watch, in a day or a week, he would have been unable to prevent the thief from removing all his articles of value.

It was going to take every penny he possessed and all his remaining strength to get to Rose's dwelling. Rendered moneyless, the journey would go from difficult to impossible.

Get there he must, for the idea of having the inscription on his tombstone read, "Died Trying," was no consolation whatsoever.

CHAPTER 8

With his head already spinning, Rudy did not want the wine. He had merely asked the boy to open it as an excuse for conversation. Nor did he think his fragile stomach would hold the bread and cheese, although he had stressed both be brought to him on a regular basis. It was all he could think of to order.

Feeling the lack of coffee or tea acutely, he perched on the side of the bed, staring with a glazed, desultory look around the cabin. As a suite, the only advantage he saw in it was isolation. The bunk was hardly better than those issued to common seamen, while the furniture was rickety and poorly constructed. No rug adorned the wood slat floor, while the oil lamp poured noxious fumes into the enclosed space.

Fearing to extinguish it and thus leave himself in darkness, he shoved it to the farthest corner, then on impulse, shuffled to the door. Picking a thread from his cuff of his jacket, he jammed it in the crack. It was an old gambler's trick, a way of determining whether anyone had ingress to his cabin without permission.

Upon returning from a long night at cards, or arising in the morning, a quick glance determined whether or not the string was in place. It was as good as hiring a boy to watch his back. Better, he mused, for aboard the *Southern Cross,* there were no Negro lads to assume the task.

Feeling more protected, and deriving a modicum of strength from that knowledge, he weaved unsteadily to the porthole. Unfastening the latch, he hoisted it upward, relieved beyond measure that his quarters were situated along the outside of the boat.

Taking in a deep breath of salt sea air, he filled his lungs then exhaled slowly, first through his nose, then his mouth, rolling his tongue over the crystalline residue, enjoying the taste. There had been a time, not so long ago, when he believed he would never sail again. Landlocked in the bowels of Tennessee, the ocean seemed tens of thousands of leagues away.

"I'm coming, Rose. Wait for me."

If he spoke loud enough, working the timbre of his voice into that resembling the old Rudy Blake, she might hear and stand ready.

"I am alive. I did not die in war."

Not in any of the bloody battles, the inconsequential skirmishes; not from a sharpshooter's rifle, or from his own cannon, exploding in his face. Not from poor nutrition, exposure to the elements, not even from a bullet, fired from a Confederate sentry's musket.

Nor had he perished from the caprice of the gods, by whom he had been driven to enlist.

"I am alone, Rose," he sobbed, feeling the discharge from his nose drip unevenly down his chin. "You were right. She would not come with me and so I was caught in the burning of Atlanta. You said so. You knew what would happen, but you didn't know it all." Shivering violently, he withdrew from the porthole, chilled and damp.

"You weren't sure, were you? Not certain I'd survive. The odds were against. But I did. I think I did."

Staring bleakly down at his trembling limbs, he stifled a shudder, then wrapped his arms around himself. With clattering teeth, speech became affected.

"I think I'm alive." Cognitive formation of ideas was difficult and his certainty wavered. "What was it you said? About how a woman knew she was in love?" Pulling back the memory, he tried a faint, ghost-like smile. *"A woman knows she's in love when she hurts; when she's in pain.* The same can be said for a man, R. B. I'm suffering. Only my love for you has kept the smoldering embers lit."

I am with you, she replied from the recesses of memory and distance. *I am waiting. Send me word upon your arrival and I shall come. To take you home. And Rudy?*

Cocking his ear eastward, he listened for what was coming.

You are alive.

It was more than he could have hoped. Crumpling to his knees, the once fierce scourge of the Seven Seas clasped his hands together and prayed.

> "Now I lay me down to sleep,
> I pray the Lord my soul to keep.
> If I should die before I wake,
> I pray the Lord my soul to take."

A child's prayer, repeated by an adult's innocent lips.

When he awoke, Rudy found himself in bed. He did not remember rising from the floor, nor undressing, though he was now clad in undergarments and socks. Craning his neck toward the wardrobe, he observed his suit neatly folded, the shoes carefully aligned beneath. A cry of dismay issued from parched lips.

"Who has done this?"

Without a doubt, Roberto, the cabin boy, had arrived at dawn. Using his pass key, he had let himself in, depositing the breakfast tray on his stand. Discovering Rudy insensate on the floor, he had dragged him up, undressed him, then performed the kind service of neatly arranging his clothes.

"Let him think I was drunk; or seasick," he added, a wry smile crossing his otherwise taut features. Ordinarily, allowing the youth to think him a landlubber would have been abhorrent, but under present circumstances, it was better than permitting him to draw the conclusion he were ill. While he had frightened the boy once, weakness would obfuscate matters considerably.

Two circumstances clouded the issue. There was no breakfast tray on the table and the thread he had placed in the door was undisturbed. Shaking his head in disbelief, Ruby tottered to his feet, desperately attempting to catch his bearings. Surely, the error was his. There *was* a tray and the tread *had* fallen. His perceptions, upon waking, were faulty.

Beginning a systematic search, he navigated the cabin inch-by-inch, going so far as to peer beneath the bunk, seeking the elusive tray. It was nowhere to be found.

Wiping beads of cold perspiration from his brow, he rationalized the situation.

"He saw that I was dead asleep. Knowing I would not awake for hours, he took back the tray, so the coffee would not get cold."

His voice was weak, almost a whisper, yet it was the best he could muster. Like a good actor, he shook his head derisively and tried again.

"He saw that I was de-" Realizing his poor word choice, he trembled, then omitted the offending word. "...I was asleep." To have left it uncorrected would tempt the gods. "Knowing I would not wake for hours, he took back the tray, so the coffee would not get cold."

Nodding in approval, for he had always been his own best audience, the thespian waved an appreciative thanks to the absent servant. He had judged well, made an ally. A simple sleight of hand and the promise of reward transformed an enemy into a friend. It was well to discover the old tricks world as well in this new world as they had in the previous.

Nagging in the back of his mind, however, was the thread. A quick glance at the door upon awakening had assured him it was still in place. That implied no one had entered.

"No," he demurred, running his hands through his hair the way drunks freshened their appearance after a night's debauch. "I am mistaken. It has fallen. My eyes deceived me."

Easier to believe that, than the contrary.

He began to dress, working his unresponsive arm through the wrinkled shirt. The material stank of sweat, curling his nose in disdain. A gentleman would never wear a soiled garment. It reeked of poor breeding, or worse, poverty.

"I am not a gentleman," he reminded himself. The old adage did nothing to quell the storm of trepidation creeping up his back and into his neck. The backs of his palms dampened, a sure indication of danger or extreme nervousness.

"Get up and check the door."

"Why should I?" he argued. "The thread has fallen."

"It is in place. You saw it, yourself."

There was no hope for it. With a theatrical sigh of resignation, fooling no one, he crept toward the portal, the tails of his shirt brushing listlessly against his thighs.

"There. You see," he indicated. "It has fallen. The boy has come and gone."

The thread was wedged in the crack, exactly where he placed it. It had not fallen. His coldness of the moment before turned hot, so that the shirt clung to his back like a second skin, while imaginary blisters from the boiling perspiration formed on his chest.

"No matter," he dismissed. "The fault is mine. I jammed it in too tightly."

To prove his point, Rudy wrapped his fingers around the knob, turning it gently. The door opened a crack. The thread slipped noiselessly to the floor.

"He has replaced it," he croaked, the words nearly choking him. "He has somehow managed to put it back."

It was a logical explanation and utterly false. Not even Rudy could believe the lie. No one had entered his room. Roberto had not brought his breakfast tray; he had not undressed him.

Who, then, had perpetrated the deed?

"There is someone here. With me. In the cabin."

That would explain the conundrum.

"Hello," he called, biding the stranger reappear. "Hello? I mean you no harm." And then, to back his friendly salutation, "I have a pistol."

The interloper did not make himself known. "I understand," Rudy tried again, forcing the words out in a pitiful attempt to deliver them with authority. "The ship is overbooked. They sold you a berth in my cabin."

No one took advantage of his offer at forgiveness.

"Come out and show yourself, damn it!"

The less inviting salutation elicited equal results. There was no stranger hiding in the suite. He had already searched his quarters, looking for the breakfast tray. The answer to his dilemma was apparent, even to him. He had awoken during the night and undressed himself. He had folded his suit and placed his shoes equidistant from one another, military style. As he had been taught at the Virginia Military Institute. In his confusion, he had reverted to early training.

The idea was as repugnant as it was frightening. He had suffered a blackout, a loss of memory. His mind was slipping away.

"I am sick," he whispered, with the full realization he was completely alone and abandoned by the world. If Roberto had come, as ordered, then he had departed just as quickly, unconcerned about the lack of a response to his knock. Rudy could have been dead on the floor for all he knew or cared. He was no ally, just a boy who had been frightened away by a parlor trick.

Rudy had been too clever, too cunning. What was twenty dollars to such a youth? He had stolen a cumulative two hundred dollars in purloined jewelry. Before the voyage was out, he would have five times that. Rather than bribe him into submission, Rudy had merely scared him away. He would not come with a breakfast tray filled with steaming coffee and fresh bread. He would not punctually deliver lunch or dinner and he most assuredly would not bring a bottle of red wine from the captain's private stock.

It was a devastating revelation.

Alone, with three thousand miles of ocean to traverse. He would never make it. Never arrive in Liverpool alive.

Alive was the key.

His body would surely arrive. How long would it take for someone to realize he had expired? Two days? A week? Not until his corpse began to smell? Would that be what prompted them to finally investigate?

"We've had complaints from the passengers, Captain. There's a terrible stink coming from one of the staterooms."

"Probably some rotting food one of those bastards horded aboard."

"It's worse than that, sir. The whole level reeks of it."

Rudy knew the captain would not want to breech his privacy. It would take a virtual uprising before he would grant permission. He would not go himself; that would be undignified. He would send the second mate. With a pass key.

Where would they find his body? On the bed, curled into a ball, arms and legs stiffened by rigor mortis, tongue lolling out the way he had seen so many dead soldiers? Or fallen to the deck, neck bent at an unnatural angle, eyes glazed with the cataracts of death?

The mate would curse; the steward would wrap a handkerchief around his mouth to ward off the stench. It would do no good. The smell would penetrate his clothes, poison his lungs. The sight would ingrain itself into his memory, until its haunting posture would taint his very existence.

"Wrap it up in a tarpaulin and stow it in the hold."

Just another side of spoiled beef.

Food for Confederate soldiers.

"We'll dump it on the wharf at Liverpool. With a name tag. Maybe somebody will collect it."

With his mind in a whirl, Rudy remembered the stories he had heard on the Mississippi. Because the water table was so high, burial beneath ground was impossible. Those unfortunates who had not the fee to purchase a crypt were shoved in pine boxes and shipped north to St. Louis. There, they were left for the local administrators to handle as they saw fit.

Potter's Field.

With no one to pay the Ferryman.

Never to reach the far shore of the River Styx.

Never to find peace.

"We'll toss him overboard."

What? Who was that speaking? Craning his neck, Rudy frantically searched the cabin, seeking the speaker. But it was only his imagination. He was listening to the captain in his make-believe scenario.

"I'm not toting a dead body all the way to England. A passenger's no different than a crewman. Sew him up in his blanket and consign him to the deep."

"Who will read the service?" The damned mate always had an objection.

"You will. Get the Bible out of my quarters."

That, Rudy knew, was what a Bible was used for at sea. That, and to solicit divine help when the hurricane waves were washing overboard and the ship was sinking.

The ship's sail maker would be summoned. "Sew him up."

But that was not right, he reminded himself, shaking his head to clear the cobwebs of his past. There were no sail makers aboard a steamer. He felt the loss acutely. Tears streamed from his eyes. All the sail makers had been rendered useless with the advent of steam.

As useless as a dead riverboat gambler.

Dead gamblers had no friends.

"We consign this body to the deep." No one there to pronounce an "Amen" over his corpse.

"Rose!"

But Rose was not there. He was alone. He was shark bait.

He remembered that, too. The scene aboard the *Lexington*.

"Give the body to us, Captain. We'll hack it up for shark bait; an arm or a leg ought to catch us a big one."

It was a way to pass the time; keep the wayward passengers occupied; prevent them from asking yet again, "How long until we round the Horn?"

The card shark, rendered into shark bait.

The irony was too great to bear.

"Oh, God!"

God, in his Infinite Mercy, was not listening.

The night passed into day, or the day passed into night. It made no difference. Time was inconsequential. Rudy no longer had time to kill.

Time was killing him.

His blackouts occurred more frequently, lasting from minutes to hours. He had no indication of their coming, knew they had left only when brought to awareness by a jolt of reality.

Items in his room were rearranged; pillows moved from the head to the foot of the bed. A blanket mysteriously folded itself; sheets disappeared, the porthole opened and closed, shirts fell from the wardrobe. Once, he woke to discover his shoes were on the wrong feet, as though a capricious giant had manipulated his body while he slept.

He had heard men tell of such phenomenon before, but those were drunks, deep in their cups, or opium eaters, suspended over hell's fires by the power of their craving. He had seen men, delusional with fever, or out of their minds from pain, yet he was neither inebriated nor addicted, burning hot or writhing from tortuous injury.

When his own mind had wandered from starvation or fear, or when in the grips of disease, reality had warped, but never abandoned him. No matter how far and wide his mind wandered, he was always brought back to reality with crashing force. The dullness, the creeping apathy, the loss of contact with present circumstances he suffered now was disconcerting beyond words.

There was no clearing of the brain, no ability to summon memory and drag back the incidents which puzzled him. He was an insomniac who walked in his sleep; a man hypnotized by trauma, performing deeds both out of character and out of sense.

Forgetting the name of the cabin boy, he staggered to the companionway and called for "Alomar," only to be informed there was no one by that name aboard. He set out his shoes to be cleaned and someone stole them. He waited piteously for breakfast and cried like a babe when dinner was served.

For a man who prided himself on being unemotional, tears came fast and furious to his eyes. Staring at the sunset through his round window on the world, he wept for the dying sun; observing a leaping fish caught by a swooping bird, he nearly choked on his tears at the loss of life.

Cutting himself with his razor, for his hands were too unsteady to shave, he crumpled into a ball, traumatized at the sight of blood. With his lips parched and cracked from unmitigated thirst, he found his water glass too heavy to hold and spilled the contents, reducing him to licking drops off the floor. Wracked by hunger, the over-dried beef clove to the roof of his mouth, while the soup, cold from inattention, gagged him, closing his throat before he could swallow.

His watch stopped. Winding it in a frenzy, he broke the spring, so that it ticked no more. The oil burned out in his lamp and no one refilled it. He mistook his chamber pot for a hat and dirtied himself. There was no place to bathe, and no one to bring him a basin of fresh water.

Occasionally a knock came at his door, but the sound frightened him and he would not answer it. Only after the footfalls faded in the distance did he dare drag himself to the door and open it, a crack, no more. Occasionally, a covered tray was set by the floor; more frequently, there was nothing.

He attempted to care but could not.

Rarely, he overheard conversations in the corridor; passengers exchanging pleasantries. They spoke in a foreign language he could not comprehend, their sentences meaningless and derisive. He determined they were laughing at him and harbored bitter resentment. He fantasied about shooting them, but had no weapon.

He craved milk but none was ever brought. He wrote a note, requesting bread and was disappointed when none came. He heard scurrying in the night and imagined rats deserting a sinking ship.

Once, he made an attempt to go on deck, hoping the fresh air would revive him. Changing his shirt so that he would not appear unkempt, he found his fingers would not work the bottoms and thus abandoned the idea, condemning him to his little prison cell.

He dozed in fits and starts, waking from bad dreams drenched in perspiration, always afraid he had died in his sleep and resurrected as a wandering spirit. Elongated shadows wrapped their clinging tendrils around his neck, cutting off air; the crashing of the waves were always the footsteps of those coming to sew him in his blanket.

The moon was made of green cheese, but he could not reach it and eat. The spray of the sea too salty to drink. He was cold and could not find his blanket. His teeth shivered in his gums and he felt them loosen. One by one he picked them out until he was rendered toothless, then woke from another spell to find them clamped shut, his jaw locked.

Sleep became his one compelling desire but he could not force his mind to rest. Always before him were images he did not recognize, incidents so vivid he could smell the fires or touch the grass, yet never was he refreshed upon waking. He called names aloud, having no idea to whom they belonged; rode horses shackled by rotting harnesses, fired cannon which blew up in his face.

His flesh became unduly sensitive, causing him to rip the cotton fabrics from his body. The wool of the bed clothes itched him unmercifully, and he tossed them aside, lying on the bare mattress. Feathers from the pillow stuck in his ear, pricked his neck, forcing him to lie flat. The weight of the oppressive humidity bore down on him so he could not breathe.

A constant throbbing in his left hand drove him nearly wild, until he found release in fantasy. With a surgeon's rusty saw in his right hand, he severed the offending limb from his body, only to discover he had exacerbated the agony by leaving himself with a bleeding stump. Tearing his sheet to shreds, he wrapped his hand, then screamed at the apparition of contorting fingers, clearly visible through the bandage.

Forcing himself to inspect the damage he had not done, Rudy observed a split and ingrown fingernail. Chiding himself for his cowardice, he attempted to pare the nail with a knife, bringing forth puss and darkened blood. When the pain grew unbearable, he held his arm above his head, alleviating the pressure. But he was not strong enough to hold it there, and when it dropped, he writhed in agony.

He thought of war and why he had not died. He recalled digging graves and dumping bodies inside, too numerous to count. He counted gold coins, none for the eyes of the dead. He wished he were dead.

In a moment of transparent clarity, he remembered the moments before battle, when men scribbled their names on errant pieces of paper, pinning them to their breasts, lest they be killed and buried in unmarked holes. Forcing his eyes to focus, he removed his red Moroccan pocketbook from his coat. With the pencil firmly attached by cord, he manipulated his hand, writing the first words which came to him.

Rose Theodore. Blake House. London.

And then he laughed. It was a deep, maniacal sound, filling his heart with dread.

When they came to take him away, it was Rose Theodore they would consign to the depths, not Rudy Blake.

The world darkened around him and he knew no more.

There was nothing left to know. With the stroke of a pencil, he had murdered that which was more precious than life.

CHAPTER 9

"The passengers have all disembarked, sir," the seaman's voice sang out.

The officer in charge checked his manifold, then shook his head. He was tired and wanted to complete the task. Only then could he get ashore. It had been a long voyage.

"What about that odd one in the Stateman's quarters? Has he left?"

"I didn't check there, sir," came the reluctant reply.

"Then do so. He hasn't croaked, has he?"

"Not the last time the steward looked in, sir."

"Well, pack his things and get him out. If he's going to die, I don't want it to be aboard ship. Jesus, I'll never get away if he's dead."

The officer waited impatiently for the crewman to return. He had just convinced himself the odd recluse had rotted in the cabin when he caught sight of him. Standing a head taller than the seaman escorting him, the passenger appeared more like a scarecrow than a human being. Walking with a decided list, his face was unshaved. Dark circles under his eyes accentuated the pallor of his skin. An unhealthy sweat covered his brow. He trembled like a broken mast amidst a torrent.

The crewman saluted his officer.

"Here he is, sir."

"What took you so damn long?"

"He was covered in a blanket, sir, and wouldn't give it up."

The officer swore under his breath and shook his head. He would far rather have conceded the blanket and saved himself ten minutes. As it was, he was not at all certain they could get the passenger off the ship before he expired.

He hoped to hell the skeleton-in-rags did not have any contagious disease. The cabins he so lately occupied were already lent out to a wealthy French businessman and his family for the return trip. If they caught something and perished, the world would be turned upside down.

He cursed.

"Did you say something, sir?"

"No... Yes. Get him off the ship," he dismissed with a derisive wave of his clipboard.

"What'll I do with him, then?"

"That's not our business."

The seaman squirmed uncomfortably.

"But if he gets trampled underfoot on the wharf, there'll be questions asked. Where did he come from? Which ship did he disembark off?"

The officer cursed aloud this time. He knew the man was right. Striding up to Rudy, he stuck his face near that of the sick man's.

"You, there – where do you belong? Where were you traveling ? Have you someone here to pick you up?"

Rudy made no answer. Eyes half shut, he did not understand the words, so harshly spoken. Having been alone so long, it was difficult to distinguish reality from fantasy.

Annoyed, irritated and impatient, the officer reached into Rudy's pockets, beginning a search. His fingers immediately encountered a wad of bills. Surprised and disconcerted, he withdrew his hands quickly, least he be accused of theft. While he was not above the deed, he could hardly be expected to conceal it from the seaman.

As though to confirm his better instincts, the tar whispered, "What was that?"

The answer was self-evident.

"Money."

"Sweet Jesus. He must be a gentleman. He croaks on us, the captain'll have our hides."

The mate did not appreciate being included in the "our."

"You look," he ordered, stepping away to distance himself from any crime, real or imagined, that might be hung around his neck.

"I am not a gentleman."

It was not the denial, but the fact the passenger spoke at all which caused both men to cry. He did not look in a condition to initiate speech. The fact he did was closer to a testimony of the resurrection than it was to the state of his health.

Stiffening his resolve, for the bosun's whistle informed him he was needed elsewhere, the mate realigned his jaw into something resembling a jut.

"Come, sir. You must disembark. Where is your destination?"

Just as the seaman's answer to "What was that?" was pre-determined by fact, so, too, was Rudy's.

"Hell."

The officer should have been prepared but was not.

"Where is that?" he demanded, before tripping over his words as realization struck. Glancing at his companion, he shuddered, then made a whirling motion with his finger. "He's gone off the deep end. The captain hears about this, well both catch –"

He did not finish his sentence. Rudy had done it for him.

Grinding his teeth in frustration, he shot a less than reverent glance skyward, then reached inside Rudy's coat, this time withdrawing his billfold. Readjusting the cap on his head, his trembling hands parted the leather tri-folding wallet.

The pencil, attached by a cord, fell out, causing him to jump back from fright.

"Thought it was a snake," he apologized, though the tar was not listening. His own face paled by the ongoing spectacle, he had moved away, wanting nothing more to do with the passenger or the mate. "Come back," he was ordered. He did so with trepidation. "Look through it."

"I don't want to touch it," he demurred, withholding his arms.

"Just see if there's a name and address."

"I can't read," which may or may not have been true. As the bosun's whistle blew a second time, the officer directed his attention toward the contents. On the right-hand side of the billfold was a tablet of paper, filled with doggerel. Not even a man in possession of a rudimentary education could decipher it.

He was about to abandon the enterprise as hopeless when a scrap fluttered out from between the pages. Catching it in midair, he scanned the penmanship, sweat breaking out on his brow as he read the words.

Rose Theodore. Blake House. London.

Shoving the note at the enlisted man, he replaced the wallet in Rudy's coat.

"Bring him ashore and put him in a carriage. Tell the driver he has money," he added, a prickling sensation working its way down his spine. If the sailor stole it all, there was just the possibility the cabby would return his passenger, demanding payment.

He knew he should go himself, to be sure, yet the idea of remaining with the man one moment longer set his teeth on edge. There was something unholy about him which had nothing to do with disease.

"But I have work to do –"

"Damn you, do as I say. It was your idea," he added in self-defense. "I'll cover for you. No go, for God's sake!"

Crossing himself, the sailor grabbed Rudy by the arm. For a moment, he thought his fingers would curl around nothing but cloth.

"Come on, mister," he pleaded. "Let's get a move on."

The bosun's whistle blew a third time. This, Rudy finally responded to. Lifting up his head, he stared wildly about him.

"Who calls me?" he demanded, the stench of his breath causing those near him to gag in revulsion.

"Rose Theodore! Blake House! London," screamed the mate, whether to elucidate the seaman or to pacify Rudy was unclear. The name worked magic, for the passenger's eyes lit with an inner fire neither would have believed possible.

"If she waits, then I must go."

Using that as his impetus, Rudy allowed himself to be guided to shore. By the time transport arrived, however, he had resumed his moody, depressed silence. Opening the door, he was unceremoniously shoved inside, striking his chin on the seat. He whimpered but no one was listening.

"Blake House; London," the seaman announced. "He has money – American. He'll pay."

Without bothering to wait for the objection he knew was coming, the man scampered away, directing his face into the breeze off the ocean. Superstition lay heavily upon him. The passenger had marked him, breathed the kiss of death on his brow. His days were numbered.

With a wail of his own, equal to any the rotting man-thing could have issued, he slunk back aboard the *Southern Cross*. Dousing his head in a bucket of rainwater used to swab the deck, he hurried to his bunk, there to lie beneath the blanket, awaiting his fate.

When death came calling, as it surely would, he would be no more ready than any other. And equally bitter. All he had done was his duty.

"Excuse me, ma'am," the servant interrupted, nervously clearing her throat. "There's a man at the door asking for you. At least, I think that's what he said," she added, a premonition of foreboding shrouding her own words. "His voice is thick and his accent strange."

Rose Theodore glanced up from the dinner table where she had just sat. Her expression mutated to one of annoyance as she contemplated who might be calling at such a late hour. From the description, it was likely some disreputable gun seller, sneaking up in the dead of night to wheel and deal in contraband.

Seeing him would not only make her dinner cold, it would be a wasted effort.

"Doesn't he know the War is over?" she declared in derision, brandishing the steak knife in her left hand like a weapon. "I'm out of that business." With her upper lip curled back, Rose shook her head, adding darkly, "There's no profit in it anymore."

"I couldn't say, ma'am."

The maid bowed, hurriedly stepping back. The action was stilted, causing the mistress to give her a second look. Seeing the obvious discomfiture prompted Rose to pursue her train of thought.

"The man is probably hawking muskets," she decided, unaccountable ire welling in her breast. "Used at the Alamo." It was a private joke, and she forced herself to laugh. "Or better yet, they're muskets used by Santa Anna's men to attack the Alamo; *those* came from Waterloo."

The analogy that the Mexican dictator's muskets had originally been sold to the army by a British arms dealer, and that she was in the same business, suddenly struck her as odd. A deep cold penetrated her tall, wiry frame. While she did not generally care from whom she bought arms, the similarity struck a chord.

The Alamo had been a slaughter, one of the truly great disasters in American history. Every man defending that former mission, including Jim Bowie and Davey Crockett, had died. They had perished against 100:1 odds, defending their principles against a general who had lied to his own people by repealing their constitution.

The thought put Rose in a pensive mood, making her less, not more inclined to see the stranger at her door. It was late and she was not in the mood to discourse on politics. Or guns. What she was in the market for now he could not possibly supply.

"I'll get one of your gentlemen to dismiss him, ma'am, if you don't mind. He don't look as though he'd take 'no' for an answer."

It was a peculiar request and one which did not sit well. She did not begrudge the servant her fear, but rather, the idea of having a man do her dirty work. If there were danger, she had brought it on herself. That made it her duty as well as her onerous pleasure to address the situation.

Replacing the linen napkin and the silver knife on the table with deliberate delicacy, Rose stood, her graceful form towering over the servant. Correctly interpreting her mistress' desire, the woman drew back.

"Shall I let him into the parlor?" she uncomfortable inquired, indicating Rose's usual place of business.

"No," came the instant reply. "I shall see him at the door." She might have added, *I doubt there is any need to invite him inside,* but stayed her tongue, lest she unaccountably be compelled to retract the thought.

With her annoyance rising at the idea of granting this stranger an interview, Rose glided, cat-like and quiet to the entranceway, the swish of her long skirt against the carpet noiseless and restrained.

The door was barred, testimony to the opinion of the servant. There was no outside light, leaving the stranger in darkness. It was an unfriendly act which would, she decided, prompt a respectable man of commerce to depart. If he truly had business, he should reapply himself in the morning, hat in hand.

With condemnation on her lips, Rose unhesitating turned the solid knob, pulling back the door. If he were gone, no loss.

He had not departed. At least not in the corporeal sense.

The lamplight, streaming in from the hall, caused rays of yellowish-white to bathe the interloper. Reacting as though shot, he staggered back, hand raised weakly to his eyes, so that his face was covered. While a natural instinct, it did not bode well for the success of his mission.

He was tall, dressed in expensive, well-tailored clothes, that did not quite fit him. The suit appeared to have been made for a man of much larger girth and shoulder, giving the impression they had been stolen from another at the point of a knife. Were the cuffs soiled with congealed gore, Rose would not have been surprised. It would, at any rate, be an excuse to dismiss him.

Yet that was not quite the scenario. There was also the peculiar air about him of a boy playing dress-up. Despite his towering height and obvious age, she could as easily have imagined him trying on his father's wardrobe in a vain attempt to appear the worldly gentleman before a gathering of ladies. That image was negated, however, by his slumped shoulders and drooped head. No man of breeding would present himself at a woman's domicile in such an attitude. Nor did his unshorn cheeks, heavy with grey-tingled stubble, or the malodorous scent of an unwashed body speak well for him. Had he actually put on the patriarch's dress jacket, he would receive twenty lashes from a hickory stick across the backs of his hands.

That, Rose decided in a flash of insight, would not have surprised him, for he was a man who knew pain. And injustice. It was that fact, and no other, which prompted a closer scrutiny.

Even in the dark of night she could see an unhealthy pallor about him, which caused a sort of glow. Disease, racking his body, had made it florescent, as occasionally happened to the corpses of those not long dead.

Completing the picture, her trained eyes went immediately to his hands, ascertaining he held no weapon in either. The fingers on his left were curled, however, seemingly representing the man in whole, who had reverted to a fetal position for comfort, rather than necessity.

Even standing several feet from him, she could smell his breath was foul, although not from drink, as was the usual cause in those who came to see her. It occurred to her she ought to step back to avoid the odor, but did not. Nothing on earth would have compelled her to move. Not until she understood this conundrum.

"Good evening, Miss Theodore," he whispered. His voice was barely audible, yet contained within was a distant call to familiarity. A smile worked its way across his sunken lips, ghastly in the presentation of so amalgamate a gesture. Wavering unsteadily, he shifted his feet to regain balance, then attempted to remove his hat in an ingrained gesture of politeness, but found his arm would not respond.

Stricken to the roots of her soul, Rose gasped, her own cry a commingling of abject horror and holy revelation.

"Oh, dear God!"

She had known. Somewhere in the back of her mind, from the moment of her servant's announcement, she had known who it was, yet refused, dared not believe.

He had come home.

Not as a conquering hero with a grin and a jaunty doff of the cap, sweeping her off her feet with the grandiose style of a rogue, but as a despised outcast, broken and in pieces.

He had come to her dwelling to stand at Death's Door.

"Rudy!"

The man so addressed nodded, his eyeballs rolling upward as the last of his strength gave out. Toppling forward, he stumbled into her arms, a puppet, whose strings had been cut by a malicious master, for whom he was of no further use.

Anticipating his reaction, Rose caught the giant as easily as though he had been that little boy wearing his father's suit and not a grown man. Half carrying, half dragging him to the dining room, she waved away the offer of assistance from the maid. No one must touch his body. It was to her hands alone he had come.

Traveling from Hell had been a long journey.

"Sit," she ordered, guiding his unresisting form down into the chair she had so recently vacated. Were it still smoldering from the fires that burned with her, it would not have been warm enough, for his body was cold, like the grave, his bones stiff and unyielding, as ones petrified from too long exposure to the ground.

Slipping her hand naturally beneath his chin, she held up his head, then kissed the brow. Not for his sake, for he was beyond understanding. The act was performed for their audience.

"Who is this man?" the startled maid hissed, bewildered by the scene. None of the mistress' callers were admitted to any room save the parlor. Breaking that covenant with such a stranger was a terrifying spectacle.

Dismissing the question as irrelevant, Rose commandingly waved a hand. "Light. Turn up the wick. Then stoke the fire. Put on water. I will have tea brewed. Then summon Mrs. Tompkins; have her fetch whisky from my den."

Making a small curtsy, Mary McGivins hurried to carry out her tasks, holding her hand to her jaw to prevent her teeth from chattering. When the room was properly illuminated and the kettle set over the burner, she scurried away, a rat only too glad to desert a sinking ship.

Not until they were alone did Rose replace her hands on his body. A mere touch transmitted to her the fact Rudy was no more than skin and bone. Even through the heavy material she felt his fleshless constitution, so weak his rapid, shallow inhalations barely moved the taut muscles of his chest.

Seeing that he would speak, she put an ear to his mouth, registering, but no longer obvious to the staleness of his breath.

"Rose. I've come home."

"Yes, baby," she cried, the words forming over numb lips. "You've come home."

"I promised."

"Hush. Say no more. You have fulfilled your vow. Now, it is my turn." Uplifting his dull, glazed eyes, he sought clarification, eyebrows knitting in a downward point. "To take care of you," she reminded him, the weight of her promise a condemnation of war and inhumanity, ascribed across the spectrum of the entire human race.

"I'm sorry...."

Kissing him again, then tugging on the unruly locks of hair at his temples, Rose smiled with the bravery of one whose new battle constituted a fight against the Grim Reaper.

"Later. Tell me later. When I have you in bed. That is the place for tall tales."

He smiled, or she thought he did, which was enough for the moment. Now, there was much work to be done, for there was very little life left in him.

Mrs. Hanna Tompkins, the head housekeeper and Rose's ostensive "chaperone," arrived with a flurry of activity. Immediately assuming command of the situation, she saw to the final preparation of the tea, directing the maid to use "the best china," then readjusting the cozy so that it fit snugly over the pot. When all was in readiness, the elderly woman chosen for her discretion as well as her domestic abilities, made a slight bow toward the couple.

"It's best to get him in the other room, ma'am. The fire's burning bright and he'll be more comfortable in his own chair. I'll assist," she offered, presuming Rose's reluctance. "He's a bit unsteady on his feet; travel from London is no' small jaunt," she added, the marked burr in her voice highlighting the Scottish dialect which she employed or not as occasion warranted.

Appreciating the fact she glossed over Rudy's condition for the others, Rose agreed. Easily slipping her arms beneath his, she whispered gently in his ear.

"We're going into the den, baby. Just a short walk. I want you to see what I've done with it."

Without waiting for a reply which might not be forthcoming, the two women got him to his feet, then guided his progress. Once situated in the great, overstuffed chair, Mrs. Tompkins affectionately petted him on the shoulder, then bustled out, returning almost immediately with the hot beverage.

"I've plenty of top cream in the pitcher. And sugar. He'll be needin' something sweet. And perhaps a bite o' something. Shall I make sticky buns? It won't take –"

Rose considered, then shook her head. While the suggestion was appealing, she did not think Rudy capable of swallowing solid food.

"In the morning. Thank you."

"Aye. Well, try a sip or two of spirits before you give him the tea. It warns the throat. I'd no' give him the whisky, though, Miss Rose. It bites a man long unused to drink. Closes up the throat. A bit o' brandy, perhaps. Or the Madeira might just do the trick."

Contemplating the wisdom of her words, Rose decided she was correct. "All right. Thank you."

The housekeeper brought the bottle and two glasses, setting them on the sideboard before making a small curtsy and departing. She did not speak again until the double doors were sealed and she was alone with the maid.

"Who is that man?" Mary whispered, shivering in fright, then drawing her shawl closer around her shoulders. "I've never seen the mistress bring such a creature into the house. And the den, no less. What's he got –?"

"Hush, child! Hold yer tongue. It's the master what's come home an' no mistake."

"The master?" she exclaimed in revulsion, eyes fluttering wildly. "Surely it cannot be."

"It tis. It's Captain Rudy Blake as I live and breathe."

"But he looks...." The maid faltered, then retreated a step, reverently crossing herself. "He's a bad one. All shiverin' an' dirty. He's no gentleman."

Shocked by the audacity of the maid's assertion, Mrs. Tompkins brought back her hand in an attitude of one who would strike a punch. It was only the latent truth of the statement which stayed her action.

"You had better get over that if you wish to maintain your employment," she retorted with a jab as vicious as a strike.

"But there's an evil spirit hoverin' aboot," the woman argued. "I kin see it."

"You see nothing of the kind. He's a good man; and a gentleman," she underscored in defense of both Rose and Captain Blake. "Besides," she added, wagging a finger then gesturing with her hand. "The doors are painted blue to keep away the spooks. Can't none get past."

Twitching nervously, the girls' eyes snaked outward, then shifted uneasily toward the windows. "What about through them?"

There was no way Mrs. Tompkins could win the argument. Stamping her foot in annoyance, she dismissed the subject, but not without a final try.

"You're new here, but I know him. He's been hurt; use your eyes, girl. There's nothing wrong with Captain Blake that a loving heart can't cure."

There were few things upon which Hanna Tompkins and Rose Theodore disagreed. While the latter's heart would have cried out an avowal of the housekeeper's assessment, the analytical portion of her being could not.

The body of Rudy Blake had come home. That, she would heal with time, medical expertise and all the potions at her disposal. His mind and his soul, however, were another matter, entirely. Those, he had left behind, on the bloody battlefields of Georgia, South Carolina and Tennessee. To heal the metaphysical would require more than all the knowledge and love in the world.

It would take magic.

Putting her squarely on the side of Mary McGivins.

CHAPTER 10

The fire crackled in the grate. Logs still wet with sap snapped like vicious dogs, as the life blood of the tree, no longer of any service, boiled and popped. After one particularly loud crack, Rudy cringed, placing his hands over his ears to block the sound.

Quickly ascertaining the cause of his misery, Rose nodded to herself. By morning, all the wood would be replaced by older, drier pieces. There must be no repetition, no reminders of the past. They would think only of the future, for that was where hope lay.

"Try a little wine," she urged, bringing the half-filled crystal to his lips. "Just a sip. It will warm you."

"Cold," he shivered, lowering a shaking hand to accept the glass. Rather than give it to him, Rose held it while he sipped, watching carefully to see he did not choke before offering a second.

"Just a little. And then some tea."

"Tea," he repeated, brows furrowing. Remembrance came slowly but with it, a sad smile. "After you pulled my tooth –"

"A poultice," she agreed. "Yes. But this you will drink."

"When.... When was that?"

His question was pitiful in its misery.

"1863. During our trip to Richmond. To see Jefferson Davis. We went to clear your name and to sell the guns you had run through the blockade." Seeing she had provided too much information, Rose spoke slower, enunciating her words with clarity. "You negotiated a new contract with the Confederacy. They paid you in gold."

He tried, but the effort was too much, causing him to cough weakly. It was not a wet, tuberculin cough, but a dry, trickily one she diagnosed immediately as stemming from a sore throat. "Some more wine to coat your insides."

"No more," he protested, shaking her off. "I... do not care to drink."

"I think, perhaps, you have forgotten how," she smiled back, making the effort for his sake. Inside, she was steaming with rage. Two weeks aboard ship and no one had taken the trouble to see to his well-being. For that, she would have restitution. "Let me get you undressed. That way, you can better feel the warmth from the fire."

He fought off her effort, drawing back into a ball. "No."

"Modesty?" she demanded, pretending pique, then ruffling the dirty, snarled strands of hair drooping listlessly down his brow. "In front of me?" When he offered no reply, she tried again. "I, who have seen you naked more times than I can count?"

She succeed in making him blush, which warned her own body, but not his.

"Have you?"

Biting her lip for fear she would cry in despair, Rose embraced his emaciated frame.

"And you have seen me the same way. If you have forgotten, that, sir, you are no gentleman." His low exhalation of air, approximating a guffaw, restored her confidence. "Very well. I see you do remember. It is as well for you, Captain Blake."

"Shall we go to bed?" he whispered, desperately dredging the long-buried years from his sodden memory.

"Indeed, we shall. But not before I have a look at you. It has been so long since I slept with a man, I wish to refresh my memory. Can the same be said of you?"

Grunting in embarrassment, he did not notice as she gently tugged at the sleeve of his coat. When she could not get it past the clenched fingers of his left hand, she tried prying them apart. As he cried in low, mewing noises, she immediately desisted.

"All right, Rudy. It's all right," she countered, using soft, musical tones to assuage his fright.

"I hurt, Rose." Staring around the room in wild abandon, Rudy appeared to seek the objects there as the source of his pain before abandoning the attempt as useless. Shaking his head, then dropping it down on her shoulder, he wept. "It's been too long. I've forgotten... everything."

"Not-every-thing."

Enunciating the words in syllables to underscore their importance, Rose bit her lip then covered his emaciated frame with a woolen Afghan, taking care that he see and assimilate her actions as non-threatening. When he was bundled and the fire stoked, she squatted before him so that even with downcast eyes he could not miss her.

"You have had a terrible journey, Rudy Blake. You are sick and you have a fever. But you have not forgotten. Your-mind-is-intact."

Rudy desperately wanted to believe her. Yet with the den spinning around him and the shapes of furniture assuming grotesque images of amorphous goblins, his faith was challenged.

"Who are you?" he whispered.

"Rose Theodore." The idea was preposterous. Curling his lips in disdain, Rudy shook his head, fidgeting nervously with the blanket. A hand on his restrained him. "I am truly and verily Rose. You are not dreaming."

"Rose... Rose is dead." That much came back to him with the force of a tidal wave. He had heard it by the campfire; Grainger and the boys were speaking in undertones, but he had clearly comprehended their news. Rose had perished smuggling gold through the blockade. When her ship ran aground in shoal water, she had attempted to escape in a dingy, drowning when the weight of the treasure dragged her to the bottom.

Rose could not make the same connection, but behind his eyes was a madness she would not tolerate. Placing the cool of her palm to his forehead, she felt the ravages of disease, the burning of fever. He was delirious. Protestations to the contrary that his mind was intact, she fully comprehended that to allow a lie to grow would implant the seeds of insanity. Ones that not even she could exorcise.

With her own heart fluttering erratically, she ran her fingers through his tattered locks, attempting to rearrange them, as well as his sodden brain, into some semblance of order.

"Rose Theodore is not dead. She stands before you, alive and well. You are in England. In the Blake House. You are not dreaming." Reacting to the smoldering flicker behind his eyes, Rose readjusted her position, her long, slim arm pointing out objects of prominence in the chamber.

"You are sitting in a chair; one I bought especially for you. I like to think of it as your throne." Smiling for his benefit, which was lost to glazed incomprehension, she continued. "That is my chair, beside yours. Where we will drink brandy while you smoke your pipe. Beyond is the grate, where the fire burns. It will keep us warm when we tussle on the floor."

"Rose... is dead," came the weak protest.

"No!" It was an angry response and she chided herself for it before reining back her desperate emotions. "Rose Theodore is alive. Some other Rose is dead."

Scanning her memory for the point of reference he had become fixated upon, she summoned back the scene in the dance hall.

"You are remembering some other lady with the same name. Think, Rudy. In Wilmington. There was a woman named Rose. The men jeered her and I was upset. I danced with one of them. It was he who died, not Rose."

"Rose. Rose. I heard them say it. 'Rose is dead.'"

"Them? Them – who is 'them'?"

"Grainger. Relly. Cavanaugh," he repeated, the way a boy recited multiplication tables, by rote, without full comprehension.

She did not know those names.

"Who are they?"

Shaking his head, Rudy rolled his eyes. Rose would know who they were. Rose knew everything. If this Rose did not know, then she was an impostor and he was dead. Died and gone to hell. This was the devil's trick. His lips curled in a sneer.

"Go away and tell your master you have failed. I will not be played for a fool."

The statement was so articulately and eloquently spoken, Rose withdrew in shock. Because she knew the way his mind worked, even ravaged by delirium, her answer was preordained. With a smug smile of her own, she laughed out loud. The sound, hollow and devoid of mirth to a more astute listener, made Rudy reassess.

"I am not Satan's minion, Captain Blake. *I* take no subordinate place in hell. I am Rose Theodore and I defy the devil. Give him your own message, if you will. But not here, sir, for within these walls, evil has no ingress."

"But..."

"No 'buts,' Captain Blake. If Grainger and Relly and Cavanaugh said I was dead, then they lied."

Her assertion was a bold one, meant to challenge. In that she succeeded, for he responded immediately.

"They would not lie. They... trusted me. I was their –"

"Captain?" she guessed, pressing closer. The reaction she obtained was not expected, but equally revealing.

"No! Not their captain! I was a private, nothing more!"

"All right, Rudy," came the rapid acknowledgment. "So you were not their captain, but a soldier. One of them. And they told you Rose had died. But they did not know me," she pursed on a stronger footing. "So it was some other. Surely," she prompted, "you asked... about Rose. You would not have let my death go unavenged."

His head bobbed eagerly, a splash of color finally lighting otherwise pallid cheeks.

"I was coming... to see for myself. I was coming, Rose," he sobbed, tears welling in his bloodshot, swollen eyes.

"I knew you would," she agreed with all the faith in God's universe. "Someone told you otherwise."

"Benjamin!" he shrieked, his voice echoing off the wood-hewn walls.

"Benjamin told you." Relief was palpable and she evened her keel by resting a hand on his thigh. "He knew. He checked for you, didn't he? And Benjamin wouldn't lie."

Grainger. Relly. Cavanaugh. Benjamin. Four soldiers, one of them catapulted to sainthood.

It came to him so vividly, Rudy's entire body heaved upward, the corner of the Afghan slipping off his shoulder.

"Rose O'Neal!"

"Ah. Yes. Rose O'Neal." Even in the far flung corners of distant England, she had heard those exploits. "Smuggling gold for the Confederacy." Brushing back her auburn hair, the real Rose smiled. This time, the expression was sincere and loving. "A hero and a fool, sir. If I had been a spy, the Federals would not have caught me – dead or alive. I had a better teacher than she."

"I thought," he groped, then lost the thought. Exhausted by the exchange, Rudy wilted into the chair which seemed to engulf him. "You are Rose and you are not dead. But surely... you have forgotten me? It has been so long."

"Forgotten you? Oh, God, Rudy, only you could ask such a question. No, beloved. I have not forgotten you. Not if it had taken the course of two centuries could I have forgotten you. You are," she added from the depths of her soul, "my life."

"As you are mine," he sobbed, losing the willpower to sit. As he toppled forward, she was there to catch him. "There was no one – no one to put coins on my eyes," he added, his bones transforming to warm rubber. "Nothing with which to pay the Ferryman."

Caught between the fluidity of time, Rudy was jerked from past to present without the volition to control the sands of the hourglass. Thoughts which had occurred weeks and months ago were as temporal as the moment.

"Just as I did not die, you, too, survived. The Ferryman will have his fare, but not for yesterday and not for tomorrow. You have come home, Rudy Blake and Rose Theodore is here to welcome you."

"You are not a haint? A ghost? Not here to torture me?"

"No more than you, sir. And if this be 'torture,' then I deceive myself." Pressing her lips to his, she kissed him, until small yellow stars obscured her line of vision and the heavens had reasserted themselves in proper order.

Having laid to rest the spirits of what were, it was time to rediscover the now.

"Come. We will go upstairs. To the third floor."

Placing her arms around him, she hoisted upward, but he protested, hardening his muscles.

"No."

"Why not?" To tease him was all she knew. "Do you not wish to check my bedroom? To see if there have been other men in it?"

He stared blankly for a moment, then a silly, toothy grin spread slowly over his cadaverous face. "Am I really home?"

There was only one reply.

"Home to stay."

Crookedly waving his hand upward, he tried to find the Rudy Blake of old. It was a poignant attempt which melted her heart.

"Have there been any other men in your bedroom?"

Laughing good naturedly, Rose reapplied her arms to his body.

"I am not going to tell you. You will have to discover that for yourself."

He grunted in displeasure, but rose easily as she pulled him up again. He felt so light she was tempted to carry him in her arms, hurry along the trip, get him safely into bed. But he was not a baby. To treat him so now, however well-meaning the reason, would damage his psyche. Pride was a delicate mechanism. Once out of balance, she would have the devil of a time recalibrating it.

"You're smiling," he observed, noting her subtle change of expression from teasing to introspection. Caught in the act, Rose reminded herself never to underestimate him. As long as there was breath in his body, his spark of life would assert itself. It was a good point to note. One she doubted not, which would sustain her in the long, convoluted weeks ahead.

"I was thinking about gold," she explained, expanding her original thought. "And the devil."

She hoped to intrigue him and succeeded. As his lips pursed in wonder, she guided him toward the stairs, making the journey more palatable and less strenuous for both.

"How so?"

Considering his close proximity with death and the lingering vision of the Ferryman, it was imperative to turn the tables on Satan. Like a good gambler, Rose weighed the odds, then played her trump card.

"Weighing gold dust, to determine proper value. How many times have you heard a prospector squawk that the scales were out of balance?"

"Every time," he scoffed, carefully emulating her as she put one foot in front of the other.

"And who did they accuse the money-changer of working for?"

"The devil!" he exclaimed in a childlike, high-pitched voice of pure joy. She had given him the equation and he had worked it out. For the first time his cheeks flushed with a healthy rush of blood.

"Since you, dear boy, never found any gold, that places you in the position of the banker. And what banker doesn't work for the devil? Ergo, you – and I, by association – are on the side of..."

She paused, allowing him to fill in the rest of the sentence.

"The greatest cheat of them all!"

"Precisely!" Indicating he raise his foot, they ascended the stairs. "'Why not try me?'" she quoted, reminding him of an oft repeated story he told about God and the devil.

He guffawed, then nearly toppled over as a fit of coughing assailed his weakened frame. His congestion was deep. It did not require a physician to hear the beginnings of pneumonia. Leaning him against the wall, Rose waited until he had caught his breath before offering a square of linen.

"Spit into this."

"No," he demurred, averting his face.

"Why not?"

"It is... impolite."

"I do not want you swallowing a mouthful of poison. Spit into it, I say." She waited for the explanation which would surely come.

"You will... look at it."

"I will 'look' at all of you before I am through, Rudy Blake," came the dire warning. "You shall have no secrets from me – neither outside or in. What do you say to that?"

She had set him up for the answer, but now that she had taken him to the point, her heart caught, fearful least he not have the mental prowess to complete the retort.

"You are in league with the devil."

Bowing her head so he would not see the tear which formed, Rose nodded.

"Indeed, sir. That is the answer."

Inspired by the compliment, Rudy sighed in contentment, then leaned heavily against her. After wiping his mouth on the handkerchief, which she promptly confiscated, they made their way to the upper landing. The journey had been arduous, achieved in baby steps and through the power of nefarious association. Opposed to the alternative of carrying him or having him crawl, their triumph was staggering.

Her silent prayer was an oxymoron.

God bless Satan.

"You know the way?" Rose prodded, positioning herself behind so that if he wavered, he would not fall.

"I have forgotten many things, R.B. but not that."

Which was the second answer to her prayer.

And more than she had a right to expect.

CHAPTER 11

"Lead the way," Rose advised, pointing down the corridor. "Slowly. I will not have you frisking like a stallion at the starting gate. We will sleep tonight, for I am tired."

Five, six, seven steps and they stood at the threshold of her room. "A moment, while I light the lamp. As you can see, I expected no one tonight. But," she added, stealing a moment to inspect the thick, blood-tinged mucus he had expelled, "your pillow rests beside mine. It has been there since you left. No one has touched it."

"You need not have kept yourself for me," he began in piteous protest. "I would not expect –"

The remainder of his sentence went unuttered. With a hand on the small of his back, Rose propelled him forward, letting him tumble onto the mattress.

"Enough of your foolishness. Should I have been less stalwart than you? Upon hearing of the death of one 'Rose, spy for the Confederacy,' did you not risk your life to go to her, whom you supposed to be me? Should I have less honor?"

Mumbling an apology, Rudy curled into a ball, drawing up his legs, then wrapping his chest in his arms. As a fit of trembling overtook his wasted body, she lit two reading lamps, one on either side of the bed. Only then did she gasp.

Seeing him clearly for the first time, the spectacle was horrific. His grey eyes were sunken so deeply into his skull they were barely visible; his cheeks, too, were hollow and recessed, while his hair, streaked with grey, bobbed unevenly on his head like corn stalks, ravished by storm.

Stubble lined his chin, white and thistle-prickly, while his mustache, that he wore "for luck," sagged beyond parted lips, the tail of the dog, sadly misplaced by a cruel sculptor. Rather than a man returning from war, he might have been a recently released prisoner, discharged from the dungeons after twenty years hard labor.

Like an infant, his neck lolled down, without the strength to hold it upright. A trickle of spittle bubbled from the corner of his lip. Panting through his mouth, his teeth, necessarily exposed, were dirty and stained.

His fingernails were untrimmed, talon-like and curled at the ends, while the knuckles on his hands protruded prominently, the veins swollen and blue.

What lay beneath, Rose could only conjecture with horror.

"Come. I will get you under the blankets, where it is warm. But first you must change. I have a nightshirt I have been saving for you; for a special occasion," she added, stroking him gently on the arm. The feel of his skin was tough and leathery.

"What occasion?"

"You have come home." While her tone was kind, behind it lay the aura of clinical demand. Reverting to his earliest training, that, above all else would elicit a response. The time for tenderness must wait until his medical problems were addressed.

"I will sleep as I am," he began without the strength to back up his refusal. Feigning deafness, Rose reached across him to unbutton his coat. Pulling it off, she discarded the garment over a chair back.

The tie around his neck had knotted, probably from being improperly affixed. Without bothering to fuss with it, she severed the cloth ribbon with a knife. Already having made the determination he would never again wear this wardrobe, there was no worry of preservation.

The shirt was crookedly buttoned and thus easily unfastened, while the vest was so large it was more a matter of pulling it over his shoulders than bothering to undue the small, intricate pearls. He wore no braces, nor any watch, making her task less complicated.

Her first idea had been to make him stand, slipping his trousers and drawers down his legs, but as his body sagged, she determined on another course.

"Be still," she whispered, making small talk to divert his mind from the operation. "Are you hungry?"

Her loving, sensitive fingers detected small tremors running through his body which were not from chill, but rather an innate sense of propriety. A gentleman did not remove his clothing in front of a lady, nor did he allow himself to be undressed, even by a physician. Of all the men she had known, Rudy was the most bashful in exposing himself.

Not necessarily, she mused with a private, inward smile, when making love, but at other, less intimate times. She had long suspected that even when alone he did not bare himself easily. This was testimony not to any shame in his body, but stemming rather from a tacit acknowledgement that what he was inside was not reflected by the shape and character he was molded into.

She recalled a conversation when Rudy had confessed seeing faces other than his own when looking in a mirror. Faces and times of long ago; not the countenances of men he knew, nor necessarily human faces, but strange, distorted, alien looking creatures. Rudy had called those apparitions "monsters," and they had frightened him, yet Rose knew better.

They were not monsters, nor creatures from the dark recesses of a tortured imagination. She had seen ones like them in her own mirror, but they had not disturbed her. Instead, they had excited her curiosity, for she knew instinctively they were reflections of her own soul, and of what she once had been.

Rudy's mind was formed by rigid Christian dogma, Negro spirituals and mythological stories he had heard, read, or created as a child. He had not allowed himself to see beyond these fantasies, often confusing or altering his beliefs as proof he was the epitome of evil. That, too, was the occasion of his upbringing, and she damned those who encouraged his immature mind with guilty conspiracy.

Rudy he did not understand religion, nor the scope of God's complex mysteries. While he was perfectly willing to ascribe onto himself the dark powers, with them came unmitigated terrors. Her comprehension went beyond conventional spirituality, past the mysticism of ancient scribes. She adhered to no bonds, acknowledging the possibilities of what lay Beyond as infinite, rather than finite and predictable. Where he dreaded to probe, she charged ahead, facing the unknown with cheer instead of trepidation.

"No," he whispered so softly she had to bend her heard toward him to understand his meaning.

Momentarily disconcerted, for she had been fathoms ahead of him, Rose forced herself back on track.

"When was the last time you ate?"

Poking her forefinger casually into the recesses of his stomach, she accessed the damage. While his muscles were firm, he was so thin she nearly reached his backbone. Anger welled anew for those who might have fed him and had not.

"I don't remember," he confessed, dropping his head in the attitude of a lost child. When concentration failed, he hopelessly shook his head.

Retrieving his coat, Rose slipped her hand inside, removing the pocketbook. Inside, she found money, his ticket and the illegible pencil scrawls he had made. Of all the pages used, only one paragraph was clear: her own name and address.

"I wrote it down," Rudy acknowledged with difficulty, trying to remember why. As awareness finally came, his face brightened. "I was afraid... afraid I wouldn't remember... when I got ashore. My mind... it's not always clear. I kept trying to remember something, trying to remember... something I had to write down. And then it came to me. Rose. I must write 'Rose Theodore, Blake House, London.' Did I do it correctly?"

The hopefulness of his query sent shivers down her own body.

"Yes, Rudy. You wrote it correctly. Perfectly." Flipping through the pages, she did not have to wonder how many times he attempted to write it before finally succeeding.

"They took it from me -- the man on the ship. He read it aloud."

"I'm so glad, Rudy."

"Did I do right?"

"It has brought you to me. There is nothing more 'right' on the face of the earth."

"Am I here? Truly here? I thought so many times... to be with you, and never...."

"Shhh," she cajoled, carefully replacing the pocketbook, then engulfing him in her arms. "You are here. Truly here. With Rose. No longer a dream, but a reality. No dream could touch you, could it?"

"No.... No. Never that."

"Then believe what you feel. And what you see, for Rose is beside you and she will never leave. That you may trust with all your heart."

"You are not...?" How to express himself? Disgusted? Repulsed? Horrified? The words piled in until they were a mosaic of meaningless concepts. She did not have to be gifted with second sight to read his mind. To ignore or gloss over his tortured interrogatives, however, was tantamount to affirmation.

Even worse would be to express her first response: that his soul held within it such beauty and light his very essence inspired her. Whether or not he believed her would be moot, for it was not inner but outer form which concerned him now. And in her heart, Rose did not blame him for so corporeal a dread. Were she in his place – were her body ravaged by starvation, disease and injury – she, too, would seek reassurance that the one she loved was not turned away by so horrific an appearance.

Assuming the stance of a naval officer at sea, legs apart, hands behind her back, head tilted forward, she scrutinized him a long moment before speaking. Not until he fidgeted under her piercing stare did she make pronouncement.

"Ruby Blake, I say onto you, that had you come to me crippled – missing an arm or a leg; had you arrived at my door missing an eye, or with your face scarred from wounds received, I would still love you. But you have not. You are wasted and sick; there is so little left of you I barely recognize that magnificent body. Yet behind the ravages of war, I see the handsome man I knew. I will heal your hurts and flesh out your body. I will shave your face and trim your mustache. And when I am through, sir, Satan will abandon claim on you, for you shall once again be my beautiful boy; an angel, if I may say so, in the guise of a man."

"Surely not that," he protested, averting his head in embarrassment.

"I have said so. No longer may you lay claim to the Dark Powers, for your beauty will shame and repulse the denizens of hell."

It was a challenge, a taunt to flatter and rekindle his spirit, for that, too, required all her healing arts, and would, in the final analysis, be her greatest postulate.

"Do you truly believe that?"

His question was heart rendering. Rose nodded with confidence, then allowed a hint of question to flicker across her taut features.

"Between the two of us it will be a hard decision: which of us is the most handsome." Winking roguishly, she added, "Depending upon whom we ask and how they answer, I will withhold my favors. Business favors," came the equally rapid clarification.

"No matter," he grinned, feeling suddenly alive. "I will give them mine." As quickly as it came, the light faded from his eyes and he sunk back against the headboard. "You talk nonsense. I am not the man I was."

"No. You are not. You have changed."

Tears sprang to his eyes, which he had neither the ability nor the will to hide.

"Rose, what happened to me?"

With the change of mood came an altered responsibility to the questioned. She had served him one truth: now she must provide another, but in a more lateral sense.

"You have been away from me too long, you rascal," she tempted, reaching out to grab strands of his long, unruly hair. With a sharp tug, she elicited a grunt of surprise. "You've been up to no good."

"No good, Rose," he repeated, torn by conflict of both inner and outer confusion. "No good."

"You will tell me and I will listen. But not tonight."

He spoke through her last words. "I went to war, Rose... It wasn't my war," came the poor protest. She prohibited further conversation by placing a finger against his chapped, rough lips.

"It *was* your war, Rudy; that's the tragedy of it. It always was."

Rose knew he did not understand; that comprehension would come with time and much soul-searching. The sights and smells of battle she could soften; the weariness, fatigue, the hurts she would cure. But bringing him around to a full comprehension of his motives – of why he was drawn into a bloody conflict, the political motivations of which he did not support – would be the hard part. Failing in that, all else would be worthless.

"I will assess the damage," she commanded, leaving him to obey her doctor's voice. As he flattened himself against the bed, she ran her professional eyes over his emaciated frame.

How much he had changed. Loose skin hung over shrunken muscle; bones protruded over excoriated flesh. Scabs and scrapes marred his body, peppering him with puss-filled, draining wounds. The wide, cross-shaped scars he had borne since 1850 still commanded prominence over his chest, although now appearing wider and uglier than she remembered. The hair on his chest was scraggly and patchy, a fact she attributed to poor diet, or possibly chafing from rough clothing; that on his arms and legs seemed rather darker and longer than before.

His feet were red and swollen, clearly having received little attention. His ribs stood out like a beached whale caucus and she counted them unconsciously, first to herself and then aloud as a remembrance of other, better times.

"Twelve pair: all intact. It is good to know you have made no 'Eves' during your long separation from me."

"Oh, God," he mumbled. "Not that."

"You have come home to the same Rose," she reminded him. "One who will never forget your excesses in religious folly."

Adjusting the lamp to cast a greater degree of light across his form, she gave him the opportunity to close his eyes. He was pale: so colorless, in fact, she wondered why he was not translucent. The blue from his veins stood out in sharp contrast to the whiteness of his skin, and where open sores still oozed blood, the red was made to appear even brighter by the surrounding field of greyish-white.

Methodically, her attention shifted to the area needing immediate care. Biting her lip against the fear of hurting him, she let her skilled fingers probe his excoriated and reddened genitals. Gently separating his legs, Rose sucked in her breath to see the large, bleeding hemorrhoids and the discolored skin around his buttocks.

Exposed to acidic diarrhea, a lack of sanitation, and unprotected by clothing, the wounds had festered, exposing him to terrible discomfort and cramps when moving his bowels. That, she determined, would have exacerbated his inclination not to eat. It was a problem she would have to overcome immediately, for he was as close to starvation as he had been at any time during the War.

There was a smell of infection which cling to his skin, expelled through his pores, and breathed out through contaminated lungs, past a dirty, unclean mouth. There was sickness inside him far deeper than mere eyes could probe. The enormity of it nearly weakened her resolve. She was not a doctor, and for the first time in her life, felt that loss acutely.

"Rose?" His soft, querulous voice caught her ear, though he had spoken barely above a whisper, and she ripped her attention away that which she had promised to remake in the image of an angel.

"Yes, Rudy. I'm here."

"Rose...." Holding out his hand, it wavered in the air like a lost sentinel, before settling lightly on her shoulder, as though he dare not touch her too forcefully, for fear she would disappear. "I lost a tooth, Rose." Tears welled anew and his lower jaw trembled in remembrance.

"A tooth, Rudy? You lost a tooth?" The idea was preposterous. "How could someone have pulled out one of your teeth?"

"No one pulled it," he miserably confessed. "It just... came out."

"Let me see."

Opening his mouth as far as he could, which was only half as far as she required, Rose bent over him, staring with stark disbelief at where his shaking finger pointed. There, as he said, was a gaping hole. It was on the opposite side of the one she had extracted, in his lower set of teeth, so there could be no mistake. Goose bumps of dread washed over her suddenly dampened skin.

"How did this happen?"

"I don't know. I... put something sticky in my mouth. When I removed it, the tooth came, too. I had scurvy, Rose," he sniffed sadly. "I... I couldn't find anything green to eat. It was winter, and –"

"Enough." She had not the strength to hear the rest. Her imagination would more than adequately supply the details.

Examining his oral cavity, she probed carefully at the base of his other teeth. All seemed ill-fitting and loose where once they had been firm and solid. His gums were an unhealthy color, while his tongue was coated and appeared moldy rather than in need of brushing.

Pursing her lips, Rose understood she must not let him lose any more teeth, especially those in the front, where the loss would show. While a gentleman could hide scars on his chest, he could not disguise so heinous a social affront as a gap in his mouth. Rudy would be accused of being a barroom brawler; or worse, a man of no breeding.

While untrue and equally unjust, the stigma would further warp his opinion of himself, propelling him further into the Netherland of devils and demons.

"It hurts, Rose," he mumbled, speaking around her finger so that his words were garbled. "Will it be all right?"

"Yes," came the immediate promise, not a lie and yet not spoken with the conviction of certainty. "You are right: you did have scurvy. Damned pirate," she chided, grabbing his nose between two fingers of her left hand and tugging gently. "That's a seaman's disease, you know. What right did you have, contracting it on land? Can I never trust you out of my sight?"

"I think not."

The reply, so sincerely spoken, nearly caused her to laugh.

"Then we are agreed upon something." Tweaking his nose a final time, she pulled back to peer into his eyes. "I will procure for you a toothbrush and some tooth powder. Remember: we once spoke of that. You shall brush your teeth every day, and I'll teach you how to rub your gums with salt water. That will help strengthen them and keep them clean."

His pout caught her off guard, although had her mind been broadened, she would have anticipated his retort.

"Does this mean I can't gargle with whisky?"

With a cry of delight at his well-meaning but misguided interrogative, she threw her arms around him, hugging him close.

"Oh, Rudy. I've got you back, and I will make you well."

Her assertion was both a promise and a threat, for in it she wagered her strength against his desire to live. He had come far, yet she doubted not the road they traveled meandered through the Valley of Despair. He was gravely ill. Time was her enemy, not her ally. His patience was as frail as his body. To delay, to fail in achieving immediate progress would plummet him over the abyss. What good then a body without a soul?

Rudy Blake had come home. To live or to die was the salient point not even Rose Theodore could answer without overcharging her account of Faith.

CHAPTER 12

The gentle rap on the door altered Rose to the fact Hanna Tompkins summoned her, and that the head housekeeper was there on a matter of domestic urgency. That, in itself, was disturbing, for the woman was capable of handling most situations by herself. If she were worried enough to intrude on a private moment, her concern was not to be ignored, no matter Rose's inclination to dismiss her.

"A moment," she warned before resting a firm hand on Rudy's shoulder. "Close your eyes and rest. You are weary and I have talked you nearly to death." The expression, though a common one, nearly choked her as she realized its inappropriateness. Cursing silently, she quieted his protest by a finger to his lips. "I shall return directly."

"You promise?"

"On my word of honor."

Gingerly resting his hand on hers, as though he had not the right, Rudy piteously scanned her countenance.

"If I am asleep, will you wake me?"

"I will."

It was as much as he dared ask. Wearily dropping his arm, his eyes fluttered shut. Kissing him tenderly on the brow, Rose stood, then briefly inspected the room. Were her absence delayed, she did not want him rising from bed and tripping on any unseen obstacles. Repositioning a chair out of harm's way, then pouring water from her carafe and setting the glass by the bedstead, she turned her back on him in the attitude of one leaving sanctuary.

"What is it?" she demanded of the servant, slipping noiselessly through the portal, then taking care to seal it before speaking.

"They're in a snit downstairs and I cannot control them," came the terse, abashed reply. Bowing slightly, she begged apology for her weakness.

"What is the matter?"

"The master. They think him..." She did not complete the sentence, letting Rose infer what she would.

"I see. I will handle this."

With an angry, contemptuous jerk of her head, tossing her long, auburn hair back beyond her shoulders, the mistress glided seamlessly down the stairs, her chaperone trailing noiselessly behind.

The servants were gathered in the kitchen. There were six in all: a cook, two chambermaids, the gardener, stableman and butler. Though the house was relatively small, the large staff not only represented Rose's status and respectability, they were necessary to assist when entertaining both invited and uninvited guests.

"I am here," she announced, warning by her tone that no foolishness would be tolerated. The assembled cowered before her imposing presence, but for once would not be placated without explanation. "What is it you wish me to clarify?"

"Mrs. Tompkins will speak for us," the stableman began, but he was immediately denied that liberty by the woman, herself.

"I will not. You shall speak for yourselves, for I have no hand in this."

The pronouncement dashed their hopes, but not the latent fear. Shifting awkwardly, then drawing back a step, for none of them were seated, Mary McGivins curtsied, then spoke.

"The man upstairs —"

"Is Captain Rudy Blake. The man *I* serve," Rose completed, words chipped and tight. "He is a seafaring man and a soldier, come from America. The men – D'Artagnan, Jack, BoBo and the rest – we all serve him. They were his crew; I his chandler. Surely, you have heard his name."

"Aye, madam," the butler acknowledged, hanging his head. "But he looks fair queer. I saw him come up to the door."

"He is sick; nothing contagious," she added, although it went against her nature to explain. "He has served his country and been honorably wounded. He has come home. This, and all you see," she indicated, sweeping her arm before them, "belong to him. This residence is called the 'Blake House,' as you are all aware. For Captain Blake. What more do you need to know? You serve him as you do me – in all things, without question."

"He came with the full moon, mistress; and the wind came up wid his arrival. Tis an evil wind, that chills the bones."

"I will have no talk of evil. I will tolerate no superstition."

"You took him upstairs."

It was a direct challenge. One she would not back down from. Meeting the eyes of the speaker, Rose's own flashed with haughty superiority.

"Aye," she mocked. "That I did. To my bedroom. Who is to question me?"

Her fury was cold and dangerous. While she wore no wedding ring on her hand, she would not permit them to stand in judgment. Rudy was more to her than husband: he was the man who had saved her from a life of degradation, raising her to a station equal to his own. Never before had she been required to defend him; always before it had been he who defended her. With the tables turned, Rose's ire knew no bounds.

"He isn't like them others; those what come to do business. Them, we know. Him, we don't."

"It is enough that *I* know him. That I tell you all is right. He is no ghost, nor spirit, but a living, breathing man. He came on no ill wind."

"How long shall he stay?"

"For as long as there is breath in my body. He is..." Rose hesitated, then dared allow a smile to permeate her marble features. "My equal. Those who will not serve him as they do me, shall pack their bags and be gone – by the full of the moon. Speak now," she warned without quarter. "Trust him as your master, or *I* shall cast a spell no traitorous heart shall escape."

It was Mrs. Tompkins who assumed responsibility for filling the void left by Rose's pronouncement.

"You've heard the word. It was as I told you. You may all stand on notice." The servants responded immediately, gasps of surprise and fear following the drooping of shoulders and defensive cringing.

"Mistress," the butler implored Rose, rather than the speaker. "You would discharge us?"

"I would."

"Tonight?" Mary McGivins pleaded, suddenly finding the hard, cruel fact of being without employ far more dangerous than the stranger upstairs in the bedroom.

"Aye," Rose agreed, the lines around her pursed lips hardening.

"This very hour of midnight; and may God have mercy on yer souls," her companion prompted, making a show of crossing herself. By itself the act was blasphemous, hearkening back to the days before a unified Protestant Church. It was a gesture Hanna would not have performed under any but the most dire circumstances, requiring not an act of faith, but extraordinary play acting.

Copying the piety with more sincerity if not less verve than her superior, Mary implored their employer, who stood suddenly between the hired help and the ghosts of the black night. Slumping awkwardly to her knees, head bowed, she quivered on the floor.

"We've no cause of complaint from you – or the master," she began, voice choked with fear. "I, fer one, beg yer pardon an' implore you to forgive our transgressions."

The threat to send them out at the bewitching hour carried more weight than the loss of wages, making the mysterious man upstairs less threatening than what might be encountered outside. It was a lesson Rose marked well. The devils a person knew were always less terrifying than the unknown, lurking in the dark.

It was not in her nature to overlook insult, but the moment had been carried. To dismiss them now would mean trouble. Seeking new situations in neighboring houses, or worse, traveling to London, they would fill gullible minds with tall tales of monsters and demons. At all costs, the Blake House must not become the center for controversy. Too many questions would arise: suspicions she could ill afford to fall on Rudy's innocent head.

That he was a marked man Rose doubted not. The American authorities, flush from victory, would soon be combing the British landscape. Rudy's exploits as a blockade-runner had surely put a price on his head. Were he to be captured without proper papers, there was every reason to assume the Federals would try him as a war criminal. Until she was certain of his status, anonymity was his only defense.

"Very well." Less than a full pardon, Rose's statement carried with it reprieve. "Return to your stations and we shall speak no more of this night. Go," she commanded suddenly, tired and drawn. "Before I change my mind."

Bowing respectfully, the men backtracked from the kitchen, afraid to turn their backs on the mistress. The women, helping Mary to her feet, curtsied, then slunk away, mumbling low apologies under their breaths.

"Useless, the lot of 'em," Hanna muttered, absently setting to rights a teacup which had tipped during the confrontation.

"Thank you, Mrs. Tompkins," Rose whispered, reaching out a hand to steady herself. The old woman grasped it, squeezing it tightly.

"Sit down; you've had a strain."

"I have," Rose bitterly admitted. While directed outwardly toward the servants, the confession rang far deeper, toward her own inner being. Rudy's arrival had shocked her, ripped her soul to its foundations. That he was not the man he was could scarcely be argued: that he would eventually resume his former status remained unclear.

"A toddy. A stiff shot o' some whisky in a glass of hot water will steady your nerves. An' when you've gone back upstairs," she added with a trace of familiarity seldom indulged, "I'll finish what you do not drink, for we've our work aboot us."

As an unlooked for confirmation of her own dread, the woman's statement was a portend of black days ahead. Black days and black nights.

For which the only redress was to fly the black flag.

Rose Theodore's pirate had returned.

"Rudy? Rudy, are you awake?"

She knew he was, for she could sense the restlessness, feel the workings of his scattered mind. The question was merely for form; for the sake of alerting him to her presence. A knock on the door was too formal; to enter silently ran the risk of shock. In his altered mentality and fragile state, the unannounced presence of a stranger might stop his heart.

"Who speaks?" came the hushed, muffled response as though the voice arose from behind a layer of blanket and pillow. If only that and she would tear the offending bedclothes off, striping with it the year of agony.

"It is I; Rose. Your Rose. Rose Bud Theodore."

"Rose Bud Theodore," he repeated, a parrot, rather than a man.

"Rrrrose Bud," she clarified, biting the skin of her inner lip, then slipping noiselessly inside the room. Shutting the door behind, for she had her fill of prying eyes, Rose crossed to him, taking within her own his thin, cold hand.

"I have been gone but a short time. Surely you could not have forgotten me?"

Averting his head from the glare of the lamp, she saw the fleeting smile of recognition before it disappeared in shadow.

"I thought I was dreaming."

"No dream, sir, but reality. It is I and no shade."

"Touch me."

Seeing he was unequal to the task of assimilating her feel through the medium of his fingers, she slipped an arm beneath his head, gently lifting it upward. Pressing her lips to his, Rose kissed them, tenderly and with the trepidation of her own horror. She need not have prayed for his ignorance of her fright, for he was well beyond the salient.

"You are a ship out to sea without a helmsman," she whispered, more from her own observation than his comfort. "I am here to set you right. To steer your course."

"Where shall we go?"

She had not expected a reply, and his question startled her.

"Where ever you like."

He thought for a moment, then heaved a gentle sigh of resignation. Even the idea of escaping with Rose on a sailing vessel taxed his strength. Unable to name a destination, much less contemplate their adventures together, the loss reduced Rudy to a shivering mass. Crying for what he had been and what he had lost, he flailed his arms then attempted, by the manipulation of his body weight, to roll himself off the bed.

"Where are you going?" Rose exclaimed in horror, throwing herself down on him the way a blanket was tossed by a hapless homesteader over the uncontained rage of a forest fire threatening his cabin.

"Away. I must get away."

Misunderstanding in her apprehension, Rose restrained Rudy, pressing her hands against his body with needless force.

"We will go, Rudy, I promise you. I said so. Where ever you like. To the South Seas. To the West Indies –"

"Not we!" came the hoarse rebuttal, as he abandoned the effort as hopeless. Rose released him, then took stock of his startling pronouncement.

"What do you mean – not we?"

Sinking into the mattress, Rudy did what he could to hide his head in shame.

"I should not have come back here. It was a moment of weakness. You have your life," he added more sharply. "I have burdened you with an invalid."

Color crept up her cheeks, finally igniting her shining orbs. Crossing her arms over her chest, her own chin jutted in defiance.

"So that is it, is it? You no longer love me."

"No longer love you?" came the horrified exclamation, costing him what energy he had kept in reserve. Sucking in air between his teeth, Rudy's already sunken cheeks assumed the outline of his skull. "I shall love you always."

"No. That cannot be. By your own admission, you wish to go your own way in the world, leaving me behind." Sweeping past the bed, Rose crossed the room, ripping apart the curtains to reveal the night landscape. "There," she indicated, the fingers of her dominant left hand pointing outward, "is your freedom. Take it!"

"Rose. Rose Bud... you mistake."

"No mistake," came the terse denial, tears streaming down her face. "You no longer love me."

"How... how can you say that?" he gasped, tears filling his own eyes, the drops pooling in the depressed sockets, before raining down his face.

"You wish to return to that other, perhaps," she continued over him, her intense anger stirred by the long months of separation and despair. "I speak of the West Indies and your heart is elsewhere."

"Damn you for saying that!" he spit, droplets of water emerging through his bloodless lips. "And damn you again for saying I do not love you!" Vainly repositioning himself so that his chin was propped by his arm, he trembled violently. "You – you are the only person I shall ever love. Truly and completely, as my own."

Suddenly frightened and confused, Rose pressed closer to the cold glass, as though it was within her power to fly, had only the window been open.

"Not we. You said it, Rudy. Not we. You shall travel the seas alone. I have waited here," she completed miserably, "for nothing."

With the blood vessels throbbing in his temples and his breath coming in ragged intakes of air, Rudy extended his free arm. While her back was to him, Rose saw the action in the reflection of the erstwhile looking glass.

"My love; my sweet, cherished second self," he began, the words a jumble of sound, syllable and tortured emotion. "I meant only that I am not the man you knew; I have changed, altered... broken. I am not pirate, nor swashbuckler." He hesitated, praying his use of a favorite word would shake her from the window. "I am nothing."

Her fright was too great to penetrate. She had supplicated, begged, cajoled God to send him back. Now that her petition had been answered, she found rejection instead of acceptance.

Unable to assimilate his own plea, all she heard was one phrase, echoing through the dark, recessed areas of her tortured brain.

Not we.

"I will make you well, Rudy Blake. I will heal your wounds, repair your body. I will doctor you, nurse you, tend you. And then I shall set you free. I claim no hold on you; neither your body, nor your heart."

Unable to fully comprehend her own motives, Rose struggled with the latch, finally pulling it back from its cold mooring. Jerking upward, she opened the window an inch, then half a foot. Not satisfied until the opening was great enough to permit the passage of head and shoulders, she felt the icy, bitter draft of wind curling through the wooden frame.

"Fly," came the low, leaden command. Whether it be for Rudy or herself went un-elucidated. "There are no bars. Leave freely all who have entered this domicile."

Rising like Lazarus, Rudy manipulated his body, pausing only to steady himself from the stiff breeze of her essence before taking fledgling steps toward where she stood. Rose did not hear him, had no awareness of his nearness. Not until his hand rested on her shoulder did she react, and that to stifle an exclamation of horror.

"Kill me," he intoned, the words a death knell to her heart. "Slay me. With your hands. Choke me; strangle me. And if that act be repugnant, use a knife. Or a gun. I shall wait whilst you retrieve one."

She saw him, in the window, the reverse image of the man she cherished and had once known better than her own identity. He had returned but in goblin shape.

"How can I kill you, when you have destroyed me?"

The sentence was chipped, terse, the way she might have spoken to a client buying her services for the night. A man, a preening, prancing, dandy of a fool, with a bulge in his trousers and a wad of bills in his pocket, thick enough to choke a horse. He, too, would have said "Not me," were she ever so vain as to believe their liaison meant more than a romp in bed.

Not me, not me, not me, until the words rang through her mind and her own sanity hung in the balance.

"Rose Bud."

"Not Rose Bud. Just Rose. Rose Theodore. You know my name. Do not desecrate it with the addition of..."

Of what? The addition of a pet name? The familiarity of shared initials? No more R.B. He was R.B. She was R.T.

No mistake.

Not we.

"You entirely mistake."

A laugh welled in her throat. He was mocking her.

"You have another. Go to her." She indicated the window. "Fly. *I* will not stop you."

Rudy's lip curled, revealing ghastly shrunken gums, prominent teeth. His breath, when he exhaled, was foul, dirty, tainted with the life which smoldered within.

Yet when he spoke, his words were neither harsh nor grating, but rather soft and warm. Were she in her right mind, Rose could have determined they arose, not through his raspy throat and chapped lips, but from a deeper well.

"Not we," he said, enunciating the words with clarity. "Because you and I are not 'we.' We are one. And in our oneness, we are 'I.'"

"You mock me, sir."

Placing his withered, gnarled hands on her taut, inflexible arms, the appendages of a wooden soldier, Rudy turned she who was R.B., for he had bestowed upon Rose Theodore that middle name and there was no possibility of rescinding such a gift. It was as tangible as a wedding ring, as real as a vow of constancy.

"Stare into my eyes," he commanded in his captain's voice. "Who am I?"

Rose obeyed because he had once been Rudy Blake.

"I know not."

A smile, thin and ironic, flickered across his wan features.

"So you see, we have come to it. Finally. Now you know."

Her brows furrowed, her whirling thoughts unable to assimilate his intent.

"Come to what?"

"If you know not who I am; you who love me – how am I supposed to know?"

"You speak in riddles."

His head drooped in resignation.

"If all the world forsook Rudy Blake, Rose Theodore would stand by his side. Is that not verity?"

"It is," she avowed.

"If the world spat on him, she would defend?"

"She would."

"If the world dismissed him from their company, she would follow him into exile?"

"Yes."

"If he committed sin so grievous God abandoned him, she would march beside him into hell?"

"Shoulder to shoulder."

"Then I enjoin you again, behold he who stands before you. Behold yourself," Rudy added in a low, gentle undertone, adjusting their positions so both could stare at the glass. Before her was a couple, a man and a woman. Both tall of stature, yet withered and stooped by storm.

"Whom do you see?" She had no answer. "Look closely. We are not what we were."

"I see... I see...."

"Take care," he warned. "For upon your reply hinges eternity."

It was not to be, for Rose would not allow it. Removing his hand, she met his gaze with the stare of one who faces the hangman's noose.

"What do you see?"

The phrasing of the question was a mistake, an innocence of misremembrance. *What* instead of *whom*. He was quick to pounce upon it.

"A conundrum."

As Rose's eyelids snapped back in shocked perplexity; while her neck arched in feigned, then true registration, he grinned. The emotion was spontaneous and life-giving. For the first time since the nightmarish stranger had appeared at her blue door, challenging her protection against iniquity, Rose knew him well.

"Conundrum," she repeated, the precious word sweetening her lips as the hallmark of the sacred duet: *in the beginning,* and *as it shall be.* "A puzzling riddle; a question with two opposing answers. A seeming contradiction of similarities."

"Explain further." Not a command but a plea.

"Life is a conundrum, for it encapsulates both good and evil. The possession of money is a conundrum for with it, a man may perform acts of charity and maliciousness. Rudy Blake is a conundrum," she continued, the strength of shared communion lifting up her soul. "For he is both gentleman and rogue."

"And you? Is Rose Theodore also a conundrum?"

It was his playful jest, a dare she could field or throw back, and therein would lay the answer, not to his question, so earnestly placed, but of his statement, *in our oneness, we are I.*

"She also is a conundrum: a harlot, made a maid; an avenger and one who is avenged. A woman to your manliness."

"Is she R.B. as I am R.B.?"

"She is."

"And is she mine?"

Throwing back her head, Rose tossed the long tresses from about her face.

"I have answered that, already. I will ask, rather, are you mine?"

The answer was preordained, for he had read it in her thoughts.

"World without end."

The completion of the holy trinity.

CHAPTER 13

Their hug was long and life-sustaining. Not until Rudy's arms began to shake, did Rose release him. Even then she hesitated, for he had been so long removed from the warmth of a human touch his body felt empty and deserted.

Working a smile onto her own wan features, she gently tussled his hair.

"Lie back down. I've waited a long time to get my hands on you, Rudy Blake, and I'm not going to waste the opportunity."

Misunderstanding her meaning, he sunk into the feather mattress, flattening himself into mere skin and bones. "I can't..." he protested in shame, the words nearly lost as he spoke them to the pillow. She comprehended, however, and countered by placing a gentle, yet firm hand on his shoulder. Rolling him back, she stared into his confused, lost eyes, reflecting back to her a deep-set misery from within the dilated grey-green colored depths.

He was a wolf, she decided: an undomesticated canine, caught too long in a trap. Deprived of freedom, subjected to unspeakable tortures of deprivation, humiliation and starvation, it had begun the process of destroying itself by biting off its own foot. In the wild, a beast could not survive without the ability to run and hunt, defend itself and its territory. A man was no different. Stripped of spirit, he was vulnerable to the traps set by his own kind as well as those devised by his convoluted mind.

The spirit was alive, yet the spark was nearly extinguished. She must release him before the hunters came to claim his pelt for their trophy case.

Shaking away the unpleasant image, Rose pressed his arm.

"That is not what I meant, Rudy. There will be time for that later, when —"

"No," he demurred, startling her by the force of his denial. "Never again." With a sob of abject misery, he gritted out the words. "I am no longer a man."

Fearful lest he had caught the fleeting images of her imagination, Rose increased the hand pressure on his body.

"I say you are a man. And if I make such a declaration, there is no one who dares dispute it, Captain Blake."

His answer, when it came, cried of misery so profound it took her breath away, for encapsulated within was bitterness beyond mere physical prowess. It went to the root of his soul.

"Private!" he spat. Spittle from his ejaculation struck her in the face, but it was not that which stung, but rather his withered self-identity which inflicted the damage. While he dreaded his loss of intimacy, the loss which was killing him ran deeper, still.

Shaking her head, Rose recalled to mind the image of Rudy Blake as she had first see him aboard the Admiral's flagship. Tall, stalwart, assured, the flush of victory on his cheeks.

Captain.

More than a title, it was the concept which drove his being, augmenting all the other facets of his personality. Were she to restore his spirit, free him from the cruel trap of pain and defeat, it was through that medium of wind and wave and command.

"No, Rudy. Whatever rank you held in war has been erased; gone. Eradicated from the *Book of Life.* Surrendered," she underscored, her words harsh and cutting to sever through the layers of defeat and degradation. "If you were a private in the Army of the Confederacy, you are no more. That has been put aside. You have come home as you left it, Captain Blake."

Leering sarcastically, his eyes narrowed in shared memory.

"I left it," he taunted, the superiority of debasement strong upon him, "a captain without a ship; a master, with no one to command."

"Yes," she readily agreed. I sold your ship. As you once sold the *Gemini,* as I recall. In New York, was it not? You washed your hands of the sea, yet she called you back, Captain Blake. How long was it? Two years, before you were once again before the mast, Captain Blake? Or do I mistake? Perhaps it was some other Captain Blake who ran the blockade; who carved out his name in the lore of pirate history?"

He attempted to turn his head but her hand on his jaw prevented the action. Drawing nearer, Rose pierced his orbs with anger of her own.

"An evil twin, possibly? A duplicate? A man calling himself Captain Rudy Blake? Was it he and not you who saved me from the Admiral and a life of prostitution? Speak quickly, sir, for my time is precious. If it were he and not you, then it is to that man I owe my life."

"It was I," he began, choking on the admission. "But –"

"I shall near no 'buts' from your lips, Master Blake, for I remember as well as you. Better," she taunted, to have the best of him. "Deny you were a captain; the pride of the Seven Seas. Deny you captured three Federal warships – or that the magnitude of the moment was still upon you when you entered the Admiral's cabin. You fairly glowed with power – with self-possession. I saw pride, accomplishment, a trace of smugness in that handsome face, Rudy. Then," she continued, maintaining sharp eye contact to note he was listening, "you were a captain, with the air of sensuality about you I could not resist. Neither could you, unless you deceived me."

In her mind's eye and the truth of her avowal came his defeat.

"I am not that same man, Rose," he miserably confessed. "All of that which you speak... you were correct. It was another man." His face twisted. In the flickering of the lamp light it seemed to age, denying her that glimpse into the past. "My lust for life has vanished, as surely as the *Reprobate.* Sold into the slavery of defeat." He liked the imagery and instinctively moved back into the shadows to highlight his ghastly smile.

For the first time in her life, Rose lowered her eyelids so as to hide his face, separate it from the years and the months gone by.

Trembling with a fit, as though she were the patient, ravished by circumstance and he the distant physician, sucking, rather than restoring life, she spoke.

"Who are you, then?"

Recalling the reaction he had so recently obtained, his answer was terse and cutting.

"Private Blake, artillerist in the Army of Tennessee. Retired," he added, knowing the bitterness would not fuel but quench the smoldering embers of her heart. "A soldier, whose name has been written in the *Book of the Dead.*"

It was then realization struck with the force of an exploding cannon shell. Rudy Blake had come home, not to live, but to die. He had promised that under all circumstances he would preserve his life. That, he had accomplished, at wondrous cost. Unable to extinguish that spark which kept his heart beating, he had returned. For her to put it out.

As cruel as it was unjust, he would destroy her love and thereby have her release him from that promise, so onerously given. Only in that way could the War Between the States and his own miserable contribution be put to rest.

With an unsteady hand, Rose poured herself a glass of brandy, downing it in one swallow. The liquor burned her throat, choked her, but she would not cough for all the world. That was the contemptible weakness of Woman, laid down upon their heads by men who were masters, not equals.

Swallowing a second shot, Rose felt nothing. With repetition came familiarity. A third would quench the fire.

"Private Blake, I am the harlot Rose Theodore. As life has destroyed you, so, too, has it brought me low. We once stood high but that was long ago. As you cannot endure the changes wrought by war, I can no longer live with degradation. As you are no longer a captain, I am no more a chandler, a gun buyer. So be it. We cannot endure what we have become. Let us end it, here, together."

He blinked and through the salt water of tears, saw her clearly.

"Die?" he whispered, which was not a challenge but a question.

"Die." Which was neither a challenge nor a question.

"How?" His mind was blank and the prospect seemed an impossibility.

"Poison." Holding up the empty whisky glass, she smiled thinly. As with hope, humor had evaded her.

"What poison?"

Her smile widened. The cards had all been dealt.

"Your gambler's ring. You have it on your finger? Give it to me."

Without waiting for his approval, Rose reached out, grabbing his left hand. There, upon the fourth finger, which would never house a wedding band of her own purchase, was his gambler's ring. Admiring the diamond and the matching rubies, she twisted the gold. It was loose and moved easily, requiring no more than a tug to set it free.

"This," she replied, "has seen good service." Placing her own fingers on the latch, she easily opened the secret compartment, revealing the small quantity of white powder. "Arsenic," she identified with the certainty of one who knew her work. "Not the most pleasant mode of self-destruction, but adequate to our needs. Say the word, sir, for we have come too far to back out, now."

"The word," he repeated with awed comprehension.

"We shall perish as we lived – in infamy."

"No. Not you. Not you, Rose," he protested, the words choking in his throat. "Not you."

"Not I?" She laughed, regaining, for the moment, her irony, if not her humor. "I, who am no more than a slut –" Rudy objected but she spoke over them. "You need no further proof than your own servants. I call them yours," Rose interjected, though he had made no move to contradict,' "for you are the master of the house. Everything you see before you was bought and paid for by your own hands."

"The servants?"

"Yes." The affirmation was chopped, the "s" dying an ungainly death. "Should I have needed a reminder we are living in sin, *Mister* Blake, I had merely to inquire of the household staff. They, as god fearing Christians, where we are not, were well content to lecture me on morality. Or, in this case, immorality."

With his complexion as livid as the impurities of his thinned blood would permit, Rudy's hand streaked out, tightening around her wrist. Rose tugged, but he would not release it, clinging to the lower part of her arm with the tenacity of a dead man's grip.

"Speak plainly," he hissed in what, in another man, in an officer and a gentleman, be construed as a command.

"I thought I was."

"Who has dared –?"

"What matter their names? Suffice it to say –"

He cut her off by applying pressure, yet she did not answer, though her fingers went numb.

"When? When was this insult delivered?"

"I see you have divined it from my face," Rose gushed, her own shame augmented by his fury. "But you need not feel left out. Whilst I was accused of admitting into my bed chamber a man not legally my husband, *you* were rendered an evil spirit."

"The devil, you say!" he cursed, neck veins distended in violent agitation.

"No; the devil, *they* say," she clarified, insensate to the dictates of her previously calm demeanor. "Blown in on an evil wind."

"Call them. This instant. Or I shall," came the dire threat. When she gave no indication of complying, he roared toward the door. "Get up here, damn it! All of you in our employ. This instant."

Shaking her wrist to ward off the false sensation of sleep, Rose flew to the entranceway, slipping her still tingling fingers around the cold, brass knob. Pulling it back on silent hinges, she bowed to him.

"Get up here, you damned bastards of worthless carrion!"

The dull tramp of feet on carpet, then a breathless Mrs. Tompkins made her appearance. Straightening her cap, she curtsied but had not yet straightened before he roared.

"Bitch! How dare you –"

"Not her," Rose interjected, placing her body between the housekeeper and the bed. "She is my ally."

Allied, not by words, but the truth chiseled on her face, Rudy bellowed, "Get the rest up here, or by God, I'll keelhaul the lot of you unworthy scum!"

Signaling with her eyes, the trusted servant disappeared, returning momentarily with the six others. When they had gathered, the maid and the cook, the butler and the hands, the sick man swung his legs over the mattress until he achieved a posture of authority.

"What is this I hear? Of judgment on your betters? Who among you has dared speak a word against the mistress?" There was nothing to say, for fear of unearthly retribution silenced their tongues. Thrusting out his arm, Rudy glowered at them with a hatred he had not felt since the burning of Atlanta.

"I blew in on an evil wind, did I? So you think? So you were well to believe." Clutching his fist until the knuckles whitened, he bared his teeth. "You would accuse this woman – this noble, unselfish paragon of virtue – of immorality? Speak, before he you also slander."

The men shifted uncomfortably while the women cowered behind them. Against the window pane the wind rattled, shaking the glass with the tempest of indignation.

"You will not speak? Then listen," Rudy threatened, his voice grown deeper, more a growl than a human utterance. "I say before you, with God as my witness, this woman, your mistress, and I are married in the eyes of the Lord. You see no ring? The devil take you," he finished, pointing at Rose to display the jewelry she still maintained. "There is your ring. And thank God you do not know the whole of it – or how close you came..." He hesitated, a sneer of condemnation spreading over his face. "...to toasting our marriage. There is a custom -- call if from the *Book of Blake* -- that the servants drink to the long life of their masters by having that ring -- our wedding ring -- dunked in champagne before we dispense it.

"What say you, Madam?" he inquired of Rose, perspiration dripping from his overheated brow. "Shall we, who so nearly completed that ritual ourselves – invite them to drink of the magic elixir?"

It was a temptation almost beyond her power to refute. With their own deaths so recently contemplated, her blood lust was acute. Steadying her nerves, which played against desire, Rose hesitated. Almost too long.

"As I would have it... I will have it not."

"Then I enjoin God to send them to hell," he damned, raising an arm and pointing toward the door. "Be gone, the unworthy lot of you. This night and not a moment longer. Take your belongings and this curse – that should I, Captain Rudy Blake, come across you in this life, or the next, your souls are forfeit. That from a man blown in on an ill wind."

Having said what he would, Mrs. Tompkins slipped back into the room, ushering out the discharged servants.

"See to it they are departed before the hour strikes," Rose added, stepping back toward the bed. "Then come to us and say 'it is done.' No more and no less. Pay them what you will from the house account and make the proper entries. And may such coin disappear from your purses as if it were no more than faerie glamor," she darkly added.

They were gone in a moment, as though they had never been. With their departure, a pall lifted from the room.

Hefting the heavy ring in her left hand, Rose inspected it thoughtfully, before offering it back to its rightful owner.

"I am sorry about the scene. I don't really know what possessed them. They were hand-picked and –"

"Possessed is the right word, Rose," he objected to both her statement and the ring. "I cannot fault them for their distrust of me. I did blow in on an ill wind."

"If you did, it was the wind of illness and not of bad luck," she retorted, crossing to the window, then drawing back the curtain which had draped over the glass. Clouds, which had been scattered before, had seamlessly merged together, creating a blanket for the stars. Moon beams, breaking through in shafts of silvery light, struck the earth in isolated patches. The resultant appearance on the ground resembled a giant chess board.

"We have played the opening moves in what was, perhaps, the greatest gambit of our lives," she addressed to the darkness, though her words were meant for Rudy. "I wish I could say the game was won... but then, life is a game, is it not? Finish one, begin another. That is the proper order."

"You put it like that and you make me smile," he confessed, shifting his weight so that she heard the bed springs creak. "I have always said, 'never play a game you cannot win.' It has kept me alive these many years. Tonight, it was you who saved my life."

"No," Rose denied, reluctant to tear her eyes from the unfolding panorama of the outside scene. "We were the players, but it was a divine hand which pulled our strings. This night we played God's game."

He clucked his tongue, creating an aura of peace over her shattered psyche.

"Does that mean we bested God?"

As his own magnetic pull increased, she turned gracefully from the window. The hopeful, almost boyish expression on his wasted face brought tears of joy to her eyes.

"To admit as much would be to swell your head. Suffice it to say we triumphed over evil and ill winds."

"The servants –"

"I will hire more," she dismissed, for that subject had been retired. "In the meantime, Mrs. Tompkins and I can perform the domestic chores. As for the rest – your boys can serve as waiters and footmen."

He mouthed the word "boys" before actually articulating it.

"The boys. From the *Reprobate?*" She nodded. "Are they here?"

"Yes. They have all crawled back."

He shuddered at her expression, the recollection of his own degradation still vivid. He did not dispute the appropriateness, nor her bitterness, for he clearly took her meaning.

"I wondered what became of them."

"Well you might have. They had not your courage... or your convictions," she concluded, returning to his side and again offering back the ring. "The South had more claim on them that it did you, yet they chose safety over principles. A lesson learned at the hands of a master, who is more adept at hiding his true feelings than conveying the honesty of his heart. They do not know you, Rudy."

"I do not know myself," he moaned, sagging back against the headboard. "I am so tired... and confused."

"Life is not meant to be easy. Lie back."

"I wish it were," he sighed, waving an unsteady hand in the air.

Placing a hand on his chest, Rose affectionately patted the protruding ribs.

"If it were, you would never fool anyone with your shell game. They would all spot your sleight of hand, and then where would you be? How, if life were easy, would you 'cheat death'?"

"I have cheated it tonight. With help."

"Yes. I have felt John Paul very closely these past weeks, waiting for you to return. I would mount his sketch on the wall as a remembrance –"

"I lost it, Rose," Rudy interrupted suddenly, the paleness of his complexion growing waxy as a thin sheen of perspiration slithered across his body. "It was in my billfold, and –"

"So we carry it in our hearts. As we do the memory of John Paul," she closed. Sensing the latent heat from his skin, her lips pursed. "Replace the ring and let me examine you. You must not underestimate your illness. We have much work ahead of us."

"You keep it. I gave it to you," came the whimpered protest, but she shook away the offer.

"Now is not the time. Nor the place. There will be another."

He shivered, his head drooping.

"How can you be so sure?"

"Because I am Rose Theodore."

That stirred him and his eyes, which had closed, fluttered apart, shining once more, for a brief second before the spark rekindled into feverish luminescence.

"And who is she?"

They had come full circle.

"A grand lady, sir, to stand beside you, a gentleman of worth and consequence. A seaman," she continued, resting quietly beside him, her weight displacing his emaciated body so that it rolled toward her until they touched. "To obey the orders of Captain Blake. But only aboard ship," she added, so he would not misunderstand her statement. "On land, we are equals. What say you?"

"I say," he began, the words already slurred by sleep, "We beat God at his own game."

It was blasphemy and it was the reaffirmation of life.

Death had been held at bay. Which was not to say they had cheated the Grim Reaper, but under present circumstances, it was the next best thing.

CHAPTER 14

Rose dozed. Watching the slow intake and exhalation of breath, the quiet, rhythmic motion, so like a ship at sea, had lulled her to sleep. It was only the sound of Rudy's gambler's ring, slipping from its tenuous perch, which woke her. Shaking her head, then carelessly rubbing the back of her neck, which had grown stiff from the awkward position, she bent over to retrieve it.

The weight of it reassured her. Gone were the associations of the hour before. What remained were only the memories of a better time.

Readjusting the lamp to cast its light on the bed, Rose took his hand, meticulously separating the fingers so she could return the ring to its proper place. Only then did she notice something terribly amiss with the third finger.

With the ease of someone handling what they most cherished in life, Rose gently but firmly straightened the swollen joints. The nail, hot to the touch, was split and blackened around the bed. Drawing it to her nose, the stench of rotting, gangrenous flesh sent shock waves of nausea through her heightened nerve endings.

"Rudy, what happened here?" His prone position and the chance to sleep had dulled his senses, however, and he shook his head with desultory incomprehension. "Your hand – the finger is badly infected. How did you injure it?"

With his attention directed toward his hand, pain flickered over his drawn features.

"I hurt, Rose."

"Yes," she agreed, wrapping her own fingers over the wound, to block his vision and salve, for the moment, what must be the occasion of exquisite agony. "It must be treated immediately; tonight. Without delay. Do you understand me?"

"Sleep, Rose.... I am so tired."

The confrontation with the servants had drained whatever reserves he maintained. Stripped of that last energy, his ability to fight had dissipated into nothingness.

"I know, baby. Be still."

Reluctantly parting with his hand, Rose raised a shaking hand to her own head, before stepping toward the door. His pitiful cry arrested her movement.

"Where are you going? You are not leaving me?"

"To summon a doctor. I will send one of the boys."

"No," he sobbed, hiding his hand beneath the pillow. "Come to bed. Lie beside me."

The idea was as compelling as it was impossible. In this instance, physician must supersede lover.

"Later," she promised. "After the doctor has come and gone."

"You... you are a doctor. You take care of me," he begged, sniffing back the moisture from his runny nose. "Only you. I am afraid."

Crossing back, then kneeling beside him, Rose dropped her brow against his. In this manner she prayed her own mounting terror would be less contagious.

"The severity of the wound is beyond my ability to treat. It requires the skill of a surgeon."

"Cut my finger off?" he wailed, before succumbing to a coughing fit. She comforted him as best she could, but her heart was not in her reassurance.

"A doctor, Rudy. I know him well. You can trust him; as I do."

"Cut my finger off?" he repeated, like a child.

There was no way to answer the question. "You'll like him, Rudy; his name is Mannering. I have it on good authority he even knows how to cook grits," she teased, finally eliciting a spark of animation.

"Oh, God, then hire him. Pay him full seaman's wages." She smiled but he could not see it through her tears. "You will not let him cut off my finger?"

"Ggggrits, swimming in butter; thick, the way you like them."

As a statement, it fell short of a promise. Kissing him again, she rose with the enthusiasm of one going to their own execution. At the door, she called huskily.

"D'Artagnan!"

The seaman, Rudy's former first officer, appeared, hair disheveled, encrustations of sleep in his eyes. His appearance was deceiving, for he had not been asleep. Because her shoulders sagged, he appeared taller than she.

"Yes, ma'am," he reported, respectively touching a hand to his head. Lowering his voice, he attempted to peek into the bedroom, but was blocked by her sudden movement. "Is that Rudy? Is Rudy here? Has he come back?"

Three questions, uttered as one long interrogative, barely decipherable save to one who knew beforehand what he would ask.

"It is Rudy. He is gravely ill. Ride to Dr. Mannering's; bring him without delay."

"What's going on? We heard the ruckus with the servants –"

"I have given you an order," she snapped, the words bringing him to attention. "I expect no questions. Do as I say, or pack your duffel and leave this house."

Shifting his hands to his stomach in the attitude of a man skewered through with a marlin pike, Jack stiffened, swallowed, then backed away.

"Aye, sir."

"Take the carriage," Rose warned. "That way, it will save time." Finally straightening her back, Rose shot him a look of pure hatred. Although the intensity of the expression was meant for the officer, the bitterness was directed upward, toward a higher authority. "Do not fail me."

Which put both D'Artagnan and God on guard.

He scurried away, the trip hammer of his heart at the double-quick. Rudy had returned but not in the guise of a conquering hero. Things were not as they should be and he was afraid. More than his master, Rudy Blake was his hero; invulnerable, invincible. It was inconceivable that he could die. Nowhere in D'Artagnan's mind had that been a possibility. To confront the inevitability now came close to shattering his world.

Which gave him more in common with Rose Theodore than he ever wished to achieve.

Returning to the bed, Rose hesitated before rousing Rudy. His light sleep appeared peaceful enough, but there was in it the touch of everlasting repose. Ridding herself of lingering ghosts and harsh words, she absently righted objects on her wardrobe before sensing the presence of an active mind. Turning once more toward the doorway, she saw Mrs. Tompkins.

"Begging your pardon, Miss –" the housekeeper began, but Rose's curt gesture silenced her.

"Not you," she began, forcing herself to modify the anger which was directed outward and not toward her companion. "Between us, you need not stand on formality."

The older woman, who had seen a great deal of life, most of it unpleasant, relaxed, slipping more comfortably into the familiarity she had shared with the mistress. Her ostensive position as chaperone was for outward appearances, only, and that to appease society. Her true position, that which she had earned by faithfulness and trust, was as a world-wise advisor.

Her place here was to mitigate the damage, right the ship, set the navigational course toward bluer waters.

"I apologize for the lot of those damn help," she began, testing the depth of Rose's anger. "I've seen them out an' they'll no' return. In the mornin' I'll go to London. Hire other servants."

"There will be no need for that," came the terse reply.

"The master will expect his household to be run in a manner befittin' a gentleman. I'll have no shame come to you for the disrespect of those low-lives."

"He won't remember," Rose dismissed, purposely avoiding the body on the bed.

"Then I'll no' have him complainin' aboot the dust on the mantel, or the slovenly condition o' the kitchen. He's a man who knows what's right, Miss Rose. A man o' breedin' an' culture. He looks to you to set it right, an' you look to me. I'll go to London."

Her insistence was a ruse, patently obvious, yet it calmed the storm, for within it lay the restoration of normalcy. If Rudy were to notice a layer of dust or pots in the sink, he would be his old self again.

"Yes," Rose decided. "You do that."

"In the meantime, I'll wager the boys can put the place to rights. Swabbin' the decks, you might say. I understand that at sea, no task is beneath a man. It's aboot time we reminded them o' their duties." When she received no confirmation, Hanna completed her thought. "Heavy work makes light hearts."

The sentiment, so like what Rudy might have said, finally elicited a heave from her bosom.

"I'll remember that."

"Aye. An' while yer rememberin'," the friend pursued, overstepping the bonds she had carefully established, "you might see to yer own work."

Rose's head snapped to attention.

"And what is that?"

"Settin' this room to rights for the doctor. He'll be needing decent light; better than you have. An' hot water; bandages. An' some o' yer own potions, for you've a fair way of healin' yerself, mistress. I've heard him say it an' I've seen it with me own eyes. Yer creams and lotions. You know what you need, there's no use askin' me," she concluded with an indignant huff, though Rose had given no indication of denial. "An' a stiff shot o' brandy to steady yer hands. T'will be a fair long night and the doctor will be needin' an assistant with a clear head."

"Coffee," Rose decided, the flavor of it swelling her taste buds. "With cream and sugar."

"Aye, you think I'd forgotten the master's tastes? The pot's et an' the tray is set. I'll just bring it up and you can let the currents o' it waft over his poor, thin face. There's nothing which brings a man outta his dreams faster than that. Except for the love of a good woman, which you are an' more, besides." Wiping her hands on her apron, Mrs. Tompkins nodded. "He's come home, Rose Theodore, alive an' kickin'. You asked fer no more, an' no more you got. Be thankful."

Rose stared in utter incomprehension for a long beat, then suddenly doubled over with the rapidity of one who had been stricken with stomach cramps. With her arms around her middle and her face a crimson red, a belch of hilarity burst forth from puckered lips.

Mrs. Tompkins' first reaction was to offer help; her second, and more accurate response was to laugh with her mistress.

"Oh, shit, Rudy," Rose chortled, her use of the uncouth slang further exacerbating her mirth. "Blessed is he who asks for nothing, for he shall never be disappointed." Losing her balance, Rose leaned against Hanna, using the woman for emotional ballast. "We are one up on that poor sod. We have asked for little and that is precisely what we received. God be praised."

Launching her fisted hand in the air, Rose detached herself from the servant's arms and danced a jig around the bed. Kicking as high as a foal which had suddenly discovered the power of locomotion, she traced the contours of her "pasture," before pausing, breathlessly, beside his bed.

"'Blessed are the poor in spirit, for theirs is the Kingdom of heaven'; 'blessed be the name of the Lord. ' 'Bless those who curse you, pray for those who abuse you. We are four times blessed." Snapping her fingers, Rose prompted Mrs. Tompkins. "Another, quickly. One for every finger of his hand."

"Blessed is he who takes no offense," she promptly supplied. From the bed where he lay, his eyes mere slits, Rudy Blake joined in the revelry.

"'Why not try Me'?"

It was a quotation from his devil's story, the turning of the tables; the choice between good and evil. Clasping her hands together, Rose applauded. Into the action went her newly restored heart and soul.

"Close the Pearly Gates, Captain Blake, for Saint Peter will have to wait for you. And damn the Ferryman. We'll row ourselves across the River Styx and take Tartarus by storm."

"Up the rebels," he replied, weakly lifting his arm to meet hers. That, too, was an old hurrah. And for the first time in five years, he could pronounce it was an lower case "r." He was a rebel but no longer a Rebel.

For Rose Theodore and Rudy Blake, it was the final shot of the Uncivil War. As the clock chimed twelve, signaling the birth of a new day, their Day of Reckoning passed into history.

CHAPTER 15

It was an hour later, at one o'clock in the morning, that the knock came at her bedroom door. Without averting her eyes from the patient, who had slipped back into a semi-comatose state, Rose motioned with her hand. Only after the petitioner coughed politely into his hand was she forced to look up.

"Miss Theodore, it is Dr. Mannering. May I enter?" Her blank stare of incomprehension prompted him to elaborate. "Your bed chamber?"

The significance had not occurred to her. The house and everything in it belonged to Rudy. Where he was, was his. Therefore, it was his bedroom and not hers. That technicality was lost to the physician, who dared proceed only on her reassurance.

"Certainly. I appreciate you coming at so late an hour."

"Mr. D'Artagnan said it was urgent," he replied, stepping gingerly across the threshold, black surgeon's bag in hand. Appraising Rose astutely to ascertain her own health, he quickly directed his attention toward the man on the mattress. The flush on the doctor's cheeks faded by the time he set his case on the table.

Beside it were a dozen bottles and jars, all meticulously labeled in Rose's own hand. Reaching out for one, he studied it with curious awe.

"What is this one for?"

"The reduction of swelling in the tissues."

"And this?" he inquired, indicating another. Snatching it from his hand with respectful familiarity, Rose replaced the bottle on the table.

"You know very well what it is."

"I ought to." Opening his bag, the physician extracted an exact duplicate. "Inasmuch as you have been supplying me with it these past several months. But this one," he continued, plucking up a small receptacle she had purposely hidden at the back, "I do not know. Although I recognize your handwriting, the artwork on the label is unfamiliar to me. Explain, please, its purpose – and the use of the liquid."

Grabbing the brown glass bottle, sealed with a tiny cork away from him, Rose hesitated before answering.

"The sketch is a copy of a tonic, sold in the States."

"A Negress?" Reading the bold printing from the bottle in her hand, he shook his head in wonder. "Mammy's Best Boy?"

"Yes."

"And it's purpose?"

"It has magical properties," she replied with a vague smile. When he extended his hand, she gave it back for him to read the printing.

"'Cures the ills of diarrhea and constipation, headache, stomach bloating, generalized weakness, fatigue and intestinal gas. Improves the eyesight, sharpens the hearing,'" he verbalized. "'Useful in cases of male regeneration. Adds muscles to the body, improves quality and texture of the hair, stimulates the flow of blood to the brain and private organs.'" His brows knit in surprise. Unlike her other concoctions, this was clearly grandiose and out of place. "Magical properties, indeed. Is there anything it does not restore?"

"Life," Rose whispered, her lower lip quivering with emotion. "Please help him, Dr. Mannering."

Turning toward his patient, the physician frowned. "Who is he?"

"D'Artagnan did not tell you?"

"He said nothing except that a man was dying and that you had summoned me with great urgency. A fact, in itself, which surprised me, as you are as well versed in the healing arts as I. Better, in fact," he concluded with respect, "for I do not have your knowledge of herbs and chemicals."

"He is Rudy Blake."

Mannering sucked air through his teeth, then nodded thoughtfully. While the man himself was unknown to him, he was as familiar with the name as his own.

"These two years I have wondered," came the whispered confession, "whether he truly existed or not. I have heard much about him, although," he sighed, "not from your lips. Rudy Blake." Nearing the bed, he appraised the man with a critical eye. "What is your diagnosis?"

"He is suffering from critical malnutrition; he has had scurvy and dysentery. His gums have retracted and his eyes are yellow-tinged."

"Liver."

"There are open sores over his body. But it is the wound on his hand I summoned you for. I fear it is gangrenous. You will examine it?"

"Certainly."

Handing her back the vial of "Mammy's Best Boy," for he sensed it gave her comfort, Mannering knelt beside the patient. Placing a hand on Rudy's brow, he quickly ascertained a high temperature.

"Fever; blood poisoning. Is he delirious?"

"His mind wanders, at once both clear and confused, doctor."

He turned to the patient and spoke soothingly.

"Mr. Blake, I am Dr. Mannering. May I examine you, sir?"

"Captain Blake," Rose's warning overlapped. "Kindly address him by his proper title. He will respond better," she added.

"Captain Blake; can you hear me?"

Rudy groaned, then attempted to open his eyes. The effort was more than he could accomplish, however, and he sunk back, breathing ragged and irregular.

"So far gone," the physician marveled, gently taking Rudy's left hand in his. "How did he get here? You went for him? To Liverpool? You should have brought him to hospital –"

"He brought himself. This night."

"Good God." Adjusting the light which Rose had placed on an end table for the purpose of examination, Mannering rapidly checked the discolored finger. "How did this happen? It is not a fresh wound but one of long standing. It should have been treated immediately."

"He was a soldier in the late American war. There was no way for him to seek help."

"Damn war and soldiers, alike. See here, Miss Theodore. The nail on this finger is split and filled with puss. The infection has gotten into the bone. It is the cause of his fever."

Without having to read his mind, for she had already made her own diagnosis, Rose nodded agreement. Unaware that rivulets of perspiration poured down her face along the lines of tear tracks, she stated firmly, "Save his finger, Dr. Mannering. That is why I have summoned you."

As though she had requested of him that he practice alchemy rather than the healing arts, his lips parted in mute denial. It was a long moment before he addressed the statement. When he did, his voice was laden with stern regret.

"I cannot. I must amputate the finger to save his life."

The determination was a slap in the face she had anticipated. Yet hearing it from the doctor's mouth staggered her. Crossing past him, her action forced him to move from the bedside.

"Then you can be of no use to me. The matter is not open to discussion. Thank you for coming at so late an hour. Mrs. Tompkins will pay you for your services. Good night."

His hand streaked out, grabbing her roughly. It was a breach of etiquette, but one in which he was temporarily oblivious.

"For God's sake, Miss Theodore, his life is at stake. The man is dying. Even were I to amputate, I am not certain I can save him. He is wasted to nothing; no reserve of strength. He may not rally from such an operation. But to delay, even for an hour, will prove fatal."

Running her hand through her hair to brush back the unruly strands and thus clear her vision, Rose shuddered, but gave no indication of a weakening resolve.

"Then he will die as he lived: a whole man."

"Surely, the loss of a finger in exchange for his life – no man would fail to accept such an exchange."

"He would," she stated with finality.

"Then he is a fool," Mannering spat with contempt. "And you are twice a fool and no doctor."

The sparks which generated from Rose's eyes might have spontaneously combusted the physician's body, rendering it to ash.

"In that, you are correct. I am no doctor. I have no formal education. That, sir, I looked for in you. That – and compassion. I have told you: there are no two ways about it. Captain Blake would rather die than suffer the indignity of disfigurement. That is his choice and I respect it. As you say, I am no physician; yet, like you, I have sworn an oath to do no harm. I know him. That is enough."

"Rose! Listen to me as you treasure this man." His use of her first name froze them both. "I will do everything in my power to restore his life, but let me operate, I beg you." When she did not answer, he continued over her deathly silence. "You brought me here, knowing what I would say. The fact is unpleasant to you; you did not want to admit it. You wished to hear me say it, and so I have. Let us dispense with the inevitable and perform our work. Upon my word, he will thank you for it."

"Go."

Releasing her hand, Mannering brushed his fingers over the bloodless indentations left on her skin.

"Upon my honor –"

"Rose."

The low, tortured voice from the bed shook them both, as though the dead had spoken. Before her eyes the physician vanished. No one remained in the room but she and Rudy.

"Yes, my darling. I am here. Rose is here, beside you."

"There is someone else? Someone you are speaking to?"

The instant had wiped the doctor from her mind. Glancing upward, Rose took in the intruder's shape and form, recognition returning slowly.

"It is no one," she dismissed. "A servant. He is departing the way he came; through the door. I have some medicine for you. Look." Removing the small brown vial, Rose held it to the light so he could see the sketch. "Mammy's Best Boy. A dose of it now and another in an hour. That will restore your strength."

With recognition came infinite gratitude.

"Mammy's Best Boy. You have found some."

"I have concocted it with my own hands; from an old recipe."

"Mammy... Mammy told you?" he asked in awe.

"Yes."

"She has been here?"

"She watched over my shoulder as I prepared it. It is a very old recipe; passed down from generation to generation. She shared it with me; for you. For her little boy; the little boy she loved as her own." Rudy sobbed. Rose bent over to kiss his feverish brow. "No one shall ever have it but you. That was the promise I made her. But you must tell me," she continued, working a sad smile onto her chiseled lips, "which remedy do you require? Diarrhea or constipation? Headache? The restoration of male potency?"

"All," he pleaded, nodding wisely. "Do not withhold a single property."

"Then I shall have you chasing me about the room, sir," she scolded, "whilst you are fighting your bowels, which are both bound and loose."

"But at least I will not suffer headache," he pointed out. The statement, so innocently delivered, brought a stifled cry from her heart.

"No, Rudy. You will not have a headache." Untying the knotted string around the cork with her teeth, Rose pressed the bottle to his mouth. "A sip, no more. Or shall I dilute it in water? Two drops in a glass –"

"Ah," he protested, wrapping his lips around the narrow neck. "A homeopath. I had forgotten you are of that persuasion."

When he had gulped a swallow she withheld the bottle.

"Your strength will be restored in a moment; but for now, you must lie still. Be very quiet. Can you do that?"

"For you," he promised, eyelids sinking slowly over protuberant orbs, "I can do anything."

"Captain Rudy Blake." The name was spoken as the tolling of a bell, dark and deep and ominous. "I am Dr. Mannering. Can you hear me?" With a whimper of fright, Rudy clung to Rose. "The third finger on your left had is badly infected. Can you tell me how it happened?"

She cuddled him, a baby rabbit in the clutches of a cruel iron trap.

"Rose....?"

"Speak, my love, if you remember."

He did not want to remember and for agonizing minutes the doctor and the healer waited as the swirling images congealed in Rudy's brain.

"Cold," he announced to no one, as the winter mind of his memory ripped through the rags he wore. And once, "Relly," which, to his listeners, could have meant "really," or "real," or nothing, at all.

Staring in dull fascination, the watchers heard the belch of artillery, smelled the overheated gunpowder, ducked as arms and legs from disembodied targets, neither grey nor blue, hurtled over their heads. Private Blake, cannoneer, did not have to speak, for his mind was an open book, a kaleidoscope of color, a daguerreotype of twisted, mutilated battlefields.

He ran through it all, the way a condemned man on the gallows reviews his crimes. It was Judgment Day and the hangman and the assistant were the sole witnesses to his confessions.

When Rudy finally did articulate his feelings, his voice served a higher master, coming, not from his own volition, but through the dictates of Ares, the god of war.

"Winter. Freezing. We were crossing the mountain. Ice and wind. Terrible. Inhuman." His demons raged within, chilling him without. "The wheel... of the piece. It slipped... over the edge. My gun. I reached for it... attempted to pull it back. It happened then... I think. As I grabbed the wooden frame. A splinter, under my nail. I paid it no heed. What," he asked, staring into nothingness, "was the point? The gun... the gun. It slipped and I could not hold it."

He sobbed, a heart-rendering noise of pain and agony. "Lost. All lost. What was the point... of any of it? No point," he admitted, answering his own question. "No point."

"You had no one look at it? No physician to treat the wound?"

Rudy shot a look of pure hatred toward the doctor.

"It was a matter of no consequence."

"But later? When you were down from the mountaintop? Not even then?"

"Who is this man?" Rudy demanded sharply, raising the level of his voice to a shout. Rose waved a hand before his face, the magician removing the trance from the hypnotized subject.

"No more, Rudy. Come back to me."

He twitched, sniffed, then wiped his nose on the sleeve of the nightshirt. A film settled over his eyes.

"He has told you all he can," she spoke to Mannering. "All he knows. A splinter of wood – or metal. In the winter."

"What winter?"

"1864-65," she identified with a contempt directed above and beyond his shoulders.

"That was six months ago – or longer. It's a wonder he's alive."

"No wonder," she retorted. "He swore an oath to come back to me. And so he has. Now it is my turn to fulfill my promise to him. To preserve his life – at no cost."

Mannering, in his ignorance, misunderstood the expression. "I will not charge him –"

"No cost," she tersely reiterated, "of limb, or digit."

"But surely now that you know – now that you have accessed the damage; the passage of time...." He faltered, then helplessly extended a hand toward her. "You promised him his life. Let me assist you in preserving it."

His use of her word did not pacify Rose's resolve.

"I have said it. He endured hell on earth. He has come to me for salvation of both body and mind. I shall not fail him."

Mannering's hand went back in the attitude of one who would slap sense into an hysterical patient. Her neck arched back, jaw extended for the blow which never came.

"You cannot force me."

"Then ask him!" the doctor screamed, using his extended arm to point toward Rudy. "Let it be his decision."

"Yes," Rose agreed, a sneer of disdain obscuring her beautiful features. "Ask him."

Gingerly gliding past her, as though it had been she and not he who had threatened violence, the physician settled on the corner of the mattress. Leaning closer, so his words would be clearly understood, he stated his case.

"Captain Blake, can you hear me?" A nod, no more, to signify affirmative. "Your finger – the one you injured. It is severely infected; the bone has been compromised. It is poisoning your blood. I can save your life, but only if you let me operate."

Rudy shrugged as if the matter were of no consequence to him. Pain, he seemed to say, is my familiar companion. Mannering nodded in approval, but Rose was not through with him.

"Explain to him what you mean by 'operate.'"

"I must amputate your finger, sir; there, at the base of the hand. To remove the source of danger."

"My finger? You must do what?"

"Amputate it; cut it off. To preserve your life. Nothing short of extraordinary means can save you."

"I think not."

Balling his hand into a fist, the doctor struck the pillow by Rudy's head, bouncing it around.

"Damn it, man! Do you understand what I am saying? It is little to trade, in exchange for your life."

Rudy smiled. The expression was ghastly, perverted. The white of his teeth gleamed supernaturally in the flicker of the oil lamp.

"I am not in the business of barter, sir," he began, barely moving his lips, forcing the doctor to lower his ear to catch the explanation. For her part, Rose moved back, so that her shadow fell across the bed. It was to that Rudy addressed. "Do you remember, Rose, the tale I told? Of San Francisco?"

"I remember," she answered.

"Returning from the gold fields. Destitute and broke. Penniless," he elucidated for the stranger. "Without a penny piece in my pocket. Without a farthing; or just that much. A poke of gold to make my stake; my way in the world. What was it I purchased, Rose?"

"A manicure set," came the prompt reply.

"A manicure set. To pare my fingernails, smooth the calluses, heal the cuticles. I am a gambler, sir. A prestidigitator with cards. I am a shell man," he added, suddenly remembering a new point. For the moment, and the moment was fading, his mind was as sharp as the blade in his gambler's ring used to trim cards and split edges. "To win, to pluck the bird," and he smiled at his own analogy, "I must have the advantage. "The bettor must stare at my mouth and not my hands." He shuddered, the lines in his mouth down-turning. "You remember, Rose. I taught you." His face clouded as other memories penetrated his consciousness. "No. That is incorrect. It was John Paul I taught."

He faltered, lost his train of thought, then rambled on, quickly, before the image faded.

"A gentleman is taught to stare at the face of the speaker; that is good manners; and fortunate for the gambler, for that is how he plucks them. While they are watching his face, he manipulates the shells." Swallowing the lump in his throat, Rudy coughed, then continued, his voice lowering to a hush. "You wish to mark me, doctor. No one would look away from a cripple. People are drawn to disfigurement. Instead of watching my mouth, they will stare at my hands. How, then, am I supposed to win?"

"A game of chance cannot be worth more to you than life, itself!"

"Banish him, Rose," Rudy declared, sinking back into himself. "You said I would like him. I like him not."

The declaration had been delivered. It awaited only to be signed and sealed to complete the formality.

CHAPTER 16

Rudy's condemnation was not of Rose's judgment, but of the doctor. Mannering looked to her for guidance, torn between obeying the dictates of his patient and common sense. Had the order come from any other, he would have taken his bag and left, but Rose Theodore held a peculiar sway over him.

****

Rose Theodore and Thomas Mannering had met over a year ago in the graveyard of the parish church. She had been gathering herbs which she placed in a reed basket. Assuming her pursuit to be culinary, he had braved a breach of social amenity by approaching the peculiar stranger and speaking before either were property introduced.

"I wonder how one could eat such plants, nourished by the fertilizer of the dead."

Raising her head with the haughtiness of one unaccustomed to being so addressed, the early morning sunbeams glinted off her hair. It was the tartness of her rejoinder, however, which startled him out of his complacency.

"In the British Isles, is it not commonplace to use the carcasses of fish, washed up from shore, in the garden? Or to spread animal offal across a field? I make no distinction between harvesting those crops and consuming what I pick here. That is," she continued, resuming her task, "were I supposing to supplement my table. Which I am not."

"But you have no flowers – so you are not collecting for a bouquet."

"Indeed, sir, I have little inclination toward beauty which will wither and die upon my table."

"What, then, are you doing?"

"Selecting ingredients for my medicines."

"Medicines?" he demanded, hands akimbo. "You are a witch, perchance? A most attractive one, I do admit."

"I have been called worse," she replied, ignoring his compliment.

"What, worse?"

"An alchemist; a conjurer of potions and tonics. But not," she added, removing her bonnet and fanning herself with the brim, 'a pill-pusher.' That, I believe, is your line."

Taken back by her obvious and less than flattering reference to his profession, Mannering drew nearer.

"I, madam, am indeed Thomas Mannering; local physician and surgeon. And your name, if I may be so bold?"

"I," Rose identified with an up-tilt of her chin, "am the local arms dealer. If you have quality rifles to sell, or perchance gunpowder of good quality, we may do business. If not, your interview is at an end."

She left him, but not his thoughts. Disturbed and disquieted by the strange apparition, he determined to make inquiry. Mannering might not have gotten past the noncommittal shrugs of his neighbors, but for a startling revelation from one of his patients.

"I see," he began, examining the healing would of John Dix, "you are recovering nicely; very nicely."

"Aye, an' no thanks to you."

"You have complaint of the suturing I performed on that cut you received from the saw?"

"You tolt me to stay off the leg. Couldna do that; there's chores to be done."

"But you must have... for the flesh has knitted well."

"T'other came to me. It were she who mended the wound."

"She?"

Dix waved a finger in his face.

"An' never charged me. No' in money. All she asked fer was to wander me fields, pickin' in her basket what she might. Leaves and weeds and whatnots."

"Her name?" he demanded in pique.

"She be the mistress o' Blake House."

Blake House. He had heard rumors about the "doings" there. Disreputable men, calling at odd hours; covered wagons, dropping off unidentified crates of prodigious weight. Odd-looking seamen with peculiar accents, traveling back and forth to Liverpool, but none of them shipping out.

"American!" he exclaimed aloud, ashamed at himself for not placing her dialect sooner. *I am the local arms dealer.* But surely not she, herself.

"Who is her husband? Where is Master Blake?" he guessed, from the name of the house.

"Don't ask what ain't none o' my business. An' don't you go messing around over there. She knows more about doctorin' than you, Mr. Mannering. If she were to take mind, you'd be out o' business in a fortnight."

Not charging farmer Dix for the "unnecessary visit," he completed his rounds, then presented himself at the Blake residence. The housekeeper answered his summons.

"I beg permission to speak to the lady of the house."

Squinting past him to the road beyond, Hanna Tompkins saw no horse. He was, therefore, not on "official business."

"What's your name and what's your ailment? And who sent you?" she added, eying his well-cut, professional suit.

"Please announce Thomas Mannering. I have a chest congestion," he demonstrated by coughing into his handkerchief. "I was sent by John Dix, for whom she cured a terrible laceration."

Hearing a noise beyond his powers to translate, the woman stepped away from the door. Mistaking that for an invitation, he moved up, only to be halted by a firm hand in the face.

"Wait here."

Disappearing a moment, she returned with a sour, guarded expression.

"The mistress sees visitors 'round back; in her 'herb garden,' she calls it."

Politely tipping his hat, the physician picked his way through a prodigious growth of rose bushes to the rear of the building. There he discovered, to his great astonishment, a huge, glass-enclosed greenhouse. Peering through the windows, he counted twenty types of medicinal plants before being accosted by a voice from behind.

"Thomas Mannering, is it? With congestion of the chest? Step inside, then, and let me listen to your lungs."

Spinning around, he beheld the woman from the kirkyard. Gasping in stupefaction, he removed his hat.

"How did you get behind me? I did not see you come out the door nor hear you follow."

Rather than reply, Rose smiled and walked past, opening the door without any apparent movement of her hand.

"You called me a witch. I should think that answers your question nicely."

Without waiting on ceremony, were any to be offered, the mistress entered first then stood back, permitting the erstwhile patient to follow. Ducking beneath an array of herbs dangling from the ceiling, then sidestepping jutting shelves filled with mismatched earth boxes and flower pots, he finally made his way safely to a small enclave.

"How do you navigate through this jungle? I think you are in need of a more proficient gardener, madam."

"Aye. Navigate is the word, for I am a member of an illustrious crew. And have taken lessons in steering by the stars. But alas, they are not yet out. I found my way by having memorized the passageways. May I add, there is no 'madam' about it, for I am unmarried." Casually reaching over to remove a stray twig of parsley, she shot him a quizzical look as he withdrew from her touch. "You have come, sir, with a complaint of chest congestion. How may I properly determine the progress of your illness without inspection?"

"But of course...."

"You thought, perhaps, I had lured you here to seduce you?"

He blushed and coughed into his hand.

"No, no. Of course not. It is just that... as you say... you are unmarried."

Rose dismissed his fear with a casual wave. "I dare say I have had cause to study the male physique in far greater detail than you."

Leaving him to ponder the implications, she reached into a drawer and removed a stethoscope. Placing the tips in her ears, she bade him unbutton jacket and shirt. His eyes snaked warily toward the instrument.

"You... have a stethoscope?"

"I am gratified to see you recognize it. Stethoscope: the word is taken from the Greek, *stethos,* meaning chest and *skopein,* to examine. Used to mediate sounds produced in the body; primarily the chest and abdomen in a process called auscultation. You use one in your own practice, no doubt."

"No, I do not. I have only seen sketches from my studies."

"Really? I find it quite indispensable. You should consider purchasing one."

"Where did you get it?"

"From Germany. Where I order all my surgical equipment. I find their quality of superior workmanship." Warming the silver casing around the obturator, she placed it against his chest. "Take in a breath and hold it. Now cough."

Intently listening to the sounds, Rose moved the stethoscope to several positions, then made him turn, placing it against his back and repeating the process. When satisfied, she used a speculum to check his nasal cavities.

"Some slight discharge but that of a clear nature. You have allergies?"

"None that I am aware."

"Ah."

Reaching behind her to a potting stand used to hold a vast array of bottles, she carefully selected one and held it out.

"Although I do not think your health was the cause of your visit, Dr. Mannering, you do have a cold. Drink this, one moderate swallow, twice daily. Upon rising and in the evening; sometime between dinner and bedtime."

Uncorking the vial, he suspiciously sniffed. "What is in it?" Her left eyebrow arched.

"Witches do not disclose their secrets – Thomas."

Her familiarly nearly caused him to drop the medication.

"Do you always call your patients by their first names?"

"No. But you are not a patient. You came here to snoop,"

"To 'snoop'?"

"An informality I resort to upon occasion. From the Dutch, *snoepen,* meaning, 'to eat on the sly.' In this case, it may be taken to infer 'spying,' or 'an informal investigation.' Have you found what you came for, Surgeon Mannering?"

Mumbling an apology, he slipped away, forgetting, in his haste, to further question her about John Dix, the cough mixture, the herbarium or her gun-buying pursuits.

The following day a potted hibiscus was discovered on the stoop of the Blake House, with a handwritten note directing it be given to "The lady of the house." The enclosed message read:

"Dear Miss Theodore: Forgive my imperious 'snooping' of the previous afternoon, and pray accept these flowers as a token of my admiration and respect. Whilst you previously indicated to me you had no inclination toward beauty which will wither and die, I did notice a profusion of rose bushes by your pathway and the sides of your house. I beg you accept this humble offering and my acknowledgment of your own beauty, which far exceeds the flowers. Your humble servant, Thomas Mannering.

"P.S. John Dix has recovered splendidly from the 'potion' you applied to his wound and I, I am pleased to relay, have recovered completely from my cold after only three doses of your medicine. I would know more about this magic. If you are available for consultation, please reply to this missive with the date and time.

"P.P.S. According to my almanac, there is a full moon Tuesday next. If you are inclined to dance under it while conjuring spells, I should take it as a great professional courtesy if you were to invite me to the ceremony. Naturally, everything I witness will remain confidential. I have never yet betrayed the *secretus* (Latin, for 'secret') of a fellow healer. T.M.

"P.P.P.S. Where ever did you learn the Greek and Dutch tongues? T.M., again."

A return note, delivered by a messenger wearing a flowing seaman's blouse, wide-bottomed trousers and a red sash, offered the requested invitation. After reading the short missive, he demanded a moment to write his reply. The man responded by curling his lip.

"I wasn't instructed to bring anything back."

"Then tell your mistress I shall certainly come."

This elicited a glare of contempt from the man who spoke with a broad Southern accent. Had Mannering been more familiar with Americans, he would have noted the play acting.

"She ain't my mistress. She's an officer of the *Reprobate*. I take her orders but we ain't familiar. Nor should you be," he growled. "There are those what wouldn't take kindly to it."

Flustered, the doctor attempted to make amends. "I meant no disrespect. It is merely a term of respect."

"Keep it up and you're likely to find yourself tossed overboard. That," he added with a toothy grin, "is the captain's way of enforcing discipline."

"A bit extreme, isn't it?"

"Maybe. But no one ever makes the same mistake twice."

Creeping back into the shadows, Jack returned home and recounted his interview. It remained a source of general merriment for weeks to come.

Arriving promptly for his "consultation," Hanna Thompson directed him into Rose's study. Accepting the proffered hand, he removed his hat and sat down amid four walls of book-lined shelves. Clearly intimidated by her library, he rested his hands on his knees so as not to knead them in anxiety.

"This is a wonderful place you have here – Miss Theodore. Is that the proper manner in which to address you? I do not wish to make a mistake for fear of having the 'captain' throw me overboard."

"Have no trepidation on that account. He is away. But in his stead, I am perfectly capable of performing the deed. And yes, 'Miss Theodore' is acceptable. I see you have done some investigating to learn my name."

"I have, but have learned little else. Your... man... called you an officer. Of a ship called the *Reprobate.* Can that be true?"

"I prize that position as one of my greatest accomplishments. Although I am not certain 'officer' aptly applies. I am still learning the craft of seamanship."

"Along with that of arms dealing?"

"I am further advanced in that profession. I suppose you have no Blakely cannon to sell?"

"I do not even know what that means. But what of this ship – the *Reprobate?* Who is her master?"

"A gentleman of the highest honor. And one who treasures his anonymity."

"I would like to meet him."

"I feel certain the desire would not be reciprocated. But you have come to conjure spells?"

"To watch you at it, rather."

"Then come and I will show you."

Leading the way through the house to a rear door, they entered the greenhouse. On a coal burning stove by one of the widows several cast iron pots boiled a variety of mixtures. Sniffing at the unaccustomed odors, he tried to guess the contents.

"Thyme? Rosemary? And something else."

"Peppermint."

"For medicinal purposes?"

"In this case, for taste. Here," she indicated, lifting up a lid, "I am preparing a lip balm. When it congeals I shall store it in a small tin, easily kept in a pocket. Salt air – or any cold air, for that matter – chaps the skin, particularly the outer portion of the lips most exposed. By rubbing on my ointment, it alleviates the condition for hours. I have another lotion for the hands. Very useful for seamen."

"An ointment of your own creation?"

"Most certainly."

"And you have others?"

"Many. For a variety of ailments. Everything you see here," she indicated, sweeping an arm across the aisle, "is of my own development."

"Then, you are a chemist."

"In my spare time."

"What do you do with the rest of it?" The gleam in her eye answered the question. "I see. You deal in arms. But how reconcile the procurement of weapons with that of the healing arts? They would seem to be in direct contrast to one another."

"One is a profession. The other, shall I say, is a hobby."

To lighten the suddenly somber mood, he inquired, "And do you also dance by the light of the moon?"

"I do, sir. But I am afraid you shall not be privy to those ceremonies. The gods do not appreciate outsiders."

Nor does the Captain remained the unspoken addendum.

Thomas Mannering discovered more than he bargained for. Admitted into the world of healing herbs and spices, salves, tonics, lotions and the fine art of administration, he readily fell under Rose's spell. Never daring to push his luck, yet not immune from fanciful speculation, he become Rose's disciple. Whenever free of an evening, he applied at her door, hat in hand, seeking knowledge of plants, chemistry and to console a loneliness he supposed to be two-sided.

With his guard thus lowered, he inadvertently crossed the line after she developed a case study and line of treatment for one of his troublesome patients.

"Rose, you are a doctor!"

Her own radiance at his enthusiasm disappeared in a flash. Withdrawing in unmitigated anger, her expression conveyed more sharply than words the mistake he had made.

"I am no doctor. Nor have I laid claim to that exalted status. I received no formal education in the art of medicine. Call me 'witch,' if you will, for such is nearer the truth than what which you have just slandered me."

Frightened and confused, he reached out a hand in conciliation.

"That was not my intent; I meant only to compliment; to praise you on your insight and healing skills."

The confession did nothing to alleviate the hard lines of her stoical face.

"A healer I may be, but not a physician. That is the realm of *Mankind,* not a proper female pursuit."

"You have been hurt by what others say," he pacified, his own emotions torn by grief. "For Mankind, then, I apologize."

Shaking her head, Rose slid away, taking care to separate herself from him.

"It is not for you to apologize; therefore, I cannot accept so noble an offer."

Tortured by her denial, he sought refuge on a different plain.

"And yet you tell me you are a ship's chandler; a procurer of guns and munitions for a notorious sea captain and his fleet. Surely that is not the realm of a well-bred woman. If you can be one, why not the other?"

He expected an immediate response, but one was not forthcoming. Instead, Rose went about tidying the room, purposely placing her back to him. Not until she finished her tasks did she speak. The words echoed off the glass walls, giving them a sad, haunted quality.

"Yes. I am a ship's chandler; and a seaman, 'worth my salt,' if *he* is to be believed. *He* has given me that posting. He, for whom I would gladly sacrifice my life to spare him one moment's discomfort."

"He.... Tell me. Please. Of this extraordinary man, for whom you would die."

Slowly turning around, Rose faced her new friend, eyes on fire.

"You would not see him as I. You would judge harshly, for he is a shape-shifter; a man who presents one face to the world and another to me."

"Give me the chance. I promise not to be hasty. Only introduce me, I pray."

She understood his words and his jealousy, which she had not sought. A smile crept across her features, finally matching the glint behind her piercing orbs.

"That, I cannot do, although not from secrecy. He is away.... Far away. He has gone for a soldier, to fight for his principles. In a war not of his making; nor of his understanding."

"To defend liberty. A Federal man. I have read of this war. To free the Africans from the bondage of slavery." Bowing from the waist, Mannering touched his hand to his heart. The act solicited an unanticipated rebuttal.

"You misunderstand; Rudy Blake does not defend the Union. He is a... Rebel. A Confederate."

Stung by Rose's terse statement, the doctor stared at her through lowered lids.

"But surely not you.... You cannot condone such barbaric beliefs."

"I 'condone' the Cause, not the man. Only one who knows him as I do can fully comprehend his complexities. I said he was beyond your powers of reasoning. And so he is."

"You cannot leave it like that," protested the interloper, deeply hurt by her accusation and his exclusion from her company that Rose's denial surely implied. "I would know more of him." When she gave no indication of forgiveness, he tried harder, pulling from one of her plants a stem and leaves. Slipping it through the buttonhole of his coat, he used that has his peacemaker.

"Make me see Captain Blake through your eyes. Reveal for me the side he hides from others."

To recruit an ally for Rudy was tempting, for he had few truly worthy of the honor. But to speak unguardedly of him was tantamount to treason. What Rudy obfuscated from the world was his affair and not hers to share.

"It is beyond my power."

"And yet you considered it," he grasped, literally swiping his fingers through the empty air. "I have a true and honest heart; I will swear my confidence. Nothing you say will ever pass my lips to another living being." What he transmitted to God, however, Thomas held back, for not even his admiration of Rose could prohibit him from prayer – and the sublime advice he might need from a higher power.

Noting the sprig in his buttonhole, she remained unmoved.

"Why? Why do you want to know?"

The reply came simply, forthright and totally unpremeditated.

"Because you are a complex woman and he had brought out in you the spark of divine inspiration. What you were like before you met him, I cannot say. But that he is a great man I readily acknowledge, for you respect him. And you would not give your approval to any but the most pure and worthy of men."

Rose heard the declaration of love in Mannering's own words and relented. But only an inch and that in a lateral direction.

"I will speak of him on two conditions."

"Only ask and they are yours."

"One, that you understand, now and forever, that I love him; that no power on earth can ever alter my affection. Between you and I lies friendship and nothing more."

"Granted," came the unmitigated promise, for he had expected such to be her demand.

"Second, you will teach me surgery; technique, theory. In exchange, I will guide you into the mysteries of herbal medicines."

"But... but that is not fair," he stammered. "You offer me twice what I gave you: knowledge of Captain Blake and your skill with plants. That is an unequal proposition no gentleman could accept. I must offer more. Ask something else of me."

"No other form of payment is required."

"Then you leave it to me. So be it."

From that day forward, a missive was left daily at the door of the Blake House. Occasionally it came in the form of a potted flower, or a freshly dug bouquet of colorful weeds. Sometimes he would copy poetry from his books, and rarely compose lyrics from his own imagination. On Sundays Thomas inscribed passages from holy writings. When the mood was on him, he drew sketches of rolling meadows, wild, skeletal trees or abandoned barns, and when he lacked inspiration, anatomical renderings of muscles, veins and arteries.

All that he did with only minimal hope of winning her love, for when Rose Theodore did speak of Rudy Blake, she highlighted it with the spark of divine inspiration.

His own words.

****

CHAPTER 17

The man on the bed did not look like Rudy Blake.

Not the daring privateer, the reckless gambler, the dauntless, yet misguided seeker of gold. There was not the air of a gentleman about him, nor of the fierce, competitive nature of a wild spirit.

Nor did Mannering see the imprint of a boy who believed in elves and faeries, sat on splintered church pews beside his beloved Mammy, rode a horse named Black like the wind, or was capable of any of the flights of fancy Rose Theodore ascribed to him.

It was not the wound or the fever or the ravages of war hiding those qualities. The mistress of Blake House had been right. Rudy Blake was beyond the powers of Thomas Mannering's reason.

"Dr. Mannering, Captain Blake has asked you to go. I can do no more than second his opinion."

"But his injuries must be treated."

"I will tend to them, myself."

Shaking like a kitten left out in the rain, the doctor took a step closer to her, resting a hand on her arm. With wet, imploring eyes, he begged her leave.

"A moment with you. In private. For a consultation," he added, fearful of her refusal. He was correct in his trepidation and it was only their friendship which gave her pause.

"A moment. No longer." Kneeling beside Rudy, Rose gently brushed her hand across his brow. "I will step out. Close your eyes. When you open them again, it shall be to rest on my face."

"You're going... away?" he cried.

"Into the corridor. Rest. Do as I say."

She did not stir until he had carried out her directive and only then reluctantly. When they were alone in the hall, Mannering bowed his head before meeting her passionless stare.

"I forgot myself. Forgive me. But," he hurried on over the objection forming on her lips, "let me help. He is gravely ill. Each, by ourselves, may not have the knowledge to save him. But together, we cannot fail."

"I will not have his finger amputated."

"That is agreed. I will remove the fingernail, only, and scrape the bone. I will cut away the infection but leave the finger intact. When I have done what I can, he shall become your patient. Use your herbs and your potions. Soothe the inflamed flesh, treat the fever as you know so well how to do. I will look in on him, change the bandages, advise where I can. Do not deny me this. For the sake of our friendship and what he means to you."

Torn by the conflict of so great a charge, Rose hesitated.

"He has dismissed you."

Mannering pressed his case with the ardency of a suitor. "He will be asleep when you return. He need not be awakened. In fact, it would be better if he does not. We will anesthetize him, so he feels no pain. Then I shall operate. In the morning, nothing need be said of my assistance."

"Deceive him?"

"Would he not appreciate the deception? He, the master pirate, who employs deception as an art? He, the chameleon you described so well – the man who changes his identity with the shifting of the wind? Who would approve more heatedly than he?"

The decision was preordained but not without penalty.

"Thomas, I cannot overestimate my reluctance to go against Rudy's wishes; whether or not he be correct. In this instance, however, I will, because he has empowered me to speak for him. As his *agent*," she stressed, already burned once this evening because she wore no wedding ring. "While we are not bargaining in the strict sense of the word, I must have your promise."

"Anything."

While Mannering blushed at his unadulterated avowal, it was Rose who broke eye contact. In his naiveté, the young physician had not enough experience with the world to fully comprehend the nuances of his promise.

"Not anything; just one thing," she clarified, thus releasing him from his foolishness.

"And that is?"

"The truth."

"I would never lie to you," he protested, raising his voice. She immediately quieted him with a finger to her lips.

"You understand my feelings toward Rudy. I have made them plain enough." He nodded, not daring to confirm the statement with even a one word agreement. "But for the duration of this night – and the dawn to follow," she stressed, "you must forget that."

"Forget it? But why? I can never –"

"Were I Captain Blake's wife; his mother, his sister – you would, by training and sensibility, withhold certain details from me. Protect me from your honest insight. Say that is so."

"Yes," he whispered, finally able to utter the word.

"That must not be. I need to know; I must have your open and full confidence. Do not think to spare me."

"Rose," he pleaded, crossing his fingers and bringing them up toward his chest in the attitude of a penitent. "You love him. What I might say to a confidant will hurt you."

Wrapping her hands around his, she negated his kindness with a terse shake of her head.

"That is exactly how you must think of me. As a confidant. An assistant."

"A fellow doctor?" His question was unfair but he would not back down from hearing her admission.

"As a fellow healer. A doctor, if you must," she relented, failing to suppress the bitterness swelling inside her. "This night, and for this night only, you are I must be equal partners. Withhold nothing, as though we were both uninvolved. Only in that way will I trust you."

"What is there to doubt?"

Releasing him, Rose steadied herself against the doorframe. Were the wood less solid, it would have bowed under her weight.

"Whether he will live or die."

"I am not God," Thomas cried, attempting to move past her. She was faster than he, and blocked his path.

"No. But you have seen death. Just as I have. Occasionally, we may be mistaken, but not often. It is the... aura. The weakening of the soul. The preparation for the flight of the spirit. I might, perhaps, miss it. You will not. If you see such a thing, you must swear to me on your honor as a gentleman and a physician, to convey such to me. Do not couch your words in sentimentality or unnecessary tenderness," Rose added, her lower lip trembling. "For I will know and despise you for it."

"And if he is to die?"

"I must make preparations."

"For... him?"

"Do not ask what you cannot bear to hear," came the sharp retort. "Take me aside, tell me the word and then depart. With my everlasting blessing," she added, averting her gaze and thus permitting him to wipe his eyes in privacy. When he had sufficiently recovered, Rose continued. "Will you swear to me?" His hesitation was too long. "I will not think less of you if you leave now. I ask much."

"I promise."

The pact was sealed. Drawing in a deep breath, Rose crossed herself the way she had seen her beloved, superstitious Rudy do so many times before, then proceeded Mannering into the sick chamber. As he had predicted, the patient had fallen into a light coma.

"We begin immediately." He had his doctor's voice on, earning him a second, albeit silent, blessing. "You will anesthetize him whilst I operate. Once he is in a deep sleep, I leave it to you to monitor his pulse and respiration."

"Yes, doctor."

"His rates will be tachycardic when we begin. If the heart action falls below fifty, you must warn me and we will give his body time to recover before proceeding. Is that clear?"

"Perfectly."

"If his intake of air becomes stridulous, or he develops congestion of the lungs, I must stop and reconsider. He is very weak, very broken down, Rose. He may not bear what we must do."

"He will bear it."

Which was as much a hope as it was a belief, and as close as Rose Theodore had ever come to letting her heart rule her brain.

Setting out his instruments on the clean linen towel draped over the end table, Dr. Mannering checked to be certain everything was in order before raising a questioning eyebrow at Rose.

"He is under the influence of the ether," she informed him, her hand resting lightly on the damp, medicated washcloth. "His pulse is rapid but strong."

"How fast?"

"One hundred and twenty per minute."

"And his breathing."

"Deeper, now that he has been relaxed."

"Then, we begin – Doctor Theodore."

Carefully withdrawing Rudy's entire left arm from beneath the blanket where he had hidden it, Mannering examined the wound for the first time with intense scrutiny. His face remained calm and unemotional. During this procedure and through all the days to come, he would play the role of teaching instructor. That was part of the bargain and one he would not break for the world, though he wished otherwise.

"I begin," he demonstrated, catching the surgical steel in the lamplight so that its polished surface glistened, "by excising the skin at the side, from tip to knuckle. Once the puss has drained sufficiently and the unnatural swelling reduced, we will have a clearer idea of what damage there has been to the muscle and bone. That," he added for the sake of his pupil, "is our primary concern."

"And if they are compromised?"

"I will cut away as much of the tissue as I dare. But not so much," came the unsolicited promise, "to hinder dexterity. You will not be sickened by the smell?"

"I have performed autopsies on bodies a week in the river," came the low, solemn statement. "I have handled cases where the bowels have ruptured. I shall not be sickened."

"Very well. We begin."

With the first deep cut Rudy stirred, twitching like a man in a nightmare, only partially capable of distinguishing dream from reality. Rose pressed the cloth closer to his nose and his body quieted.

"Hush, my love. I am with you. Rose is here."

"He must be steady."

"Cut away," she ordered for both the patient and the assistant. Mannering flicked the scalpel in his hand, adjusting the instrument until it had the right feel, then resumed his task. As he slit the taut, edematous flesh, releasing the accumulated poison of months, the room filled with a toxic, almost gaseous scent. He coughed, cleared his throat and proceeded. She remained as mute as a sphinx.

Using the cotton bandages set out for him, Mannering soaked away the bloodied fluid, dropping them into a basin on the floor as they became unserviceable. After reducing the pile by nearly one third, he bent lower, starting into the cleared field.

"Come and have a look at this, so we may both judge."

Reluctantly leaving her position at Rudy's head, Rose stared coldly at the incision.

"Remove the nail," she ordered, "and extract the metal shard."

"As you say."

Staying his hand until she had resumed her place, the doctor began the slow, careful exhumation of the fingernail. When she saw perspiration roll down his face, Rose swabbed his brow, then brushed aside the stray locks of hair. As the fingernail came loose, she accepted it from his clamp, the way a believer would have taken a piece of the True Cross. Covering it in gauze, she caught his eye.

"For study," came the explanation. "When I have time, I shall sketch it. For my journal. I keep a record of all my... patients."

"Very good. I approve."

Tantamount to his acceptance was her belief she would have the curiosity and the strength of heart to perform so gristly a task.

"Now: look at this. It is as I suspected. The splinter of cannon has been in place so long, the bone has begun to grow over it. There is gross infection. I do not know if I can remove it without seriously damaging the innate structure of the finger."

"If you cannot, I will."

"Look!"

Ignoring the disapproval in his voice, Rose examined the foreign body, so long imbedded it had literally become a part of Rudy's finger. Holding out her hand, she took the blade in her left hand, hefted it, then replaced it on the table. Selecting one with a longer, more delicate curvature, she probed the area. Rudy jerked spasmodically, then groaned.

"Give him more ether." When Rose had applied several more drops of liquid over the cloth and the patient breathed easier, Mannering lifted imploring eyes toward her.

"For God's sake, let me amputate the finger. Now. If we attempt to remove the metal, there is no guarantee of getting it all. Even the most microscopic fibre will re-infect the bone and destroy our good work."

"Then we must be certain to remove it all."

"Use your eyes, woman! The bone is compromised; rotten. It cannot be saved."

Brushing back her own hair, Rose met his gaze with a steely one reserved for rending wood to ash.

"Then we may say we tried our best. I do not hold you responsible for a negative outcome, Thomas."

"I hold myself responsible!" he cried, abandoning his calm.

Pulling back so that her hands no longer rested on Rudy's body, Rose met Mannering's loss of composure with icy stillness.

"Have you never, in your practice, come across a case – say that of a miner, badly crushed, the bones of both legs shattered beyond repair. You may, or may not have the skill to save his life, but to try, you must cut off both his legs. Being a cripple, the man will have no work. His family will starve. Feeling useless, your patient will grow to hate himself and those around him. He will take to drink; beat his wife and children. Berate the life you so conscientiously preserved. He will sit on his porch and curse the other men – once his friends, who now shun his company. He will curse God when once loving hands pick him up and tote him from that porch to his bed, where he will lie and rot. Have you never faced such a situation, doctor?"

"I have."

"The stumps of his wounds may heal, but his heart will be forever corrupted. How have you benefited your patient, doctor, by saving his life, but destroying his soul? Or," Rose pursued, leaning nearer, until her breath stung his cheeks, "have you stayed your hand from that healing touch? Have you, perhaps, considered the alternatives, and acceded to his wish to die a whole man?"

Blinking once, then letting out a sorrowful breath of air, Rose shook her head. "There are worse things to befall a human being than death, Thomas. That is why, I believe, that the Lord, in His great wisdom, gave us the power of free will. We make decisions, whether good or ill, based on what we think in our hearts to be the proper course. No one ever said they would be easy ones. They are not. Once made, we tear ourselves apart, never knowing what might have happened had we walked the other path.

"I believe that every man and woman has the inalienable right to choose his destiny. What is precious to one is not so to another. What one man accepts, another condemns. We are all individuals, doctor. Rudy was fortunate in that he was able to make his own choice. Had he not been, I would have made it for him."

"Which would you have chosen?"

She would not answer. It was not his privilege to know.

"He has spoken. Proceed. Cut away the splinter and scrape the bone. He will live or he will die. In either case, he will be what he was. A whole man."

"You will die with him," the physician moaned, eyes watering. "You as much as said so."

His statement, so agonizingly pleaded, caused Rose to react in a manner he had not expected. She smiled.

"Then I will die, for he has given me life. I choose to follow his body to the grave and lie beside him, for only then will I find eternal peace." Seeing his misery, her smile widened. "Do not grieve for me, Thomas, for I believe Rudy and I will resurrect together, standing at the Pearly Gates, hard-bargaining St. Peter for admittance. Rudy will play high card with him, whilst I pick his pocket. That," she added with a determined stake of the head, "will give us a stake at the celestial poker game we will surely enter."

"Amen."

Recommencing his work, the British doctor pried the metal chard of cannon away from the former Confederate private's finger. Extracting the largest of the pieces, he caught the New Yorker's eye.

"Nasty."

"Save it for me."

Placing it alongside the fingernail, he went back to work. He had barely begun when he cried out, jerking his head back, but not fast enough. A stream of bright, watery-pink blood struck him in the face.

"Bleeder," he gritted. "A damned severed vein."

Without waiting to be instructed, Rose immediately grabbed a tourniquet, tying it tightly around Rudy's left arm. On his look, she tersely explained, "Pressure."

"Very good. Hold him, while I have a closer look."

Restraining Rudy, who trashed his feet while attempting to free his hand, she observed with clinical fascination as Mannering examined the damage. His exhalation was palpable.

"Just nicked the bugger." Realizing, too late the inappropriateness of his language, he shuddered by way of prefacing his apology.

"I'm sorry. Forgive me."

"No apology needed." On his surprised expression she added, "I've heard worse. And for less cause."

"A man who swears in front of a lady is a dog."

Give a dog a bad name and you might as well shoot it.

Something Rudy had said once, in reference to himself. The remembrance of it made Rose's eyes flutter shut as she controlled her own pain.

For the second time, the doctor misunderstood.

"I'll control the bleeding. It's a terrible sight, I know."

"It wasn't that," Rose affirmed, reopening her eyes. Thinking quickly for an excuse, she lamely added, "He's so pale. His blood is thin and weak." Reaching out, she touched her finger to the soiled bandage used to soak the blood, then brought it to her lips before he could stop her. "So little iron. It's no wonder he's so weak and colorless."

"Iron? What has iron to do with it? That is not a component of the red coloring."

"Iron is integral to healthy plasma. Have you never tasted it in blood?"

"Never," he admitted, momentarily diverting his attention from the open wound. "Nor was I ever taught of such a thing. How it is ingested into the body?"

"Red meat." came the prompt reply. "Have you never prescribed a diet of red meat for someone suffering from anemia?"

"Bloody red meat," he agreed.

"But why?"

"To transfer blood from one being to another."

"Not blood, itself, but the building blocks of blood. So that the patient may take from the meat the nutrients necessary to stimulate the formation of blood in his own body."

"Where did you learn this?"

"Through my microscope; and through observation."

Mannering shook his ground, obstinate. "Then we might as well eat iron shavings. Or have this iron in Captain Blake's hand dissolve into blood components."

"The body cannot absorb it that way, or it would have."

"I would know more of this."

Redirecting his concentration, he quickly cauterized the vein with the tip of metal, heated by an open candle flame. When he was certain the narrow vessel was sealed and pulsating, he changed instruments, this time selecting what appeared to be a small pick.

"For your '49'er," he explained, attempting to regain his equilibrium.

"For luck," she agreed.

Mannering removed three more pieces of decayed metal splinters, then resumed his scraping operation before his brows knit and his head twitched. Misunderstanding, Rose went to wipe his brow. Shaking her off, he stamped his foot in mock annoyance.

"What do you mean, 'for luck'? I thought he never found any gold? Or are you suggesting I will find gold as well as iron whilst I am digging in his hand?"

She understood this was his way of relieving tension and was only too glad to answer. Pointing toward the table where she had laid Rudy's ring, she followed his gaze toward it.

"There was, indeed, gold 'about' his hand, but alas, I removed it. Too late for you to excavate."

"That is the largest ring I have ever seen. Is it really gold?"

"Really and truly. While I cannot say for sure, I assume it is California gold."

"How much is it worth?"

"Oh," Rose carelessly dismissed, "the gold is only a tenth of its value. The real worth lies in the diamonds and rubies with which it is studded. And, of course," she amended slyly, "in its intricate design."

"And the sum total?"

"One the order of five thousand dollars."

Had Mannering less fortitude, he would have dropped his instrument.

"If he is that wealthy that he carries a fortune around on his hand, why does he want to be a gambler?"

"For the same reason a man born with two good legs wants to walk. Because that is what he was created for."

"And you? Do you also gamble?"

Switching her line of vision from the gem-covered ring filled with cyanide to the man on the bed, Rose moved her head slowly, up and down, exactly opposite the pendulum of a grandfather clock.

"Yes."

Mannering grunted and resumed his work. After another half hours work, he set the pick down and sunk wearily into a chair.

"Enough," he declared, steadying his hands by placing them on his thighs. "Let the patient rest a moment while I catch my breath."

Making a final check of Rudy's pulse and respiration, Rose joined him, drawing up another chair so she could sit beside him.

"Do you want anything? A drink of water? Some brandy? A light refreshment?"

"No. Just some time to compose myself. The work is delicate and my back hurts."

"I will rub it," came the immediate offer, but he quickly indicated she remain seated.

"I didn't say that for you to offer. I beg your pardon."

"I know you didn't. But I am your assistant and I do not mind."

Stretching his tight muscles, then rubbing the back of his neck, Thomas sighed before answering.

"Under other circumstances, I would take you up on the offer and pray for better times. But you know I cannot." He blushed, then coughed discretely into his hand. "He is a lucky man, you know, your Rudy Blake."

"There is luck, and there is luck," she hedged. "How do you mean?"

The reply was blunt and sincere. "To have you."

"I am not the prize you think I am. Take that as a warning and ask no more."

"And if I did?"

"I would be forced to tell you that although my parents were both teachers, who trained me to follow in their footsteps, I chose to go another way. A far less honorable path. One, you may take for granted, they would not have approved. I became a working woman."

He did not catch her subtlety for it was not in his nature to consider the worst of anyone.

"A seamstress? A tutor for a disreputable landlord?" Her silence was ominous. "A land speculator? A card player? Is that why he was attracted to you? Where did you meet – over a card table?"

"In a bedroom."

The bluntness of the statement, offered without excuses, caused him to fall heavily against the back of his chair. Whatever jocularity he had expressed, or expected her to counter with, vanished as quickly as the air in his lungs. With a hand to his face, he covered his eyes.

"So now, perhaps," Rose Theodore continued, her voice steady and unemotional, "you will heed me when I say not to ask what you do not want to hear."

"Good God. I'm so sorry."

"Sorry? Sorry for what?" Rising from her seat, the lady wandered the confines of the room, hands held stiffly at her side, the way a prisoner faced the executioner. "I am not sorry. In this life, I have few regrets. That is not one of them." Pausing to face him, she ended, "I made my bed and I shall, figuratively, sleep in it all the days of my life."

"He... he bought you? That is how you met him?"

Rose startled the young doctor by laughing.

"On the contrary. Rudy rescued me. From a Federal admiral's ship – where I was plying my 'unholy' trade, if I may be so bold. Opening that devil's safe, Captain Blake paid me for services not rendered to him, personally. Seven hundred dollars. Far more than the Admiral had promised. That was only fifty dollars. Captain Blake gave me that money to make a point."

"And that was?" Mannering whispered.

"That I was worth far more than either the Admiral or I thought. Yes, Thomas. I became Rudy's 'lover.' Willingly and with malice aforethought. I would have been content to let it go at that, but he was not. He saved me from a life on the streets; made a 'respectable woman' of me. First, I became his accountant and then, on the voyage over from Charleston, a seaman – a member of his crew. Once on British soil, I have worked for him as his chandler. Outfitting his ships; purchasing guns and munitions. But you knew that. Did you never wonder?"

"Wonder... about your relationship with him?"

"That. And why I wear no wedding ring."

The words were harsh and mean.

"Yes. I wondered."

"Then wonder no more. He is married – to a woman he does not love. He cannot marry me. And yet we are married, if marriage be a union of two like souls. From now until eternity, he is my husband and damn the wedding ring. For you see," she added sarcastically, "I have no reputation to ruin."

"Do not say that!" he cried, jumping from the chair and in his haste knocking it over. The crashing sound it made sobered them both and put an end to the conversation.

"We had best get back to work before he wakes."

"Yes," Rose agreed. "Before he wakes."

It was clear enough.

CHAPTER 18

With a sigh of weariness from the heart, Dr. Mannering replaced the scalpel on the table, then indicated a curved needle.

"I've not much of a hand for suturing; not the delicate areas. My fingers are too big."

While Rose doubted the assertion, she nonetheless accepted his offer.

"I would like to do it. Sit down and rest." Noting the fleeting expression of pain cross his face, she quickly recanted. "Unless you would rather go home. You've been up all night and I have no doubt a waiting room full of patients. How thoughtless of me."

He temporarily allayed her fears by dropping down onto the chair.

"If I thought that, I'd dance a jig all the way home. Why do you think I spent so much time here, teaching you – and learning of herbs and chemistry? I'm young and the folks hereabouts are suspicious of any physician who isn't balding and grey-bearded."

She understood what lay beneath his words and realization stung. Under other circumstances she might have let the words go on face value, but her own pride was stung.

Threading black thread through the eye, Rose studied the instrument a long beat before speaking.

"Thomas, I never lied to you. Never once did I encourage your attentions of a more personal nature."

He had not expected to be challenged and flushed, miserably regretting his bitterness.

"The foolishness was one sided; I apologize Miss Theodore." Glancing down at his hands, he forced a wry grin to his face. "I hoped to charm you away from the mysterious Captain Blake by diligence and my vast knowledge of physiology. What I neglected to take into account was the anatomy of the heart."

"You will like him." Averting her back, Rose began the intricate operation of mending together the thin, frayed skin around Rudy's finger. "When he is well and on his feet, you must spend some time with us. Get to know him. He is a generous man, and –"

"I need no other payment than your gratitude," Mannering blurted, then covered his face with his hand so his next words came out muffled. "You called me in as a physician. I treated him with my utmost skill. I would do no less for any patient."

"There are men who say a doctor should never operate on his family; those close to him, because affection rules common sense. I have never agreed. It has been my experience that I think far more clearly when one dear to me requires a healing touch. I witnessed that in you this night."

"If he had died, I would have done everything in my power to save you."

"I know. Your tender emotion means a great deal to me. I do not dismiss it with Rudy's arrival. I treasure your friendship and I will miss your visits if you do not come again."

"I have taught you all I know. You are as qualified a surgeon as any presenting themselves for examination at the Royal Academy."

She would not be diverted from what she had to say by useless discussions. "I have told you what I was. My past is well documented. Every man here knows my history; or at least enough to spread idle gossip. They were all part of Captain Blake's crew when he rescued me. Even you must realize such a wife would be a hindrance and not a help to a young surgeon, just starting out on his career. Reputations have been lost for less."

Dropping his hand, Thomas rose from the chair, partially obscuring her light. Rose waved him back, which served the dual purpose of separating them.

"I hardly know whether or not to believe you," he confessed. "You were, perhaps, sacrificing yourself to spare my feelings."

"In the eyes of the world, Rudy Blake is a reprobate. Do you know what that means?"

"A scoundrel; a man of ill repute."

"Indeed. Like I, he has no reputation to lose by associating himself with a fallen woman. If anything, we complement each other. We are both... conundrums." Rose hesitated, a small, radiant glow expanding her life force as she contemplated the idea. "Do you believe in God?"

"I do."

"Then, possibly, you believe, as I do, that no deed, no act committed, no thought occurs without some divine purpose."

He did not see where she was going, or he would not have been so ready to agree.

"Yes. I see God's hand in even the worst tragedy."

"Then believe this: I had free will to choose my path. Unlike so many unfortunates, I entered the... oldest profession... fully aware of what I was doing." Rudy stirred under her ministrations and she calmed him with a hand to his forehead. "Hush, baby. Not long, now, and then we shall both sleep."

Drawing the thread around the needle, Rose tied a knot, then reached for a jar of cream. Daubing her finger into the cloudy, semi-fluid material, she carefully administered the medicine to his sutured wound.

"Perhaps not fully," she continued to Mannering, "but fully prepared to accept the consequences. I thought to save my money and start a school for girls. Or 'retire to the country,'" she added with a darker inflection.

Wrapping a thin gauze bandage around his finger, her mind whirled with possibilities.

"He and I – we are so very much alike. I had not thought about it until now, but circumstances have opened my eyes."

"See – what?"

"My boy, here – this very worldly man – scorned by the very people who should have loved him – sought respectability by the vast accumulation of wealth. If he were the richest man in the world with his castle atop a grand mountain, no one would dare hold contempt for him. They would envy him, worship him. No matter his 'evil deeds,' he would be a gentleman in their eyes. Such is the power of wealth."

Her voice lowered into a wondrous softness. "Perhaps I thought the same thing. With money, I could do what I wanted, with no one to shake a finger at how I obtained it. Money is the root of all good." Her smile widened as her flesh prickled with thousands of tiny goose bumps at the familiar quotation. "I could have been a teacher like my parents; live in humble dwellings; scrap for money to pay the rent. There is a quiet dignity in that. But I wanted more. Much more. I wanted freedom."

Pausing in her reminiscences, Rose turned toward Thomas. "Shall I further bandage his hand or leave it open? I have only a loose dressing on it to admit the air."

Crossing to the patient, the doctor considered, deep lines furrowing his brows.

"Will he pick on it when he wakes?"

The question might have been asked of a child, and Rose's familiarity with Rudy's childlike qualities washed warm love through her soul.

"Without question."

"Then heavily bandage his hand, up to the elbow. It is best to leave the wound undisturbed. Then elevate the arm in a sling."

"So it is above his heart," Rose agreed. "Making it easier for the heart to pump blood to his affected limb. That will ease the throbbing and make it less painful for him. Thank you for reminding me."

Although he had not, Mannering took credit for the observation.

"Here. Tie the sling across his chest at top and bottom. With it immobilized, he will find it more difficult to –"

"Investigate," she finished for him, quickly strapping Rudy's left arm close to his chest.

"Good job," came the approval. And then a prompt. "Finish your thought. About money," he added tenderly, draping a hand across hers.

"I was referring to security which comes from it," she easily resumed. "With riches, I could do what I wanted. Trade English lessons for bookkeeping instead of coin. Treat the sick without taking their last penny. Indulge my researches. Travel. None of that would be open to me if I were poor."

Pursing his lips, Mannering brought his head close to hers.

"Are you asking my forgiveness? Or God's?"

Jerking away, Rose shot him a look of intense defiance.

"Neither. I am drawing a parallel between myself and Rudy Blake. One I had not seen as clearly as I do now. My life as a prostitute brought me into contact with him. I should hardly have found him otherwise. It was God's will; God's plan we should find one another."

Finishing on a strong note, Rose washed her hands in the basin, then carried the bowl to the window. Holding it in one hand, she pulled up the glass, yelled a merry "Man overboard," then tossed the bloodied contents through the frame. Cocking her ear to one side, she listened, her imagination easily supplying the yell of surprise as the water doused an unsuspecting head.

"We are two sides of the same coin, Dr. Mannering. Bless you for helping me realize how melded we are to one another. And how proper and fitting it is we are bound to one another by love and commonality."

Biting his lower lip, the doctor bowed.

"I will examine the patient, now. For other wounds, before I take my leave."

Assuming a calm demeanor, he pulled back the sheet covering Rudy. With the hands of one accustomed to looking at flesh as a disease distinct from the patient, he removed the nightshirt.

"He is greatly emaciated. He will need... red meat."

"I will start him on strong beef broth the moment he wakes. And tea. For its restorative powers – and fluid. He is as dehydrated as malnourished." Pinching Rudy's skin, she watched as Mannering observed the poor compliance.

"That is your test?"

"As good as any I know."

"I think, perhaps... Miss Theodore... you are a more capable doctor than I."

The time was past for her to accept such a compliment.

"We both have knowledge. Tonight, I needed yours and you came. I shall forever be grateful."

Gently lifting Rudy's arms and legs, the physician searched for obvious cuts and bruises. Finding none which demanded immediate attention, he indicated Rose roll Rudy over on his side while he inspected his back. Prying a finger between Rudy's buttocks, he made a low, deprecating noise.

"The skin here is badly excoriated. Raw from exposure. He suffers from a severe case of piles. Those swollen, exterior ones should be excised before they cause more excessive bleeding."

"Yes, they are bad. I feared as much. Eating irregularly with poor hygiene has exasperated the hemorrhoids. I will have him soak in a sitz bath, filled with warm water and soothing herbs. That should reduce the inflammation. Careful diet and regular habits ought to reduce them in size, so surgery is not necessary."

"You are speaking of a lengthy recovery. It will be months before he is capable of evacuating his bowels without pain."

"He has come home to me; time is one thing God has provided. One race is over: we begin anew."

"You have the patience for this? Having a sick man..." His thought, "in your bed," died on his lips, replaced by, "in your house, is tedious. It causes wear and frayed nerves. When progress is slow, tempers flare."

"Are you suggesting I send him to hospital? Or perhaps deliver him into your care?"

"It is a suggestion." Shifting uncomfortably, the physician began washing his instruments as a means of avoiding her glare. "I am concerned for your household. There are women here. Wracked by delirium, he is capable of great violence."

"At the moment, there are only two women present," Rose tartly informed him. "The others have been dismissed. He will have little contact with Mrs. Tompkins, and that, well supervised. She," Rose added significantly, "is not afraid of him."

"And you?" Mannering tried, failing to conceal his concern and skepticism. "In such close quarters? A blow from his arm could break your jaw. In his suffering, he might mistake you for an enemy. It is not uncommon for gravely ill men to take out their frustrations on those helpless females attending them."

Rose choked back a guffaw, then wiped the smirk from her face.

"You think I am helpless?"

"Not helpless," he quickly assured her. "But overcome, perhaps, by your affection and your need to provide comfort. Such emotions cloud the judgment; make one careless or obscure the dangers others clearly see."

"He will never hurt me."

"But that is exactly what I mean," he tried, discarding an instrument in the water to face her. It made a sharp, pinging noise as metal struck metal. "There are no absolutes in medicine. Your mind is not open to the possibilities of unexpected violence. Your judgment is clouded by gratitude and a need to repay this man for –"

Anger swelled in Rose's breast. With her fists clenched, her jaw jutted outward.

"For what? Services rendered? That, sir, is an insult. Once even a former prostitute cannot bear."

Retreating from her own flare of unanticipated violence, Mannering held up both hands in impotent defense.

"You misunderstand. I meant only that –"

"I know what you meant. You need not search for lies to soften the intent. My mind is as clear as it was the moment I first met Captain Blake. Which is more than I can say for you, sir. You wish him out of my house. Or, as we are speaking of absolutes, out of my bed. You are jealous, though you have no right to be."

Shoving him aside in unladylike possession, Rose began the task of cleaning the surgical tools he had abandoned.

"I saw the look on your face, Thomas, when I told you of my former occupation. You were shocked, dismayed. More than that, you were disgusted. You imagined me a pure and chaste lady of unusual scientific knowledge and I sadly disillusioned you. Now, you wish to eradicate my past by taking Rudy from me. What would you do to him in your surgery? That which I have forbidden? You know his weaknesses. What would it take for you to disfigure him so that he would not wish to live? If he takes his own life, jumps out a window and breaks his neck, what then, doctor? Have to me yourself? Go back to pretending I am a gentle woman and not a whore?"

"Stop!" he roared, but Rose had no fear and great indignation.

"I will 'doctor' him and I will cure him. He will not die and he will not be disfigured. So says Rose Theodore to any God or gods which may be listening. And to you, doctor, I say, keep your place and mind your manners, for I shall tolerate no disrespect for Rudy or for myself under the roof of my own dwelling."

Shaking like a newborn calf, her words chastised the young man into humble obedience.

"I only feared for your safety. And for your mind, should he never fully recover. I have seen such events and they are devastating to one who... feels so deeply."

"You have never met one who feels as deeply as I. Yet I view my love as a strength, rather than a weakness. And so it is. Stand on your guard, for you totter on the edge of making me your enemy."

"That I should never wish," he cried, covering his face with his hands. "All of this... has been too much. I stagger under the weight of..." He could not find the right word and so let go the thought. "Let me be your friend. Always. As it was before."

She shook her head, denying him that grace. "Not as before. We must begin anew – now that the cards have been placed on the table."

Grimacing under her gambler's expression, Mannering reached out a hand but did not touch her.

"I am tired. The long, arduous operation has fatigued me; caused me to speak unguardedly. Please forgive me again and let me recommence my examination of the patient before he wakes, for the ether is wearing off. It would not do for him to hear arguing in his sick room. I am physician before man, Miss Theodore. Trust that, if nothing else."

Rose could not believe him, for she knew better. No man or woman had the capacity to place their occupation above basic humanity. No dedication, however sincere, lifted the practitioner beyond the tenets of their personality. But she did not say so. To argue was to digress from the moment.

She therefore relented, but did not absolve.

CHAPTER 19

"Do as you will," Rose relented, shifting her gaze from the doctor to the patient. He was her love. His life was in her hands and she would see to it all that was necessary was done to preserve that which was most precious to her.

Palpably relieved, Mannering tugged at the tails of his suit coat, then ran his hand across his breast, as though to wipe clean the slate. Lifting up the chair, he repositioned it beside the bed, then gingerly settled into it, facing Rudy.

"I will examine your mouth, sir," he began, less aware than Rose of the semi-conscious mind working within the prone man's skull. He expected no response and was therefore surprised to note a flicker of awareness as the patient's eyes rolled under half-open lids.

Taking the small lamp, the doctor adjusted it for better light, pressing his own tongue against his front teeth in reaction to the retracted gums of his patient, which gave Rudy's teeth the appearance of unnatural size.

"Will you hold back his lips for me?" he requested of his assistant.

Complying without hesitation, Rose divined permission from Rudy's silent signal and carefully pried open his oral cavity. Mannering made quick work of his inspection.

"His teeth are rotten; decayed. See where they are blackened and loose. I know of nothing which will save them."

"With care, they will stabilize. Trust me when I tell you Rudy's teeth have very long roots." On his surprised expression she added, "I pulled one, once. Not long after we met. It was quite an ordeal. One I should not care to repeat."

"Then, you have the strength of a man," Thomas flattered.

This was a compliment she could easily accept. But not without further clarification.

"I should have said, I assisted in the removal of the tooth. D'Artagnan, Captain Blake's first mate, actually wielded the pliers. I held the patient down. Which was the harder of the two tasks."

Barely hiding his shock, the doctor withdrew, needing breathing room.

"You will hold him again while I extract them?"

"We will deal with his oral care another day," came the chipped assurance.

"And that means you will save them the way you saved his finger?"

"Yes."

"Ah. I am learning. But the gums," he pursued, not quite ready to abandon the point. "They will not hold teeth – even those with long roots."

"I have salve; and other means of restoring circulation."

"Pray, tell me."

Regardless of whether there was sarcasm in his demand, she was eager to elucidate him.

"Salt water to begin. As you know, salt purifies. It will cleanse his gums, remove the accumulation of slime and scum. Followed by a rinse of baking soda, flavored with extract of peppermint. That will sweeten Rudy's mouth, make the task more pleasant. That way, he will be more inclined to keep up with the treatments."

"He won't have the strength for that. You'll have to have a servant assist him –"

"Not a servant. I shall do it."

"You? Put your hand in his mouth? Daily?"

"Oh, no," Rose lightly dismissed. "Not daily, Dr. Mannering; five times a day. Once upon rising, after each meal and at bedtime. The more often we perform the operation, the sooner the flesh will heal."

"And yet the teeth are rotten; the enamel is compromised and cavities have formed. Surely disease will enter and destroy the inner bone."

"It appears that way," Rose conceded, unconvinced. "But I believe what you observe is no more than outward stain. Like the outer man, once bathed and clean, they will present a much more hopeful picture."

"And you shall bathe him, yourself? Without aid? Water will sting his..."

"Private areas," Rose supplied. "I have both a shower bath and a custom-made tub in which he may soak. He will do as I tell him, for he knows I have the power to relieve his suffering."

"Then he has great faith."

"More than other men."

"In you," Mannering clarified.

"I took your meaning. His journey here, across three thousand miles of water would have killed another. What sustained him was his belief in me."

"He knows you for a physician, then."

"He knows me for many things. A healer, for I will not use that other word, nor allow him to employ it. He knows I love him. It was a lesson hard-learned, for he is not a man to trust easily. Life has been cruel to him."

"But not," Mannering tried, "as hard as on you."

"We have both walked through fire. We have both been manipulated by circumstances beyond our control. And yet, tempering has strengthened us. Neither he nor I are what we might have been. But who, sir, can say otherwise? And who is to complain if they use their free will to enhance God's plan?"

"You believe that?"

"I have said so."

Leaning back, the doctor turned the shade of the lamp so it shone away from Rudy's face.

"If you know so much, tell me what God's future has in store for you."

The question seemed to deflate Rose, for her stiff resolve weakened and her shoulders slumped. Leaning against the bed frame for support, her head hung in weariness which might have been interpreted as depression.

"I cannot say."

"You do not know, or you dare not verbalize what you know?"

"I lay no claim to special powers, Thomas. I know the world. That is enough."

"Explain what that means?" he pleaded, turning toward her with sudden pity.

"'My Kingdom is not of this Earth.' Christ's words."

"Meant to convey there is no happiness to be found here?"

"True joy is to be achieved in heaven. That is the gift the Lord bestowed upon all His creatures. That was Jesus' message. The happiness we find here is transitory."

"You sadden me."

Recovering what strength she yet possessed, Rose forced a smile to her otherwise drawn and pinched features.

"That was not my intent. I have been happy. I am thankful now for the blessing I have received. Rudy has come home. We will be happy again."

"But not forever," he prodded.

"Not... continuously," she hedged, irritated to be forced into elaborating. Staring upward, past the rough-hewed ceiling to the imagined sky beyond, she added, "There is trial and suffering ahead. But it is not wise to dwell on such things. The gods will hear."

"The gods?"

This time when she smiled it was a dismissal. "Rudy's gods; those on Olympus who have made him their special pet. He would tell you they listen to the conversations of Man, waiting their chance to catch their favorites in a slip of the tongue. A boast; a brag. A belief in everlasting happiness. It is best to keep one's thoughts to oneself."

"That is not a Christian belief."

"And who created the 'lower heavens,' if not God, for nothing is thought or dreamed which does not have his approval."

"His plan."

"As I have said," she sighed. "Go now, please, for I am weary. I must sleep."

"Beside him?"

"Enough, before I lose my patience and throw you out," she cried, raising her arm and pointing toward the door. "That will destroy my gratitude for what you have done and I have promised you that, if nothing more."

"We are both tired," he agreed, gathering his instruments and replacing them in his black bag. "I will say good morning to you, then, madam." He hesitated, then tried a softer farewell. "With your permission, I will check in on the patient in a day or so. But if his fever rises, you understand –"

"There are no guarantees in life, sir. I will deal with that situation as I see fit. For his life is as precious to me as my own."

Bowing a good-bye, Thomas Mannering crossed the threshold. Pausing between the wooden sides of the oak frame, he made a final *adieu*.

"One day, will you explain about the water? Why you tossed it out the window?"

"It is a good story," Rose Theodore acknowledged. One she would share again with Rudy and no one else. It was something they could laugh about. In private, under God's watchful eyes. "Good-bye."

Padding quietly down the stairs, Thomas Mannering again found himself in familiar territory. While he had never been upstairs, his entrance into the lower level of the Blake House had become a matter of course. While it was true he used it only as a conduit to the herbarium and Rose's green house, once she had invited him into the parlor.

The night had been cold and even the warmth generated by her stove, with its system of pipes and vents had failed to keep away the chill. On her suggestion, they retired inside, to sit before a roaring fire and drink tea. Stifling a shiver now, he glanced around himself, confirming the fact he was alone. If it were true Rose had fired the servants, then he had the place to himself.

Abandoning his manners, Mannering strolled into the living room, loath to abandon the woman he had come to look upon as more than a friend. He was disturbed and that disquietude would not allow him to leave without a reckoning, at least within himself.

Unlike his previous foray, no fire burned in the grate. The room was depressingly empty. His footsteps, absorbed by the plush carpet, seemed to draw, rather than augment life. Glancing around like a thief, rather than merely an intruder, his eyes took in the furnishings. A piano sat in the corner, around which were placed several chairs. Beyond, closer to the chimney were two couches, each with delicately constructed end tables. It was on one of those from which she had served him the hot beverage and shortbread with her own hands.

He had imagined much that evening, dreamed more. Rose Theodore was as unlike any woman he had ever met as snow was to rain. Beautiful, alluring, intelligent, charming, they had talked of medicine, spoken about foreign lands, touched upon a myriad of subjects which made his head spin, as though the drink they consumed was aged brandy, rather than East India tea.

There was not a subject on which she was unfamiliar; not a topic he broached that she did not have an opinion. Listening to her discourse on New York City, with its tall buildings, massive manufacturing plants, crowded shipyards and teeming population, or being enraptured by her descriptions of Bermuda, he had fallen in love with her.

Rose had briefly touched upon the mysterious Captain Blake and his mighty clipper ship, but in Mannering's ardor, he had dismissed the man as no more than another story in her vast repertoire. Whoever he was, Blake was gone, abandoning her for private plans of his own. She had not said what, nor had she known when, of if, he would return. That had been the doctor's avenue for hope.

Rudy Blake had returned, not the swashbuckling pirate he expected to see, but a pitiful, downtrodden wreck of a man. It was not injuries which demeaned him, but his uncouth demeanor. Healthy and vibrant, he might have appealed to a woman, but not Rose Theodore. To be her equal, he would have to be a gentleman, a man of high moral standing, something Mannering decided he was not.

Settling himself on the couch, he closed his eyes, letting memories of his previous evening assail his better judgment. She was unique, a treasure, a woman destined for happiness and a loving husband with whom she could share his triumphs and his children.

Rudy Blake was married. She had said so, herself. That fact he had not known and clung to with the tenacity of a retriever. His future was with another. He could never wed her, never place a ring on her finger; dare not give her children. Those were things only marriage could bestow.

Thomas Mannering did not believe Rose's story of her past life. It simply made no sense. She was too educated, to genteel, too refined. Hers had been a life of culture, breeding. He did not doubt she knew of hard times, but those had only tempered and stiffened her resolve for what was pure and pristine in life. She deserved better than an American rogue.

What was it she had called him? His brows knit as his weary mind replayed the scene in that bedroom, her bedroom. A reprobate. That was it. He nodded, confirming the assertion to himself. Rudy Blake was disreputable, foreordained to damnation. No matter the circumstances of his birth, he was lower class, inferior. He had no mind, no sensibilities.

She had only told him those stories about herself to shock, to make him stand back, reevaluate. That was her way of warning him: Captain Blake has a hold on me. One I cannot break. It is best you step aside, or he will hurt you.

Thomas Mannering was not afraid. Not when that man stood between himself and the woman he loved. He would fight for her, defend her from the scourge which had so unexpectedly reentered her life. She had been trying to save him, yet it would be he who saved her. That was the proper order, the way it was between man and woman.

Crossing his legs, he wondered at his own acceptability. He was not rich. His practice was small and unassuming. But that would change. With Rose as his wife, they could travel to London, set up an office, attract a better clientele. With her knowledge of herbs and potions and his skill as a surgeon, his name would become a household word. Patients would travel across Britain to seek out his opinions.

That was his destiny; what he had longed for all his life. He was more than a country doctor. Within his hands were life-giving ministrations. She spoke of God: let her see this was God's plan, not that she should waste her affection on a man who had nothing to give the world but grief.

She was a religious woman. Living in sin with a married man could not set easily on her conscious. His duty would be to make her see the true path. In that he would have divine assistance, for there was no doubt in his mind the patient would die. The infection in his hand was too deep, of too long standing. His blood was poisoned. Despite his best efforts, scraping the bone and excising the destroyed tissue was not enough.

Even amputating the finger would have only prolonged the agony. It was too late. The body was rejecting life, slipping toward the depths beyond which no man returned. His breathing was labored; soon it would become stridulous. Air would no longer fill the lung sacks. His fever would rise, burning the organs, destroying normal function. When they failed, Rudy Blake would slip away as though he never were a living man. In a week, he would be buried. In a month, he would be rendered no more than memory.

Dr. Mannering knew his duty. In this instance, it was not to the patient but to his nurse. He must make certain she placed no blame for Rudy Blake's death on her own shoulders. The patient had simply come too late. It was sad, but a fact of life. Surely, she would understand.

She must get over his loss. If she owed him a moral obligation, she had satisfied it. Not even she could put death off indefinitely.

How little Thomas Mannering knew Rose Theodore.

CHAPTER 20

Righting the room was more than a matter of tidying up after the medical ministrations. For Rose, it was a return to normalcy. Once the basin and the bloodied table linin were removed and the chairs set back in proper alignment, it would feel like home, rather than a hospital. Without obvious signs of sickness and disease to remind them of his illness, both she and Rudy could begin the second stage of their life together with a fresh slate.

Gently replacing the soiled nightshirt he wore with a fresh one, she changed into a long flannel one before crawling in beside him. Her added weight depressed the mattress enough to rouse him from his uneasy, drug-induced lethargy. A low, mournful groan escaped his dry throat.

"Rudy, it is I. Rose."

Awareness was slow in coming.

"Rose?"

"Your Rose. I have come to sleep beside you."

"Rose? My Rose?"

There was only one way to convince him. Leaning on one elbow for height, she bowed her head so that their lips touched. Kissing him lightly, then increasing pressure until the act was one of sensuality, Rose waited until he responded with equal passion before reluctantly breaking off.

"Does that convince you?" she whispered into his face, so the heat of her breath would continue their shared warmth.

"My Rose," came the contented sigh. He tried to rise into a sitting position but a hand quickly restrained him.

"You have had enough excitement for one night. Now, we must sleep. I am so tired, Rudy," she added with conviction. "My head is swimming with exhaustion. Close your eyes and follow me to the Land of Nod."

"I will follow you anywhere."

She believed him and that assurance washed waves of comfort through her tortured soul. Wrapping her body over his, she radiated heat into his wasted frame. As his feet shifted beneath the covers she heard his breathing regulate. In a moment he had slipped away, snoring lightly to the accompaniment of her own exhalations.

Protestations to the contrary, sleep did not come as easily to her as she hoped. Lying beside his body only increased her awareness of how little life force remained inside his shattered shell. While his skin felt cold, that was an external delusion. Inside, fever waged a fierce war. While she and Mannering had done all they could to remove the source of his injury, the physician was correct: the battle was far from won. The slightest trace of metal left within the finger would reignite infection, burning away what strength remained. She did not have to be reminded the safest, surest course would have been amputation. Yet even that was not assured. Blood poisoning was an insidious disease. Removing the cause was no guarantee of health.

While her decision was a foregone conclusion; one she had fought with the determination of a Rebel soldier, neither the analogy nor the outcome placated her. She had waged terrible war, but the odds were against success. The enemy, like the blue-coated soldiers he had faced, were unconquerable. Strike toward the center, they came at the left flank. Turn in that direction, and hordes raced from the right, scattering depleted forces into panic and rout.

"Stop!" she ordered herself, clenching her fists, then bringing the blanket closer to her throat. "The War is over. Put it behind you."

Yet she could no more forget the terrible civil conflict than could Rudy. It lay between them, a wedge separating their existences in the same way his fever dragged him down toward death. Even if she were able to cure the ravages of bodily ills, his memories would continue to haunt, tainting his mind with images of destruction and defeat.

Long before Rudy knew his fate, she had understood destiny.

It was his mind she worried about; that delicate, frightfully misunderstood instrument which housed his personality, his desire to live, his struggle for life.

Beyond the physical horrors, it was the emotional sights, sounds, smells and sensations which would leave the deepest, most enduring, yet least comprehensible scars. What Rose lacked in specifics she more than compensated for by knowing one irrefutable fact. Rudy Blake had thought himself impervious, and discovered, to his shock and consternation, he was not.

To put the pieces of his shattered life together, the man lying on the bed, tortured by soul-shattering nightmares, the form and shape of which even he could not identify, would have to come to grips with those unendurable scenes. More than that, he would have to make peace with them. For if he did not, she did him no service by saving his life, for death would be preferable.

In this, time was their enemy. What he remembered of the year which separated them was already tainted. While some of his experiences he would recall in sharp detail, much more were shrouded by numbing repetition. What had been new and acute once, was now buried under a layer of routine, forgotten, or dismissed as irrelevant.

His pride was such that when he told a story, some of that which he relayed would be twisted to make him into the hero or the villain. No one could tell a tale better than Rudy: no one was better at hiding the truth from himself. He was a master of embellishment, adding and subtracting incidents so skillfully only a listener attuned to the ways and mannerisms of his obfuscations would ever detect a deviation from the truth – a lateral move to port or starboard that even the storyteller did not realize he was making.

In that manner, he was no different than anyone else: two witnesses to an accident would have ten different accounts to relay: stories, which, over time, would subtly change and alter in their own minds into facts and incidents far different than what actually happened. The passage of months, the exchange of fright for temperance, the audience he was playing for – all went into playing a part in the subtle reshaping of one man's history.

Rose knew she had to guard against such reweaving; she would have to make judgments based not on what he said, but how he told a particular incident, the inflection of his voice, the fire in his eye. She knew most of his tricks, understood the workings of his mind. Depending on circumstances, he could as easily make himself out to be the hero of a scene, or the goat. If honor were involved, he would invariably choose the latter; if the telling concerned some rascally pursuit, the former. Yet, on another day, if she could maneuver him into retelling the tale, it was equally likely he would alter the outcome, even to the point of making himself the gentleman. It was her job to sift through the lies, half-truths and misrepresentations, to discover what had actually happened.

Historical facts he could not dispute. Those she would ascertain through research and investigation. Men with names and regiments she might track down and interview.

That was the easy part. Then followed the necessity of making Rudy accept and live with what he had done, as well as witnessed: of putting back together this man who had come to her so shattered and confused.

No, she warned herself, as sleep finally came. *He is not the same man. He is a better one.*

Making him believe it, however, was nearly as futile as spitting in the wind.

It was predawn, the darkest hour of the night. The room was preternaturally still, without the telltale swaying of a ship at sea. That indicated he was on land.

Flaring his nostrils, Rudy attempted to determine by smell, where he was, for even acclimated to the pitch black, his eyes were unable to decipher familiar objects.

Body odor, male. Commingled together with another; perspiration of a man, the gentle, fading scent of cologne. Parting his lips then breathing through his mouth, Rudy vainly attempted to place the distinctive smell. It struck a familiar chord, yet was too faint to register.

Light breathing beside him alerted him to the fact he was not alone. Stiffening his muscles, he listened to the sleeper. The intake and exhalations were regular, easy. Whomever it was dreamed with a light conscience.

He was sharing a bed with someone but identification went no further. Clenching shut his lids, he attempted to pull memory from his sodden brain.

Atlanta? Had he taken a hotel room already shared by another man? No, that could not be right. He had a private suite of rooms. No one, friend or stranger, had ever been invited to spend the night.

Charleston? Wilmington? He concentrated, breathing again through his mouth, the tip of his nose quivering with anticipation. His eyes snaked toward the window, where a gentle breeze ruffled the curtains. No tangy salt air alerted his senses. He was inland, therefore, and not in a coastal city.

Traveling. He had a vague awareness he was on a long journey. He thought, or thought he remembered, a stage coach. Peddlers. Hawking... what? It was beyond his power to retrieve. No matter.

This, ten, was a wayside inn, or a tavern. That would explain the shared occupancy. It would be his ill luck to wake his companion, setting him on yet another foray into tinware, or statues, or life insurance.

Rise slowly, he warned himself. *In stealth.*

Shifting his weight toward the side of the bed, Rudy nearly lost his balance. His first instinct was to right himself by flailing his arms. It was then he realized his left arm was immobilized. With a shudder of dread, he quickly slipped his legs to the floor, then ducked, waiting a blow from the man who had restrained him.

Frozen, a deer caught in the glare of a hunter's lamp, he waited. No movement. He had not aroused his captor.

Slowly, painstakingly, he inched from the bed, cringing at the spring of the mattress. While the identity of his roommate was unknown to him, he had obviously been singled out by thieves. Somehow they had lured him, caught him in a trap. No doubt they had robbed his purse, then tied him, waiting until the dark of night to dispose of his body.

Only good fortune had spared him. Waking with a full bladder, he had caught the murderers unaware. Without doubt, another slept on the floor, or in a chair. He would have to be careful not to wake them.

Creeping to his feet, a wave of vertigo assailed him, nearly causing him to lose his balance. Glancing downward, he ascertained not only had they tied him, they had shot him, first. That explained his grogginess, the sharp, searing pain in his arm.

Bloody bastards.

Tiptoeing toward the door, Rudy rested his hand on the knob before working up his courage to turn it. If it were locked, or if there were some warning device attached, he would have to fight his way out.

Blessed was his spirit to discover the handle turned. Steadying himself against the frame, he regulated his breathing, concentrating on the task rather than the agony shooting down his frame. To get out, to escape, to find help. That was his primary concern. He would have his wound tended to after he was safe.

There was no one in the hall. A wall lamp burned at the end of the corridor, illuminating the stairwell. Using that as his signpost, he crept out, taking care to close the door behind him. With luck, he would be gone before the villains were the wiser.

Hurrying toward the landing, Rudy misjudged his strength, nearly pummeling, head-long down the steps. Grabbing the bannister, he clung to it for dear life, madly struggling with the black spots appearing behind his orbs as though they were the enemy and not merely an inner manifestation of illness.

"Steady." Right the ship. Bring her into the wind.

He was delusional, aware that his mind was clouded, twisted, spinning out of control. That frightened him more than the hurt, more than the fear of being attacked.

"Rudy Blake. I am Rudy Blake."

He was sure of that but nothing else.

"Down the stairs. One at a time."

Without conscious direction, Rudy's legs responded. The right foot reached out, hovered over the edge, then snaked downward, taking an age to reach the next rung. It righted itself, found firm footing. The left followed. He had progressed, but not fast enough.

"Move!"

He was no longer certain whether he was descending the stairs of a hotel, or creeping into the bowels of a ship, nor whether the slats were wooden or rope. Thoughts crowded in, one upon the other. His sense of direction failed. Should he be descending, or looking for an escape hatch topside?

Rutledge. He remembered climbing up onto the deck of the slave trader's ship.

Chalk. Once, he had ascended steps, discovering a bucket of chalk residue in an abandoned school room.

War. His entire life had been spent in one fight or another.

The handrail was to his right. Using his one free arm, Rudy clutched it for dear life, making a crutch of the solid oak railing. For better or for worse, he was going down.

Nine. Ten. Eleven. He found himself counting. Once, he had taken stairs two or three at a time. No more. Bypassing the second floor without a look, he began the last leg of his descent, reaching the bottom before Time ran out.

Another lamp burned in the foyer. Kerosene. He identified it by smell. The wink was trimmed, turned low. A night light.

Four more steps and he was at the door. No clerk dozed behind a counter. He was not in a hotel, then, but a private residence. No help from any quarter.

Life, repeating itself in nightmare.

Tightening his groin muscles, for the urge to urinate was becoming overpowering, Rudy sidled toward the entranceway. A narrow brass chain served as a lock, keeping intruders out. Apparently, his captors had not considered the possibility of someone escaping from within.

Nodding to himself in grim satisfaction at this child's play, he slipped the chain, then attempted to ease open the door. It did not budge. A prickling of electricity raced down his back as a rivulet of sweat rolled from beneath both arm pits.

"Bolt," he whispered huskily. *Search. Find it.*

While the illumination was better on the lower level than it had been upstairs, it was by no means adequate to the task. Running his good right arm up and down the frame, his fingers detected no exterior lock. He had been wrong, misjudged. Someone had taken care to secure their treasure.

He was to be held for ransom, then. That was the answer. He had been kidnapped, injured in the struggle, then removed to a hiding place until money could be raised. Doubts assailed him. Had they made him write a letter to his banker, requesting the deposit of funds into another man's account? Or had they demanded a sack full of gold, dropped off at a secret location?

If that were the case, his days were surely numbered. Once the thieves had their money, they would have no use for him. Although he could not remember their faces, he had surely seen them. With fear of his identifying, then testifying in a court of law, the only recourse open was to kill him before any of that transpired.

How much was he worth? It seemed an odd question for a man at death's door to worry about, yet the moment he thought it, Rudy became obsessed with the idea. He could not remember; had no concept. If only he knew the year, he could calculate.

How old was he? Another question for which he had no answer. If he were a youth, then whomever had kidnapped him was seeking money from his father. A laugh nearly choked him. Charles Blake would never pay ransom. In all probability, he would have offered money to have his son removed from the line of succession.

Was he a seaman, then, on his way to the gold fields? The idea was preposterous. Common tars had no more than a few pennies rattling around in their pockets. A prospector? That was even more ludicrous. No one but raw boys believed in the faerie tale of discovering chunks of gold as big as one's head.

A land speculator? He had success in San Francisco as a wheeler-and-dealer, but not the kind for which men risked hanging. A gambler? Waves of grim satisfaction washed over the man standing by the locked door in his nightshirt. River rats were always on the lookout for an unwary sharper. Had he made a killing at the tables and been absconded by crooks?

Memories assailed him. He had been stalked by a predator; that much was true. By a blond haired wisp of a man with a crippled hand.

Rudy's gasp was sharp and painful. Twisting his body to stare upward, pain radiated through his left arm. That must be the answer. It was he, that shadowy figure from his past. What was his name? No moniker came to mind. Perhaps he had never known it.

David. That was it. David, the scroungy reporter who had followed him around, like a dog, smelling meat. He had laid in wait in an alley, or hidden inside his room, waiting his chance. Catching Rudy unaware, he had led him off at gunpoint, bringing him to this deserted hideaway.

David, the cripple. Because his right hand was useless, he had perversely wounded his captive. Share, and share alike. Yes, that was something to which David might agree. David, the disinherited sketch artist, eking out a living selling scurrilous articles to bespectacled editors.

He had done this. Closing his eyes, Rudy found he could easily imagine his soft, gentle accent, his bright blue eyes, the long strands of yellow hair falling over his eyes.

Tell me the story of your life, Rudy Blake, while we wait for the ransom to be delivered. Tell me how a riverboat gambler cheats; explain to me your tricks. I want to get it down; put it all on paper. I'm writing your biography. It will make fascinating reading. Especially the ending. No one wants a happy ending. Not for the likes of you. My readers will want justice served. It's a moral story I'm telling, Rudy Blake. Evil must be punished. Remember Edward Rochester?

It had been a moment of weakness on Rudy's part. He and David had been speaking of classic literature and he had brought up *Jane Eyre*. David had loved the book, but Rudy had hated it. Not the story and certainly not the characters, for they were etched in his memory as clearly as though he knew them intimately. What he loathed of *Jane Eyre* was the very fact which David now espoused: the morality.

Charlotte Bronte had purposely mutilated her hero for the sake of conventionality, rather than necessity. Losing both a hand and an eye was excessive punishment for attempted adultery, especially when the author, herself, had taken such great pains to justify it. Rudy had pitied Rochester, raging inwardly at his disfigurement by an unloving, unsympathetic God.

It was that which put him off *Jane Eyre,* turned him away from the tender love story, setting a wedge of bitter resentment deep within his heart. His conflicting thoughts had never allowed him to blame Jane for her sudden, complete departure. Reading the novel as a boy, he held out for her right to be a faerie bride, yet that, in no way, hardened his heart against Rochester, the tortured hero. It was the writer, assuming the role of a deity, whom he loathed.

While Rudy's opinions fluctuated as he grew older and more worldly, they never changed a wit against Bronte. God may take a life He has created, set him in an uneven contest with the devil and have no blame placed against Him. A god might swallow his child whole for fear that son would shine greater in the heavens that he; a parent might ruthlessly sell a child's beloved Mammy and be judged kindly by the world. A husband might keep himself aloof, cruelly disciplining and controlling the lives of both his wife and children, and society would declare him a fair and good provider. All these things Rudy Blake had seen, or at least thought he understood.

What he had never fathomed, however, was an author's merciless mutilation of a beloved character. It did not matter to Rudy there was a larger issue at stake in Bronte's work. Moral issues had no right supplanting the health and well-being of a living, breathing character. For the sake of pacifying society and its harsh, unrepentant judgment of one soul over another, Rochester lost a hand and an eye. He had endured the wracking pain of abandonment, tortured by three years of near total blindness.

Where was the fairness, the justice in that? Hers was a senseless, needless act of barbarism. It added nothing to the plot, yet condemned a sensitive man to hell.

For all eternity, Edward Rochester would roam the planet and its upper and lower regions, either in corporeal or spirit form, a mutilated, disfigured, hideous, scarred shade. No repentance, no matter how sincere; no prayers directed to any God or god; no argument, pleading, fit of anger, or rain of hot tears could ever return to him what he had lost.

Never would he be able to fasten a button, tie his tie, cut his meat, shuffle a deck of cards, hold his children and feel their tiny fingers within those of his left hand. Never would he have the eyesight of an eagle, the ability to see peripherally, or in dimension. Not for one single second could he look into a mirror and forget he had become a monster.

Rudy had felt then, as he did now, that life was not worth living in so disfigured, so hideous a form. If a loving God, a loving *creator* had placed him upon this earth, then that deity had the right, the *obligation* to care for what it had generated. The fact It *would* not, as opposed to *could* not, had always disturbed him.

If God were capricious, merciless; if He played favoritism, clearly bestowing riches, wealth and happiness on some, but not off of His children, Rudy wanted no part of His Kingdom. Let others worship: let them *fear*. Perhaps they had good right. But love? Never. It was not possible a human being could both fear and love the same lord. A person either quivered for life in humble, frightened submission, begging for mercy without the slightest chance of receiving it, or he loved.

Charlotte Bronte had cast her fate in with the former and for that, she received no forgiveness from either the boy or the man named Rudy Blake.

David, the erstwhile author, had not understood. They had argued the point together, spittle flying from their lips. In the end, neither had swayed the other and it was that retribution David sought now. At the point of a derringer, or the tip of a blade, he had slunk, undetected, into Rudy's stateroom. There, with the perversity of God's avenging angel, he had equaled the score.

"A hand for a hand and an eye for an eye. First, I cripple you, then I blind you. And then, I take all your worldly possessions. Like God, like Charlotte Bronte, I, too, can play the Great Avenger."

That must have been how it was. In his childlike ignorance, Rudy had trusted the writer, admitted him into his life, only to discover he was no different than all the gods in Olympus, all the authors playing God. Like all the pitiful supplicants before him, his faith had been denied.

CHAPTER 21

Rudy's head hurt and his mind wandered. David was not David but John Paul and John Paul would not have kidnapped him. If any man alive held contempt for money, it was John Paul.

The fact he had seen John Paul die was irrelevant.

Bursting through the door the way Rebel soldiers attacked a well-fortified field position, Rudy sprinted across the open yard, ducking and weaving, then jerking sideways, toward the rear. Dodging bullets, nostrils wide to the stench of blood and burst bowels, pupils distended, tongue pressed against the roof of his mouth, he screamed silently, tripped and wept aloud.

Landing awkwardly, he fell on his right side, instinctively protecting his wounded left. Jamming his shoulder into the ground, his teeth ground with pain. His ankle hurt. Unbalanced, he rose again and ran, seeking cover of a more permanent nature.

An outhouse, a small, undistinguished outcropping of building, little more than four walls and a roof, appeared out of nowhere. Growing up around it were prickly bushes, green-leafed foliage with thorns. Beyond it, a stand of trees, the exact type he was unable to distinguish.

Although his need was acute, with bladder close to bursting, Rudy was afraid to enter the unexpected cell, more mirage than reality. Inside might lay a Federal soldier, waiting to blow off the top of his head, or gut him in the stomach with his cold steel bayonet.

Worse, and far more damning, the shed-like structure might contain the remnants of his artillerists, the dead and dispirited boys of Battery B.

He had almost convinced himself to move on, to crawl to safety among the timber, when a cat or a dog or a small rodent crossed his path, hissing with ferocity at the appearance of so unwelcome a stranger. Fearful least it give away his position, Rudy mounted his courage, ripping open the door, then rode inside on the wings of desperation.

The outhouse was darker than the night, with only a small, open half-moon atop one wall, for ventilation. The earth smelled damp, moist, with a commingling of lye, used for sanitation. A tall, high-seated commode sat perched above an unseen hole. What lay beneath he did not care to contemplate.

Pausing to catch his ragged breath, Rudy listened for telltale signs of occupation, cocking his ear to one side in a vain attempt to distinguish his own exhalations from those of dead men. Raising his arm, he waved it across the enclosed space, dreading with supernatural anxiety, to encounter the touch of rotting flesh.

Nothing.

He was alone.

Outside, no sounds of firing; no discharge of cannon. No tramp of boots, no weary, guarded whispering, "Who goes there?" or "Identify yourself and your regiment."

No ghosts, no haints, no twisted limbs, no blue-jacketed enemies.

Yet, war surrounded him and peace was an illusion.

"Hello?" and then, more hopefully, "Benjamin?" No answer. "Hello!" and then, more forcefully, "Benjamin!" No reply.

He had gotten lost, then, strayed from the front. War was where you found it, and he had discovered temporary reprieve.

A cry, then silence. Freezing in his tracks, Rudy nearly lost control, tears springing to his eyes in lieu of passing water. A night bird, nothing more. Trembling from humiliation, he shuddered, the dire warnings of childhood coming back to haunt. There was no greater sin than the soiling of one's clothing. Better to endure the agony of an exploded kidney, or a ruptured colon than disgrace oneself in public. Such was the price a boy or a man paid for gentility.

He had seen it on the battlefield, knew it to be true. Men, lying on the ground with their legs blown off, weeping, not from the fact of their dismemberment, but from the idea of having soiled their trousers. Boys, fresh from school, howling in distress. Not because they had killed their first man, but stemming from the incidence of having wet their trousers in the process.

It was a rite of passage, a ritual of battle from which few men were immune. Rudy Blake, daring sea captain, resourceful gunrunner, arrogant gambler, had not been spared. With death and destruction his constant companions, even he had succumb to that least forgivable of all sins.

He had forgotten and now he remembered. Wailing aloud, he draped his arm across his face, weeping for what he had lost and what no man or gentlewoman could ever replace. Gone forever was his adulthood, replaced by a form of pseudo-childhood, where parents and schoolmasters crouched behind every tree, clutching rifles instead of birch switches, as punishment for his crime.

In the annals of humanity, War was the Great Equalizer, rendering men to boys and boys to corpses.

Death before disgrace.

The man who had written that had never been to war.

Fumbling for the buttons of his fly, Rudy vainly attempted to disengage the fastened sides of cloth, to no avail. Gritting his teeth, he abandoned the effort, attacking, instead, the binding across his shoulder. He must free his hand, prove to himself he was whole and not dismembered. Only then could he begin to reattach the scattered remnants of his life, reforming the youth he had been into a new and convoluted stranger.

Even cloaked in dream, Rose knew he was not there. Casting aside the chards of sleep-induced fantasy, she expended her senses, poking and probing the room for his presence and discovering only emptiness.

"Rudy? Rudy?"

It was not that she expected an answer. Duty, the last trace of civilization before panic set it, compelled her.

Sitting up, Rose extended her hands the way an octopus might, utilizing the tiny sensors at the tips of her fingers to aid in her penetration of the dark. No displacement of air from breath, no waves of electricity, generated by brain activity, returned to her probing digits.

Gone.

Her first concern had arisen over the danger of Rudy rolling out of bed and injuring himself on the floor. With that immediate fear alleviated, she drew the obvious conclusion. Awaking with the need to relieve himself, he had somehow managed to wander away in search of a privy.

Throwing off the covers, Rose flew from bed, checking first the window. Discovering it only partly opened, too narrow for a man to slip through, she whispered a silent prayer. That, at least, went in her favor.

Grabbing her robe hanging on a hook attached to the door, she scrambled into the corridor, scanning both the landing and stairs with a sweeping glance. Determining his absence, she padded toward the "Head." Politely knocking, she drew back the door, hoping against logic to find him there. The small chamber was empty, without indication of having been recently used.

Leaving the door ajar, she headed for the steps, taking them one at a time. While her eyes had acclimated to the gloom, haste was her enemy. It would not do to trip over him, had he descended half way, then fallen, blending into the shadows of night. Never must she forget he was a chameleon, with the powers to disguise himself. Lost and confused, he could disguise himself as well as any four-legged amphibian.

"Better," she mused, allowing a flicker of pride to decorate her otherwise taut features. And then, louder, for his benefit, "Rudy? It is Rose? Are you here?"

The lower level was as quiet as the tomb. The servants were gone and Mrs. Tompkins' room was toward the back. It was too early for even her to be awake.

Two steps took Rose toward the living room before her peripheral vision detected the front door, slightly ajar. Her supposition had been correct. He had gone outside, then, in search of the outhouse.

Hurrying across the yard, then around the corner of the house, Rose's sharp eyes detected movement before her brain registered an identification. Halting immediately so as not to alarm him by sudden movement, she raised her arm in greeting.

The tall, gangly man, his back silhouetted by the rim of the sun over the horizon, hesitated at her gesture, flinched, then glanced furtively to his left, poised for flight. With his nightshirt blowing in the breeze and his long, untended hair falling across his brow, Rudy appeared more spectre than man, capable of dissolving into memory faster than a rabbit could run.

Implicitly believing what her heart registered, Rose stayed her impulse to run to him, instead extending both hands in peaceful greeting.

Look at me, she commanded. *I am unarmed. I mean you no harm.*

"It is Rose."

Remember me, as I remember you.

"Rose?" The question was poised with hesitation, disbelief. Behind the interrogative, however, was unmitigated relief. "Rose!"

That was her impetus to race. Engulfing him in her arms, she showered kisses on his stubbly cheeks before grabbing the locks of hair and playfully tugging them.

"When, sir," she demanded, "has any man been so warmly received after a short foray to the outhouse?"

He grinned sheepishly, then rolled his eyes the way he used to, igniting hope in her breast.

"Never, I wager," came the embarrassed confession. And, more daringly, "What is my reward?"

"A basin of warm water to wash your hands before you sit at my table," came the smart rejoinder. "And then a tour of the house. Don't you remember? There are indoor facilities – much nicer than this. Where you may sit – or stand – at your leisure, without fear of being consumed by insects, overcome by odor, or having your protection blown away in a wind storm!"

"No. I – I don't remember," he confessed, flushing at the admission. "Where am I?"

"You are in England. You have crossed the Atlantic in a ship and come to my door last night in a carriage. This," she demonstrated, indicating the vast property, "is the Blake House. Where I live. Named after someone very special to me. Can you guess who?"

His brows furrowed in concentration, but she would not let him struggle. "You. Rudy Blake. Blake House."

"Why... why isn't it called the... Theodore House?"

An apt question which would admit of no dalliance.

"You bought it for me. Because this is where you shall live. Where you have come home to."

"Home?"

"Home," she repeated with the authority vested in her by love and commitment.

"How long... have I been away?"

"A year and a day," she quoted, wrapping her arm around him. She did not have to see him react to know he identified the line. "Time for secrets to be confessed. It was Edward Rochester's promise to Jane Eyre."

His face contorted in pain. "Where have I been?"

"To war. But now it is over. Peace returns to a bloodied land."

Staggered by the overwhelming influx of sharp, piercing memories, he wavered, nearly losing his balance. Only her close proximity saved him from toppling.

"Yes," came the gritted acknowledgment. "But we were separated, while Jane and Rochester were happily married. There is no child between us which will bind your love to me when I confess my terrible secrets."

Damning her inadvertent mistake, Rose propelled him forward.

"March. Toward the house. You have much work to do."

A light flickered behind his eyes as his mind was diverted.

"What task is it you set before me?"

"The ledgers I have so diligently kept: of my business activities. The double entries, where I have hidden my dealings, skimming money off the top for my personal gain. Surely you have not forgotten your promise to find me out?"

His interest intensified, yet confusion reigned.

"Yet you said the war was over –"

"Only recently concluded," she carefully reminded Rudy, while gently steering him toward the house.

"Who... who won?"

Halting in his tracks, Rudy's half-closed green-grey eyes turned westward, toward the ocean and three thousand miles of water, across which lay the land he so recently fought for.

"The Federal government has prevailed. As you predicted it would, so many years ago. The South has lost; it has been brought back into the Union. Slavery has been abolished."

A low moan of intense agony wracked his shattered frame.

"Slavery, Rose. The greatest of all evils. And I... fought to preserve it." Dropping his head into his hands, Rudy wept, tears unabashedly gushing from beneath swollen lids. "How can you ever forgive me?" She let him cry, for there was no other way to wash away the stain of guilt. "How can Mammy ever forgive? I have betrayed."

"You did not fight for a Cause, Rudy Blake, but for an oppressed people. And for the land. That, we both condone. As you know in your heart," she added with resolution. "For we were beside you. Begging God to spare your life."

"You? Mammy? Beside me?"

"With every breath you took. Did you not feel our presence?"

"Yes," came the low, hesitant avowal. "I felt you."

"Then you know there is no question of forgiveness. Only love, which transcended time and space. Now come. Into the house. If I do not feed you, I shall be considered a poor mistress."

Meeting her gaze took more courage than he believed he possessed. Her eyes locked on his, held the nearly translucent orbs, transmitting more than either had words to express. Only then did he sigh in tepid resignation.

"We shall see."

It was as much as he dared conceded. She would ask no more.

"What we shall see about is getting some hot nourishment in you. Come. Are you too weak to walk? If so, lean on me."

Gingerly trying out his feet, Rudy took a step, hesitated, then swallowed uneasily. "I have leaned on you too much, already," he whispered, words tinged with shame. Pursing her lips, for she understood a plea for help when she heard one, Rose easily slipped his arm over her shoulders.

"Equal partners," she reminded him, moving forward before he could object.

One step at a time, they made their way back toward the house. Kicking open the door she had only partially sealed, Rose stopped in the doorway.

"Do you want to eat downstairs, or shall I serve you breakfast in bed?"

Rudy hesitated, clearly torn, then directed his vision toward the rear.

"I am not presentable. The servants –"

"There are no servants," she interrupted. "For the moment, only Mrs. Tompkins is present. You remember her? My chaperone; the one you insisted a 'lady of quality' should have. To keep down the gossip when gentlemen came to call."

He frowned, confusing past with present tense.

"I recall someone of the sort. Has it worked?"

Rose was tempted to say "Too well," but bit her tongue. "Yes. I am as well regarded in England as though I were high born."

"But only one servant?" His brows furrowed in consternation. "I seem to recall –"

"We will hire more. Now that you are home. Alone, my needs are simple. Tell me your pleasure."

"I would like to feel... normal."

"The kitchen it is. That is where I take my meals."

Guiding him through the narrow opening, positioning herself sideways so he might enter first, she sat him in a chair, noting with concern as he cringed.

"Your buttocks are sore; I forgot. Let me get you a cushion."

"No," he pleaded, restraining her before she could escape. "In a moment.... Some other time. Do not leave me." On her puzzled look he added, "I am afraid if you go, you will never return." And then, piteously, "Please do not think me weak."

"I think you and I are very much alike. I feel the same way about you. When you are out of my sight, a loneliness assails me that no one else can console. Sit there while I make coffee."

Patting him carefully, she fussed a moment, then crossed to the sink. Easily pumping water into the pot, she set it on the burner, then proceeded to set the table. Selecting Blue Willow mugs, Rose placed them within reach, then brought out a matching sugar bowl and creamer.

"Are you hungry?"

"No," Rudy confessed, rubbing his stomach as though the reminder brought pain. "I have not craved food since...." But he could not remember how long and left the sentence dangling.

"We will have a light meal; eggs and soft bread. Shall I poach them for you?" Taking his silence as agreement, she placed four eggs into a pan of water, then set it beside the coffee pot. "For dinner, you will have broth. But that is for later," she quickly amended as he crinkled the corners of his mouth. "In the meantime, drink this."

"What is it?" he asked, critically inspecting the glass she handed him.

"Water. It has curative powers."

Taking a sip to appease her, Rudy set the glass down, his arm shaking badly.

"If that were true, the Confederate Army would not have starved."

"Magic water. I have put drops of medicine in it." Settling in beside him, Rose rested her hand on his. "You must tell me all about it."

Closing his lids, Rudy shook his head.

"I will tell you. But not all of it. It is beyond... words."

"I will have it," came the warning. "But not now. When you are stronger."

Slumping back, Rudy grimaced, a cry of pain escaping his compressed, bloodless lips. "My hand – what has happened...? Was I – shot?"

"An old wound," she explained. "A splinter of metal, wedged beneath your fingernail. From a cannon you tried to save."

He sighed heavily, then trembled. "I saved nothing."

"You saved yourself. That was all I asked of you." And then harder, "That was all either of us had a right to expect."

Forcing open his eyes, Rudy stared at her, droplets of moisture wetting his cheeks.

"Why, Rose? Why did I do it? Of all men, why did I go to war?"

There were too many answers. The path down which they led was the way to madness. They would travel it together, but not before his body had a chance to heal. Only in that way could it withstand a second scraping to the foundations of his soul.

"You asked about your wound. I will address that concern. Will you listen?"

"Rose," he sighed in absolute sincerity, searching for an appropriate comparison, "I would listen to you read the Bible."

Her unguarded guffaw brought an unsolicited grin to his face.

"I stand corrected," she retorted, basking in the glow of his humor. Snatching the boiling eggs off the stove, she dropped them into wooden cups and began slicing bread. "Allow me to rephrase: will you pay attention?"

Flashing her the little-boy smile which had become waylaid during the course of his life but never lost, he agreed.

"Yes."

Returning to the table with two steaming mugs of coffee, Rose placed both out of his reach. Not until she added eight sugar cubes and top cream to his did she slide it over. With hers in hand, she offered a toast.

"To our partnership. Long may it endure."

Curling his cup around so the handle was toward his fingers, Rudy demurred.

"I have a better one. To our love, which will endure forever."

Like the War, that was a subject she would rather have let lie. "Love" and "forever" were words married couples shared. Her too-recent sparring with Thomas Mannering had left her gun-shy.

Reading the hurt, Rudy responded by offering his arm. To refuse his gesture would be convey more falsehood than truth. Taking it in hers, Rose kissed the knuckles, one- by-one, and in that way appeased him.

"I love you, R.B."

"I love you, too, R.B."

They would plow the field another day, even if it were after the seeds were sown.

Carefully extracting herself, Rose sipped the coffee, then deftly excised the tops off both his eggs. He observed her like a hawk, as though her actions bore significance to him he did not care to share.

"Tell me about my hand."

She did not touch her food until he had begun his and spoke only after he had swallowed.

"There was great infection; swelling and puss inside the affected finger. Dr. Mannering removed the fingernail, cutting down to the bone. He then removed the corrupted tissue and four tiny pieces of metal. The operation was delicate and dangerous. He believes your life to be in danger."

Dropping his spoon, Rudy stared down at his bandaged arm, lips moving soundlessly in horror.

"Against his advice, I refused further treatment. Your hand is intact; your fingers all present. Are you paying attention?" He nodded. "You are feverish and gravely ill."

"Is that... why my mind wanders?"

"That is part of it."

"And the rest?" he asked, without daring to meet her eyes.

"Your sensibilities have been stretched past the point of endurance. What you have witnessed and what you have done in the name of honor and justice," she hurried on over his protest, "have further weakened you. We must put both to rights before you can be well."

"Is it possible?"

"You know it is," Rose replied with simplicity. "Or you would not have returned to me. I know it is, or I would not have let the doctor lay a hand on you."

"How long?"

"As long as it takes."

"Will I die?"

"The expression, I believe, is 'over my dead body.'"

"That I do not want; I would never seek!" he cried, attempting to rise from the table. A wave of dizziness struck him, however, and he groaned, slumping dejectedly backward. As his eyes rolled to the top of his head, a stream of saliva drooled from his lips. Suppressing her own vision of horror, Rose wiped it away with a table napkin, before tucking the cloth away, under her chin.

"Your reclamation, sir, will not be easy. Nor will it be pleasant. There is much pain to endure – on both sides."

"How, Rose? How can you hope to reclaim a –" She attempted to stop him, but in vain. "A reprobate?"

"By acknowledging beforehand we are both imperfect beings. Does that suit you?"

"You are perfect –"

She would not argue the point. "Does that suit you?"

For once in his life, he knew better than to disagree. It was a milestone in their relationship.

"I agree to your terms." And she conformed to his rephrasing of her question.

"How, and if, you regain full use of your finger will depend upon your following my instructions to the letter. You will not pick on the bandage; you will keep your arm elevated in that sling. As the flesh begins to heal, you will soak your hand in warm water. I will give you exercises; you will do them without complaint."

"You ask too much," he protested to deaf ears. "It is the right of every free man to complain."

"Then pretend you are back in the army and I am your superior officer," came the uncompromising reply. "You may grumble behind my back as long as you do what I say."

"Will I... ever be normal again? Able to deal cards?"

"That is my intent."

"Will there be a – scar?"

"Yes. But not an obvious one. Underneath. No one will ever see it without close examination."

"You will know it is there."

"So God will have marked you a second time."

"Why?" he whispered, withdrawing into himself.

"Once for Himself and once for me."

That was the answer and it came to her, unbidden. It would stand instead of a wedding ring.

As though Rudy had been reading her mind, his answer was as prompt as it was unexpected.

"I accept that."

Overcome by emotion, Rose picked up his fallen spoon and offered it to him. Taking it in his right hand, Rudy immediately attempted to transfer it to his left. Having been raised in the European fashion, his habitual response brought pain to his face.

"There is much we both must overcome. When soldiers write their life stories, they neglect to mention the true aftereffects of war."

Seizing the opportunity to lighten the mood, Rose smiled gaily.

"What glorious exploits will you put in yours? Will you tell about making fools of the Union Navy as you slipped through the blockade? Or, perhaps, of the 'Gentleman's Surprise' you tricked them with?"

Uncharacteristically, he shook her off. "I will not pen any such stories. Let the past be buried; with my biographer."

His reference to John Paul and his journal saddened her.

"I'm sorry, Rudy. I didn't mean to stir up those memories."

Stabbing at the egg with a desultory motion, he accidentally knocked over the wooden cup. Growling in displeasure, he flung the offending utensil across the room, listening while the metallic pinging noise rebounded against the floor.

"Being a ship's captain and gun-runner was child's play. That was not war; it was no more than superior seamanship. I fooled myself into thinking it gave me a taste of battle. I was wrong. Dead wrong. As wrong as I have ever been about anything in my life." Taking the remaining knife in his hand, he wielded it in front of her face. With a grim stare, he leaned across the table until they were nearly touching. "Shall I show you how a soldier eats?" Without waiting for a response, he stabbed the blade through the bread, then picked up the egg. "Like this." First bearing his teeth, then opening wide his mouth, Rudy stuffed the food into it. With a furious disregard for any social amenities, he chewed it whole, shell and all. Swallowing it nearly intact, he started on the second before her cry of distress waylaid him.

"Stop it!"

"No. You wanted to know what war was like. It strips a man bare; reduces him to base elements; to those of an animal, until he is no longer a man but a beast." His hand streaked out, grabbing the bread. Tearing a slice in half, he wedged that, too, into his mouth, so his cheeks were distended.

Chewing open-mouthed, regardless of the bits of wadded mass falling from his lips, he finished one piece, then started on another. He would have consumed the entire loaf had she not finally grabbed away the plate.

"All right, Rudy. You've made your point."

"No, madam," he leered in licentious gravity. "I have not yet begun to fight."

And suddenly Rose understood that she had become the new enemy

CHAPTER 22

Rose recovered faster than she would have believed possible. Eating her own breakfast hurriedly, she poured them both a second cup of coffee before speaking.

"Is there anything else you want?"

Rudy had not expected civility and her tone disconcerted him. Amid conflicting emotions, he belched, started to excuse himself, then crinkled his nose.

"I am a stranger. You do not know me. I am not the man I was."

It was meant as a challenge and she could accept it as nothing less.

"Nor am I the woman you knew. Twelve months alone has changed me. I have dealt with unsavory characters, bought and sold guns and munitions; skirted the law. I have kept your books, making double and triple entries for my own gain." Her leer matched his own former expression. "I have functioned in society as a lady of means and worth. Like you, I have fooled them into thinking I am a gentlewoman. I have attended parties of titled noblemen; received and given invitations.

"While I may not be able to match you, evil deed for evil deed, I am no longer the whore, fresh off the streets of New York or Washington. Nor am I the grateful, submissive chandler you set foot upon English soil. Circumstances have mutated both of us beyond recognition. You think to shock me? You will have to try harder, Rudy Blake."

It was too much for him to assimilate. With a sigh of resignation, he hung his head, breathing deeply. When he finally did speak, she failed to catch the word.

"Say again?"

"Pineapple. I would like a pineapple. May I... have one?"

Had he said, "I would like a loaded pistol," she would have obliged. Possibly with the same enthusiasm, for her own nerves were as raw as his.

"Yes. Certainly."

"You have one?"

His question came with a whimper of false expectation. As pity washed over her, Rose nodded.

"I have always remembered that as your favorite fruit. That," she added with a faint smile, "and peaches."

The remembrance touched a chord in his mind.

"I had one, once. Benjamin and I... found a can. In a general's wagon. The boy ate horehound while I had peaches."

"Seems a fair exchange – inasmuch as you do not like horehound."

"It is poison," he declared, rolling his eyes the way he had teased Benjamin. "I promised him better."

"And did you get it for him?" she gently asked, praying for a reply in the affirmative.

"I don't remember."

More disappointed than she could account, Rose placed a hand over her lips to hide her expression, then hurried into the pantry. Returning a moment later, she produced a large, prickly yellow pineapple. Rudy's delight in seeing it nearly mitigated her former unhappiness.

"Where did it come from?"

"I grew it in my greenhouse."

His hopeful reply caused her to regret the joke.

"Really?"

"No, but I've considered it. Look, Rudy," she demonstrated, making small talk to keep her own mind from wandering. "Did you know that if you cut the top off and set it in a shallow pan of water, it will grow?"

Rubbing his fingers together the way a banker detected counterfeit bills, he considered for a moment.

"I may have heard that. But I've never been in a position to try. Usually, I order pineapple out, and it is not served whole." Before the words were out of his mouth, his lips pursed and a cloud settled over him. "Take it away. I do not want it."

"But why, Rudy? What's wrong?"

"It is rotten. To the core. I do not even want to see you cut into it. I know."

"But it's fresh." Tapping the fruit, she listened to the muted sound, the offered him the same opportunity. "Try for yourself. And look: there are still streaks of green at the top; an indication of quality. It is not over-ripe."

"It is, I tell you. All the pineapples in the world are rotten. Like me."

Sensing a recent experience which failed to live up to expectations, Rose glossed over his objection. In so doing, she allowed herself the opportunity of ignoring his last assertion. With a deft maneuver, she cut into the heart of the tropical fruit, revealing firm, juicy flesh.

"Smell it," she ordered, filling her own nostrils with the sweet scent. "Perfect."

Quivering from fear of discovering what his eyes related as true, Rudy drew in the rich odor, only then convinced. As his mouth watered, he smiled sadly.

"In Richmond," he explained. "After the War –"

"It was probably a leftover from a shipment you brought in in '61," she complained. "Too expensive for anyone else to buy, it sat on a shelf in the restaurant, waiting for you to reclaim it. Never mind. You will have all of this one."

"What... will it cost me?"

She did not think the interrogative as unusual as it sounded.

"Much more than you paid there. The price of a kiss. Can you afford it?"

"Yes."

Puckering his lips, Rudy pressed them against Rose's cheek.

"When you want something – really want it – and it seems within your grasp – no matter how insignificant – the loss is... irreparable."

"Not irreparable, my love, for I will make it better. See?" Quickly peeling away the outer skin and core, Rose cut the pineapple into small, mouth sized chunks before serving it. "Try a bite and tell me if it is to your liking."

Picking up a piece with his fingers, Rudy held it in his mouth, savoring the flavor. As it stimulated his taste buds, he shoved more inside, until no more would fit. Only then did he chew, and that quickly. Suddenly ravenous, he consumed the entire pineapple. As bits of fruit fell from his lips from open-mouth chewing, he scooped those up as well, inadvertently smearing juice over his fingers until they finally stuck together. He did not notice, however, until Rose offered him a damp washcloth.

Accepting the towel, he gaped at the mess he made, sniffing in dismay. Registering first disbelief then horror, he attempted to wipe his fingers, then irrationally flung the linen from him.

"What's happened to me?" he sobbed, holding his good right arm to his breast. "I'm eating like an animal. Before... I was showing you. Demonstrating... making an act. I knew what I was doing. But this – My God, I am an animal!"

"No, Rudy," she hastened to intercede, retrieving the washcloth. "You were enjoying the fruit." Seeing his expression of disdain, she hurried on, willfully altering her tone to one of stern professionalism. "The pineapple contains elements your body craves." When her words held no effect, Rose grabbed his face, forcing him to look at her. "Listen to me. When a seaman is suffering from scurvy and you set before him a jar of pickles, what does he do?"

"He stuffs them into his mouth," he began before making the connection and stopping cold.

"Correct. He eats the whole jar without worrying about manners. And why does he do that?"

"Because he is dying.... Because –"

"His body is starved for green vegetables. Were you to set before him a dinner plate of beef and biscuit, a bottle of rum and a pickle jar, which would he choose?"

"The pickles."

"Every time," she agreed, consciously wiping his fingers. "A well man would eat the beef and a lands man would drink the rum but a man deprived of proper diet eats what he knows is best for him. Just as you did. Without standing on ceremony. Afterward," she hurried on, delicately returning the soiled linen to the counter, "when he has recovered, he will stand back and laugh at his lack of etiquette. But not before. Tell me I speak truth."

"You are right," came the begrudged acknowledgment. "But I am not starving."

Nearly laughing at his protest, Rose encircled him in her arms.

"But you are. Your body, so long deprived of proper food, grabbed its chance to eat. You told me yourself," she added, "you suffered from scurvy during the War. Since that time, you have not eaten property – or in sufficient quantity. It takes time – months – for the body to recover from such devastation. Trust me," she pleaded, carefully wording her sentence, "for I am your physician, and I know of what I say."

"My physician," he repeated, engraving the word on his fervid brain. "Yes."

"You came to me to cure you and so I shall. But you must give me time. And you must also be kind to yourself. That, sir, is part of the prescription."

Slumping back in his chair, Rudy's head lolled. It was time to end the discussion.

"We are both tired. Come. Give me your hand and I will take you to bed."

"It is only just morning," came the weary protest.

"Sleep, too, is part of the cure."

"Will you sleep with me?"

There was much to do, yet to refuse the offer was not without complications.

"Yes, beloved. I will sleep with you."

Helping him to his feet, Rose guided Rudy toward the stairs. Their progress was slow, awkward and noisy. Before they reached the first step, Rose caught sight of D'Artagnan coming in from the parlor. Jerking her head in negative denial, the boy offered a silent protest before obeying orders.

Now was not the time for reunions. It was inappropriate to have Rudy's former crew view him in a weak, confused condition. Unable to maintain his swashbuckling image in front of Thomas Mannering, she would do everything in her power to keep that illusion alive for others. All things considered, the youth's devastation would be greater than the doctor's. That, she was in no mood to tolerate.

At the landing, Rose paused before the necessary.

"I want you to remember where the bathroom is. There are indoor facilities here for you to use. Running water, both hot and cold; a flush toilet. A bath tub, large enough to accommodate two," she teased, hoping in that way to ingrain the room in his consciousness, "and a shower stall."

"Was this here the last time I visited?" he inquired, his voice soft with wonder.

Flinching at his word choice, Rose shook her head.

"No. I had it all installed to my specific orders. Won't you have a look inside?"

Propelling him forward, Rose allowed him a thorough look, pleased at the growing astonishment rippling across his features.

"This is as great as a first class hotel; better, even, than any riverboat I ever sailed upon. Is that where you got the idea?" he asked suddenly, turning to her with pleading orbs. She was only too glad to fulfill his wish.

"Most certainly. You described the boats in such detail, it was simple for me to copy. Of course," she added, running her hands across the Italian marble lining the walls, "I added some details of my own. To personalize it."

"I approve." Copying Rose's example, Rudy touched the cool of the stone. "I remember first seeing marble on a riverboat. Not in the stateroom privies, to be sure, but on the dance floor. I wondered how it could stay afloat, carrying so much weight."

"No problem with that here. The floors are solid oak. Come: look at the faucets."

Turning the brass knob clockwise, she waited until the water flowed hot before guiding his arm beneath it. His exclamation of joy filled her heart.

"When you wake from your nap, I will soak you in the tub. No need to carry buckets upstairs. The water is heated by a separate apparatus in the closet, there," she pointed.

"And how is the water drawn upward from the source?"

"Through pipes attached to an outside pump. When we go for a walk, I will show you."

"So much has changed in so little time." Catching her reflection in the mirror, he addressed that image. "I feel as though I have been removed from the world for ages; decades. A man... out of time. And yet, so little actual time has passed. Is that not so?" he demanded, finding he could not recall the exact passage of weeks and months.

"I have not laid eyes on you in the flesh since September 13, 1863 when you sailed from Liverpool. It is now June 25, 1865."

"How is it that I have missed so much?"

"The world is revolving around a new technology. Machinery has replaced manual labor. You saw the beginnings of it; the Northern factories mass producing shoes. Paper mills. Modern printing presses."

"Where have I been?" he cried, covering his face with his hand. "Marching endless miles, barefoot. Reading orders written by hand. Cowering behind bushes, freezing to death." Attempting to push past her, he sobbed, "What have I done to myself? Where is Rudy Blake, the entrepreneur who was abreast of everything?"

"He stands before me," came the cool response.

"No! He is gone forever! He died at Nashville; perished at Franklin. He surrendered life at Durham Station!"

Grabbing him by the hair, Rose forced him toward the mirror.

"Look in the glass," she ordered. "What do you see?"

With a cry of shame and humiliation, Rudy stared at the hollow-cheeked, aged man peering back at him with dull, uncomprehending eyes.

"A stranger." Shifting his vantage point, he took in her image, nodding his head slowly in recognition. "I see a destitute, broken soldier and a beautiful woman. You," he accused, "I recognize. You are Rose Theodore."

"Standing beside Rudy Blake." Brushing back the long, greying locks, she straightened his shoulders then tilted his head into a jaunty angle. "Nearly two years older, a century wiser. Knowledge is not without cost, Rudy, but what you gained more than compensates for what you lost. You are thirty-seven years old. Beneath the signs of illness you are a young man. Give me time and I will prove it to you."

"Time. Always time. Time is running out for me. Look for yourself," he charged, spittle flying from his lips to mar the purity of the glass.

"So now we both know that war is hell. A lesson hard-learned. I suggest neither of us attempt it, again."

The drollness of her statement caused him to blow air through his nose. Wiping the tip with the back of his hand, Rudy caught himself, grimacing at the uncouth act.

"A year ago, I would rather have cut off my hand than wiped my nose with it."

"That, sir, I seriously doubt," came the acerbic challenge. "Or I have seriously missed my guess? "Without a hand, you would never again deal cards. And to save you from that fate, I have risked much." Tapping the sling, she bared teeth. "My professional standing in the medical community. You either fully recover, or I shall never again practice medicine."

"A foolish expression," he admitted. Glancing upward toward where he supposed Olympus to reside, he erased the statement by waving his hand across an imaginary chalkboard. "Which I recant."

"The gods are warned," came the ready approval. "Now: while I have you here, I will teach you proper mouth care. Sit." At his silent question came the answer, "On the commode."

"With, or without my trousers?"

"That depends on what business you care to perform in the presence of a lady."

He promptly sat, fully clothed. Reaching into the medicine cabinet, she extracted a small, green-glazed pottery bowl and a soft cloth.

"After every meal you must rub your gums with salt water," she instructed. "Dip your finger in the solution, then gently work it into your gums, top and bottom." She demonstrated by swirling the pointer finger of her left hand in the tepid water, then bringing it to his mouth. "Open up."

He did as ordered, permitting her to rub the alkaline mixture into his red and swollen flesh. Even that gentle touch shot excruciating bolts of electricity down the roots of his teeth, however, and he clamped on her finger, eyes wild with fright.

"I'm sorry, baby. I didn't mean to hurt you. I see how tender your mouth is. But this will help."

Shivering from exposure, Rudy swallowed the excess moisture, gagged on the salt, then drew away, simultaneously releasing her hand. Ashamed of his weakness, yet unable to control his lack of willpower, he begged a silent apology. Only after it was received did he pry open his jaws for a repeat treatment.

Understanding more clearly than Rudy the latent dread of pain, which had accompanied him without remission for the past twelve months, Rose carelessly sloshed water over the rim of the bowl. Stooping down to wipe it, she allowed him ample time to recover before speaking. By not mentioning his seeming cowardice, they could both pretend it never happened.

"To begin, we will treat your mouth five or six times a day. When it starts to feel better, we can reduce the frequency. All right?"

"And what is it for?" he asked softly, having forgotten her explanation.

"To clean and strengthen your gums; and to reduce the lingering effects of scurvy. If you are patient and brave, your teeth will firm and hold fast. So the next time you are in a bar room brawl, you will emerge not only victorious but with all your choppers."

"Is that really so? It is not too late?"

"To get in a fight or to save your teeth?" she teased, reapplying the salt water to the roof of his mouth.

"Either," came the gloomy, muffled response.

"Within a year I will have you back to normal."

"No, Rose," he demurred, jerking spasmodically as her finger touched an exposed nerve. "I wish to God that were so, and if I were half a man, I would hold you to that promise. But I am not. I am no kind of a man at all."

Taking the bowl, Rose washed it under running water, then dried it with a hand towel, set out precisely for that purpose. With her hands thus occupied, she could avoid facing him.

"You have been wounded and you have scarred. That tissue is dead. But around it will grow fresh skin. That is the nature of healing."

"I am not speaking of –"

"I comprehend you," she interrupted, finishing her job, then setting the pottery down on the tile with a resounding crack. "Neither was I. I referred to your mind. In a figurative way. In a manner you could fathom. Your mind, Rudy," she continued, wrapping the towel between her hands into a twisted rope, "is no different than your body. It has been hurt but not irreparably. Mark me, for I do not lie."

Not to you and not in these circumstances, she transmitted through the medium of her flashing eyes. "If I thought for a moment you were beyond – what shall I say? – redemption – I would not have summoned the doctor. I would not have tried so hard to save your finger."

"What would you have done?" came the low, frightful whisper, summoning up the ghosts of her past.

"I would have overdosed you with laudanum, then crawled into bed beside you. When your breathing stopped, I would have administered the same dose to myself. Is that clear enough?"

"You... would have done that?"

"I have said so. I have made that promise. My life is tied to yours. If I did not believe that somewhere, deep inside, you were the man who left here a year ago, I would have put us both out of our misery."

Slowly unwinding the towel, Rose straightened out the wrinkles, then hung it on the rack.

"When the time is right, we will excise that scar tissue; cut it away so that you bleed afresh. Then, when you are nearly bloodless, I will cauterize the wound, allowing it to heal. In that manner, we will have fresh scars, but not the same as those we carry now. Different ones; ones which will reform, ever present, but more narrow and in a new configuration."

He had pushed her to the brink but even in his confused state, Rudy Blake, consummate gambler, knew when to fold his cards.

"While you are at it," he began, working his face until a trace of a smile shaped, "will you see what you can do about the scars on my chest? I hate those damned things like the plague."

She was beyond humor but not appreciation.

"No, Rudy. That cross is yours to bear for life. But think of it, if you will, another way: I do not wish to take you back to a time before you had them. That was not *my* time. Those intersecting scars were on your chest when first we met. I saw them. Remember?"

Lowering his head, Rudy nodded.

"Of all the things I would like to forget, that is not one of them. That memory has sustained me through hell."

"Then accept them, Rudy. As I do."

"You are a hard taskmaster."

"I shall be worse."

With it was carried the hope of time. Tomorrow and tomorrow and tomorrow. All things considered, Thomas Mannering had offered her considerably less.

CHAPTER 23

Rudy slept soundly, due, in no small part, to the drops of laudanum Rose put in his before-bed drink. She lay beside him until he drifted off, then got up and settled herself in a rocking chair placed by the bed. Her nerves were too restless to permit easy slumber and to disturb him would only augment the probability of nightmares.

Sleep waxed and waned through her own brain as she relived the past twelve hours. Over and over she received word of a stranger's arrival at the door; twenty times she opened it to see him standing there in the hall light, tall and gaunt and wasted.

Every third or fourth time Rose imagined the settling, it was not Rudy who came calling at so ungodly an hour, but some other fellow. A peddler, hawking rifles, or wheeling and dealing get-rich quick schemes. Once, the man of her semi-conscious wanderings presented himself as an undertaker, selling burial plots "at half price for good customers." Slamming the door in his face, Rose woke herself, to discover her body covered with a clammy sheen of perspiration.

Waving her hand before her face to dispel the image, she found it would not go away. The mortician's features were vaguely familiar, haunting her wakeful memory with its summons to the past. Who was he? Replaying the voice over, she attempted to identify it by accent or intonation. In that, she failed miserably.

When that effort promised no relief, Rose threw the covering from her legs, then sprinted downstairs, returning almost immediately with pencil and pad. If she could not place the man by memory, she would sketch his features for Rudy. If, upon waking, he did not recognize the spiritual visitation, she would store the image away for future reference. That way, if they ever encountered such a personage, they would be forearmed against danger.

What emerged from her pencil drawing was a picture of a corpulent man with fleshy jowls pushing up the skin around his eyes, making them appear beady and small. The image of a pig was augmented by a thick black, bristly beard covering his cheeks, more disguise than vanity. Of average height, the loose black broadcloth coat he wore, its tails reaching beyond his calf, obscured the fact he was muscular, with powerful shoulders.

As her writing instrument across the page, a quantity of cheap cigars emerged from his breast pocket. A thick gold chain spread across his abdomen, bringing attention to the fact his shirt was soiled and missing buttons. While she had not seen his cuffs, Rose added loops of string, rather than links through the openings. He was a man who did not possess money, but strove, within the limits of his budget and taste, to appear well off.

The mystery man wore a stove top hat, battered around the edges and dented on the left, the result of wear and improper care. Perhaps he had fallen in a fight and damaged the brim; a drunken, barroom brawl where he had come out the loser, only to hide in the shadows of an alley, waiting his turn at retribution.

His hair, if she guessed right from the unequal illumination of her vision, was dark. Too dark to be natural. Clumps of a damp, sticky substance snarling his locks made her think of boot black. He was, therefore, in his late forties or early fifties, attempting to hide his birth year. Such an attempt was antithesis to the undertaking profession, for those men usually wished to strike the prospective coffin-buyer as aged and wise.

His breath, she seemed to recall, was unobtrusive, smelling vaguely of fish, which he had undoubtedly eaten for dinner. There was no scent of alcohol, or of peppermint, the common remedy for a drunk's telltale giveaway, indicating the slight bulge in his lower right coat pocket was not a flask of whisky. A gun, perhaps? She did not think so. Yet there was something there.

Directing her mind's eye toward the protrusion of cloth, Rose ran over the possibilities, sensing the discovery of the item would lead to an identification. A pocketbook? A journal? Neither were the right shape. A deck of playing cards? Too small.

"No," she said aloud, then glanced guiltily toward the bed where Rudy slept. Her voice had not disturbed him and for that she raised her eyes heavenward in gratitude. "It was a flask; or a bottle." If he did not imbibe himself, then possibly he kept it for his customers. To steady their nerves.

But not while selling coffins or grave plots. That was the incongruous detail. In her dream she had put those words in his mouth, warning herself he was a harbinger of death.

Of evil come calling.

Not totally satisfied with the sketch, yet loath to add details she could not be certain were summoned from dream, rather than association with tangible men, Rose set the paper against the lamp, using the metal base as a backrest. What she inadvertently created was a glow, or halo effect around the figure's head. Without instilling holiness, it gave the pencil lines a life of their own.

"No," came the rapid determination. "You'll not watch us through the medium of my own hand." Without actually seeing them, Rose knew the eyes moved. It was a phenomenon familiar to her, for often, when she drew likenesses of people, her ultimate determination of the picture's quality was the shifting of the pupils. If, by her own talent and the subject's psychic ability the orbs looked back at her, then she knew her aim had been achieved by capturing the essence of the individual.

On more than one occasion, after sketching from memory, the man or woman she drew had dropped some innocent remark into a subsequent conversation. A comment on a dress she owned but they had never seen; an observation of a book on her nightstand. Once, a close friend she had not seen in years wrote her a letter, dated the evening Rose had sketched her, confessing a desperate desire to renew their old acquaintance.

Divine inspiration? Witchcraft? A link, merging the two parties through the invisible medium of air? Rose did not have the scientific explanation but she had the faith. If the eyes in her portrait moved, then the stranger was alive and real. She had been sent a vision.

"Who is he?"

With her mind concentrating on the picture, Rose's senses had not detected the subtle alterations in Rudy's mind, indicating a return to wakefulness. Without flinching, though she was startled, Rose craned her neck in Rudy's direction, scanning his countenance with sharp scrutiny.

"He is unfamiliar to you?"

Squinting, then moving aside to deflect the errant rays of the lamp, Rudy concentrated, lips moving in silent thought preceding his words.

"Who is he?"

"Tell me first if you recognize him," she prodded, catching her breath. Her fear was of equal weight: that he would know him and that he would not.

"He is someone."

Which matched her impression precisely.

Someone.

"Who?"

"I do not know his name. In fact," he added, with an almost embarrassed grin, "I cannot say I have ever met him. And yet... he is familiar." Leaning on his elbow, his head moved in mute denial. "One of your gun-selling customers?"

"No."

"Not a man you met at a party; not a man with a title, or status. He is too vile for that. Nor a man with money. He has hungry eyes."

It was an apt description.

"What else?" She was hesitant to probe him, yet his first impressions were the ones she would store away with her own. What came later would be rationalized, reworked, altered to fit the situation rather than the moment.

"A card shark? No," he dismissed, blinking to ward off the image. "I never forget the face of a man with whom I've played cards. But perhaps... I never played him. Possibly I only watched him play?" She did not answer, for she did not know. "Or a tradesman? No," he answered his own question. "Nothing that... honest. Whoever he is, he's a thief and a liar." His nose crinkled. "Not a common, everyday murderer; not the type who accosts you to your face. The kind who knifes you in the back.

"What he is, Rose," Rudy decided, a chill of certainty settling over him, "is a man for hire when there's dirty work to be done. An underling without scruples. A front; a caricature; a man without a face. Or, a man with many faces. If I have seen him, and I cannot say with certainty I have, he did not look like that." He shrugged. "I may have known him clean-shaven; or with a mustache. The beard is a disguise. Is it real, or false?"

"Take your pick."

"Give it to me."

She hesitated, not from worry closer contact would jar his memory, but from trepidation the "underling" would seize the opportunity to put the mark on them. If they did not know him, it stood to reason he did not know them. She did not wish to forearm the evil with any salient details he otherwise would have no way of determining.

To refuse, however, was to lose the final opportunity of picking Rudy's brain. Taking up the paper by the corner so as not to touch the face, Rose handed it to him. As he took it, Rudy cried aloud, quickly withdrawing his fingers.

His first thought, but not hers, was that the pain had been occasioned by his wound. As that idea subsided, a sneer of contempt, mingled with dread, overcame him.

"He may be a gambler, but not with cards. Yet certainly a prestidigitator. A manipulator. Where did he come from?"

"A dream."

"Tell me."

"He came to the door –"

"This door? The door downstairs?" Rudy interrupted.

"Yes. But I have transposed time. He will not come here." She knew, without knowing why.

"What was he doing?"

"Offering to sell me a coffin: at half price, for good customers."

"Customers? Plural?" he demanded with so acute a longing, Rose nearly forbore answering. When the answer came, it held the same alarm he felt.

"Yes."

"Then your premonition was meant for both of us. He is not from my past, nor from yours. He is no one we have accosted together. That I would remember. Without a doubt," he emphasized, with full awareness his memory was clouded. "He is a harbinger of the future. Someone we will meet in unpleasant circumstances."

"Enough," she decided, clutching the paper, face inward, to her breast. "I will put it away."

"Where?" he asked. "Where will you put it?"

Her only thought had been to hide the sketch for the moment. Long term arrangements had not arisen. Seeing that he had a suggestion, Rose repeated his question.

"Where?"

"In – I was going to say my billfold," Rudy faltered, shaking his head. "But that will not do. Fold it and put it in your wallet. Carry it with you – the same way I carried John Paul's drawing of – me."

Seeing him cringe, Rose creased the paper into fourths before getting up to retrieve her billfold. He spoke over her activity.

"Perhaps he and I – this man and me – are two of the same animal, Rose Bud. Just as he, I was in disguise. We are both... chameleons."

"You are forgetting, Rudy Bud," came the firm, resolute correction. "The caption of John Paul's sketch: 'Rudy Cheats Death.' Deny it if you will, but David was a man of gifted insight. He knew. It was not just a shell game he was depicting – there were much larger implications than that. Because he wrote 'Rudy cheats death,' I believe it. Who or whatever this bearded stranger is; whatever he threatens us with, or holds over our heads – we will ultimately triumph."

"Do you believe that?"

"As truly as I believe anything."

"Then I will use your hope to sustain me. Remind me," he added, kicking his feet beneath the covers, "when the time comes, for I will need your faith. I am not the man I was."

Spontaneously engulfing him in her arms, Rose kissed him, first on the brow, then on the cheeks, before finally placing her lips to his. As the essence of his being radiated through her, she reacted the way a body would when struck by lightning. Enjoying the sensation which made the ends of her hair fly with static electricity, she snuggled closer. His weak protests only served to increase her hold.

"I've waited a long time to get my hands on you, Rudy Blake and I am not to be put off."

Mistaking her meaning, he cried aloud, a low, shameful moan of resignation. "I cannot," he began, then dropped his head back and howled with frustration. Grabbing his long locks with her left hand, she forced his face back so that her eyes could penetrate his greenish-grey-streaked orbs. In them were confusion and deep-set misery.

He was a wolf, she decided, caught too long in a trap. A wolf, deprived of freedom and subjected to tortures of deprivation, humiliation and starvation. Rendered a beast by the massive, unmitigated slaughter of its pack, the wounded animal-man had lost its fighting spirit. Yet not the spark of life. That she would preserve, though the ill winds of time and hot air of men would try to extinguish.

"That's not what I meant, Rudy. Time for that later –"

"No," he snarled, baring teeth, then as quickly dropping back, afraid of his own passion, which was anger and not love. In frustration he let her go, then fought bitterly with the sling restraining his arm. She waited until he had freed the limb before holding it down, her own ire dousing the flames of his fire.

"If I say a thing, you had best believe it, Captain Blake."

"Private Blake! Or artillerist Blake! Or Mister Blake, but not Captain Blake. Put that title from your mind, Miss Theodore, for that man is gone. He has changed. He is dead. Perished."

"Really?" she demanded, pulling back to ascertain the truth of his words. "Dead, is he? Dead of body, or dead of Manhood? For if you are right and truly gone, then you are meat for the grave-worms, and I shall nail you up myself, cold and stiff and unyielding to my kiss. But if you are merely unable to meet my advances, then I shall take hope, for –"

"There is no hope!" he screamed, spittle flying from his wet mouth. "I have lost it; it is gone. It has been too long. I have... forgotten –"

Reading him aright, Rose arched her shoulders, eyebrows descending with scorn.

"Where others have remembered? Do tell me; titillate me with your experiences." Her contempt was rampant. "Enthrall me with stories of how other men sought camp followers, while you cowered in the bushes. Did you peek on them, like some curious boy? Did you hunker around the campfire, listening to their tall tales and salivate like a dog?

"And even if you did witness those soldiers rutting around like mad dogs – which I doubt – why must you take that as some slur on your own prowess? What have they to do with you?"

The question was damning but not nearly so heavy as his confession.

"I have lost all desire... all thought of..."

"Intercourse? Come: let us use the proper word, for surely we are not speaking of love, but of lust." He flinched, giving her the impetus to continue. "Is it the animal drive you have lost, perchance? The willingness to copulate with any warm hole which your nose has detected from afar? Are you saying the scent of a bitch in heat does not arouse you?"

Eschewing her language, which frightened and repulsed him, Rudy sobbed, flapping his bandaged left arm in the air as if it were a broken wing, preventing him from flying.

"Listen to me," Rose ordered, taking his chin in her two hands. "Has it never occurred to you this change of which you speak reflects on the state of your mind, rather than your body?"

He blinked, then attempted to focus on her face, without success.

"I do not take your meaning."

"Then hearken to my words, for I shall not repeat them." Settling back against the mattress, Rudy flattened himself out, waiting for the onslaught which came to him, not as crushing wagon wheels or horrific cannon fire, but as gentle rain.

"When I was a woman of the streets – a prostitute, a lady of the evening, a Cyprian, if you will," she added, raising a brow to underline his own word, "I used to dream about how life would be like when I had the money to... retire. Granted, this was a fantasy, for no one in that 'oldest profession' ever 'retires,' but I thought about what my life would be like. Never again, I decided, would I sleep with any man. God knows, I had enough of that to last a 'good woman' a lifetime.

"It is a common misconception, Mr. Blake, that women choose such a way to earn a living because they are deviate – there is in their nature that which compels them to seek the company of men. A perversity... a sickness. Hush," she added, finger to her lips to prevent him from interrupting. "I have heard it said. By learned men. Of course, there are just as many scholars who declare the opposite – that women have no – what shall I say? Bedroom drive? But I will dismiss them as fools... and worse."

Moving her hands up to her head, Rose loosened the fastenings with which she had bound her long auburn tresses, releasing them. Baring her shoulder, Rose draped the straight, full-bodied hair seductively, so that the ends hung suggestively into her cleavage.

Horrified at what he knew too well to be a temptress' art, Rudy tried to avert his head, blinding himself from the spectral. This was not to be permitted. With firm effort, Rose drew him back, gripping the back of his neck as she swayed above him.

"Come, Mr. Dansforth; or Mr. Black, or Mr. White; whatever name you are using to hide your identity from so lowly a personage as a whore," she purred with syrupy sweet tones of insincerity only a paying customer would believe. Had she spoken a string of curse words, the meaning would have been as patent. "Let me undress you, kind sir."

"No! Please, Rose," he impotently protested, further weakened by her mesmerizing performance.

"Please do, or please don't?" she laughed, taking false delight in his predicament. "You say you have lost the art... the knack of 'love'? Let Rose remind you. For twenty dollars, gold, I will rekindle the flame of passion."

"Stop!" he shrieked, nearly gagging as her breasts swooped down over his open, gaping mouth.

"What is that you say, sir? That your wife no longer pleases you? Put it from your mind. She is old and wrinkled from too many children. What you need is fresh, vibrant flesh." Twisting seductively, Rose slipped the clothing from her other shoulder. "Oh?" she pursued, offering a hardened nipple for him to suck. "Your wife is in the family way and you cannot touch her? No matter; you are a man, and a man has needs."

Curling her fingers around the blanket, Rose draped it back from his chest. The sight of it caused her eyes to flutter with appreciation.

"So muscular... so manly, Mr. Jones. Any woman would melt at your feet."

Extending her pointer finger, Rose inched it slowly down the blanket, increasing pressure as she reached his groin.

"You are on a business trip, Mr. Smith? Far away from home? No matter. You will find all the comforts of your hearth here, with me. And who is to be the wiser? Mrs. Smith is distant and innocent of your dalliance. What she does not know cannot hurt her. Am I not correct, Mr. Smith?"

Giggling coyly, the weight of her palm rested on his male anatomy. Rudy groaned in shamed misery as her fingers probed his delicate area. This served as an impetus for her to flutter her hands before her eyes.

"You deceive me, sir," she prattled, beginning a steam of professional verbiage. "Why, this is the largest 'horn' I have ever felt. You are a giant among men, sir, a god of old. And you say you have lost the art. Shame on you, gentleman, for deceiving a poor working girl! Let me see what you are hiding, least I explode from anticipation."

"For God's sake, Rose, stop, I beg you!"

His effort at keeping the blanket over his body was futile, for she knew her business and all the legions from hell could not have restrained her.

"I beg you, too, kind sir, for you are a man of such gargantuan proportions, I am sorely afraid that your organ my rupture me. Just look at it!" she continued, stripping him of the covering to reveal his nakedness. "Oh, my! Such prodigious length! Surely, sir, you are famous among men. A legend. The progenitor of a legion of bastards!"

Gripping him firmly, Rose kneaded the stiffening flesh, pulling, then gently releasing, before squeezing his testicles until he trembled with desire.

When she had aroused him, Rose worked upward, her mouth agape in sensuous desire.

"But you are an experienced lover, Mr. Stone. You, undoubtedly, desire my very best efforts before you impregnate me with seed. Come, darling, open your mouth, for I know a gentleman like you is well versed in French kissing. My tongue is long and daring, sir; show me yours."

"Rose.... Rose," Rudy pleaded through clenched teeth. "Stop this. You are frightening me."

"Frightening a big, strong man like you? You tease a poor working girl, Mr. Stone. Why, nothing in this big, terrible world could scare you, sir. Not with a manly body of your possession. There is nothing you could not do! Why, the very beasts of the field, the mighty lions and tigers of the jungle would cower before your manliness."

"Please, not like this," Rudy cried, face reddened from the horror of her performance. Finally drawing back, Rose eyed him sharply, her eyes in slits.

"Not like this? Whatever do you mean? Love is where you find it, Captain Blake. Women are for the taking. Cross my palm with gold and I am yours. It is the nature of the beast, is it not, Captain Blake?"

Her use of his true name frightened him more than her prattle.

"A man is a man, and a man has needs. Tell me that is untrue. A man has desire and it is in the nature of the world for him to sate his needs. At any time, at any place. With whomever he wishes, be she serving wench or countess."

"No," he denied, mind whirling with conflicting emotions. "I have never said that."

"No?" came the retort, for she was not finished yet. "You? The rogue of the Seven Seas? You, who has bragged of your conquests across the continents of the world? You, who keep a soiled woman in a house of Ill Repute in Atlanta for your especial use?"

"Cora? Cora Sommers?" he gasped, tearing through the layers of memory to grasp her out from the shadows.

"Yes, darling. You know it is true; that you brought her from New Orleans, not because the war was on the horizon, but to service your desires. And that brat of hers – you educate him under your own name to keep her pacified; so she would give you the performance of a lifetime."

"Rose, do not do this to me!"

"To you, darling? For you, I would do anything, for you have risen me above a life of sin and degradation, to play the lady. Just so you may take me into polite society and show me off. I am quite a prize, am I not?"

Fussing with her hair a second time, Rose rolled it up over her head, then batted her eyes.

"Or that wife of yours, Captain Blake, who is no wife to you, but is untouched by your hands. You are saving her, like a piece of chocolate, for the denouement of your courtship."

Rudy gagged, then began a tortured coughing. Not until he composed himself and his breathing had grown steadier did she relent. Dropping her hands, so that her locks fell gracefully over her back, Rose replaced the fabric over her shoulders, covering her breasts. When she spoke, the tones of the working girl were replaced by her normal voice. The irony, however, remained.

"So, young gentleman, I have given you pause, have I? And now, perhaps you see why I dreamed of 'retirement'? To abandon the male half of the world to their dirty minds and filthy bodies? Why I swore I would never again sleep with another man? Because I –"

Rose bit off her sentence, rethought her words, then finally settled in beside him, gently grasping Rudy's hand in hers.

"Rudy, you tell me you have changed. That you are not the same man which sailed away from Liverpool so many months ago. I accept that." He squirmed, trying to speak, but she would not let him. "Hush, baby. I, too, have changed. That is the nature of life. D'Artagnan, Jack, BoBo – they, too, have changed. The world is not the same. How could any of us expect to be unaffected? We have seen and done things beyond our wildest imaginings. We cannot alter the past, Rudy. It is done. Over. Finished. Now is the time to mend; to assimilate what we were with what we are. There is no going back, yet together, we may forge ahead, into a new and different arena."

He moved again and this time she lay beside him, face to face, bringing them closer.

"You are Captain Rudy Blake. You will sail again. Not as a gunrunner to South America and not as a blockade runner through Federal lines. Who knows what it will be next time? As a trader to the West Indies? As an adventurer, seeking pirate treasure? I do not know, but one thing I do grasp: we will be together. And that is where my story takes me."

Readjusting the pillows so they both rested more conformably, she drew the blanket across their bodies, sharing its protection.

"You cry, because you think you have lost the ability to be a man. So you turn away from women the way I once dreamed of spurning men. But you have overlooked one salient detail."

"Tell me," he pleaded, shivering under the blow which he expected, but not from the direction it came.

"During the War, you saw men go to camp followers; you heard their grunts of 'delight.' You saw them stagger back, a sneer on their faces. Did you really wish you had gone with them – that you, too, had rutted with a dirty, despised woman? A mulatto or a Negress? Or snuck off to town, there to pay your penny and relieve your need? Tell truth," she warned.

"No," he mumbled into the wool.

"Why? Because you had lost the urge or for some other reason?"

"Tell me."

"I will say what you already know in your heart. It is merely that you have lost touch with yourself."

"I know who I am... what I have become."

"You do not. And therein lies your conflict. Something has happened to you, Rudy Blake: something so wondrous even the great sea captain does not comprehend. An alteration so powerful it has left you confused and lost."

"The War?"

"Not the War, for this change is no change at all, but a reckoning of your true self. Much to your surprise and consternation, Rudy, you have discovered two things. One, that you are a good man and not a reprobate."

"And the second?" he pleaded, pressing the side of his head against her so as to hear with only one ear.

"You have fallen in love. As impossible as that may seem – as much as you scorned the concept, denied the possibility – you are a man whose heart has been given to another."

"To you, Rose."

"To me," she acknowledged. "You did not expect it; this tenderness of emotion was not in your plans. It did not fit your self-image. Yet it happened. And that, beyond battles and death, has made you into someone you do not recognize. And so, you have 'changed.'"

"And you?"

Rose finally laughed, and the sound of her merriment was clear and bright and uplifting.

"I, too, have found myself changed by love. My dream of abandoning mankind for a life of solitude has melted away. The difference is, my dear boy, that I have kept part of it, while expanding the rest."

"What part... have you kept?"

"The idea of making love with you. Mind when I say love, for therein is the key which opens both our souls. Love, Rudy. Not lust. For the rest of my life – for as long as I live – I will never willing lie with a man other than you. That much of my dream I keep."

"And me?"

Rising up, she stared at him with tender, yet piercing eyes. As she moved, the pillow beneath his head jostled him, forcing him to realign himself to look up at her.

"Do you expect me to say you will once again be that rogue you were? I will not and cannot. As you say, that man is gone." Suddenly uncomfortable, she sat, wrapping her arms about herself. Not to ward off chill, but rather, future events, the control of which neither had the power to avert.

"I will not hold you chaste, Rudy, for your life is not my life. You love Cora, and to deprive her of your most loving company would be a cruelness. For in that relationship, too, there is love and tenderness. Whether or not you will lie with her again, I cannot say. But I give you leave.

"As for that other, your wife, I shudder to think of it. But in so doing, I bow out. You have married her; you have feelings for her I acknowledge without condoning. God and your own free choice will dictate what is to become of you. But this I promise." Grasping him around the shoulders, Rose brought him up into a sitting position, for her sentiments were not to be said to a man lying down. "It is I you love and that love has separated you from the rest of Mankind. Between us, it is holy and sacred. Trust yourself in this and do not look back but only ahead. Glorify in the changes love has wrought, for in them you have found your own true self."

Weeping quietly, Rudy kissed her on the cheek, then attempted to place his arms around her. Unable to move his left arm, restrained by the sling, he wiped his face on her shoulder, then picked at the bandages.

"Will you remove this, so I may hug you?" he asked, again that boy who was being reformed from child to man.

"No."

It was not the first of her refusals. It would not be the last. Would that it were, she prayed, for other denials would be far harder.

CHAPTER 24

"Come, Rudy," Rose declared, opening the curtain so light poured in. "We have work to do."

"The books?" he inquired, weakly lifting his head from the night-soaked pillow.

"No. Although that was a good thought. There are two items on our agenda which cannot be put off. I leave the order of them to you."

"Tell me?" he begged, the dread of making a decision nearly overwhelming. Hurrying quickly back to him, she threw her arms around his shoulders, then kissed him lightly on the cheek.

"Nothing so terrible that you cannot make the decision," came the careful declaration. "You must bathe and you must eat. Which is your pleasure, sir?"

"Tell me first what our work is." The piteous entreaty caught Rose, held her in its insidious grip, so that for a moment she was nearly as paralyzed as he. With great willpower did she resume her buoyant attitude.

"I have said: a bath and a meal."

"That is not work," he demurred, then let his head loll backward as his eyes fluttered. Supporting him with her hand, Rose debated the wisdom of her choices, then shook him gently.

"I think we will both find it so. Breath regularly and the faintness will pass." Obeying her implicitly, the color slowly returned to his wan countenance. "I'm sorry, baby; you moved too fast."

"No," came the denial as he trembled with fear. His voice, unusually soft, lowered even further. "We cannot simply do these things without permission." Forcing open his eyes, he stared in dull incomprehension, waving a hand in the air. Grabbing it with both of hers, she held it firm.

"Rudy, you are home. In this place, you may do what you will. There is no one to counter your desire."

"Rose... who will go for food? Whose turn is it? Where are the wagons –?"

Applying more pressure, she inched closer until nearly touching his nose.

"Rudy, the war is over. You are free. You are in Eng –"

"Where are they?" Pressing past her, he attempted to penetrate the fog of his mind. "I do not see them. We have gotten separated." His wail of distraction forced her to grab him by the ears. She would not slap him and argument was vain. Forcing command into her voice, she addressed the wayward soldier.

"Who, Blake, is your commanding officer?"

It was a gamble, a risk she did not wish to take, for to further indulge his trance was to encourage disorientation. Yet to ignore the circumstances of his fear was a greater danger.

"Lieutenant Montgomery, sir," came the prompt response. Something in the way he spoke the name evoked images of tenderness and love. Lieutenant Montgomery. Surely not the boy who ate the horehound? The one to whom a fine dinner had been promised? She would have it, for to guess wrongly bore dire consequences.

"His first name?"

"Benjamin," came the startled reply.

Waves of vertigo passed through Rose's own brain. Benjamin Montgomery. A piece of the puzzle. A boy officer.

Which rhymed with "toy" officer. And made her shiver.

"We will ask Benjamin whether you shall have permission to bathe or not."

His snort through the nose surprised her nearly as much as the association.

"He will not refuse."

"Ah," she cried, delighted at his bold assertion. "So he refuses you nothing?"

"He is keen on bathing... in a creek." Rudy's eyes crinkled as time swirled past them in eddies of passing days and months. "But not in a tub."

"Then we shall surprise him, for I have the grandest shower-bath in all of... in all the world. I suspect he would appreciate it if he were to discover you immersed in bubbles."

"He would laugh himself silly."

"Then that is what we shall do; prepare a feast for his eyes before setting his table with good things to eat."

"He will eat anything," Rudy snorted again, then wiped his nose against her blouse. "I once saw him eat a worm."

Despite herself, Rose guffawed. "We shall ask cook to prepare better. He will not complain?"

Wrapping his fingers about her arm, Rudy squeezed with surprising strength.

"Benjamin. Where is he? Is he here? Boy? Boy?" he called, then heaved a sigh and released her, letting his arm fall listlessly to the bed. "No. I left him in Richmond. What day is this? What year?" he demanded, one eye wandering while the other sought her face.

"Sunday. June 25th, 1865. The beginning of summer."

"Fall, you say." He tried to comprehend but the concept of time was obscure. "The medical college will not begin classes until the dawn of 1866. He is with... I have placed him with Doctor...." But he had forgotten the name. "Doctor Somebody. That was right, wasn't it, Rose?"

"Yes, Rudy. It was exactly right. He wanted to be a doctor," she divined.

"To give back the lives he had... taken." His voice lowered to a hush. "He need pay no penance, Rose. Tell me that is true."

Piercing beyond the vail of his torture, she nodded, lips compressed in absolute sincerity.

"He need not. As Benjamin would remind you of the same."

Rudy's eyes narrowed but he made no comment. She interpreted that to mean what was good for a boy was not necessarily the same for a man. She would argue the point, but not at the moment.

"Describe him to me," she asked instead, grasping Rudy's hand and pulling him up. Working over his words as a diversion, the pair began the trek toward the door.

"He is good-sized for a boy, lanky and strong, with the kind of muscle earned by hard labor, not flashy or of the type which would catch a lady's eye. He is a tumbleweed sort, with a good growth of hair and a bit of a widow's peak." Pausing for breath, for the effort of walking tired him, Rudy sketched Benjamin from the thousand and one hours he had spent by his side.

"What color hair? What color eyes?"

"Brown hair, brown eyes; not deep and rich, but almost hazel brown. With streaks of yellow, which flash when he is angry."

"Is he angry much?"

"Hardly ever," Rudy scoffed, repositioning his arm about her shoulder and forging on. "He's a ready grin and the bubbly voice. Not deep and manly but somewhere between that of a child and a youth. He'll grow a bit of stubble on his face but not the type which makes a man. He has growing to do, Rose."

"And because of you, he shall have that opportunity."

"No," he refused, sagging under the weight of what, to him, was false accusation. "I do not believe there ever was a Yankee bullet meant to fell him. None with his name on it, Rose."

"Yet you worried about him," came the prompt as she guided him down the hall.

"Now could I not? He was here, he was there, he was everywhere." Again his footsteps faltered and she gave him time to rest. "A sprite of a boy; a wild Gypsy boy. With freckles, Rose. Not the profusion of a redhead, but a scattering about his nose. I had forgotten that," he added, attempting to penetrate the mists of the past. "Untamed and uneducated but with a will to learn. And an indomitable spirit. A baby animal, Rose; a fledgling or a colt or a kitten, crawling over the top of its box, little nose quivering with the excitement of the chase.

"A boy after a butterfly, leaping and bounding and falling down and tumbling head over heels." He smiled and tears came to his eyes. "Not a soldier but a boy. A boy grown old in the service to a country and a cause beyond his comprehension. A puppy dog, Rose, chained and starved and tortured until it learns cunning."

Rudy shivered and she cradled him in her arms.

"Another step or two. We are almost there."

He obeyed because that had been his ingrained nature, tottering, then righting himself against the wall before continuing.

"The exuberance remains but the innocence is gone. The dog feigns friendliness, but behind the wagging tail hides bared teeth."

She halted him so suddenly they both nearly lost their balance.

"I have asked you to describe Benjamin and you have given me an accounting of yourself. You fool yourself but you do not deceive me. I grant you the wiles of a hard life, Rudy Blake, and the charm of a wolf cub, set upon a barren waste to hunt its supper, but that is where I draw the line."

Kicking open the door to the facility, she stepped aside so that he might enter first.

"Your Benjamin has lived through war and that war has changed him. But he will not have you say he bites the hand which feeds him. Yours is that hand, sir, and his is an adoration for life. Nor will he fight again the boot which kicked him, or the strap which lashed him. His is a gentle nature and from butterflies to bullets, he had gone to bandages. Say that is truth and I shall know him anywhere."

Rounding his shoulders into a concave act of contrition, Rudy dropped his head against her arm.

"There is no boy like him in the world. He is the son we shall never have, Rose."

"Then he is the child of our wild youth," she cried, blending tears of laughter with those of pathos. "You have set him on the path of knowledge and he has preserved you for me. Hardly an equal bargain; one which I will owe him restitution the rest of my days. Come: here is the tub. I can hear Benjamin now. He is clapping his hands with amusement."

"What... what is he saying, Rose?" Rudy pleaded, gaping with awed wonder at the huge porcelain bath dominating the necessary.

"Captain Blake, the tub is big enough for both of us, but I would as leave have you fill it by yourself!" she cried, envisioning the scene with perfect clarity.

"Yes! That is exactly what he would say. And soap, Rose. Do you have scented soap?"

"As many 'bars' as you have been in," she teased, running her hands up and down his spine, subconsciously counting the vertebrae. He clapped with pure joy, then took a step inside, daring to stand on his own two legs in a gesture of bravado. It was only for a moment, but as the challenge was won, he sank happily into her arms.

"Just a minute, Captain," Rose spoke, guiding him toward the large water tank. "Whilst we 'right your ship,' we must also haul down your sails for general cleaning and repair." Poking him in the back, she ordered, "Put up your hands."

"Is this a robbery? On the high seas?"

"Aye, but it's no treasure I'll be wantin', matey, but yer nightshirt."

"What value has that to anyone?" Rudy protested as Rose hoisted the material up and over his shoulders.

"Inestimable," came the prompt reply. "If you happen to be a lady. I'll use this as my standard!"

Maintaining hold of him by one hand, Rose swung the nightshirt over their heads with the other.

"But what shall it mean? Everyone knows to what the skull and crossbones refer, but a nightshirt?" he demanded, ducking away from the missile.

"Gentlemen, be-ware! Gentleman be-bare!" Laughing at her own joke, Rose guided him slowly across the room. With his mind occupied on her words, the journey was accomplished without mishap.

"All men wishing to board my ship must do so without 'pomp and circumstance,'" she continued, putting his hand against the wall so he could steady himself. "Buck naked or not at all. Those are my terms."

"And if they refuse?"

"My seamen will shoot their 'privates.'"

"Then they shall no longer be gentlemen," Rudy protested, balking at the enormity of the tub and his sudden fear of taking a bath.

"True. Well, we will have rendered them 'gentle-eunuchs,' and their behavior had best express their new status, or I shall throw them all overboard."

"A harsh mistress," Rudy complained, squinting his eyes.

"Nonsense; I've done no more than take a page from your book. If the cook cannot prepare a proper bowl of grits, throw him overboard! If a man disobeys, toss him in the drink; a cloudy day? Make sacrifice to the gods by offering up one of you scurvy lads!"

She was so caught up in her own act, Rose did not notice the cloud of worry descending over his brows. Not until Rudy moaned did she stop and truly take in his tortured expression.

"What's the matter, Rudy?"

Averting his face, he attempted to hide his confused emotions by holding his hand over his own eyes.

"Did I really say all those things? Did I have men thrown overboard?"

"Of course you didn't," she soothed, caught off guard by his instability. "You spoke about them often enough, but that was threat and not reality." Covering her pangs of shame, Rose directed his body toward the tub. "A good soak and you will be a new man."

Too late she realized her mistake. Lowering his neck and shoulder, Rudy hesitantly glanced up at her.

"Does that mean you wish me to change?"

"What I want is for you to wash away the ingrained dirt," she articulated carefully, warning herself to choose words with better care. With his mind focused on literal interpretation, he was unable to grasp either broad-based generalizations or references to a past he only vaguely recalled.

Seeing her conflicting emotions, he shrunk from her grasp.

"Rose, you will bear with me? I have altered in ways even I do not understand." Turning his gaze from the tub, he seemed to shrink. "I am afraid."

"Rudy, listen to me." Taking his head in her hands, Rose attempted to pierce the layers of convoluted past. What she realized, as clearly, was that she spoke for her own sanity as well. "You have been through a terrible ordeal; a living nightmare, from which you barely escaped. Your mind is weakened from the effects of deprivation. Dr. Mannering said you were on the verge of death. You will recover. That much I have sworn. That it will take time, we must both acknowledge."

"You do not know me, then," came the hurt, yet gentle protest.

"Better than you know yourself."

By itself, her avowal was not an answer. Steadying his nerves, Rudy threw back his head the way he had done of old. It was a gesture, a bit of play acting, but it served to hone his intent.

"I could not live without a finger and I cannot exist without my mind. Tell me how long; set a date." She professed not to comprehend, but his meaning was clear. "A week or a year. When we reach that time, if I am not recovered – if I am not Rudy Blake, but a shade of what he was – you must swear to tell me. I will know what to do."

There was no denying him. In her heart, she could not refuse.

As she said before, she said again. "A twelve-month, minus one day."

He sagged. "So long. Very well. I accept."

The terms were yet another act of surrender. Not as far-reaching as Durham Station or Appomattox, but equally devastating.

The War Between the States had left its indelible mark

CHAPTER 25

Inching forward, Rudy peered forlornly at the tub. His body shook and he took no pains to hide his trepidation. "Tell me why I am afraid."

"It is formidable. And deep. I shall not fill it completely," Rose promised, patting him on the shoulder and understanding his fright. "I am right beside you."

"It seems such a small thing; settling oneself in water. Of no consequence. I have taken baths before and never have I..." His head lolled as memories came hard and fast. "In Atlanta. I remember... brooms and mops and back issues of *Harpers.*" A sad smile crept slowly across his lined features. "And a troop of... Blake's Brigade."

It was simple to dwell on the positive; easy to let him recall the little Negro children with their loving countenances and undying faith. But that would have been to lie. Or worse, to liken his fear to those blameless individuals. They were not the source of his dread.

Nor, she suspected, was the outcome of that innocent encounter. But to let it remain unsaid was to offer him no plausible explanation. Gripping her fingers together, Rose forged ahead.

"Yes, Rudy. And a challenge you made. To the gods."

"And lost," he shuddered, moaning beneath his breath, then leaning back and howling. "It comes back to me. Her. That woman. I have condemned myself –"

"A year. You promised me a year," she reminded him, quickly drawing the nightshirt over his head. She had done her duty. More she would not do. "Within that time, we will formulate a plan."

He stopped her, digging his fingernails deep into her flesh.

"What do you know that I do not?"

Catching a glimpse of herself in the mirror, Rose spoke to her own image rather than to the man demanding an answer. Watching her lips move was easier than facing his, from which no sound emerged.

"Only that she survived the War. She and her parents. From Atlanta, they returned to Charleston."

Tightening his grip, she felt the pulse in her wrist throb.

"Who has told you this?"

"D'Artagnan. After the surrender he went there, looking for you. When she had no information as to your whereabouts, he came here."

"D'Artagnan." Rudy rolled the word over on his tongue, tasting its varied complexity. "He is here?"

"With the others."

"What does he want?" When she would not speak, he glanced into the looking glass, reading what she would not say. "Money. The chance to make a fortune, the likes of which he has already squandered. He will not give me a year, Rose. Nor a week. In his eyes, I will have become –"

"I shall burn his eyes out with a hot poker, if that is what he believes," she interrupted, for she did not want to hear whatever expression Rudy would have chosen. "I have dismissed a household of servants; I shall not hesitate to give him his 'discharge.' He owes you much. It is time to pay the piper or be forever banished."

"So. That is the way it is." With resignation came acceptance. "I will take my bath now." Tossing down his arm, he stood naked before her. The glint in his eye spoke more of madness than anger. "Do you know what a gentleman does when he is deprived of the opportunity to bathe?"

"Tell me."

"He smothers himself in cologne to hide the odor." His mouth twisted crookedly. "And the outcome of that tactic?"

"A richly-scented stink pot?" she guessed.

"He becomes an attraction for all the winged and crawling insects of the world."

"A winning hand. But I would rather have you clean so that you may palm a card under your cuffs without causing excitement. Can you lift up your leg?" Rose continued, indicating the height of the tub. "Or shall I help you?"

"Am I to bathe without water?" he answered instead, staring questioningly at the dry receptacle.

Accepting that as a "yes," Rose guided him closer to the yawning cavity, then adeptly scooped him in her arms, raising him over the edge. Like a frightened calf, he did not struggle but merely accepted the act, which was beyond his comprehension. Once she had set him on his feet, a gentle pressure against the back of his knees prodded him to sit.

Without the ability to balance, Rudy listed to port, his heaving bandaged arm dragging him down.

"Bend your knees, then slide forward," she guided. "I shall hold you from behind."

Had he been at full weight, she would not have been able to manipulate him with any control. Being mere skin and bone, however, she managed the task without undue stress. As he flopped onto the bottom, Rudy groaned from the stinging pain occasioned by his hemorrhoids, then rolled his eyes into the back of his head.

"You'll never get me out of here."

"We'll cross that bridge when we come to it. You may find the waters restorative. Now, stretch out and wiggle your toes, so that I may see I have properly calculated the size of the tub to fit its most prized occupant."

All arms and legs and disjointed body parts, Rudy did as requested, looking more like a crippled bug than a man. The fit, when he finally extended himself, was perfect. Seeing her pleased expression, his own soured.

"This is not good at all."

"How so?" came the worried interrogative. "You are not comfortable? Lean back and you will see how you can rest your head against the back."

"You mistake my meaning," he tried in an overly patient voice. "*I* fit in it quite nicely. But I fail to see how one sniveling boy, or one mast-tall woman would find appropriate accommodation."

"Oh," Rose dismissed, vastly relieved by his attempt at banter. "I shall lie atop you quite comfortably. As for Benjamin, I leave those arrangements to your discretion. Perhaps you could play high card to see which of you assumed the 'butt up' position."

Over his loud and nearly raucous groans, Rose turned the taps, allowing an inflow of hot and cold running water. With a deft hand, she adjusted the temperature to lukewarm before dousing his head with a thick, dark amber solution.

"What is this?" he cried, tongue snaking out in childlike fascination to taste the obnoxious-looking substance.

"Liquid soap. A private concoction of my own. With medicinal purposes," she elucidated. "Made from coal tar." At that exact moment, he spat, producing a large, transparent bubble. Without the least qualm, Rose broke it with the tip of her finger.

"Coal tar?" came the exasperated complaint. "I feel, rather, as though I'm being tarred and feathered," he complained, ducking under a glassful of water Rose poured over his head. "Perhaps it will not wash off and I will be compelled to go through life a sticky blob of a man."

"That being the case, the bees will love you. Leave it alone while it works its way through your tangled masses and raise your arms."

"Why?"

"The answer to that should be obvious, even to the most hardened of riverboat gamblers. Your body odor proceeds you by half a mile. Look, Rudy," she continued, forcing his mind to concentrate on his words so that the newness of the experience would not unduly frighten him. "This is called Oatmeal soap. It is made in Scotland. Whole oats act as a gentle abrasive."

Eying it ruefully, he spoke through compressed lips to avoid a repetition of having soap leak into his mouth.

"If you had given that to me as a soldier, I would have eaten it."

Taking a soft cloth, Rose lathered the material, then draped it across his back. His sigh was her impetus to begin. Working slowly and carefully, she rubbed tenderly, comprehending it was far more important to get him used to the feel of being touched than to scrub off dirt. Obliging her, he leaned forward, allowing her better access to the broad expanse of taut skin, barely hiding the protrusion of spine and ribs.

Assuming a cheerfulness she did not feel, she chatted as she worked.

"I'm going to have to put some meat on your bones, Captain Blake. Even wild dogs would pass on a stick man such as you've become."

"Not the wild dogs I've seen," he grunted. His words, softly spoken, were nearly lost due to the close proximity of his face to the water. "Nor the wild boars, either," he added with a shudder. "I heard stories – and saw for myself – how those beasts unearthed shallow graves with their tusks to tear flesh off the newly buried."

"I'm sorry anyone had to see something like that."

"It was gruesome, Rose Bud," he pursued, fulfilling his own need to explain by horrifying her. "You could hear the bones cracking as the hogs crunched them for marrow. Of course," he added, painting the scene with the vivid reality of living color, "they went for the tender areas first, tearing muscle the way a butcher slices sides of beef. A soldier told me he had seen gut stretched over a quarter of a mile. I guess the damned thing got hold of it and tried to drag it somewhere."

His throat contracted and he gagged, swiftly swallowing the bile which regurgitated into his mouth. Rose let him compose himself before changing the subject.

"Lift up your arm," she ordered, gently tapping the biceps of his injured wing. Working beneath the sling, she washed the pit, then rinsed it with fresh water. "It wouldn't hurt you to clip some of this hair," she decided, tugging on the underarm growth. "I'm very much afraid it is beyond hope."

"You can't," he protested, turning to face her with shocked eyes. "You know what happened to Samson."

"That was the hair on his *head,*" Rose sagely observed. "And you know I would never ask you to cut *that.*"

"Not even if it grew past my shoulder blades?"

He meant her to smile, which she did.

"Not even if it were to reach your waist. If such long tresses bothered you, I would tie your hair back with a black ribbon."

"Then I'd feel as though I were in mourning," he protested, knowing full well Rose's proclivity of long masculine hair.

"You wear black suits, don't you?"

"Not recently," he quipped as she tugged on his wet strands.

"Yes. Well, we shall rectify that. I will order an entirely new set of clothes. Those I saved for you in the wardrobe are all too large. Once clean and properly scented, new attire will do you handsomely."

"Is that possible?" he whispered, the pathos of his fear touching her emotions.

"As possible as bluffing a win with two tens over jacks and queens."

"It's funny you should say that," he remarked as she drizzled more of the dark liquid over his head. "I knew a woman once. In New Orleans. Her surname, it turns out, was Jackson, but everyone slurred it... in that peculiar accent they use," he added for Rose's benefit, ducking away to avoid another mouthful of suds. I always thought they were addressing her as 'Jacks and Queens,'" he grinned. "Say it fast: 'Jacks-un-Queens.' She was quite a gambler."

"What else did she ply?"

"As to that, a gentleman never tells." This time, he failed to avoid the soap which Rose deliberately sloshed over his face. "Aside from its obvious uses as a fuel source, and a punishment, what benefit am I supposed to derive from coal tar?"

"It cleanses the scalp; relieves itching. Shall I wash it off before it has time to work?"

"No. I itch all over," came the guarded response. "You are sure?"

"I tried it on your boys, to good effect. Of course, they 'changed sides' for several weeks after my treatment was complete, but eventually the black color wore off. I didn't hear any of them complain about it."

"That's because they didn't dare, for fear you'd leave them permanently stained."

"An interesting thought," Rose conceded, kneading the lather with skilled, artistic hands. In a moment she had created two large, pointed devil's horns atop his head. Standing back to admire her handiwork, she nodded in satisfaction before retrieving a small hand mirror. "Here, Master Blake – take a look. Now you resemble that creature to whom you're always comparing yourself."

Staring at his reflection, Rudy registered shock before grinning sheepishly. Vainly, he reworked one of the horns so that it stood taller and more pointed.

"The devil. Now, you see my true shape."

"Not yet," Rose promised. "But I will." Slipping her hand between his legs, she tugged on his male anatomy. "I'm much more interested in *this* shape. What shall we call it – the Confederate Underwater Experiment?"

"No. That 'experiment' died an ungainly death," he tried. "I guess if I ever use it again, we'll have to style it the Merger of Two Countries."

"You will, and I approve. Now bow your head, so I may rinse it off."

He complied, reluctantly offering up his symbols of evil to the god of bathing. When they were washed off and the soap irrevocably merged with the bath water, he signed in resignation.

"Was I really that bad, Rose? To be accorded Satan's status?"

"That depends on whom you ask," came the guarded response. "And to what time frame you refer."

"Begin at the beginning."

Because she did not feel equal to speaking without using her hands, Rose began a systematic cleansing of his chest and back. She chose her words carefully, although the ideas were well-ingrained in her consciousness.

"As a child you were sweet and innocent. Whatever 'sins' your father ascribed to you were no more than reflections of his own dark soul. As a cadet at the Virginia Military Institute, you were honorable and trusting. You were entirely blameless for what evils occurred at that school."

Dipping her hand in the water, Rose gently swirled it, making small waves.

"For the remainder of your life in Charleston, you were the victim of circumstance. None of the 'working women' with whom you... consorted... would think you bad. I have that from your own lips," she warned before he could interrupt. "The duel and your subsequent flight were no more than necessity."

"I killed a man."

"In a fair fight; and not one of your instigation," she reminded him. "One in which you actually defended your father. No blame could fall on your head from that travesty of justice. Although, I dare say," came the more chilling retort, "the man you shot was a worthless boy. The world is better off without him.'"

"Can you rightfully say that of anyone?" Rudy whispered, shuddering as the temperature of the water chilled him. Responding immediately to his need, Rose turned the tap, admitting more hot water to the bath. She waited until he had placed his fingers under the flow before continuing.

"Some men are born evil and some men allow themselves to be captivated by evil deeds." She made a low noise, then used her forearm to wipe away droplets of water splashed upon her brow. "While it is not for either of us to say they should never have been born, their exit from life cannot be mourned."

"Even in such a fashion? I was the better shot. I knew I would kill him."

"You knew you *could* kill him. There is a difference."

"And the dolphins, Rose? Surely murdering them was an evil act."

"We have had this out before." Her statement was hard and absolute. "You know my feelings."

"Go on," Rudy urged, conceding the point by running his fingernail across his stubbled cheek.

"Whatever schemes you hatched in San Francisco – after you had abandoned your quest for panning gold – were no more than the accepted norm. The fact you did not remain in that city and establish yourself as a major figure on the political scene amazes me. There, you might truly have become evil."

He hung his head in shame, comprehending the idea as a slur on his wickedness.

"That was not what I wanted."

"So, you see; a chance abandoned. Hardly the stuff of penny dreadfuls."

"And in New Orleans?" he prodded, wishing to hear it all.

"I have heard of no perniciousness deeds performed in that city. Being a riverboat gambler was a means of livelihood, not a black mark on your escutcheon."

"Captaining the *Gemini*, then," he tried, kicking his feet to make ripples. She responded by taking the lathered cloth and running it through the spaces between his toes.

"Your dealings, such as they were, were fair. I am hardly in a position to condone you for arms dealing, inasmuch as I, myself, am an arms procurer."

"And John Paul?"

"He is in heaven, praising you to God. I am afraid, sir, that points more toward saintliness than evil."

"He always was a fool."

"Then you are twice one. Give me your other foot."

He obliged, watching her actions with abstracted fascination.

"Then we have come to the War. I was a profiteer." The assertion was bold and challenging.

"Alas, then, Captain Blake, we have come to it." He groaned and averted his head, giving her the opportunity to draw it back, so he could not avoid her stare. "You are not a perfect man. The truth is out. There shall be no walking on water for you, this lifetime."

"But that was... evil."

"It was bad. Again, grant me the difference. You saw the war for what it was: what any war ultimately is. An opportunity to make money. Deny that, if you can."

"But speculating on food –"

"You give yourself too much credit. Your interests were in manufacturing and government contracts. Your 'food speculating,' as you call it, was no more than an arrogant whim, perpetrated in a city ripe for the plucking. Your renown came from blockade running, which, if I may admit as much, I helped you accomplish. If that be evil, then I am equally guilty."

"No, never! You are the epitome of good!"

"In your eyes," Rose conceded, feeling her cheeks grow red. "Which is something I never encouraged. You put me on that pedestal, Rudy; others judge more harshly."

"Show me the man and I will skewer him with a rapier."

For the fact he responded with vigor, thrusting his good right arm in the air, she was grateful. For the rest, she would as leave put it aside. Unlike Rudy, she had no penchant for dwelling in the past. What was done was done and best put aside. For her, if not for him, that was her path for survival.

"I spoke in generalities. I have no specific person in mind."

Flapping the sling the way a crippled bird strove to fly, he shifted positions in the tub, bringing his face close to hers.

"I know you better than that, Rose Bud. You have been hurt and the memory is fresh." Seeing she would not speak, his eyes narrowed. "I hold nothing back from you. Why, then, do you wish to spare me?"

It was an honest question and a fair challenge. He had every right to expect honesty from her. Yet to speak openly was to lose Thomas Mannering's assistance for good and all. Once confessed, he would never be allowed to cross the threshold of the Blake House.

"The servants; they did not approve of me admitting you, a man not my husband, to my bed chamber. I have dealt with it."

"Bloody bastards," he cursed with bitter ire. "Who are they to question their mistress?"

"Or their master?" she quickly added. "For that is your place in his dwelling." Sucking air in between her front teeth, Rose dipped her hand into the water. "People are people. They judge others by their own morality. That it is not ours we must accept."

"I curse them to hell."

"They will not be the last," she suddenly wavered, shivering as though a cat had walked across her grave. "We are not married."

"But we shall be. That I promise. You said," he tried, taking her submerged hand in his, "you would formulate a plan. Within the year. To shed me of that evil temptress –"

"Enough of evil!" Rose cried, extricating herself from his grasp. "I will not have you judge a woman in that manner. If she had made you unhappy, the fault, dear Brutus, is in yourself and not the stars. Call her father evil, if you must: blame Zeus. But do not overlook your own weakness."

"But you promised..." he began, stunned by her vehemence. Cringing away, Rudy bowed his head, shamed and frightened.

"To extricate you from that family. Without violence or bloodshed."

"How, then," came the low whimper.

Throwing back her head, Rose stared defiantly at him. "By employing the 'root of all good,' Master Blake. Surely you, of all men, can comprehend my meaning."

"Money?" he tried, holding out a hand while envisioning a clump of wet, gold coins.

"What else? We have it to burn."

Suddenly retracting his hand as though the imaginary coins were melting through his fingers, Rudy gasped.

"How... much?"

"A king's ransom." But she had had enough of the conversation. One year, minus one day. Time enough, she prayed, to formulate a plan. "Let us put aside unpleasant thoughts."

Wiping away the bubbles in one fell swoop, Rose rinsed his hair, then began work on his right arm. Using a bar of triple-milled, rose-scented soap, she deftly kneaded his wasted muscle, marveling at the latent strength remaining from the ravages of starvation.

This was strength hard earned, not the flash and show of male prowess acquired by birthright. Yet the sinews and fibrous knots were ill-placed and misshapen. His hands appeared too large for his arms, and his legs ridiculously long and ungainly. Rudy's stomach presented a sunken appearance, giving Rose the unpleasant sensation of a grave, where dirt had finally settled, creating a concave, cadaverous appearance.

His eyes, too, had receded into the sockets, making them seem larger and slanted at the corners. His nose, already long and noble, now gave the impression of sharpness and over-length, of being too large for his face, as if he had not quite grown into it.

Gently stooping to kiss the unnaturally curled fingers, Rose sensed pain, yet beneath it, an uncomfortable anger, as though abandoning relaxation was yet another sacrifice he had made to the War.

As his legs shook, Rose worked with additional pressure, massaging away his impatience.

"I won't take much longer, Rudy. This is your first bath. I'm only trying to get off the surface dirt."

"My brain is jumping," he confessed. "It makes my foot and leg jerk; I can't stop it."

"Your leg always jumps when you're tired. Do you remember?"

"No," he admitted miserably. "I don't remember much... of anything."

"It will come back," she assured, believing it implicitly herself. "Has the water gotten too cool?" He debated her question, tried to decide, then helplessly shrugged, unable to make the decision. Rose graciously made it for him. "Let me show you how easy it is to make the water warmer."

Turning one of the taps, a stream of hot water poured from the spigot. Forgetting he had seen her perform such an operation only minutes before, Rudy withdrew from the flow in momentary fright. While such a phenomenon was not new to him, his absence from any form of civilization had woven a tapestry of amnesia through the myriad convolutions of his brain.

As awareness slowly returned, he dared touch the metalwork, staring at the miracle with wondrous delight.

"This is your work, you sorcerer," he intoned with reverence.

Flattered by the compliment, Rose easily admitted her complicity. "Yes; I've improved the system, designed my own type of water heater. It works quite nicely, don't you think?"

"Yes. I do. It is a modern marvel." Drawing nearer the warmth, he savored the temperature before daring to increase the water pressure. "Technology had progressed so fast, Rose. I feel as though I have been awaken from a deep sleep; a trance. Rip Van Winkle. The world has altered while I remained the same."

"It is true," she guardedly admitted. "We live in a time of change. Mechanical innovation I can teach you; political and social changes must be absorbed more carefully."

"Here? In London? I could not bear to think –"

"You are safe here, my love. But that other place.... Even I can only guess what is transpiring. We must take care."

"I shall never go back," came the angry protest as he abruptly turned off the water. "I have witnessed some of your 'change,' but it is not, perhaps, what you imagine. Nor might desire. I thought," he continued, leaning back against her, "the War would destroy the South and all she represented. In that, I was less seer than hopeful man." His face grimaced in distress. "Who would have believed?"

"I would have."

"More the fool, you." Craning his neck to enable him to absorb her face, his teeth bared. "I am a man without a country, Rose. I fit nowhere."

Drawing back, she reached for a towel, then held a finger to her lips.

"You thought that once before, and were wrong. We will speak no more of it. You will go back. Because you must."

"Alone?" came the piteous demand. For that, she had no ready answer. With a sigh, Rose draped the towel over his head. Only when his features were completely obfuscated did she offer a reply.

"Where you go, I shall follow."

Without knowing why, it was an expedition she dreaded more than death.

CHAPTER 26

"Give me your arms."

Rudy complied as though responding to an order. The color of his eyes dulled and Rose could feel his mind shut down the way an engine without proper steam lost the power of forward progression. There had been a time when Captain Blake would have refused compliance for no greater grounds than he was master of all he saw. Adherence to the discipline of army life and the hopelessness of his situation had done more than strip him of rank.

It occurred to her to slap his face; bring back the spark of anger. She did not want a soldier but a feisty devil-may-care officer whose first reaction was to spit rather than obey. That was the man she remembered; the man with whom she had fallen in love. To resurrect the old Rudy Blake, however, would take more than temporary pain. To that, he had become inured. It would require a challenge far greater than that presented by a woman in a bathroom.

"Lift your foot."

This time, he did not move, offering her a spark of hope. It was short lived.

"Which one?"

Tapping him on the side nearest her, he raised his left. Grasping it without further conversation, Rose hoisted the appendage over the side of the tub.

"Lean on me while you bring your other around."

Too many words, too complicated a maneuver. Grimacing from her own doubts, Rose wrapped her arms around his bare chest, hoisting him bodily upward. He tipped, attempted to right himself, then plunged forward. Only her quick step backward and the planting of her own feet against the tile of the floor prevented a total collapse.

"There," she said, steadying them both, then pushing back to straighten him. "You are out. A free man."

For a moment, however brief, that look came back to his eyes and his chin jutted.

"Free?" he demanded, lowering his voice by habit if not remembrance. "Will I ever truly be free?"

Because Rose did not know precisely to what he referred, her answer was succinct.

"Yes."

"And may I hold you to that?"

"If you do not 'hold' me, we shall both fall on our backsides. And that will make a pretty picture."

"But, alas, there is no one here to chronicle it," he joked, startling her more than if they had, indeed, tumbled to the floor. Ruffling his wet hair, she guided him toward a seat.

"I shall do it, myself. For half a crown: and sell it to the London *Times.*"

"How shall you caption it?" he demanded, settling himself down.

"'*Shipwrecked,*'" she promptly supplied. "The edition will sell out faster than hotcakes. In fact, I would go so far as to say they would have to print an extra for overseas sales."

He almost, but not quite, made the connection, compelling him to ask. "Why is that?"

"Every admiral and seafaring dog in the Union Navy will need a copy. Backdating it, of course, to prove they were the one who brought down the infamous Rebel blockade-runner."

"You will not draw me naked?" he cried, easily envisioning the melee.

"If I do, it will give you something in common with another disgraced officer of our acquaintance."

Groaning loudly, he shook his head in protest. "That is not fair, Rose. *He* was drawn with a barrel around his midsection."

"But you are much more handsome. If I am to grow wealthy from these multiple printings, I shall wish to appeal to the ladies, as well as the – gentlemen."

Staring down between his legs, Rudy blushed, the color in his cheeks finally instilling a dash of life to his wan face.

"I am hardly at my best... advantage."

"That, sir," she laughed, squatting down to grasp a foot. "I shall sketch from memory. And dare I say being 'well hung' in the male anatomy category is a sight better than being drawn with hemp around your neck."

"Being hanged, I should at least not be naked." Gripping her shoulder with force, he compelled her to stare up into his distended pupils. "Which edition would sell out faster, Rose? My 'prowess,' or my death?"

The earnestness of his demand was heart rendering, forcing her to choose between a light quip or dire truth. One would prolong the moment, the other dispel it.

"Either would enhance your reputation. But considering the times and the scarcity of good men – as opposed to the likelihood of disposing of 'war criminals' – your state of undress would be far more popular. So much so, I would say, as to require you to go on tour. In a traveling circus."

"As what?"

"As possessor of the world's largest –"

"Stop!" he shouted, drowning out her word in a display of shocked breeding. His protest only occasioned laughter.

"Rudy Blake, you are an impostor!"

"You mean I don't have the world's largest...." He faltered, unable to complete the sentence.

"As to that, I should enjoy being judge. Charging a dime for every man who wished to compare himself to such a – rogue – I would soon find myself in the enviable position of having to establish the Bank of Rose Bud."

"And what interest would you charge?"

"At whatever sum, it would not be equal to the 'interest' you occasion." Noting his expression of hopeful joy, Rose smiled. Flattery and money were the easiest ways to a man's heart. "Although," she continued, sighing with resignation as she grabbed one of his feet and began drying it. "I shall be compelled to charge the ladies two bits – the sum total of twenty-five cents – for the privilege of watching so dramatic and far-reaching a contest."

"Why is that?" he protested, rolling his eyes in pleasure at the gentle, abrasive effect soothed the skin between his toes. "It is so unlike you to place a disproportionate burden on women." If he feared another digression into the subject of "we have all changed," he need not have bothered.

"I am just being practical. Think, my sweet, of the expense. If the admission fee were a nickel or a penny, affording every lady entry, I would have to place you in a monstrously large tent. On a raised podium," she decided, envisioning the scene with pleasure. "It would be jam-packed. Pushing and shoving for the best view. You might even occasion riots, for which I, as your promoter, I would be responsible."

"Do you think so?"

"Oh, most certainly."

Switching to his other foot, Rose was tempted to apply cream to the blistered areas to alleviate his itching, then thought better of it. She possessed no magic potion to cure his throbbing hand, nor immediately relieve the pain from his sores and open wounds. Those, he would have to endure until the healing process was complete.

Itchy feet, however, occasioned the opportunity for instant gratification. Satisfying one discomfort with a vigorous scratch was a form of positive reinforcement. Not only did it offer pleasure, she could use it to take his mind off other, more pressing hurts. Only if it became chronic or began weighing on his mind would she treat it.

She would have to do something about the cracks, however. They were deep-set and would make walking painful. It was not difficult to imagine how he received such wounds, nor the bone bruises and bleeding occasioned from marching and counter-marching.

"I should not like to think the poorer classes were left out of the spectacle, however. Any who present themselves to our ticket-taker without shoes," she continued, wiggling his big toe, "will be afforded a private showing. Does that satisfy your sense of fairness?"

"Yes," came the sad reply. "To be without shoes is a terrible thing. One I brought on myself, Rose."

"Why do you say that?" she whispered, lowering her head to avoid his gaze, for she knew the answer.

"I owned and personally supervised leather goods factories, that is why. I had an eye only for profit, Rose. If the shoes... or the artillery harnesses passed the government's nominal inspection, I sold them at full price. I did not look beyond the almighty dollar."

"Nor did anyone else," she was loath to point out.

"Does that make it right?"

"No. It was a lesson hard-learned. But you were caught up in the temper of the times. Quantity was more important than quality." Swallowing the lump in her throat, Rose finally lifted her head. "It also enabled you to mass produce such items. Ironically, you did some good. Poor shoes and harnesses were better than none. Or do I misstate the situation?"

Groaning under his breath, Rudy found it impossible to answer. His head drooped while his eyes scanned the swollen condition of his lower extremities. When he could read no message of exoneration encapsulated within the red and puffy tissue, he shrugged helplessly, lips trembling.

"I went to war wearing a light jacket and dress shoes, fit for a pleasant ride in the country, not campaigning. I should have known better, but my mind was in a whirl. Although I anticipated – nay, predicted to a week – the fall of Atlanta – without regret, Rose," he added with vinegar, so that his mouth puckered, "I was caught as unprepared as all the other... fools. You were right. I should never have gone there. I was on a... fool's errand. One which could only end in disaster."

"You tried. And for that, if nothing else, I shall always respect you. Your being there was an act of great courage. What you did after was...." She searched for the right word. "Sublime."

Rudy snorted and withdrew his feet, absently running the flat of one foot between his toes on the other.

"Hardly that. I did no good."

It was not a discussion she wished to revive. Nor could she leave it without one offering him one mitigating circumstance.

"I do not think your friend Benjamin Montgomery would agree."

He reacted so violently Rose withdrew from him, studying his angry countenance with a commingling of shock and pity.

"Why do you say his name? What is he to you?" Waving his hand, Rudy attempted to stand, then fell back, unable to flee. "What do you know of him?"

"Only what you told me. That he is a good man. And saved your life."

A wave of dizziness caused Rudy to slump forward. Rose caught him, carefully massaging the back of his neck to assuage the waves of vertigo while warily watching his hands. As he had been unprepared for the fall of Atlanta, so, too, she had failed to discern his sudden suspiciousness.

"Yes. Yes," he mumbled, absorbing both the dizziness and his own doubts with equal disdain. "I'm sorry. I didn't mean to snap at you like that."

"There's no need to apologize. I think I understand," came the thoughtful answer.

"Then tell me," he miserably pleaded. "No matter how it sounded, I don't distrust you."

"No, you don't." Choosing another towel, Rose ran the fabric lightly across his back, noting absently that most of the water droplets had already evaporated or been absorbed into his dry skin. "I could say we need a little time to readjust to one another, and that would be true. But the answer lies deeper than that."

Rudy raised his arms and she wiped beneath them, then changed her mind and offered him the towel, believing that the more he did for himself, the stronger would grow his resolve.

"You've just spent the most difficult, identity-wrenching year of your life. You've learned that in order to survive, you had to use all your wiles. That meant questioning everyone's motives." Rudy dropped the towel in protest, but she replaced it back in his hands before continuing. "I said questioning: not necessarily disobeying. There is a difference."

"But," he tried, wiping his face as a means of hiding. "You are Rose. Rose Theodore." Speaking from beneath the cloth, he finished, "You are, aren't you?"

"None other. I am Rose Theodore. And between us, you need have no fear of betrayal. But you were placed in a position where survival was based on instinct, Rudy, not logic. You learned there was a fine line between friend and foe. Making that distinction kept you alive. I would be the last to condemn."

"But I don't want to feel that way toward you."

"You don't. You spoke without thinking; as a means of protection – for your own feelings and Benjamin's safety. As time passes, your brain will relax and things will be as they were."

"Are you certain?"

"As certain as I am that you will live." Placing a hand on his forehead, she determined the extent of fever, then fussed with his bandage. Noting an area of fresh blood, she rubbed her finger over it then brought it to her lips. The taste was unfamiliar, as though it were not blood at all, but a perverted, watered-down substance, corrupted by infection and an improper balance of chemicals.

Noting her expression, he pulled away, frightened and upset. "What is it?"

Rather than answer, Rose pinched his skin, pointing to how the flesh remained peaked, rather than immediately merging back into his arm.

"Look," she directed. "You are badly dehydrated; in need of fluids. You must drink water and beef tea."

"I prefer Scotch," he pouted.

"No doubt you do," she agreed, offering him a clean pair of drawers. "But I wager that if I put a pitcher of water next to a bottle of fine old bourbon, you would opt for the carafe."

His amazement was satisfaction in itself. "How much will you bet?"

"Inasmuch as I have already given you the answer, nothing. But if it makes you feel better, I will wager ten pounds. But not until you have forgotten the conditions."

Putting his legs through the dual openings, Rudy allowed her to pull the undergarment upward. "I forget easily, don't I?"

"You have a mind sharper than anyone I know. But you are tired, now. A tired man will make mistakes a well-refreshed one would not. When I win my bet, I do not want it said I cheated you."

"I wouldn't mind, if I were in your place," he protested, sucking in his stomach muscles as she tied the strings at his waist. "Winning a bet is all that matters."

Offering him his shirt, Rose wondered if that were so and if he would ever look at gambling the same way again. After coming so close to losing the greatest wager of his life, nothing would ever be a sure bet again.

"Once you are dressed, you can go downstairs and sit by the fire, or I can take you back to bed. What is your pleasure?"

"Neither," came the prompt response as he held his arms out for her to fasten the cuffs. Before her quizzical expression could transform to words, he promptly supplied, "I haven't brushed my teeth. You told me I must perform that operation six times a day and I cannot remember when the last time was. Or am I wrong," he suddenly demurred, ashamed by his failing memory that was not, as she stated, the superior to anyone she knew.

Tapping him lightly on the head, Rose glossed over his unspoken embarrassment.

"You are right. *I* had forgotten. We are, as they say, Captain Blake, both in the same boat. The result of having too much on our minds, as opposed to too little. Slip into your trousers while I draw fresh water into your cup."

"My spitting cup," he happily recalled. "It is not every day a gentleman is invited it spit before a lady."

"Your rinsing cup," came the tart correction. "You will spit, sir, in the sink." Thrilled that he had remembered, Rose quickly prepared the necessary accouterments, handing him a glass, half filled with warm water. "Do you remember what to do, now?"

"I dip my finger in –"

"Yes, that's right," she replied cheerfully, overlapping his sentence. "But first we have to add salt, making a saline solution." He nodded thoughtfully, observing her with eagle eyes as she dropped a generous pinch into the liquid. "Now," she concluded with a flourish, "what is the best instrument with which to stir the contents?"

Rose gave him a moment to consider her lightly-asked question, then reached across his body, grasping his left hand. Deftly maneuvering the digits, she held the pointer out, making sure he registered that information for a later date when his mind was clearer.

"A finger!" he exclaimed with a broad grin. Wiggling it suggestively, the way a child would when contemplating a particularly naughty breach of social etiquette, he dove it into the water. Whirring it around to the accompaniment of his tongue, vibrating against the roof of his mouth, he nodded in satisfaction. "What, next?"

Rather than reply, she pantomimed the action of rubbing his gums. Leaning forward, Rudy carefully observed her technique before attempting it in his own mouth. Although his hand shook from the exertion, his delight in performing so important a technique raised her spirits.

"Again," she urged, motioning that he refresh his finger with solution. He did so, cautiously seeing that no drops spilled onto the floor before reengaging in the cleansing. Three times was all he could perform, but she was well satisfied. "You did wonderfully, Doctor Blake."

He beamed with pleasure at the compliment, reminding her of a time, not so long ago, when she had been the pupil and he the master. They had talked of ordnance, muskets, long arms, gunpowder, ships, seaman's knots and a myriad of topics, now ingrained upon her memory as if she had known them all her life. He had praised her progress then, and those words of kindness had touched her deeply, making the lessons a joy she anticipated with impatience. Enabled now to give back some of his own "medicine," she decided, again, there was no substitute for caring and respect.

"Enough," she declared, gently removing the glass from his hand. "Now, back to bed, I think."

"No," he pouted, licking away the residue of salt water from his lips. "You said I might go downstairs."

"To sit in the den. If that is your wish, we shall go."

Peering at her from under hooded lids, he contemplated the trip. "Is it far?"

"Down the stairs, across the hall and into the den. Forty paces," she calculated.

"And to the bedroom?"

"Ten."

"I might trip," he reneged, growing fearful.

"Yes," she agreed, eying him with playful suspiciousness. "I am sure there has been a time or two in your life when you have fallen down stairs. Not, perhaps, from the effects of salt water, but another form of liquid refreshment, perhaps?"

Her tease eased the awkwardness of his fright. Taking him by the arm, Rose led Rudy out of the necessary and guided him back toward their bedroom. When he was seated on the mattress, she started to draw up the blanket when he stopped her.

"I am not tired. I want to help."

"With what?"

"Your books; or whatever it is you had planned for the day."

Seeing that his eyelids were sinking past the Dardanelles, she nodded wisely, rubbing her hands with exaggerated glee.

"Very well. I planned on doing some reading on the components of blood. Let me take a fresh sample of yours and we will analyze it together."

That served to open his eyes, if not alleviate his weariness.

"Why would you want to do that?" he gasped in what might be construed as horror.

"To cure you."

Waving her off, he attempted to sway her mind. "Surely there must be some other way."

"No scientific method," she decided. "But there may be another way you can assist in my research."

"Anything!"

Retreating to the wardrobe, Rose extracted a small leather pouch. Deftly untying the knot, she returned to the bed, dangling it before his face.

"Open your eyes."

He did so with trepidation. Reaching inside the miner's poke, Rose grabbed a pinch of invisible dust.

"What have you got there?"

"My humble attempt at duplicating the Sandman's magic. It is a sleeping potion. As yet untried," came the cautious warning.

Putting a hand up to stop her, he squinted curiously.

"Where did you get the recipe?"

"Oh. That was the easy part," she dismissed, sprinkling the mixture into his orbs. "I picked his pocket for a handful, then placed the dust under my microscope."

Rudy blinked furiously, then yawned.

"Good for you. I approve." And then, after a second and far mightier yawn, "I would not have thought it possible."

"Anything," Rose avowed with conviction, "is possible for those who believe. And remember," she added, putting the latigo together with her teeth, "A boy who goes to sleep under the influence of the Sandman's dust is allowed only peaceful, quiet dreams."

His lips moved in silent acknowledgment before he dropped backward onto the pillow. In a moment he slept. Kissing her finger then pressing it to his lips, Rose slipped away, content and grateful for the power of magic and two minds supple enough to take faith in its power.

CHAPTER 27

A firm rap on the door of her private study alerted Rose to the fact she was summoned. While half a dozen choices presented themselves, she identified the intruder as D'Artagnan. One knock, short and hard, shielded the veneer of good breeding, but behind it lay concealed an arrogance even she could not fathom.

Some of it was the youth's own fault. Although Rose had no specific knowledge of his background, nor even his proper name, that he came from a moneyed, aristocratic Virginia family she deduced from his dialect and education. Born with Rudy's proverbial silver spoon up his derriere, D'Artagnan had been raised along the Old Ways. Of English stock, he carried with him the superiority of those who had immigrated with the families of George Washington and Thomas Jefferson.

Tutored from childhood, he had undoubtedly attended one of the major Southern universities before facing the grim reality of his position as second or third son. With a name, connections, and a taste for the finer things in life, he had eschewed law or business for risky, albeit more lucrative ventures.

Where Rudy first met him was sheer conjecture. On the riverfront, or while conducting one of his own shady transactions, she supposed. Protestations to the contrary, he would have been drawn to the boy's background. While openly condemning those whose lineage and social upbringing closely resembled his own, he was drawn to it as a moth to open flame. Sensing a streak of dishonesty and a taste for money, he would have seen himself in D'Artagnan's eyes.

Spinning yarns of adventure and greed, it would have been a small matter to bring him under his wing. Exposure to Rudy's fanciful attitude, brash daring and unrivaled success had made a disciple out of the neophyte. The man behind the door, recruited in those early days to crew the *Gemini,* had been an apt pupil.

Along with his new moniker, bestowed upon him by Captain Blake to signify his status as one of the chosen: a musketeer, booty and prosperity eradicated whatever gentleness had once been harbored within his slight frame. D'Artagnan was, for all intent and purposes, Rudy Blake without the sentience. Rose could damn him for it, but not with utter condemnation. He was, after all, only trying to emulate his hero.

The fact D'Artagnan missed the gentle side of Rudy's nature was not surprising. That closely guarded secret was as well protected as the combination to the captain's safe. Rudy wanted his crew to see only his hard exterior: took pains to weave the identity of a world-wise, impenetrable pirate. Money, he preached, was the root of all good. If they believed him, the fault lay in his acting and his own bitter self-deception.

Carefully wiping the pen tip with a piece of cloth, Rose set the instrument between the pages of her book before looking up. She would have preferred to put off this confrontation, but now that is was upon her, there was no delaying the inevitable. How she handled it would determine not only the youth's fate, but his master's, for reinstalling belief in his prowess was the greatest task that lay before her.

The irony was, it was her wish to remake Rudy Blake over in his true image, rather than that of others. She must make D'Artagnan and the rest of his crew who had drifted into her employ travel the same road, without realizing how greatly their destination had altered.

"Come."

The words were spoken with Rudy's authoritative inflection, denoting little tolerance for interruption. Without being the captain of the ship, she must act the part until he was ready to resume command.

Permission granted, the door swung inward, casting a shaft of sunlight from the outer windows. Rose waited until the rays were obliterated by the passage of D'Artagnan's body and the rough sound of wood touching wood to slowly turn her head. Arching an eyebrow, she wordlessly sought the nature of his call.

"Is he here?"

Although she understood to whom the youth referred, "he" was as unacceptable as it was disrespectful.

"He?"

"Rudy." As her eyebrows furrowed, the correction quickly arrived. "Captain Blake."

"Yes." It did not behoove her to explain, but drawing the amenities out was less to her taste.

Sensing failure, D'Artagnan nervously licked his lips, then took a step forward, bowing slightly in the presence of a lady.

"I was hoping to see him. Is he all right?"

"He is not. He has a grievous injury to his hand, as well as other ailments requiring intensive medical care."

To lie would serve no useful purpose, though she would have had it otherwise.

"Is he – going to die?"

An evil smile curled around Rose's lips. "Eventually. As will we all. Yourself included."

Coughing cautiously into his hand, the petitioner retreated.

"I mean... is he going to die now? Soon?"

Moving away from her desk, Rose stared him down with a look even a total stranger could have comprehended as dire warning.

"He is not."

Breathing a sigh of relief, the young man relaxed, arms swinging loosely at his sides. "Good!" She immediately put him back on guard.

"Explain, please, the purpose of your questioning."

The request was a trap into which D'Artagnan plunged, head first.

"Now that he's back, we can buy another ship and do some mercenary work along the South American coast. There's good money in that; and you can supply us with guns," he added magnanimously. "Revolutionaries in those kind of wars aren't as reliable as the Confederate government, but they still pay in gold."

Rose did not have to wonder what Rudy's reaction to such a comment would be. She shook her head, harboring no compunction whatsoever in bursting his bubble.

"I very seriously doubt Captain Blake will have any interest in that sort of 'adventure,'" she warned, taking perverse pleasure in seeing his face fall. Inching nearer, D'Artagnan waved his arm around the room.

"Then what's he doing here?"

"Just possibly," she tartly snapped, "he came to see me. And also, as I have already advised, to recover from the considerable wounds he sustained during the 'Late Unpleasantness.'"

"But if he wasn't shot," D'Artagnan stubbornly protested, "How long can it take him to recover?"

"Shall I 'give it to you' in medical terms?" came the sarcastic inquiry, predicated upon a full understanding he would refuse her offer. In that, she was not disappointed, for he stared down, mutely shaking his head in denial.

"No. What I mean is, when will he be better?"

"You have a timetable to keep?" she demanded, offering a second pitfall for him to avoid or plunge into. He dared grin, arousing her ire.

"Time's wasting; there's money to be made," he bragged in subconscious imitation of his master. "If we don't make it, there are plenty who will."

Rose started at the youthful, boyish face, the unwrinkled countenance, the shining eyes, the slender hands held out, as though ready to seize the moment, and her heart sank. She wondered if Rudy would see the indelible mark he had imprinted on this youth. A scar, as surely as those emblazoned on his chest, encompassing all his lust, impatience and callousness, totally devoid of his humanity, compassion and appreciation for the gentler side of life.

Her question was rhetorical, for she already knew the answer. In defying his own inner goodness, he denied it to his "boys," as well. The result was what she saw before her.

Rose had kept those of Rudy's crew who had drifted back to her. She had employed them, fed and housed them; attempted to reform them into something just slightly better than the larcenous, immoral, selfish men they had become. She thought she had made inroads, but the look in D'Artagnan's face informed her otherwise.

Not all the blame lay at Rudy's feet. No one had told her of his inner self, yet she had spied it the first moment they met. That he was not what he seemed was as evident as his swagger and sparkling grey eyes. The difference between herself and the crew could be summed up in one word. Intent.

While Rose wanted only to help, the others sought to advance themselves.

Squinting up at the first mate, Rose wondered whether the true separation between them stemmed from a more obvious cause: gender.

Being a woman, am I more inclined to nurture? If I were a man, would I have seen through Rudy's disguise? Would I have wanted to link my life to his as a means of advancing us both, or would I have stooped to the degradation of idol worship to benefit my pocketbook?

The answer came so sharply to her consciousness Rose started D'Artagnan by slapping her left hand down against the desk. Fear and dumb curiosity kept him rooted to the spot.

"While I cannot speak for Captain Blake, I will speak for myself. What I have to say is best presented *en masse* – in mass," she translated, failing to disguise the disgust behind the explanation.

"Yes, ma'am," D'Artagnan responded, taking the opportunity to retreat a step. "I know what it means. Shall I gather the crew?"

Smiling at his vanity, she curtly gave permission. "Now. Without delay."

Bringing his hand to his head, the mate acknowledged the order and disappeared. Left to her thoughts, Rose debated the wisdom of her action, then shook away the lingering doubts. Before the "crew" was reunited with their commander, there would have to be a reckoning. Rudy's reformation would be handled in private, over the course of his convalescence. The boys required a more immediate and sterner forum to shatter their expectations.

Getting up to stretch her legs, her mind worked with cold fury on the coming confrontation. She might have made it easier on herself by working in subtleties before Rudy's arrival, but his appearance and weakness had caught her unprepared. It was not the emotion she lacked, but rather the words. Those would have to come on the fly.

As Rudy would say, an officer learned first by observation, then by putting those lessons into practice. In her life, Rose Theodore had been taught by masters.

She heard them first outside the door, whispering among themselves. There was nervousness behind an overriding anticipation. One, she would augment. The other she would shatter. In the coming confrontation, it would be best for all involved if no one forget she possessed the skill of a master marksman.

Although the day was warm, a fire burned in the grate. She had prepared it for Rudy, knowing his thin blood would cause him to shiver with the slightest breeze. Although he had not come down, she had lit the kindling as a reminder of his presence. Pausing to stoke the wood into an engulfing flame, Rose crossed the room, opening the door before any had the chance to knock. Each man backed respectfully away: all but D'Artagnan. He would be the spokesman. As a substitute for Rudy's former mate, the lamented John Paul, he was a poor second. In more ways than either he or Rudy imagined.

"Enter."

They came, one-by-one. D'Artagnan was first, squaring his shoulders with righteous pride in his position. Close on his heels came Jack, the helmsman; Canary, the signalman; Smartmouth, the auctioneer; Forty-Niner, the boy born in 1849; the ever-present BoBo; Copperhead, the red-haired fellow. The stalwart seven. They did not comprise the entire contingent of the *Reprobate,* but these were the most prominent, the favorites.

Most had been with Rudy when he captained the *Gemini,* years before the War. These were the ones who knew John Paul, formally known as "David." While none, to her certain knowledge, originated from New Orleans, home port of the jointly-owned ship, all had spent considerably more time with the captain than had Rose. It was ironic, then, she knew him best.

But not, she intoned silently to the invisible master, *surprising.*

She would have sold the lot of them for a handful of figs.

That she could not was a double-edged sword. These men were tied to Rudy by bonds greater than any of them knew. To dismiss even one would be to cut a heart string.

Something even the late, lamented Ringo, would have to agree.

It was her prerogative to sit, but she did not choose to take advantage. She would address them standing, using her superior height to carry home what emphasis did not.

Physical domination she had learned, long before any of them had come into her life, was an asset never to be ignored.

"As all of you know, Captain Blake has returned." Pausing while they exchanged glances, she allowed them a moment of jubilation before continuing. "As I explained to Mr. D'Artagnan, he is suffering from a grievous wound to a finger on his left hand. A splinter of metal lodged beneath the nail, causing massive infection. He is also suffering from loss of blood, which has caused generalized weakness."

Walking counter-clockwise, Rose began a circuit of the room, hands behind her back. Those she approached too near immediately stepped aside, avoiding confrontation.

"Dr. Mannering, the local surgeon, whom you all know from his regular visits to the Blake House, is of the opinion Rudy's injuries are life-threatening. He suggested the finger be amputated."

BoBo crossed himself with the intensity, but not the piety of his master. The rest, less inclined toward outward manifestations, hung their heads or stared upward, through the ceiling.

It was Jack who dared step forward. Clutching his empty hands before him in the attitude of one with bared head, seeking penance, he pleaded for himself, as well as the others.

"You don't believe that. You won't allow it."

In lieu of D'Artagnan, who inexplicably remained mute, Rose should have expected Jack to be the spokesman. What she had not anticipated was the dire certainty in his voice. In another, she would have interpreted it as respect and realized, to her shock, it was both.

Recovering slowly, it was Rose who backed down. Not emotionally, but physically. His close proximity to her, radiating the type of belief she had seen offered to only one other in her lifetime, gave her pause. Preparing herself for battle, she had overlooked faith.

Resuming her walk, this time clockwise, her mind whirled over the altered situation. It was not possible she had misinterpreted D'Artagnan. Nor BoBo. Canary, Smartmouth, Copperhead and Forty-Niner could be expected to follow their lead. Unless, she realized, with a start, one amongst them took an opposing position. Forced to choose between two warring factions, which way would they go? She was no longer certain.

Was Jack strong enough to bring them to his side? And if so, why had he cast his lot with her? Because he felt she could restore Rudy to his former self, or for a purer motive?

She longed for Rudy's consultation. He would know. Or would he? Watching surreptitiously from the corners of her eyes, Rose suddenly doubted that he would. Between the two, her judgment in human nature was more astute than his.

Unconsciously squaring her shoulders, Rose completed her course before crossing to the hearth. Placing her back toward the radiating warmth, she reassessed, never suspecting this was her first council of war.

CHAPTER 28

"No, Jack," Rose began, choosing to address the speaker directly. "I did not permit Dr. Mannering to perform the operation." His chin jutted out, silently confirming his opinion. "What we did was remove the fingernail, extract the splinter and scrape the bone. I have medicine of my own, which I placed over the wound."

"Good." He unclasped his hands, dropping them to his side. The action offered her the impetus to continue.

"Exposure, malnutrition and fever has weakened his constitution. His mind will require time to heal. He has seen much atrocity; marched through hell. Those deeds and images are not easily set aside."

"He did," Jack hesitantly began, meeting her gaze with unwavering conviction, "what none of us had the heart to do." Turning to his companions, the third mate addressed them with a guilt so suddenly upon him, the words nearly choked him. Stumbling over the first word for reasons Rose did not comprehend, he stated, "We are all – Southerners – yet we viewed the War from a distance. We took risks but for other reasons."

"Rudy always said the War was for making money," BoBo tried, running the back of his thumbnail across his cheek.

"And so it turned out to be. For us. We made our fortunes and were content to let it stand at that. I am not judging you," Jack pursued, color rising into his cheeks. "I could have joined and I didn't. I did not see that as my... place." Shamed by the confession, he tapped his forehead. "Rudy saw differently. He was in Atlanta. The city fell around his feet. People were burned out of their homes; herded outside like cattle. He did what a brave man would do. He offered himself. Not for the Cause, but for his homeland."

A staggering pronouncement. Feeling the heat of the fire too hot to bear, Rose instinctively moved away. Unleased by her removal, a cascade of warm air filled the room.

Forty-Niner, the youngest of the assemblage, reached out a hand, resting it on Jack's arm.

"He was brave, wasn't he?"

"You know he was."

"But why," he pleaded, as only a boy could, "did we lose?"

It was Rose's turn to answer. Her smile was one of acknowledgment for innocence, rather than ignorance.

"Rudy did not join the Confederate Army to help it win," she replied, moving her head from one to the other, so as to make eye contact. "There must be no misunderstanding his motives. Even if he," she decided, working out the problem in her mind, "was unclear."

She was not tired, but suddenly her chair beckoned. Lightly descending onto the seat, she placed her arms on the rests, palms downward.

"He fought against unwarranted aggression. For a people, like he, who were downtrodden and defeated."

"But he always said," D'Artagnan protested, shoving his way forward, "Never play a game you cannot win."

She was ready for him. Her smile curled into an expression of derision.

"But you mistake, Mr. D'Artagnan. Both of the 'game,' and the outcome. Shall I tell you?"

Six pair of eyes turned to the first officer. Suddenly uncomfortable, yet not ready to admit defeat, he nodded. "Yes. Tell all of us."

It was a challenge. The first shot of a dual. *Rudy,* she thought, *would appreciate the similarity to another duel.* In this one, too, he would emerge the victor. Yet like that other contest on the Field of Mars, it would not be without cost.

"The game was not about winning. It was played for honor. Duty. An acknowledgment of his place in the world – as a gentleman."

"What did he 'win'?"

"The lives of Southern soldiers." Memories of a boy she had never known washed over her. "Friendship. Camaraderie. Faith in himself."

"Distinction?" Copperhead whispered, shifting his gaze to the fire so as to avoid her eyes.

"That, too. Great distinction."

Because she did not have specifics, Rose spoke from her own faith. *Details,* she wryly decided, *to follow.*

"Was he promoted? Made a major or a colonel?"

It was a boy's question, a yearning to have his hero acknowledged in the eyes of others. She would have to be careful how she answered, for their expectations were not hers.

Drawing the French knots of Confederate rank up her sleeve, Rose closed her eyes, summoning a consciousness of memory she did not know she possessed until that moment.

"There is only one rank to which Rudy ever aspired: that of sea captain. Who here would dare disagree he is the greatest in his chosen profession?"

D'Artagnan, who might have seen through her diversion, was shouted down before he spoke a word.

"Hurrah for Rudy Blake!"

"Three cheers for the captain!"

Waving their arms and stomping their feet, the crew paraded around the room in joyous good spirits. Rose let them have the moment before bringing it to a cautious halt.

"Gentleman: the times are not what they were. Priorities change. What Captain Blake will, or will not do, depends on circumstance. He needs time to heal." Turning so that she faced D'Artagnan, Rose leaned forward to emphasize, what to him, alone, was a warning. "I cannot rush the process, nor shall I do anything to risk his well-being."

Signaling out the mate, Rose indicated the door with a casual sweep.

"If any of you have come here, waiting the moment Rudy will charge off into the fray of gunrunning or mercenary work, I tell you now: you have deceived yourself. That *he and I* will seek high adventure you may presume. Whether any of you are invited to participate will depend entirely on yourselves."

A bubble of sap burst in the fire, hurtling thousands of minute sparks across the rug. Gliding toward a particularly large ember, Rose suspended her foot over it, letting the significance of her action burn into their minds, then savagely crushed the orange glow into black ash.

"Conduct yourself with decorum and integrity." She did not see him flinch, but felt D'Artagnan's skin crawl. Singling him out, Rose was tempted to wrap her hands around his neck and squeeze the life out of his body. The action would have suited her present mood but not her temperament. Instead, she reached out, placing a hand on his shoulder. While the touch was light, he sank beneath it.

"Those are the watchwords, gentlemen. Mark them well."

Struggling from beneath her arm, the ranking officer distanced himself, his face a contortion of anger and confusion.

"So you say," he began. Despite his resolve, his lower lip trembled. "Where does Rudy stand? Has war made him righteous?"

It was a stunning condemnation of the man she loved. A man who had played his cards too well; etched his image of *reprobate* into the very souls of those who chose him as their stone god.

She could not blame D'Artagnan and yet she did. Like the fish which had swallowed the hook, he had entangled himself on the line. Her choice was to cut him free or allow him to work his own way out of the trap.

Blinking twice then reattaching herself to him, Rose softened the inflection of her voice.

"I remember a time, sir, when you posted a letter for me – against Captain Blake's express wish. For that deed, you were unfairly punished. Do you recall such an action?"

"I do," he admitted, swallowing nervously, for unlike Rose, he saw no chance of freeing himself.

"I respected you for that. But now I must ask: why did you do it? Because you knew what I requested was right? Or merely from a sense of... disobedience? Were you a man on a mission, or a boy, defying the will of his elder?"

With his mouth hung open, the youth struggled for an answer and could not find one.

"I don't know."

Rose surprised him by smiling.

"A fair and honest answer, which I accept." As the moment of confrontation passed, the crew shifted positions, breathing easier. Jack leaned against the back of Rose's chair, while Canary and Smartmouth rubbed shoulders, seeking tactile reassurance from one another. BoBo, separated from the rest, stooped down to wipe away the soot from a spot on the carpet.

"I reiterate. The times are not what they were. Which does not mean there is no adventure or... money-making schemes in which to participate. Those who can bide their time, and are willing to see what the future brings, may stay. There is work enough for you. If there are among you individuals who wish to strike out on their own, I invite you to do so. Now. You have heard my terms. They are irresolute. This, gentlemen, I speak in Rudy's name."

"You have more to say?" Smartmouth inquired, braving the silence to nod upward, in the direction of Rudy and Rose's shared bedroom.

Crossing to the window, Rose opened it, filling her lungs with the sharp morning air. Though the sea was far distant, a reminiscence of another room, filled with salt air, and a council of war, not her own, filled her mind.

"Two years and three months ago, Captain Blake made me an offer, inviting me to join his crew. When the question of my acceptance was put to the vote, all of you here had the opportunity to say nay. You did not, for reasons only partially understood by me. Since that time, I have given the matter considerable rumination." Pausing to observe how the breeze ruffled the curtain, Rose drew strength from the ocean, which lay far beyond. "You thought to replace another in Rudy's heart by his attraction to me. I was the woman of the world – she, who understood men and money. The other was childlike... and childish, preferring dolls, as I recall the verbal report, over *her husband.* Am I correct, Mr. D'Artagnan?"

Slapping one hand over the back of another, in the attitude of one who thought to catch a fly, D'Artagnan pressed flesh to flesh until his knuckles whitened. Whatever his actual thoughts were, he responded, "Yes, ma'am."

"'Miss Elspeth,' as we shall call her, was, in your minds, distracting Rudy from his true responsibility – that of making money for his crew. And incidentally for himself," she bitterly added. Raising her hands, which were free from encumbrance, Rose settled back in her chair. "In my 'book,' gentlemen, that is a selfish perspective." Challenging D'Artagnan, she asked, "Who would care to comment?"

Massaging the junction between hand and forearm, the first officer hesitated, then slowly peered under his fingers. The fly, if there had been one, escaped.

"Rudy always said the War was for making money. As much and as fast as possible, for it wouldn't last forever."

"Ah," she sighed, turning her attention to BoBo. "So we have heard. "And you believed him?"

"Why not?" The answer was so forthright, she was compelled to smile. The expression, however, lacked good will.

"So. There is nothing, in your mind, more valuable than the pursuit of wealth? I will answer that for you," Rose continued, leaning forward. "No. There is not. And that, Mr. D'Artagnan, is a sin."

Flushing madly, the boy shot out a hand, pointing it at Rose. "It's what 'Captain Blake' preached," he accused, pouting like a child. "It was he who gave the order to shoot Ringo. Not me."

Settling back, then crossing her legs, Rose appeared royalty before swine.

"And yet it was you who carried out the deed. You, who shot your best friend in the back of the head."

"Yes," he sobbed, suddenly overcome by emotion. "He made me do it."

"And you resent him for it?"

"Yes!"

"So you do have some values, sir. You are capable of making moral judgments. But tell us. Why did you obey?"

Startled by the unexpected turn in the conversation, D'Artagnan shifted his weight, staring from one to the other of the assembled crew.

"Because Rudy ordered me to. Because Ringo had betrayed him."

"And so he had," Rose approved. "But he never followed you; never sent BoBo or Jack or Canary to spy on you. You might have spared your best friend, but you did not. Why, D'Artagnan, did you obey such an order against your heart?"

His mouth agape, the man tried to summon forth an explanation satisfactory to himself and Rose. His reply was a long time coming.

"Because you said so. Because Ringo had betrayed him; followed him in secret."

"No," came the solemn correction. "Betrayal was your word, not mine. Although, I would not disagree," she added, rocking slowly. "Yet you might have let him live. Beyond the warehouse, in back of a stand of trees, by yourselves, no one would have been the wiser. 'Go,' you might have said. 'Run for your life. Go away. Disappear. Never show your face again.' But you did not. You.... What did you do? Tell us. We have all wondered."

Sucking air between his teeth, BoBo distanced himself from his friend, but never took his eyes from his face. Jack moved toward Rose, hands stuffed into trouser pockets. Smartmouth coughed, then rolled his eyes.

"Yes. Tell us."

"Why? Why do you want to know?" D'Artagnan screamed, dashing toward the door, then halting a foot from his obstacle of escape. "This isn't fair! I don't want to say!" Jumping straight up, he shivered. "Rudy made me do it! Your Rudy!" he accused, shaking his head as perspiration rolled down his brow.

"Rudy gave you the order. You obeyed. Was it from fear, D'Artagnan?" she asked, leaning forward, eyes bright with the intensity of the moment. "Did you believe if you let Ringo go, Captain Blake would find out and have you shot, instead? No," she answered her own question. "While that idea might have passed through your mind, that was not the reason. Explain, please."

"I don't know," he pleaded, cupping his hands together. "Please. Let it drop."

"I am afraid I cannot," Rose apologized with a tenderness none of them expected. Rising to her feet, she left the comfort of the chair to stand alone. "Were you frightened that Captain Blake would know of your hesitancy and dismiss you? Consider you a coward and ban you from his crew? What would that mean, D'Artagnan?" she continued, walking forward. The crew parted, letting her pass unmolested. "A loss of status? A missed opportunity for making money?"

"No! It wasn't that, either!" he wailed, spittle flying from his lips. As she continued to approach, he held out his hands, hoping to keep her back.

"No. It wasn't any of those things." She had finally reached the point of her lesson. The teacher in Rose Theodore steadied herself for the hardest taught exercise of her career. "You shot him because Ringo had done something terribly wrong. He had – betrayed – the faith Captain Blake held in him. In all of you." Turning to face the crew, this time from an opposite perspective, Rose met their pained eyes with steadfast resolution. "Amongst a working, cohesive crew, there is no greater crime than treachery. Fear, even cowardice may be overlooked, but not the willful act of unfaithfulness. That is the severing of a bond so absolute, only death may remedy. You understood that, Mr. D'Artagnan, and acted accordingly. I do not condemn you."

"Then why," he faltered, eyes misty, nose watering with tortured guilt, "do you bring this up now?"

"To make a point." Motioning he move away from the door, Rose placed herself between the men and their egress. "On values. And judgment. On what is the ultimate purpose in our existence."

"Tell us," Forty-Niner whimpered, crossing his boy's arms around his chest. Jack put a hand on his shoulder, drawing him closer.

"You killed a man in cold blood – I will not say 'murdered,' for your act was the administration of justice. You killed a man because he placed money above honor. Ringo was suspicious and greedy. He saw cross-purposes in Rudy's actions, rather than avarice. That, he could not tolerate. Nothing must be allowed to stand in the way of making money, that holiest of all possessions. He clandestinely followed him, hoping to discover, and ultimately reveal, the cause of his wavering from duty."

Copying Jack's example, Rose placed her hand on D'Artagnan's shoulder. To his credit, the boy did not flinch.

"All of you understood Ringo's motive. You knew of it because he told you. That none of you prohibited him is a mark against you. But let that stand. When called upon to pass judgment, you sided with morality, rather than evil. You abandoned money for justice."

Squeezing D'Artagnan's shoulder, Rose moved away, walking toward the open window. All eyes followed her. mute with expectation.

"All of you have been put through the fire; all of you understood what was at stake. There are values in this world more important than wealth. I understand that. Rudy understands that. Perhaps he does not have the ability to express such noble sentiments in words, but you must look to his actions.

"Why," she continued, parting the curtain to reveal the expanse beyond, "did he, of all gunrunners, refuse to arm his ship? Because such armament took space away from precious cargo?" Her lips curled in derision. "You know better than that."

"Why, then?" Canary whispered, his stare fixed on the rolling landscape revealed through the panes of glass.

"Because he is not a murderer. How many times did you hear him say, 'This is not my war'? He did not wish to kill in the name of the Cause – or of plunder. He opted for daring – for adventure – rather than taking the chance of destroying what, to him, was innocent life. Rudy Blake was playing a contest of wits, gentleman, not war. Had none of you guessed?"

"No," Jack confessed, hanging his head.

"Then think of it now. Despite his wild protestations, Rudy Blake does not worship money. While he may sometimes be confused on that point," she continued, shaking her head in soft negation, "there is a... line in the sand... he will not cross. Life has been cruel to Rudy; it has beaten him down, but he has risen from the ashes." Indicating the fire, which radiated with red-hot embers, Rose nodded. "Given a choice between right and wrong, he will choose to stand on the side of righteousness. That," she sighed, warring between weariness and exultation, "is why he went to war. Not to defend a way of life, or a Cause, or to amass glory. To protect a land and a people defeated by the insane greed and aggression of their leaders. Now," she pursued, moving to the hearth and grasping the poker in her left hand, "that war is over. Rudy has done his duty. He has come back. He is not the man he was; he never was the man you thought him to be. That he is far greater I pray you will discover."

Stirring the nearly consumed logs, Rose watched as latent flames, given new life by her action, rose to prominence. The heat seared her cheeks, scorching them a beet red.

"You have heard what I have to say, gentleman. Make your own decisions. Accept Rudy as he is and as he will be, or pack your bags and leave. There is no place in this – crew – for betrayers. One week," she added, propping the poker against the brick before turning to face her rapt audience. "Meet him: speak with him. I will not prohibit you. I have done what I can to protect. The rest is up to you – as individuals. If you find him too unlike that godlike image you created, I adjure you to bow out. Gracefully, as befits men who served under the Skull and Crossbones."

It was Jack who moved first. Gliding gracefully toward Rose, he guided her toward her chair, seeing that she was properly seated before turning to the others. Without a word, he indicated the door. Forty-Niner, the sixteen-year-old man, scurried to open it. BoBo was the first to leave. Canary and Smartmouth followed, then Copperhead, Jack and D'Artagnan. The crewman, who was not nicknamed for the gold rush where a prospector named Rudy Blake discovered no gold, was the last to depart.

Rose Theodore had given them one week. She had offered Rudy one year, minus a day. The clock was ticking.

Like war, time was a both friend and enemy.

CHAPTER 29

Returning to her pursuits, Rose found she could not concentrate. The words on the page blurred, further increasing her irritation. With an annoyed snap of the wrist, she closed the book, then bundled it together with pen and paper. Escaping through the side door, she stepped outside, her study material clasped firmly to her chest.

The air was warm and humid, yet it felt cool to her after the stifling heat of the fire. Pausing a moment to draw in a heavily scented breath of air, she identified a mixed perfusion of roses and wild grasses. Her gardens were not the typical mix of English flowers, planted along well-cultivated rows, but rather an abandonment of order in lieu of color and scent. Cobbled paths led around the property, emboldening a curious wanderer with a mixture of awe and disbelief.

It was her faerie garden, sprinkled throughout with mints and herbs, berry bushes and miniature shrubs. A wee elf, on his journey to collect exactly the right mixture of leaves and fruits with which to make wine, could not discover a more pleasant and successful place to gather.

This was Rose's Eden, her garden of peace. Yet it would mean nothing if Rudy were not there to share it. Tugging listlessly on her blouse, then blowing across her exposed skin to cool her overheated flesh, she crept quietly, like a mouse surveying its kingdom, toward the rear of the house. Disengaging the lock, she let herself into the greenhouse, shutting the door behind her to bar intruders from the sanctuary.

No one but Mrs. Tompkins and Mr. Mannering had ever been invited inside. Of the two, only one would be welcome again. It was not a depressing thought, but one of resignation. Like Rudy Blake, Rose Theodore did not belong to the world of polite society and gentle manners. They were outcasts, as atypical to drawing rooms and family gatherings as weeds were to civilized bouquets.

While either could function within the realm of silver plate and fancy balls, their true nature lay among meadows covered with dancing bluebells and bowing buttercups, crashing, white capped waves, salt-sea air and smoke-filled parlors, alive with the clink of whisky glasses, the riffling of cards and sundry, backroom deals.

Life was adventure, spiced with mischief. It was challenge and fair play, double-dealing and righting wrongs. It was not meant to be spent, but enjoyed, and the greenhouse was part of that existence, a hideaway, a tarrying point between galloping chases and fast getaways.

It was one side of their multi-faceted personality. At the moment, it served double-duty as her study.

Sweeping away a cluster of papers and horticultural books, Rose settled down at the rough wooden table, her pen dangling between her lips the way Rudy held his pipe. Sucking inward, imbibing the flavor of his tobacco, so well ingrained in memory, she continued her pursuit.

"BLOOD," she began, reading aloud from the lexicon. It was a habit she had developed at an early age, always cognizant of the fact someone, somewhere, was listening. It had taken her over twenty years to put a face and a name to one listener. The others, she suspected, preferred to hide behind a cloak of mythology, some temporal, others spiritual.

Together with the first and most significant, they would solve the mystery of blood poisoning and make him well.

"'*Sanguis.* A red homogeneous fluid, of a saltish taste, and somewhat urinous smell, and glutinous consistence, which circulated in the cavities of the heart, arteries and veins. The quantity is estimated to be about twenty-eight pounds in an adult; of this, four parts are contained in the veins and a fifth in the arteries. The blood is the most important fluid of our body. Some physicians and anatomists have considered it as alive, and have found many ingenious hypotheses in support of its vitality.'"

Deftly removing the pen from her mouth, Rose inspected the point the way Rudy often fussed with his briar, before dipping it in his tobacco pouch. Mimicking his action, she dipped her pen in ink, carefully underlining several key words, consciously disregarding the rest as she resumed her recitation.

"'The *cruor,* or clot of the blood is essentially formed of fibrin, and coloring matter. In distillation it gives out a great deal of carbonate of ammonia, and a vast quantity of carbon, the ashes of which contain much phosphate of lime, a little phosphate of magnesia, carbonate of lime, and carbonate of soda. A hundred parts of fibrin are composed of: carbon 53.360; oxygen 19.685; hydrogen 7.021 and azote 19.934.'"

Looking up, the pen suspended between page and chin, she shook her head with bemused wisdom.

"Sounds more like the components of gunpowder, Rudy," she remarked to her sleeping companion. "If you had only known, you might have suggested a way to extract that vital commodity to the Confederate high command. Blood was one item they had in plentiful supply."

Grimacing at her own joke, she returned to the text, scanning the small print with an eagle eye for a modicum of useful information.

"'It is of importance to remark, than in none of the parts of the blood are any gelatine or phosphate of iron found, as was at first supposed.'"

Slapping her hand down, a drop of ink dripped onto the paper, slowly absorbing into the fibers. Rolling her eyes in disgust, she dusted the irregularly shaped mark with sand, then glanced upward, through the ceiling.

"'Blood-black ink,' I believe you once called it, Captain Blake. I see now, you were not far off the mark. You have missed your calling. The medical profession is filled with ignoramuses!"

Her immediate chuckle served to lighten her anger, as she responded to his silent protest.

"Yes, I suppose I am calling you an idiot. But you are exonerated, sir, inasmuch as you have never professed to actually lecture on the components and usefulness of blood. This man," she continued with scorn, flipping to the title page and reading the name, "'Robert Hooper, M.D., F.L.S.,' is not only twice an idiot, he is dangerous. *Lexicon Medicum* is more black magic than science. Good Lord. You would suppose that in 1842, 'Harper & Brothers' could have found better material to print."

Scanning the four-point text, her nose curled in derision. "Also by Samuel Akerly, M.D., formally physician to the New-York City Dispensary, Resident physician to the City Hospital, late Hospital Surgeon to the United States' Army, Physician to the New-York Institution for the Instruction of the Deaf and Dumb, &c. &c."

Repeating "Late Hospital Surgeon to the United States' Army," Rose shuddered and resumed her place under the "B's," with a *sotto voce* remark that it was just as well Rudy had not joined the Federal service, for he would have been no better cared for.

"'The importance of the blood is very considerable; it distends the cavities of the heart and blood vessels, and prevents them from collapsing; it stimulates to contraction the cavities of the heart and vessels, by which means the circulation of the blood is performed; it generates within itself animal heat, which it propagates throughout the body; and lastly, it is that source from which every secretion of the body is separated.'"

Closing the hard-covered book, Rose scanned her greenhouse, finally discovering that which she sought. Grasping the tome with two hands, as befit its prodigious weight, if not its import, she deftly raised a flower pot, depositing the book beneath.

"Now, you serve a useful purpose: 'enlightening' my plant, which is struggling for sun. I will read no more today."

Rubbing her red-rimmed, bleary eyes, occasioned by lack of sleep, rather than the study she had anticipated, Rose sensed a restlessness growing within. Shackled by misinformation, her mind sought release. With a resoluteness born of desperation, she abruptly crossed the room, seeking refuge from an old friend.

Reverently removing the chamois cover, sewn with her own hand to protect that which lay beneath, she revealed what Rudy had once described as "one month's wages" – her microscope. Hefting it carefully by the curved brass frame, she carried it toward a small, round table, set by the window. Shoving aside a series of slides made from smears of Rudy's blood, she selected an unused rectangle of thin, polished glass.

With a penknife from her pocket, Rose pricked the tip of her own finger, waiting until a tiny bubble of red fluid had pooled before rubbing it across the surface. The answers she sought would be contained within a comparison between the life fluid of a feverish man and a healthy woman.

Minutely redirecting the polished mirror to catch the rays of the sun, she devoted herself to sketching a world hidden from the naked eye.

Working with a pencil, side ruler and calipers, she copied the miniscule circular shapes, pausing only to move the mirror or the microscope for better light, as the great outside orb worked its way across the horizon. Lost in concentration, she did not hear the door open.

Clearing her throat in a masculine way of announcing herself that she had developed from her mistress, Hanna Tompkins made known her presence so as not to startle.

"I thought you might like some coffee, Miss Theodore."

Given permission to address her employer by her first name was a privilege the servant seldom employed, and never upon announcing herself. Familiarity was not her place, and while invited to step beyond her role, she never did so without cause.

Glancing up from her work, Rose's eye fell on the pocket watch she had suspended from a nail by the window.

"So late. I hadn't realized."

"Aye. Lost in your research, time has got the better of you," came the calculatingly droll response as Hanna officiously cleared a place for her tray. "Schillings to pounds, that watch hasn't been wound in a fortnight."

Her intent, however accurate, was not meant to make Rose smile, but rather to draw her cautiously from her work. The ploy succeeded, for Rose lay down the writing instrument in exchange for the timepiece. Putting it to her ear, she listened in vain for the telltale ticking.

"I see that you are correct. You might have wound it for me, or at least made note," came the chipped response, "inasmuch as you have had 'two weeks' to correct my error."

"Oh, no, madam," she demurred, forming a grimace to her face which did manage to elicit a grin. "I'll not be touching any of your confounded instruments in here. Not after what I've seen. There's things alive in here what only God, Hisself, and His appointed advocates are privy to know." Removing the green and white-striped covering from over the tray, she absurdly wiped her hands. "I don't want inny of 'em jumpin' out at me."

"You've a stronger stomach than that," Rose countered, pointing toward a plate of cheese and crackers. "It hasn't kept you away from dining on that very substance I showed you under the microscope."

"You mistake, mistress. The cheese is for you to eat. As for me, I've 'eliminated from me diet' that which is crawling with... bugs."

"That is a falsehood and you know it. I have seen you eat cheese pie a dozen times since I showed you the components of dairy products."

It was a game they played; one which bonded them together as two individuals cut from an uncommon cloth. No other of Rose's acquaintance, when shown the living organisms of cheese, would ever sup again on such lively fare.

Hanna Tompkins was her treasure and her friend. Two commodities rarely found among those walking upright on two legs and claiming to have descended from the Creator's loving hand.

As a stalwart companion, Rose would have chosen her above any of Rudy's crew.

"You'll have to drink yer beverage from a chipped mug, I'm afeared, and you've no one to blame but yerself," Hanna fussed, sweeping her arm across the room. "You've turned this... laboratory... into an island of castoffs."

Quietly suppressing a shudder of acknowledgement, not at the vast array of abandoned and forgotten cups, glasses and mugs, but at the unintentional reference to a sanctuary of misfits, she put on her blandest expression.

"Why, whatever do you mean?"

Elevating the contest to a new height and thus, she hoped, setting her mistress on a course well defensible, Hanna singled out one of the many shelves. Marching forward with matronly contempt, her own jaw jutting with superiority, she struck the first blow.

"Let us take an accounting. Here we have," she continued, lifting up a pitcher, "last month's lemonade. Grrowing, I might add, a multitude of wee beasties to put a righteous head of cheese to shame."

"Let me see that," Rose demanded, snatching the vessel from willing hands. Peering inside, the lady of the house readily confirmed the diagnosis.

"Mold."

"Disgusting, is what it tis," issued forth the declaration. "Enough to put a good housekeeper to shame. And this – count them, Miss Rrrose. One, two, three, six, seven, two hundred and forty eight drrrinking vessels, wid more o' the same inside them. Is it any wonder I'm forced to serve you with cracked china?"

"Indeed. Very careless of you to leave so many undisturbed for so long a time."

Throwing up her hands, while incidentally thrusting several of the mugs into Rose's hands, Mrs. Tompkins continued her management inspection.

"And what," she shrieked, "do you call that?"

Following the direction, Rose calmly identified the object.

"My good madam, it is a candleholder."

"Candle holder, is it?" snapped the rebuttal, as grasping fingers clutched to themselves a wine bottle, strewn with layer upon layer of melted wax. "From the French Revolution, I've no doubt. Patriotic colors, have we? Red, blue, white, an' green for Ireland, on top o' the mix. Next, you'll be knitting a cap to keep the flame warm!"

"Before I chop off its head," came the cheerful response as Rose grasped the bottle, adding it to her collection. "What else offends your sense of propriety?"

"Never say you didna ask, for I've a list as long as yer arm!" Highlighting her varied dialects came a cry of discovery as sharp as a pencil point. "Drrried leaves, hangin' like condemned men an' not a one fit to consume. You might as well make good use as bad with all these – specimens – but, nooo, they're for 'experimental purposes,' only. Not a sprig o' parsley or bundle o' thyme in the lot."

Affixing her gaze on the ceiling, Rose counted twelve such lines, strung from the four corners of the room, each filled with plants in various stages of drying. She might have pointed out that more than half the "specimens" were fated for the pantry, but did not. Convinced Hanna's eye was as astute as any shopkeepers, there was little use delineating the names of eatable herbs with which they were both familiar.

"An' what's this, now?" Marching with the practiced easy of a general inspecting troops, the servant, hands on hips, surveyed what might have been, if property cleaned and polished, a dining room table. Atop it were clustered an assortment of apothecary bottles and jars, some corked and tired with string, others sealed with cherry-red wax. Displayed without obvious order, taller in front of shorter, fine, tinted, Spanish-blown glass with bas-relief vines and grapes, side-by-side with murky, bubble-infused jars, the whole resembled a deranged tinker's stall.

Eschewing that for another shelf, Hanna's nose curled in obvious distaste at the assortment of instruments displayed for ease and frequency of use.

"If you were a butcher, I'd say 'have at it, misses,' but you're no but what we call a 'scientist.'"

"A scientist?" Rose questioned, drawing nearer to observe her own well-beloved tools. "And where, pray tell, did you come by that word?"

Snapping around so that the hems of her skirt flayed around Rose's ankles, squinted eyes proceeded the pronouncement.

"On me father's knee, if you're a mind to be haughty about it, Miss Theodore. Well I can remember him saying to me as a lass, 'Beware of bad men, for they'll steal your purse or take your heart. An' avoid those who wear the black, for behind that dress may lurk the devil. But worse of all," she whispered, lowering her voice while bringing her lips toward Rose's offered ear, "are the *scientists.*

"'What are those?' I asked in me innocence, an' he responded wid a shiver an' a finger to his lips, 'They be the ones who discover things. Like as not they view the body naked, with an eye toward cuttin' to see what makes 'em tick, rather than fer throwin' 'em in the pot fer Sunday supper!'"

"A wise man," Rose observed, deftly ducking as a dried bouquet of parsley was plucked from overhead and thrown at her. "But what, madam, is your point?"

"Aye, dinna you know we're short a good roast fer supper, an' I've come to offer me services, should you care to 'operate' on one of them 'boys' who hangs around and does not have the wherewithal to sing fer his porridge."

They had come to the "point," and the gratitude which welled in Rose's heart was second only to the affection she felt for the woman, retained, at Rudy's behest, as her chaperone. Hanna Tompkins had been the first person Rose ever hired and were she to hire one thousand more, none would ever equal this faithful servant.

As the smile faded from her lips, her head bowed in reflection.

"I thank you."

Dutifully retrieving the parsley and restringing it exactly where she plucked it, Hanna made a small curtsy, then pointed toward the tray she had brought.

"Drink your coffee while it's cold, or I'll not be taking responsibility. I've said what I've come to say."

"I shall put your words in my pipe and smoke them," Rose thanked her, raising her hand in fond farewell as the woman departed. She might have responded with a more apt correction, that she would drink her coffee while it was "hot," but the distinction of opposites, like her upside world, appealed to her.

She was, after all, a mad scientist. Which was, in her existence, if not Hanna's father's, far better than being a bad man or a preacher.

To that, she was absolutely certain, Rudy Blake would agree.

CHAPTER 30

The cry was inaudible to human ears. Raising her head sharply, Rose cocked her ear upward and toward the left. Listening. The sound was not repeated, yet she knew she had heard it. There would be no more work done this day. Rudy's mind had summoned her from dream-sleep. He must not wake up alone.

Methodically wiping the tip of the pen, then blotting her work with blotting paper, she cast an eye about the room, seeing all was well before departing. The pale little plant sitting atop the *Lexicon Medicum* had already stretched its feeble limbs toward the glass. It would make a good story. Both naughty and hopeful, Rudy would be amused by the tale of how such a useless tome discovered its true potential.

With three long strides she was across the room. Opening the door in one fluid movement, she glided through, without thought of locking it behind her. No one would venture within. As burglar alarms went, "witch's weed," *Aconitum lycoctonum,* commonly known as wolfsbane, and a microscope, with the capacity to turn a man's stomach contents upside-down with its powers of revelation, were better than dead bolts, dogs and crossbars.

No one was about as she marched through the foyer, which was as well for them. Idle hands, the boys had quickly learned, were soon put to unpleasant chores.

Taking the stairs three at a time, her accustomed mode of ascension, stemming from her earliest days with the fearsome Captain Blake, Rose hurried down the corridor. The entranceway to this room, as well, was shut, but not bared. No one willingly entered the chamber of a sick man. Unless they had business, or went by the name of Rose Theodore.

One glance rewarded her presence. Rudy lay on the bed, the blanket tossed aside, pillows dropped to the floor as he canvassed the depths of Nod. Ascertaining that he was not yet awake, she readjusted the window to admit more air, then gathered in the pillows, before perching by his head.

One touch was enough to assure her his fever had not broken. Stooping lower, she sniffed inward, absorbing his stale breath into her own mouth. Slightly acidic and sour, she was relieved to detect no lingering traces of infection. Dr. Mannering had been incorrect in his hasty assessment of

Rudy's oral care. The odor arose from a sick stomach, rather than gum disease. That, she could cure without loss of teeth.

Shaking him by the shoulder, she attempted to rouse him, without success. Exerting greater energy, she spoke, summoning him back.

"Rudy. Rudy – it is Rose."

With a start, his body went rigid, the muscles tensing for struggle. As his pupils contracted to the light, they fixed on her as his mouth clamped shut.

"Rudy, it is Rose. You are safe. I have awoken you from dream."

Struggling against her touch, he tugged against the sling before raising his right hand, first to wave across his brow, then to tighten around her arm.

"Where am I?" he hissed, voice both angry and confused.

"You have come back, Rudy; to the Blake House. You are in England. With Rose."

Frowning against the impossible, he squinted, trying to bring her features into focus.

"Rose? Rose Bud?"

"None other," she responded, smiling in comfort.

"You are not... a dream? A figment, come to torture me?"

"It is as well for you, sir, you did not ask if I were a nightmare." Leaning over, Rose placed her lips against his, gently kissing his chapped pair. As his eyes grew bright, she increased the pressure, until he responded with desperate need. When it was over, she drew back, but not far.

"No," he protested, straining upward. "Wake me again!"

Embracing his emaciated shoulders, she lifted him upward, showering his face with hundreds of tiny kisses. That, finally, elicited a sigh of relief.

"Is that better?"

"Much better." Struggling away from her restraining grasp, he stared around the room, familiarizing himself with the furnishings before looking back. "I can never be certain," he confessed, wiping away a stream of saliva from his mouth. "So many times I woke to find myself alone."

"Never again," she promised in a rare exaggeration, permitted only by the occasion.

"I am... hot."

"Yes. You have a fever. That is to be expected. It will pass." Enunciating carefully, in short sentences, she pinched the neck of his nightshirt. "You have soaked this through."

"I always was a good sweater," he unexpectedly bragged, grinning proudly, like a child.

"And not a bad snorer, either," came the happy agreement. "A lesser house would have come tumbling down."

"But it will not?" he whimpered, suddenly afraid. Silently cursing herself for the careless statement, she soothed him by resting a hand on his chest.

"It will not. I was teasing."

As his brows furrowed, Rudy shook his head in sad depression. "You see, I cannot be certain. So much bad has happened... I expect the worst." Indicating that he wished to sit straighter, Rudy sighed in fear. "That is so unlike me, Rose. To be so... scared. Why is this happening?"

"It is the effects of the fever. Were you to feel otherwise, that would be cause for worry."

"Really?"

His question, so hopefully asked, tore through her insides as though it were a scalpel.

"I have said so. And one thing you may be sure: what I say, I mean."

Averting her head, for shame at her former pronouncement that he would never wake to find himself alone, Rose attempted to compose herself by fussing with his bandage. Blood had soaked through the gauze, some of it fresh and red, but most of the dampness was nearly colorless, tinged around the edges by an unhealthy brown.

"Come. Let me help you remove this soiled nightshirt, then I will change your dressing."

"You make me sound like a turkey," he protested, as a means of delaying the inevitable. She rumpled his hair, then shook her head.

"I know it will hurt, but the longer we put it off, the more it will stick to the healing flesh. It is better not to wait. Let up your arms."

"No."

Because she expected such a refusal, Rose was prepared for action. Before the word had departed his lips, her fingers poised over his armpits, wiggling suggestively. His flared nostrils bore testimony that he fully comprehended her intent.

"No doctor would threaten to – tickle – a patient."

"Nor would a doctor kiss one awake. Shall you have it by the book, or would you prefer a more nontraditional method?"

"Why do you always have an answer?"

"I know how your mind works."

Without latitude for a rebuttal, he wearily lifted his arms, allowing her to slide the damp cloth over his head. Taking in the sight of his protuberant ribs and concave stomach, she mentally prepared a list of tasks to perform. First among them was to order him a new wardrobe. By no means must that be put off. While there was no immediate need, any less might prompt the "gods" to strip him from her. That, as punishment for taking his survival for granted, by assuming she had all the time in the world to see the work performed.

Clucking her tongue, Rose rolled her eyes heavenward.

"We must always be on guard against the gods."

"What?" Rudy asked, tugging frantically on her blouse. Startled that she had spoken aloud, Rose quickly apologized.

"I was talking to myself."

"What about the gods?" he demanded, fingers clutching her downward. "What were you thinking?"

"That you have only just arrived, and already I am beginning to sound like you."

Partially appeased, he relented, falling backward toward the mattress. "How?"

"Worrying about your 'gods.' Zeus and the others. Watching from Olympus. Never give them an edge. I was chastising myself," she stressed, lightening her mood to alleviate his concern. "While there are worse things I might have thought and still sounded like you, there are also *better* ones."

"Have you appeased them?"

"I have. They shall never get the better of us. Not," she added in an undertone, "when we are together."

Stopping herself from dropping his nightshirt on the rug, Rose carried it to a hamper and deposited it inside. She did not want Rudy's clothes laundered with the linen from the household. Until she was certain his fever was organic and not contagion, it was best to err on the side of caution.

Retrieving a small leather medical bag from the wardrobe where she had earlier placed it, Rose carried it to the bed. Under Rudy's suspicious yet curious eyes, she unbuckled the fastening, situating the case so that he could not miss the monogram imprinted on the side.

"R.B.!" he cried, his mouth circling into an "O" of unmitigated pleasure. "You have bought yourself a – what do you call it?"

Secretly pleased at his cleverness, she did not dodge the trap he laid for her.

"It is a physician's kit," she remarked, positioning her face so he could read her embarrassment. He nodded wisely.

"I see. A physician's kit. For... physicians?"

"I had it made to specification. It is not an official kit," she added, wiping her eye with the back of her hand. Of all the people she had known in her life, only Rudy intuitively understood her reticence at using equipment for which she held no proper title. And only he, by his joy, could make her feel ten feet tall by the acquisition.

"Of what is it made?"

"Calf skin. Tanned butter soft and stained black."

Leaning nearer to have a better look, but without the license to touch, he nodded.

"I approve. With what did you purchase this doctor's bag?"

Again, a trap.

"My salary. That which I am paid for being a member of your crew."

"And?"

"Chandler for the greatest sea captain ever to set sail upon the briny waters."

Sighing in contentment, he let the compliment slide, for his mind was on more important matters.

"So. I am indirectly responsible."

"No, sir," she corrected, grasping his left hand, then cutting through the bandage with a pair of rounded-edged German steal scissors. "You are directly responsible."

What she did not say and he would never know, was the correlation, far greater than payment of money, of his involvement. One of the presents Thomas Mannering had left on her doorstep had been a surgeon's bag. His note explained that inasmuch as she was "tending patients," she ought to look "official." The sentiment had been appreciated but the initials he had inscribed over those of his own, carefully scraped off, had not been.

"R.T." was what he had placed on the leather. "R" for Rose, "T" for Theodore. He had no way of knowing that "R.T." was no longer the initials under which she worked. Those represented a woman with a checkered past. And while it was true she had "practiced medicine" under that name in the past, it had never been as a doctor, but merely a woman.

"R.T." belonged to the streets and alleys of New York City and Washington, D.C. They were symbols of what was. Rudy Blake, and his baptism of equality, had bestowed upon her a new sense of identity and a fresh pair of initials.

Rose Bud. "R.B." The same as his. Short of giving her his name, it was the most precious gift she would ever receive.

"R.B." Theodore was anything she wished to be. Crewman, arms dealer, a procurer of goods and wares. Under certain circumstances, R.B. Theodore could even be a doctor; something Rose No-Middle-Initial Theodore could ever be.

She had kept the bag out of courtesy, but had placed it away, in a box, tired with string and sealed with wax. One day, she would either return it, or give it away to a more legitimate practitioner. To assuage her own equivocal feelings, she had ordered a new bag made. One with compartments for tonics and potions, medical instruments, bandages, little trinkets for tiny patients and candy for big ones.

Prominent among her supplies was a jar of peppermint sticks. For the exclusive use of the man who believed she was a healer, with the title of "doctor" and the initials of "R.B."

She had never before used it. For like herself, it needed a baptism to be reborn into a useful tool of her trade.

Carefully prying back the top layers of gauze, Rose determined to wet the remainder, so as not to hurt him by its removal. Daubing a mixture of water and mineral oil over the linen, she let it set, then turned back to her patient with a carefully laid trap of her own.

"Rudy, who is the god of healing arts?"

"Hermes," came the prompt reply. "His winged sandals helped him track down deadbeats who refused to pay their doctor bills. He is also the god of thieves. A good combination," he declared, staring with fixed dread at his arm.

"Wasn't he in charge of something else?" she prodded, not for her own edification, for her mythology was almost as good as, if not as interpretative, as Rudy's. Rather, she wished to probe his memory and his state of mind.

"Hermes, or Mercury, if you prefer, is the Divine Herald. He guides souls to their final destination in the underworld."

"Ah. I thought as much." Deftly placing her hands on his head, she redirected his gaze away from her work, absorbing his pride at being able to supply her with so necessary a piece of information. For as long as Rudy spoke of the denizens of Olympus with knowledge, and in the present tense, she would always know his mind was alert and that life stirred within him; a flame of the moment, and a will to survive.

That was the criteria she held him to. When, on a far off someday, he answered differently, either with despondency or doubt, she would know a new situation and a further reckoning would be necessary.

Her position in life was to keep him alive, but not beyond his mortal span. She would see to it he lived his full extent of time on earth. But when the immortal spirit within him communicated that he was finally too tired to fight the human struggles, she would let him go. Not one second sooner. That would cheat her, and not even Rudy Blake had a right to do that.

Gingerly testing the gauze and finding it softened, she removed the remaining protection, baring his hand to the air. His groan of pain alerted her to the fact such exposure brought with it a throbbing hurt. Blowing gently on the open wound to add heat to the flesh, she prodded with her instrument, checking for the presence of infection, or any obvious signs of metal chards, left behind by the original operation.

Using all her senses, Rose inhaled deeply, running the odor over her tongue, before he stopped her by placing his good arm to her face.

"Why are you doing that? It's nauseating."

"It is a means of ascertaining how you are healing. Would you have me stand back and guess?"

"Yes," he decided without further contemplation.

"That is why you are the patient and I the –"

"Doctor," he quickly supplied, scrunching his nose in distaste. "It is a dirty business, Rose Bud."

"I have done worse. Shall I tell you where?" she inquired with an edge of hope to her voice which silenced him on the topic forever.

"What does it look like?"

"Better than it did," she responded, caught between giving too much and too little information. Being incredibly suggestible, planting even the hint of danger in his mind would complicate matters, prompting his imagination to wild and horrible consequences.

Placated, but not yet satisfied, he raised his eyes, scrutinizing her countenance with the gaze of an innocent babe. "When is it going to be better?"

Her first impulse was to chide him for his impatience, with a tart reminder that it was his life she was trying to save, not concern herself with timetables. Yet that would have been as petulant and childish as his plea was childlike. Reminding herself that he had been in pain so long, every moment mattered, Rose rallied her optimism.

"Not today and not tomorrow."

Wincing from the delay which seemed interminable, he pouted, exposing his lower lip. Rose impulsively reached out and batted it playfully with her fingers.

"What's that for?"

"The sheer pleasure of having you here."

"To torment," he finished, staring distastefully at his hand. "Are you finished?"

"I have not begun," she gently reminded him, lightly covering the wound with a fresh bandage to hide it from his inquisitive inspection. "Has it occurred to you, Captain Blake, that patience is not your 'long suit'?"

"Yes," came the immediate and somewhat mollified response.

Leaving him on the bed, Rose held up her hand, palm outward, signifying "stop." Disappearing, she returned almost immediately with a basin of warm water. To keep his mind occupied while she worked, Rose resumed their former conversation.

"I shall not give you a definitive answer to your question for two reasons. The first is because I cannot. Medicine is an art, not a science. Every patient heals at different rates. In your case, matters are complicated by the time separating the occasion of your injury and the removal of the splinter. I have told you, you have a fever. We must cure that, before expecting to see a great change in your finger."

"And the second," he prodded suspiciously.

"You will hold me to a date and count the days. That is where you will place your concentration. I prefer you use that energy into getting well."

"But it will get better? You said."

"A promise made is a promise kept. The nail will grow back. Look."

After cleaning the operation site, then soaking away the free flowing blood, Rose indicated the area of interest. "There are more nerve endings in your hand than in any other part of your body. That is because you need an acute awareness of tactility."

"For dealing cards," Rudy tried, attempting to absorb what his healthy mind would have grasped without asking.

"Exactly. For that and other things. Remember when you were a prospector. Immersing your hands in freezing cold water, day after day, then scraping away at silt, your skin became rough and insensitive. Did it not?"

"Yes," he strove to remember, thoughtfully rubbing his thumb and forefinger together.

"When you abandoned the gold fields for more lucrative pursuits, the first thing you did was buy bear grease to soften the flesh. Slowly, you recovered your sensitivity. We will do the same now."

"With bear grease?"

"I have better lotions than that," she smiled. "You remember my telling you about the aloe plant?" Shaking his head sadly, she nodded in commiseration and hurried on. "It is also known as the Century plant. It grows in warm climates. You must have seen varieties when you were growing up around Charleston."

"Thick, flexible stems....?"

"Correct. Mammy and her people may have used a form of it as a very powerful laxative, which may be why you are familiar with it."

"You are going to dose me with –"

"No. My purpose is to extract the gel and use it as an emollient; a skin softener. The scent is not unpleasant and you will find it much better than bear grease."

"Warm climates?" he questioned, furiously trying to follow her reasoning.

"I grow it here. In my greenhouse, where the temperature is warm year-round. It is one of my 'magic plants.' Do not ask me more, for that would be telling. You know, it is like the huckster's trick. Once explained, it is obvious to everyone, and no one is impressed."

"That I understand!" he agreed, bobbing his head.

"I thought you would. We are two of a kind, you and I. Now close your eyes and clamp your jaw, for I am going to put some very powerful medicine on the sore. It will sting like the devil."

"That is good," came the firm declaration. She inferred his reference was to the devil, but he surprised her. "Only medicine which is strong enough to hurt can cure. That is a truth, Rose. One I have learned."

She did not doubt he had learned exactly that. In Rudy's world, pain equated to pain. One could not hope to advance without suffering.

To her shame, it was a sentiment with which she did not entirely disagree.

CHAPTER 31

Stiffening his resolve, the only sound Rudy made as the ointment was placed over the exposed nerve endings of his finger was a low groan. Working as fast as she could, Rose applied pressure to the lowest joint, then blew on the wound to dry it. When that was completed to her satisfaction, she bent over to kiss his forehead before beginning the arduous process of re-bandaging the hand.

"Why did you kiss me?" he asked, trying vainly to keep his mind focused.

"Your hair was mussed. It needed some spit to make it behave."

"I hope that means *I* don't have to behave," he complained, eyes riveted to her labor like a moth to flame.

Pausing a moment to kiss him a second time, she grinned happily. "No, but that one does."

"I never held much stock in kissing," he groused as the six-year-old boy whose fascination with the art was still a decade away.

"Oh, there is a great deal to be said about kissing," Rose scoffed. "Enchantments can be broken with a kiss. As you well know," she reminded him. "Or, a 'sleeping beauty' can be awakened from trance by one."

"Something I would never try," Rudy sourly demurred. "Can you imagine what her breath must have been like after all those years of repose?"

"I said 'sleeping beauty,' without mentioning a gender," Rose corrected, winding a narrow tie around her handiwork. "Don't you think I might find a slumbering prince and wake him with a kiss?"

"It doesn't work that way."

Shaking her head, Rose tied the string with a double knot to prevent tampering.

"If it works one way, then it works the other. Just because men see things to suit their own fancy doesn't make it right."

"It's never bothered me," Rudy announced with startling honesty. Then grimacing in pain, he attempted to shake his hand, in the errant hope of flinging aside the discomfort. Grasping it tenderly in her own, she held him back. Without an avenue of escape, he turned wet eyes up toward her.

"Tell me a story. I need to concentrate on something."

"Oh, Rudy, you're the storyteller. You tell me a story."

"No," he protested, as perspiration broke out along the ridge of his hairline. "I can't think of any. You make something up."

"All right. If you won't have 'Sleeping Beauty' my way, I'll amuse you with another. But first, put your arm back in the sling. The higher you hold it, the sooner it will stop throbbing. Because," she added, reading his raised eyebrow, "it is closer to your heart. It is easier for blood to get to the affected area."

"I'm sorry I asked."

Sinking down into her arms, he closed his eyes, willing his heart to pump faster.

"Once upon a time, there was a little boy, small for his age. But what he lacked in stature, he made up for in energy, for he was constantly moving, exploring, investigating. He always had a thousand questions on the tip of his tongue, and no answer ever satisfied him, for it was never detailed enough. He was, in fact, a little fellow who wanted to know everything."

Speaking as she walked, Rose selected a fresh blanket from the wardrobe. Returning with it, she spread it over him, deftly tucking in the corners around his chin so he might not be chilled.

"What was his name?"

"His name was... R.B.," Rose decided. "And it didn't take long for everyone he knew to shun his company, for they tired of his eternal questioning. His parents were far too busy to answer him, being involved with business or entertaining; his cousins didn't know the answers, and the servants had many chores to accomplish, and no time to explain the unexplainable."

"Yes," came the sleepy acknowledgment. "That is true."

"I thought it might be," she confessed, caressing his body. "And so it came to pass that one day R.B. was out playing in the meadow. It was a wonderfully wide and rolling meadow. There were tall grasses, waving languidly in the slight summer breeze; the sun beat down, big and yellow and round, suspended in the sky like a huge, unreachable ball."

"I can feel it," he whispered, snuggling closer as she increased her gentle massage.

"It was a hot day, the kind which keeps grown-ups indoors, but which never affects children. Young people have a greater tolerance for temperatures, haven't you noticed?"

Rudy nodded and smiled, imagining Rose's mystical meadow and the little boy named R.B., who just happened to look a lot like him.

"There was a delightful odor of flowers," she continued, drawing her images from his body warmth. "The subtle perfumes of wild daises and dandelions filled the air, and R.B. breathed deeply of it. He could smell the land, with the traces of musky dark earth; he could feel the gently prickling of the grasses and sticks as he lay down and stared into the sky."

Closing her own eyes, Rose transported them both back to another era of innocence and fantasy.

"All around him were the sounds of nature: a bird chirping, without expectation of answer; the droning of a flying insect, first near, then very far away; the rustling of the grasses as their heads, heavy and bent with seed, brushed against one another. The little boy could even hear the ants at work, as they wove their way through the thousand and one intricate trails only insect eyes could ever detect."

Across the chamber of a three-story house, situated outside London, which was also earning the reputation as a place of refuge and dreams, a gust of wind billowed the curtains. The shimmering, light beige material plunged inward, imitating sails. Rudy and Rose's arms entangled in a seaman's embrace, which might have been called Cockscombing, or French hitching or overhand grafting. Strands of mussed hair mysteriously intertwined into a Turk's head knot, decorating the pair with a tar's eye for beauty.

"And suddenly," Rose whispered, alive to the possibilities, "my R.B. heard a different sound: the tinkling of a million tiny bells, sweet and enticing. The youngster rolled over on his stomach, trying to penetrate the grasses with his eyes, seeking the blue bells or the lily-of-the-valley which must be making such enchanted music. But he could not see any flowers that resembled bells."

Although she could not see his expression, Rose felt Rudy's features slowly melt into wondrous expectation.

"Hurry up," he pleaded, trembling with anxiety. "I want to know."

"Yes," she breathed back, her eyes twinkling with certain knowledge. "You always have." Squeezing him lightly, she resumed the narrative. "His little face puckered into a frown.

"'Don't do that,' a miniscule voice, coming from Somewhere, suddenly warned. 'Or you'll grow up and have wrinkles.'

"R.B. looked around himself in astonishment. Who – or what – had spoken? But there was no one about. He was completely alone. He must have dreamed it.

"'Do not look with your eyes,' the tiny voice admonished with a trace of smugness. 'You cannot see anything with your eyes.'

"'Then with what am I supposed to see?' the impatient little boy demanded. It does not take long for certain diminutive children to become familiar with magic, and take it for granted," Rose chided. To her delight, Rudy wiggled his legs.

"Go on!"

"Low and behold, a tiny, humanoid creature emerges from the flora. But that is not right," she sharply corrected herself. Tell me why?" she demanded, allowing Rudy space to readjust his position.

"In the beginning, there was the elf," he promptly supplied, a student correcting the master. "An elf cannot be said to resemble a person, for they were here first. It must be put, 'A tiny being, upon whose perfect body shape the larger creatures were patterned,'" he stated.

"Precisely," Rose commiserated, well pleased. "Our elf is no more than three or four inches high, dressed in a wild abandonment of field browns and leaf greens. He has high-topped boots that curl at the toes, arching around in a circular fashion; a meticulously woven jacket of the finest quality; with fold-back cuffs," she added, "and a high, emerald-hued, floppy cap, ending in a point. Is that correct?"

"You forgot the silver buckles on his boots; and the buttons of burnished gold," came the prompt response.

"I omitted to state those details. But of course, you are right. Ours is a very fancy elf. A dandy, you might say."

Rudy's body quivered as he laughed. "An elf-about-town."

"Exactly so. Our individual has piercing, bright brown eyes, long, delicate fingers and a contagious, mischievous grin. His most outstanding characteristic, of course, are the pointed ears, poking their way upward, from the sides of his cap."

"No elf ever covers his ears," Rudy agreed with verve. "They mark him for a superior being."

"And are extremely attractive," Rose supplied, carelessly forming Rudy's soft, silken hair into points, so that, he, too, might be extremely attractive, as she first remembered him. "Now note: this particular elf is a bit of a rake, for he sports a tiny meadow flower from a button hole, and has another tucked in the band of his hat."

"Buttercups," Rudy sighed. "When he tilts his head just so, he can see the yellow reflection on his chin. That means," he added authoritatively, "he likes butter."

"And all sweet things. It would not surprise me a bit if he had a pocket full of peppermint leaves upon which to chew."

Rudy's intake of breath was all the reward she needed.

"Just as I carry peppermint sticks!"

"And how, my boy, do you think you acquired the habit?" she teased.

"I had never thought of it. But you must be right!"

Feeling goose bumps spread over her face and body, Rose continued.

"Without responding to the little fellow's question of how he were to envision the world without eyes, the elf points to R.B.'s head. This indicates he must look with his mind, rather that his startling grey-green orbs. Then, with a wink and a silvery laugh, the elf vanishes."

"Poof! But he will come back?" Rudy cried in a low, sad undertone.

"Shhh. Do not get ahead of yourself. Of course," the story resumed, "protestations to the contrary, R.B. clearly understands the message. He ought to, for he is the type of little fellow who has witnessed many wondrous, magical things upon occasion. But he is also a very stubborn little tyke, and turns back to stare – not with his mind, but with his eyes. And, of course, he does not see anything."

Rudy grunted in annoyance, but could offer no protest, for truth was truth, even in a faerie tale.

"As though to belie his efforts, the meadow comes alive with a symphony of celestial music. He hears strings and lutes and mouth organs, all commingling in harmony with a chorus of little elf voices, raised in song. Music floats on the air, as weightless and ethereal as a cloud, then slowly drifts away, in the same manner as the breeze dissolves the light blue, puffy image of a sky dragon."

"Which a fellow might hurry along with his pretend sword," Rudy envisioned, as his right arm moved across the pillow. "But never to inflict damage, but rather... as a game. Is that the right word, Rose?"

"I think, more, as a disappointment, that the dragon refused to give our boy a ride," she thoughtfully replied. "But dragons are like that. They are persnickety beasts, for all that."

"I will ride one, one day," he promised, grasping the pillow as though it were a pair of reins.

"Of course you will."

"But I will have to sneak up on it, Rose. When it is dozing... or setting small patches of fire to the winter grasses. Dragons do that, Rose. Do you know what 'people' call the phenomenon?"

"Spontaneous combustion," she answered, grimacing at the idea of so preposterous an idea.

"Fools, they. Tell me more," he yawned, reluctantly letting go the reins to lay his head upon the pillow.

"There are words to the elf songs, which R.B. understands on a higher plane. He does not use his mind to translate these words of joy and praise: he comprehends them instinctively, for he was gifted with secret knowledge on the day of his birth."

"How, Rose? How was this gift bestowed upon me? How," Rudy begged, digging his hand into her arm in urgent wakefulness, "did they know I was born? Who told them? Was it you?"

"So many questions. You see, my love, you have not changed so very much, have you?"

"More than I wanted," he sighed, wiping an eye. "But answer. Please. Was it you?"

"No, darling. I wish I could take credit for so momentous a deed, but I was not yet born. I am younger than you. Remember?" she prodded, brushing back an elfin lock fallen over his eye.

"Who, then?" he persisted. Then, in a harsher voice which sent chills of a different nature down her spine, "No one of my acquaintance."

It was a chance for Rose to put in a kind word for his mother, but she could not do it. *Knowledge,* she silently rued, *gave to its possessor both the good and the bad.*

"No person, Rudy Blake. The Family of Faerie requires no human intervention to alert them when a child of extraordinary goodness is born."

"Then I am not the R.B. of which you speak," he cried, lifting himself off the bed. With the strength of a giant, Rose pushed him back, her eyes flashing in anger.

"You will say the elves have made a mistake? Speak loudly, so they may hear and tremble at your disavowal."

"No, no, it is just that –"

"Hush!" she warned. "Or I will speak no more and the story has ended."

Gambling on his love and his need, Rose relaxed as Rudy retreated from his position, his madly roving eyeballs hidden behind shuttered lids.

"Go on. I am listening."

Dropping herself closer to him, she resumed the narrative.

"Their songs are sometimes silly and irreverent ditties, filled with mischief and playfulness. Others are ancient tunes, hearkening back to an age when the world was inhabited by wee people and fire-breathing dragons. There is wisdom and adventure, cloud castles and treasure hunts, glamor and magic, for their consciousness extends to the beginning of Time, for they are God's playmates, and as such, are good in His eyes."

"Before Adam and Eve," Rudy responded and it was only the glint of mischief in his own eyes which stayed her hands.

"The difference being," she relented with pleasure, "that elves are real, while 'Adam and Eve' are faerie tales, conjured by a race to explain creation in a universe beyond their comprehension."

"So you have explained," Rudy winked, rubbing his side. "I do *not* have one fewer ribs than you."

"I am gratified to know I have had some positive effect on your re-education, sir," she acknowledged. "And a hard road is has been to travel."

"More!"

Waving her arm to clear away the scene, Rose brought back the meadow and the flowers and the whispering grasses.

"Suddenly, without warning, the little, innocent, loving boy is surrounded by elves. He can see them clearly now, for he has put aside the guise of hatred and suspicion inherent in his species, assuming a shape more akin to a child of nature. Invited to join them, he lifts his voice in song, attesting his human birth, but fairy breeding. The meadow swells to life, so that even the great trees seem to lose their moorings and dance, on the tips of roots, to the swaying of this other-worldly tempo."

"I know that meadow," Rudy whispered, but it was not with joy, nor filled with longing. Pausing to study his face in the irregularly cast shadows from window and lamp, casting wrinkles of time across his brow, she found, disconcertingly, she could not read his expression. Without an adequate answer, she replied, "I somehow thought you might."

Eyes misting with tortured remembrance, Rudy bowed his head, the epitome of a mighty oak tree, torn asunder. Without the power to replant him, Rose lay a hand on his shoulder.

"What is it, Rudy?"

"I know that meadow," he repeated, his voice hollow and distant. "I've seen it. Men have made war in that meadow, Rose. They've shot each other with muskets and cannon.... Arms and legs flying where once elves danced. I've dug in that precious earth, Rose Bud, burying the dead and mangled beneath that soil. I've fallen on my hands and knees and wept like a baby for the evil perpetrated upon so sacred a spot."

Throwing back his head, Rudy Blake, child of nature, howled with grief. Sobbing uncontrollably, he lashed out with his one good arm, pushing back the innocence of a bygone day.

"They've ruined that meadow, Rose, and all the other meadows like it. There are no more elves and faeries, Rose. They've gone away, for Mankind has waged War on their earth and taken away their songs."

Intellectually stunned, yet intuitively aware her story had brought them full circle, Rose stiffened her muscles, hardening her heart. Grasping her hand into a fist, she shook it to the four winds, lamenting the loss of innocence.

Her beloved Rudy had gone to War, returning from the Land of the Dead inalienably altered. The blatant inhumanity had warped his mind, indelibly scarring his sensibilities, damaging his soul.

Stifling a scream, she tore at the sheet, clenching it between her teeth in rage. She must not that those festering, poisonous wounds scar, for to cure his body without preserving the uniqueness inside was to create a monster – a three-dimensional dragon of the mechanized, inhuman race.

"No, Rudy, no. Together, we shall look for the elves and the faeries. They are as they were. Only, they have gone into hiding from Man's cruelty, abandoned the meadows. But we will listen – you and I – for their songs upon the wind. Elves are of God, Rudy, and God has not abandoned us." Her breathing grew more rapid. "The faith of a mustard seed, beloved.

We will dig into the earth and replant the flowers. They will grow, and with them will come a renewal of faith. You will see."

"I will see no more."

"Come to me, little one," Rose crooned in a gentle, loving voice as old as the oceans.

"I am not a little one," Rudy denied, entrenching himself in the bed, from which flowed no solace. "I am a man, and I have stared down, beyond the rim of the Pit."

"Then we shall fill it in," she retorted, the muscles in her jaw jumping as she figuratively cast in the first spadesful of dirt. "And mark this, for I am Rose, a child of Our Lord's garden: You shall always be *my* little one."

Rudy's anger slowly seeped away. His fresh nightshirt, drenched in cold sweat, clung to his body, a second skin to be peeled off, layer by layer, until he was bare and exposed. Yet, like the snake in the tale of the Garden of Eden, he was not capable of absorbing the Word.

"If you had seen what I have seen...."

His sentence dangled, the last gasp of a shattered man.

To tell him she had seen: that through his mind she had traversed the long trail beside him, would have been demeaning. She had not been present in flesh. But through the medium of Second Sight, belonging in the category of elves and mustard seeds, she had witnessed the travesty.

Where once there had been cracks of musket fire and booming of cannon, now lay the deathly silence of blood-soaked graves and crushed grasses. The pall of gunsmoke had dissipated, absorbed into the hazy blue sky and the amorphously-shaped clouds.

Life, such as it was, would return to Rudy's meadow, and others like it. Birds and crickets and ants would replace grave worms and mournful winds of devastation. Graves would turn to mounds, and mounds to grassy knolls. Saplings would grow where ancient oak trunks had been seared away. Spring flowers would dare lift their heads, sprinkling red and crimson and cherry of a different nature across the landscape. The stench of gunpowder and ruptured bowels would fade, replaced by scents of a gentler nature.

The earth would eventually return to what it had been, and life would go on. There would be one difference, however, and Rose knew Rudy understood it. No wee people would ever dance and sing and send their joyous messages upward, for the land had been poisoned by the inhumanity of Mankind upon it. Never again would the folk in green play hide and seek amongst the tall grasses, sip elf wine from beneath the shade of a giant mushroom cap, or float down the sparkling blue, bubbling stream encased in the upturned half of an acorn shell.

A corner of the Earth, which once housed innocence and child-love had been scorched by fire. But there were other places. Rose would take Rudy by the hand and together, they would seek the untainted. But never, ever again would the meadows and rolling hills of the South beckon Rudy Blake to sit upon his native soil and become a child once again.

War had destroyed that.

CHAPTER 32

The face staring back at him was that of a stranger. Although the features vaguely resembled those of whom Rudy Blake was intimately familiar, the eyes were not. Reflecting back from the looking glass, he noted the dull grey irises, streaked with green. Totally devoid of emotion, the orbs gave him the disconcerting impression he was staring at a corpse.

So clear was that image, he jerked his head around, thinking, perhaps, that someone had played a practical joke on him by propping a dead body behind him.

He was disappointed. And with disappointment came fear.

His intentions had been honorable. After Rose left the room, quietly tiptoeing away so as not to disturb him, he had risen. The effort had been difficult, more so than he anticipated. The wound in his hand throbbed with a pain so acute it had nearly turned the room upside down. Moving carefully, with the steps of a man accustomed to having his world rock beneath his feet, he had shuffled to the wardrobe, selecting a black, silken robe.

Forgetting, for the moment, his disability, he had tried, unsuccessfully, to thread his left arm through the sleeve, discovering after several tries, that he could not. The sling, holding his arm up, close to his heart, had been fastened in the back.

Tying the belt had proven equally impossible. Once, he could have managed a knot with one good hand, but that time was past. Such dexterity required a steadiness he did not possess. Abandoning the attempt, he had left the front open. Feeling naked and exposed, he had, nonetheless, decided to pursue his course of action.

Sixteen baby steps took him to the door. The effort cost him much and had been forced to lean against the wall, breathing heavily to catch his breath. When his breathing regulated, he had tried the knob, sweating profusely, least it be locked. Luck had been with him, for it opened easily.

Peering out, like a thief in the night, he had found the coast clear. No one was about. Beneath his feet he felt a slight vibration, freezing him before he identified the source. Someone on the second level was moving about. Reassuring himself there was little chance one of his former crew would venture further upstairs, he moved out, nostrils distended in fear. Slowly, ever so slowly, he made his way to the indoor privy.

He had meant it for a surprise. If he could prove to Rose he was well enough to shave himself, she would be proud. Seeing the flash of her eyes, the quick, lightning smile, her head bobbing in approval, he would know, truly know, he was all right; that the War, with all its horrors, lay behind him.

Shutting himself in, he found his shaving equipment without difficulty. Not the razor and brush he had brought with him, but new items, fresh and unused. She had seen to that, perhaps with the idea she would help him. How great would be her astonishment to discover he was well enough to perform the simple task alone.

That was before he had looked in the mirror. One glance was enough to stay his hand forever.

He might have come to accept the sunken eye sockets, the sharp, protruding cheekbones, for he knew he had lost weight. Even the cruel streaks of white, salt-and-peppering his hair he could have lived with, for that was correctable. A pair of tweezers and a strong hand could pluck them out, restoring to him a semblance of youth he still claimed as his own.

The creases around his eyes, the deep indentation at the point of his chin, the strong nose, made all the more prominent by his wanness, were acceptable changes in a face no longer boyish. And the scars – the deep-set splattering of indentations, gotten so long ago – were not the end of the world. They were as integral to his countenance as his lips or nostrils.

The mustache, too, was there, offset by a growth of stubble, but present and accountable. He had worn one so long, the very idea of being without was tantamount to nakedness. Whether, as Waterbucket had once suggested, it had changed his "luck" was open to discussion.

What was not, were the eyes.

A man might go to war and lose his arm. He might suffer the tragedy of having his leg amputated by overwrought, under-skilled surgeons. Dysentery could render him to the point of flesh and bone; poor diet cause his buttocks to become excoriated. The appearance of hemorrhoids torture his bowel movements. His fingernails might not grow and his teeth fall out, but one thing that man had a right to expect, amidst all his failings, was to recognize his own face.

A man, waking from a coma, knew who he was. A prisoner, solitarily confined, kept his identity. A youth, stripped of his name, still maintained the right to his own image. Even a murderer on the run, attempting to hide his features behind a beard, did not fool himself.

Only Rudy Blake, a little of all those men, was denied.

"No," he whispered, a hoarse, tortured exclamation. "That is not me. This is some trick."

Staggering away from the looking glass, all thought of shaving abandoned, he fell against the tub, losing his balance. Without two arms to steady himself, he plunged, headlong, into the receptacle, striking his head. The blow was sharp, rattling his teeth. His lip bleed. The blood tasted weak, insipid, lacking savor.

Flailing his legs, he tried to right himself, succeeding merely in entrenching himself inside the porcelain walls. Thus close-confined, he huddled, shivering, no longer a man but a kitten.

He did not want to get out. Behind him, in the mirror, he knew those eyes still stared. Fixed. Lusterless. Waiting to claim him for their own. The eyes of a fallen angel, without free will. The orbs of an underworld minion, too long deprived the sight of God.

Tears rolled down his face, from those self-same eyes, tasting warm, yet flavorless. Without being certain, he could not tell whether it were actually the dampness from weeping, or more blood, seeping from a cut on his forehead.

The difference was moot.

She had told him he would recover, but she had not mentioned his eyes. Now he knew why. A body might grow strong. Muscle cover bone. Flesh fill in hollows. Fingernails grow, covering exposed nerves. But never, ever, would those eyes recover. They had seen too much.

He had died and no one had told him.

The cards riffled, one end meeting another, so that both sides merged. The deck was stacked, tapped, then dealt. Five to a man, all down. Idle banter filled the room as inquisitive faces scanned their hands. Tongues clicked. Throats cleared.

"Who can open?"

"What are we playing: deuces or better?"

A polite scattering of chuckles.

"I can. I open for two."

A pair of pennies was shoved into the pot. More noises, some disparaging, others amused.

"Big man."

"Your bet."

"I'm out."

"I'll meet you two and raise you... three."

"Five. An unholy number."

"I'll meet you."

"We'll never get rich this way."

The strike of a match, then the intake of breath. The odor of smoke. A pall of smoke hung over the players.

"How many?" the dealer asked.

"Three."

"That must be some hand you have there."

"I'll take two."

"Three for me."

Play passed around the table. The player who had dropped out leaned back, the two front legs of his chair raising off the floor. He was content with his decision.

The sound of glasses being raised, lips sucking liquid. Quietly.

"What you have?"

"Two queens."

A disgusted snort, cards being tossed aside. Hands reaching toward the pot, drawing in the ill-gotten gains.

"A penny saved is a penny earned."

"Who said you were going to save it?"

Crude, uninspired laughter. The game was dull. Listless. Without inspiration. A way to pass the time.

"Your deal."

Cards were scraped together.

"Let's make something wild."

"Yeah. Threes. That's all I ever get."

A chuckle. Humorless.

"Are we playing aces high or low?"

"A good time to ask."

More riffling. Unskilled hands.

Hands which had never been taught. The master held his secrets close.

They did not hear him enter. They were too engrossed in their dull, listless game. It was not until his shadow passed over the playing table that one looked up. A hush descended upon the room.

"Rudy."

It was odd, he thought, they recognized him. It did not speak well for their collective souls.

"Rudy," he repeated, more for his sake than theirs.

"My God, it's good to see you."

He knew a lie when he heard one. He was not deceived.

It was not an encounter of his choosing, but rather one of his making. A resignation. Or perhaps a test. He had heard them upstairs, from his trap. Talking among themselves. The words had been indistinct, but he knew their voices. D'Artagnan. BoBo. Canary. Smartmouth. The litany of lost lives.

"Sit down."

"Do you want to play?"

There was hope and fear in their voices. More of one than the other.

An eerie expression, fleetingly amused, insanely disturbed, passed across Rudy's face. Glancing from one to the other, without letting any get a fix on him, Rudy slowly shook his head. As though he were a mechanical man and not a living person, his neck creaked, muscles in need of oiling.

"I can hardly be expected to hold my hand." Pausing half a heartbeat, he added, his voice rumbling from deep within his chest, "And I wouldn't trust any of you to hold it for me."

"We're only playing for pennies," BoBo objected, uncertain whether to be flattered or insulted. Bringing the legs of his chair down to earth with an awkward scrape, he stood, made a small, embarrassed bow, then offered his hand. "Would you care to sit?"

"No."

Again, the low rumbling of a volcano, threatening to erupt.

"It's... good to see you," D'Artagnan offered a second time, less certain than the first. He squinted up, the way a man glanced at the sun. Sideways, taking in the glare with peripheral vision.

"Is it?"

"We thought... maybe you weren't coming," Smartmouth intoned, afraid to be the last to speak.

"What would detain me?"

Shifting to his left, away from the cigar store Indian, D'Artagnan dropped the cards on the table.

"Thought you might have business." It was lame. Flat. Uncertain. "Jack would like to see you. He's not here."

It was an opening for Rudy to ask where Jack was. He seemed to miss the point.

"What business?"

The War had not prepared these noncombatants for such an encounter. Smartmouth coughed, turning away, then swallowing that which had risen into his throat.

"And Forty-Niner. He was speaking of you just the other day. Hoping you'd come. And here you are."

"And what did you answer him, just the other day? When Forty-Niner was speaking of me?" Rudy asked, beginning a walk around the room.

"I said you'd be here soon," the mate replied.

"Go on with your game."

His shadow fell over BoBo. The youth shivered and moved aside, so that the shade hung threateningly across the table.

"We're through," Smartmouth decided for the group.

"Yes," Rudy agreed. "You are through."

If the statement were meant for a threat, it served its purpose.

"You look good, Rudy," Canary tried, feeling it obligatory upon him to make some comment.

"Do I? Do I look good?" He stopped by BoBo, breathing heavily down the man's back. While he was not a dragon, his breath stung, little tendrils of fire searing the treads of BoBo's shirt.

"You look good, compared to others," he offered.

"How would you know? Tell me," Rudy prompted, shifting his attention back to Canary. "How do I look good to you?"

The man shrugged, regretting his rashness.

"You're alive. You've got all your limbs. Rose – Miss Rose – she said you're going to recover."

"Recover?" Rudy's head shot back as his back stiffened. "Recover from what?"

"Why, from your wound. Your hand," Canary reiterated, nodding toward the sling. Rudy's lips curled slowly around exposed teeth, a leering skull.

"You," he challenged D'Artagnan. "You tell me how I look good."

"I didn't say it," he protested, shoving the cards across the table in an attitude of one who has suffered greatly at another's hand.

"No," Rudy agreed. "You didn't say it. "You said I'd be here soon. Are you glad?"

"Glad of what?" came the exasperated interrogative.

"Glad-that-I-am-here."

"Yes! I am glad you are here."

"Why?"

D'Artagnan recklessly stacked his pennies by his side, counting them into rows of tens.

"So we can be together again. So things can be like they were."

"How were they?" the man who was standing inquired, purposely bumping the table so the stacks toppled.

"We had a ship. We were making money."

"The War is over."

"I know," the mate whined, crinkling his nose, then wiping it with the back of his hand. Before he could drop it, Rudy's right streaked out, catching it in a vice-like grip.

"I detest bad manners. Who taught you that? Not your father. Where did you pick up so disgusting a habit? Have you no pocket linen about you?"

D'Artagnan was so startled by the action he assumed the speaker incapable of, he cried, attempting to withdraw his limb. Discovering he could not, he raised his left, waving it before the other's face.

"Yes. I have a handkerchief. I beg your pardon. It is the times," he added hesitantly, afraid to be struck.

"Ah. It is 'the times.' Well spoken." His grip tightened.

> "In the tides of Life, in
> Action's storm,
> A fluctuant wave,
> A shuttle free,
> Birth and the Grave,
> An eternal sea,
> A weaving, flowing,
> Life, all-glowing,
> Thus at Time's humming loom 'tis my hand prepares

The garment of Life which the Deity wears!'

"Faust," Rudy clarified. Goethe. *The song of the earth spirit.* I have heard it."

"Heard what?" whispered the boy, rolling his shoulders the way a man adrift attempted to stabilize his world.

"The earth spirit. Crying. 'Alas, no more.' Do you understand?"

"No, Rudy. I don't. Please. Let me go."

Unwilling or incapable of complying, the former sea captain glared at BoBo.

"Pick up the cards." He did so for fear the hand of death would find his shoulder. "Shuffle them."

"We're done with our game," he tried, his voice below a whisper. Had he only thought the sentence, Rudy would have heard.

"Do as I say. You invited me to play. Or did I mistake?"

Glancing around the gathering, he applied his dull, lusterless eyes to the boys, one-by-one, the way a hangman sought volunteers.

"All right. I'll shuffle them."

When he had complied with the order, Rudy Blake made a grotesque flapping motion with his left arm.

"Spread them out – in your hand. Face down, so all the cards are accounted for." BoBo made an awkward attempt to do as he was told. When he held the grouping out, Rudy winked at Canary. "Draw a card."

"Which card?"

"Any card. The one which represents your destiny."

"My destiny?" Canary's voice cracked as he backed away. "What do you mean?"

"I am going to play a game with you. As I was invited. Not the same game you were playing." His grin widened, revealing red and swollen gums. "A different game. You do not object? You, who have waited so long for my return. Well," he announced, loudly and menacingly. "I have returned. To... weave your fortune. A talent, perhaps, you did not know I possessed. So. There are many things you do not know about me. Draw a card."

Running his hand through his long, wavy hair, Canary tugged relentlessly on a loose end, using it to augment his denial.

"I don't want to," he pleaded, gulping down saliva. Rudy's eyebrows arched in mock surprise.

"You don't want to?" he faithfully repeated, but without the fright. "Why not?"

No easy answer, nor glib reply sprang to bloodless lips. Dropping his arm listlessly to his side, he applied for solace from the remaining three. As well aware that death followed life, none were eager to intercede. If not Canary, Rudy's skeletal finger would point to one of them.

In the struggle between what was and what would be, none wished to know what lay beyond the veil.

"Could it be," the master drawled, enunciating slowly, so that even were their hands about their ears, the crew would hear, "that you are... afraid?" One third of a dozen heads dropped simultaneously. "Afraid?" Rudy reiterated, underscoring the word with shock and contempt. "Four men, hale and hearty, afraid to have their fortunes told?"

Placing his tongue behind his front teeth, Rudy sucked air, making a tortured, strangulating noise. Once again, he resumed his walk, this time taking care to lift his feet, occasioning no sound, so that he might have been traveling on cat's paws.

"Can this be so? But I cannot believe so... evil of you." Abruptly terminating his sojourn behind BoBo, he shot a look of pure hatred at his mate, so named for his beauty of voice. "Pick-a-card. Now."

Trembling with a fit of ague, Canary did as he was told, hesitating long before drawing one of the fifty-two pasteboards. When he made no attempt to reveal the underside, Rudy threw back his head, a god of old.

"Show the card."

"Please, Rudy.... Captain Blake. This is all – nonsense," the youth pleaded, sniffling back a cry.

"Show it. That is my... wish."

Placing one hand over the other to steady himself, Canary turned his wrist, the veins distended in his neck as though the feat required tremendous energy. With a low moan, he dropped it, revealing the suit and number.

"The two of diamonds," D'Artagnan read without comprehension.

"Deniers – or coins," Rudy more aptly identified. "The two of deniers." Bending at the waist, he studied the card, the reddish color reflecting back on his cheeks the way buttercups shone under the chins of inquisitive children.

"The divinatory meaning," he continued, savoring his knowledge like fine wine, "signifies difficulty in beginning new projects. A difficult situation arising. New, unlooked for trouble. Or troubles," he added, moving slightly to the side to indicate possible uncertainty. "Pick it up and hold it out, so that I may more closely observe the images."

Canary did so, without once resting his eyes on the diamonds.

"Ah. It is difficult to tell with precision whether it is upright, or the opposite. What do you think?" he inquired of the reluctant petitioner.

"I do not know."

"Let us consider: were it reversed, the meaning would be literary ability. Agility in handling matters." He cleared his throat. "Simulated enjoyment. Enforced gaiety. That is pertinent, is it not?"

"If you say so."

"Yes. I think that is it. We will leave it at that. Enforced gaiety with the possibility of a difficult situation arising. It is, you see," he added, rubbing his fingers together, "quite likely there is a bit of both predictions about you." Affixing his stare on Smartmouth, he indicated the deck. "Draw a card."

Smartmouth, so called from his ability to draw crowds and entice listeners, made the sign of the cross over himself, then picked from the extended deck BoBo had spread. Without order, he revealed the face.

"The seven of spades," D'Artagnan, the designated speaker, advised.

"The seven of epees," Rudy said, savoring the image. "The divinatory meaning is new plans. Wishes about to be fulfilled. Endeavor. While the reverse," he added, lifting his chin in the attitude of a wolf on the prowl, "is arguments. Quarrels. Uncertain council or advice. Interesting."

"Which is it?" Smartmouth whispered, locking his feet to the floor to fortify his foundation.

"Again, interpretation is in the eye of the beholder. Quite interesting." Lifting himself on tiptoe, Rudy surveyed the gathering. "Now, who here, I wonder, would give you bad advice? It is something to ponder. But then, again," he grinned, "you may be in for a 'share' of – what would you say? Adventure? But beware, my friend," came the admonition from a man who had seen too much. "Adventure is a double-edged sword."

Sighing deeply, but without regret, Rudy addressed his second in command.

"Your turn."

D'Artagnan, the faithful musketeer, demurred.

"I will go last."

To everyone's surprise, Rudy was amenable. "Very well. Master BoBo, named after your grandfather, a hero of the Late Revolution, once removed, pick a card. Any card," he cajoled, using his sing-song, huckster's intonation.

Laying the deck of cards on the table, BoBo spread them wide, so that the ones on the end were separated from the pack. Balling his hand into a fist, he dangled it over the grouping, moving up and down with life in the balance. When he finally chose one, it was from dead center.

"The ace of – deniers," D'Artagnan pronounced, hoping to forebear a further explanation.

"Ah, so. The *lowest* card in the suit," Rudy agreed, shattering his companions delusion.

"What – does it mean?"

His hopeless fear caused the reader to smile.

"At first you did not want to know and now you demand an answer. Let me see." Placing his right hand to his forehead, Rudy selected the interpretation. "If the card is upright – and I do not say it is – then what we have here is perfection. Attainment. Ecstasy. Treasure. An appropriate card for a pirate, wouldn't you say?"

"But I am not a pirate. Not any longer," BoBo, the namesake protested, quivering beneath the weight of his disclaimer. "What is the other meaning?"

"Oh." Rudy shrugged, maintaining his wafer-thin grin. "A matter of no consequence to one such as you." He paused, then lowered the boom. "Prosperity without happiness. Misused wealth. Wasted moneys. Corruption by money. You should not have given up your turn," he replied to D'Artagnan. "Perhaps that was *your* card he chose."

"No. I will not have it," the youth rebelled, standing back from the table. "But if you think so, return all cards to the deck and let me pick fresh."

It was a challenge no one but Rudy expected.

"Do as he suggests," he ordered. "Let there be no mistake." Hurriedly rushing to obey, BoBo gathered in the three loose cards, jammed them back into the deck, then shuffled. "No," he was abruptly halted. "Let he who will seek his fame and fortune in the ancient mysteries shuffle his own tarot."

Handing them off with a whimper of resignation, BoBo wiped his hands across his shirt, dampening them by the accumulated moisture of the cloth. D'Artagnan handled them carelessly, knocking the end against the table, before beginning a two-handed riffling. To belie his claim to superiority, several of the cards fell out. With a growl of anger he replaced them, before spreading the complete number, face up on the gaming surface.

"That's not fair," Canary complained, knocking against a leg as he leaned forward. "You can see the faces."

"What difference does it make?" the officer shouted, his face flushing from excitement. "As none of us know these meanings – if, in fact, they have any, which I doubt – you cannot say I draw one knowingly. I wish to face my future with open eyes."

"I approve." Rudy Blake, master sharper, put an end to the discussion. "With your eyes open. It is fitting."

Curling his lips in disdain, D'Artagnan, cavalier of olde, selected a royal suit.

"Here," he demanded, thrusting the card at his master. "I have chosen your card; the king of hearts, to represent me. Give me my fortune."

"Are you certain, my little minion, you are brave enough to hold my card as your standard?" Rudy asked, orbs black with storm. "I give you a second chance to amend your future. Speak now, or bear my fate as your own. And free me," he added, his voice barely above a whisper, "to choose another."

"I so choose."

"Very well." Turning to scan his audience, Rudy appeared to be counting. Not the uninvolved three, but multitudes. His lips moved, making words. Darting a look at Canary, Smartmouth questioningly hitched an eyebrow. *One hundred? Two hundred? What is he doing?*

Blinking a coded "I don't know," for he had been the signalman aboard the *Reprobate,* the seaman cast his eyes down. Whatever the message, he did not want to know.

Finally satisfied with his matriculations, the seer directed his unmitigated attention toward D'Artagnan. An aura of light seemed to have settled over Rudy, so that when he held out his hand for the card, it followed him, not a shadow, but its otherworldly opposite.

"The king of hearts. *Roi de coupes*. Within it lies your fate, Mr. –" Frowning, Rudy placed his hand to his head. "Forgive me. I have forgotten your name. What is it?"

The question, spoken softly, kindly, sent a chill of dread through the small company.

"D'Artagnan," the mate replied, shifting his weight unevenly from foot to foot.

"The name with which you were christened."

The breeze, blowing through the open window a moment ago, died. It was an ungainly demise. Instantly, the air grew thick, heavy. Quelling a sudden impulse to run, BoBo sank back, placing his hand where an arrow might have struck.

Of all the unwritten rules aboard Captain Blake's ships, the one most prominent had been the cloak of anonymity. None of his crewmen knew the other's true identity. They had signed aboard with nicknames dispensed by the commander, at his whim and free will. Never had the crew breached this secrecy. For reasons of their own, dusted, perhaps with a particle of fear at breaking honor with he who had named them, they had kept their own council.

Now, in the face of three others, Rudy himself was shattering the code of silence.

As a beginning, it portended termination.

CHAPTER 33

Stiffening his back, D'Artagnan faced the inquisitor in the guise of Rudy Blake. Without fear or honor or betrayal, he spat out that which had never before been spoken to such an assemblage, upon any occasion, good or ill.

"James Christian Carver, III."

Rather than lesson the mood, the revelation deepened it. Smartmouth licked his lips, then fanned his face, rolling his eyes upward toward the ceiling. With the attitude of a man dealt a bad hand at poker, Canary drummed his fingers on the table, his nose flaring in distaste. Silence deepened into grave-like omnipresence.

The ticking of a pocket watch became the dominant sound in the room. Steady, even, persistent, it marched away the seconds. As Rudy had the moment before, Canary counted. Ten. Fifteen. Twenty.

Twenty-one.

Twenty-two.

"No!" BoBo screamed, shattering the silent recitation. All eyes riveted to his flushed countenance. "He is lying. That is not his name!" Before the man could protest, BoBo shot an accusatory finger toward him, sealing his lips. "I know his name, Captain Blake, and that is not it."

"You know his name?"

"I do."

Hands extended, palms upward, Rudy appealed to him.

"Pray, enlighten us."

Pushing back in his chair, BoBo stood, savagely kicking the seat with the tip of his boot. The chair tottered, then regained its balance.

"His name is D'Artagnan. He has no other. I swear it, on my grandfather's grave. That," he continued, waving at the man to his right with wild abandon, "is Canary. And he is Smartmouth. The others – Forty-Niner, Jack, Copperhead, Tar Fish... all of them. Ringo," he added, nearly choking in his haste. Those are their names. The ones they were – christened with."

"So I am their deity?" Rudy inquired, leaning forward, eyes nearly closed in concentration, pulling from BoBo, by the magnetism of his personality, the answer.

"I know nothing of gods." Stifling a sob, BoBo clutched his arms around himself. "You are Rudy Blake. I am BoBo. Remember me?" he pleaded, suddenly dropping his arms and interlacing his fingers before him. "The man with a name – how did you put it – the man with a name so ridiculous, not even you could come up with better."

"Yes." The admission was easily won. "I remember. BoBo."

"BoBo. BoBo. BoBo. Mister BoBo. Read him his fortune!"

Rudy shrugged, his face a reflection of inherent sadness.

"How am I to read his fortune, when I do not know the identity of he I read it for? Is he D'Artagnan, or James Christian Carver, III? Or is he Rudy Blake?" he demanded, searching the four walls for an answer. "He had chosen my card."

The three mute crewmen could not have answered for their lives. Only BoBo was empowered to speak.

"I have told you, sir. His name is D'Artagnan. He is a musketeer. He is not that other man. He is not Rudy Blake. If he has chosen your card, he has assumed responsibility for its divination. Give it to him."

The pocket watch reassumed its ascendancy over the room. This time, no one counted.

"As it was *not* in the beginning, is now and ever shall be," Rudy confirmed, his words echoing off the warm bodies of those pressed close. "Amen." Shrugging his shoulders to indicate the matter was closed, he faced the man who had lied about his identity.

"The King of Coupes," he explained for those without eyes to see, "holds a small scepter in his left hand. In his right, a great cup. His expression is kind and considerate. He gives the appearance of being levelheaded and responsible."

As though actually seeing the lower arcana card, instead of the traditional king of hearts, Rudy smiled. A benevolence settled over him, augmenting the impression of aura.

"Upright, this card indicates a man of integrity. Learned. Responsible. In some circles, he may be considered artistic. Always reliable. Considerate of the needs of others. A man trusted to lead. Is he a fighter?" Glancing toward the open window, Rudy hesitated. "That is more difficult to answer. I would say, he is a king who would seek redress for injury and right wrongs. But only after determining the... fairness... of such action."

His smile widened as he communed with those invisible to naked eyes.

"He is seated, one leg behind the other. That implies he may not be what he seems; or rather," he added, brushing a hand across his pale, sweat-stained face, "he does not reveal all of himself to those he rules. There is something held back, in reserve."

Reaching down to touch the card table, Rudy ran his fingers over the grain, pausing briefly to dig his fingernail into a particularly deep spot.

"He leans against a table, implying casualness, yet that is a private farce. He is far from relaxed. Again, the king is displaying for the portrait-painter one of his many faces. You recall I said he was an actor. And so he is. Or, a performer. That is, perhaps, a better word. His eyes," he described, fixing his own against the backdrop of his imagination, "are staring straight ahead. But no, that is not precisely correct. While his gaze may be taken for that, he is actually peering slightly upward. What he sees, no one else may envision."

Finished with the table, Rudy wandered toward the chair BoBo had displaced, gently resting a hand on the backrest, as though to comfort the wooden piece of furniture.

"There are lines of care about the eyes. Time has taken its toll. Yet he is not old." Touching his own face, Rudy contemplated the inevitable. "His mustache droops; his lips downturned. He has been to the looking glass and seen the past."

Running a hand through his hair, Rudy dallied a moment, striking a rakish pose before continuing.

"His arm rests upon a table; a fine, intricately carved table, to be sure. This indicates wealth. He has amassed a fortune in his lifetime. He will accumulate more. Yet he spends – graciously. Possibly even lavishly. To maintain his station, for he has learned that image is much in this world.

"Upon his head there sits a crown. It is golden, signifying status. He understands the value of *gold*," Rudy added, his voice reflecting, for a second, a tinge of bitterness. "For he has sought it in unlikely places." Patting the chair, he bade BoBo sit.

"The cup – symbol of attainment – is empty. Does that mean he has lost his wealth? No. For he is rich – beyond his wildest dreams. But dreams," he emphasized. "That is the key. He is a dreamer. He had not yet fulfilled his dreams. Some have led him astray. Others have faded. New ones have replaced the old. These he shares with no one. He is alone. Yet, not alone, for we know there is a *reine des coupes*. His queen. Hidden. Unseen.

Where is she?" he demanded, turning quickly, with an agility beyond his capacity, to point toward the closed door. "She is in the deck, of course. Waiting her turn to be dealt. She, too, holds a scepter and a great cup. But we have not come to speak of *her*. But of you, sir."

Holding the king of hearts in his right hand, Rudy manipulated the card so that it sang, twirling with magical properties between and through his fingers. With a low chuckle of delight, he played with it, eyes gleaming with anticipation. When it finally appeared the pasteboard would spring from his person to take flight and escape through the window, he gave a high-pitched cry and flung it to the table. The card landed face down.

The men around him gasped, their spirits, at once soaring with the card, cruelly dashed to earth.

"And then we have the obverse." His voice deepened, grumbling in his throat like raining thunder. "Let us consider." He paused dramatically. "The reverse meaning of the king of hearts is double-dealing. Dishonesty. Scandal. Loss. Ruin. Injustice. Gone," he continued, sweeping his hand out across the table, "is our trusted leader. Shattered is our faith in humanity."

Reaching out, Rudy grasped a whisky glass, engulfing the drinking vessel with his powerful hand. Although, by outward appearances, he strove to shatter the glass, no one in the room believed that to be his true intent. Rudy was acting for them, dramatizing a part. It was not his skill which failed to carry the deception, but their overwhelming fright of the outcome.

With a lusty bellow, Rudy heaved the object away from him. It hit the wall, shattering into fragments.

"There!" he cried. "It is done. The gods are alerted. The – card – has been passed."

"No, Rudy, no!" D'Artagnan shrieked, greatly moved by the unfolding scene of which he played so great a role. Sniffing back moisture from his running rose, he made half a step toward the broken chards, then abandoned the attempt with a wail of hopelessness.

He was not to be let off the hook so easily. Dancing with a litheness of spirit they could not believe he possessed, Rudy danced about the room, hearkening to the sound of faerie wings apparent to his ears alone.

"Look!" he commanded, exposing the face of the card, which had, for eight shining orbs, taken on the shape and image of the *roi*. "See how he has changed. "Gone are the stress fractures of age. He has regained his youth, but lost his wisdom. What he has learned has been wiped away in an instant. The days of yore beckon; life's brutal challenges thrill, rather than temper."

"Send him back! Send him away!"

Reaching for the simple king of hearts, D'Artagnan attempted to right it, but Rudy was faster, most skilled. Grasping the paper with the tips of his fingers, he held it down, forcing the youth to pry it from beneath his hold. With a terrifying wail, he ripped it in half, then in quarters, spitting as he did so, a wet, hissing, back-arched cat-cry of thwarted fury.

"I renege! It was a jest; an innocent fooling. I am not you. You are the king of hearts. You, and only you!"

Rudy froze so suddenly D'Artagnan nearly vomited from the blow which never came. Clutching his stomach, he staggered back, eyelids lost inside his skull.

"I?" came the astonished interrogative. "I? You say I am the king of hearts? The roi de coupes? I – Rudy Blake?"

"Yes. You. Rudy Blake, and no other."

The passage back was not to be so easy.

"I? Think again, Master." Holding a finger to his lips while tapping his mustache lightly, Rudy stalked himself, turning to the left and right before staring straight ahead. "This is your chance. You have thrown the gauntlet, and I – I have failed to pick it up. You won the duel without firing a shot."

"I swear to you, Rudy, I was having a joke with you. I do not want to be... those things. I am not a double-dealer. Why," he laughed, the sound empty and hollow, "I cannot even win at cards." Rudy's iron-hard features did not flinch. The mate swallowed, breathing rapidly. "I am not dishonest."

The denial caused the ruby-red of falsehood to rise to his cheeks. "At least, no more than the next man. I fear scandal and ruin." The boyish strength of youth seeped from his pores. "I fear death." And then, in a tone barely audible, "I do not wish to rule. You... you are the captain of the realm. Blake's Kingdom," he tried, his jaw quivering.

That, finally, elicited a response. The lines around Rudy's cheeks deepened as his eyes sunk deep into their individual sockets. His hair assumed a greyish tint, while the old battlescars on his face sharpened into craters from the glint of fading light from the distant window.

"You call me the captain of the realm," he repeated with the frailty of an ancient deity, unearthed from a long forgotten grave. The scent of mold and mildew reeked from his parchment-like skin, yellowed by the unendurable passage of years. "Look around you, sir, at 'Blake's Kingdom.' Not here," he jeered, as D'Artagnan shifted his eyes around the room, catching him in an even greater foolery. "But there – there! Beyond these damned four walls, you minion of dust and mites! Across the miles. Three thousand miles and more. Do you see?"

Vainly striving to envision that which the king referred, D'Artagnan numbly shook his head.

"I am trying to."

"You are trying to," Rudy repeated, a parrot, mocking its master. "But you cannot. None of you can see, for you are blind. Blind beggars, all, you deceitful worms and grave crawlers. You – lice."

Stamping his leaden feet, Rudy marched in place. His back bent, his head drooped. Only his voice crackled with the intensity of hell's fire.

"You wished to be king. Why is that? Because the old king is dead. You are the heir-apparent. And a poor specimen, at that. No seed from my loin," he added scornfully. "You sent the king to battle. Yes, yes," he mumbled, more for his own edification. "Rudy King Blake. I am the king. Level-headed and responsible. It was I who witnessed the fall; I who responded to the call. I who crawled through Hades on my belly, more dead than alive. I who cried, with an ache in my heart sharper than any bayonet." Tears spilled down his cheeks, covering the scars with a new layer of agony, so that he was, at once, both youthful and aged.

"Turn your swords into plowshares," he mocked, not at himself, but at them. "You awaited my return – the reemergence of the king, untouched, unscathed, unburned by horrors of war. This, I know," he pronounced, lifting his head, like a turtle, from its shell. "You wanted it to be the way it was. Purple and gold; silks and trumpets. 'The king has returned; long live the king!' But the king is dead. Alive but dead. That," he leered, "is a conundrum. Something," he dismissed with the finality of eternity, "which you could never understand. No matter."

A fit of coughing overcame him, shaking his frame to the roots, so that the once mighty oak slipped off its foundation of earth.

"You wanted it the way it was, but when you saw that could not be, you rebelled. Richard against Henry. I know." His head shook. "I have seen war. I have tasted evil and spat it out, leaving the dogs to eat my vomit."

BoBo gagged, then covered his face in his hands.

"I have killed and I have been killed. I am not the man I was. I sit on my throne, holding an empty cup, leaning against a table. The part of me which was hidden from sight, you never saw. The crown on my head is tarnished. Why, D'Artagnan, why, did you pick my card?"

The question was a plea, a broken-hearted wail, an investigation into the depths of a man's soul.

Without explanation, Smartmouth sunk to his knees. Placing a hand on his shoulder, Canary followed suit, so that the two of them rested on the floor. Rudy ignored them, for his attention was directed solely on his mate.

"And why, in the name of God, did you destroy it?"

"The card, Rudy. Not you. I never meant to hurt you."

He did not believe the denial, but inexplicably accepted the apology. With it came resignation and an acute awareness of his surroundings. Trivial details stood out in stark reality. The woodgrain of the playing table. The length and texture of the carpet knap. The scent of men, gathered together. The odor of flowers, twisting on strings of air current, at once pungent and vague. The assertive chirp of a distant bird, stalking its territory against intruders.

Crashing under the blow of too much input, Rudy grimaced in pain, pressing his left hand against his chest, willing the insidious pain, boring a hole through his consciousness, to subside. A curtain of darkness descended over his world.

"I must sit down."

Instantly D'Artagnan reacted, grabbing a chair and carrying it around behind him. Setting the seat against the back of Rudy's legs, he gently prodded him to sit.

"Here, sir. Rest. You are ill."

Blindly trusting, or perhaps not caring, Rudy lowered his spare, quivering body. As his weight rested against the shallow, convex seat, he sighed, allowing tense muscles to relax, so that it appeared he were melting.

With the restored king on his throne, BoBo spontaneously joined Smartmouth and Canary on the floor, curling his legs beneath him, in the attitude of a child, awaiting wisdom from his elder. Catching D'Artagnan's eye, he bade him join them. Without a sound, the fourth complied, so that they formed a semicircle around the master.

Had lightning struck the house, destroying its frame so that the roof collapsed, none would have moved. They could not, for they had cast the fates with Rudy Blake. Their day of reckoning had come.

The silence was prolonged, but not uncomfortable. The boys were content to wait. Not until BoBo's stomach growled did they react. Not with annoyance or disdain, but with childlike grins at the unavoidable *faux pas* of their companion. It was that which brought Rudy Blake back from the land of beyond.

"You were afraid," he began, slowly rubbing his right hand over his left arm, not to alleviate his suffering, but rather to acknowledge to himself the suffering he had endured. "You made a mistake."

"Yes, sir," D'Artagnan murmured, the words oddly enunciated through shamed, twisted lips.

"In one brash act, you made a stand. From impulse, or anger. Or false superiority. You wished to be the king."

"Sir," D'Artagnan protested, but Rudy waved him quiet.

"I know," came the tortured admission, the deep crevices around his eyes haunting his features. "I have done the same. Not," he corrected, a wan expression of self-deprecating humor decorating his mouth, "a sin of arrogance, but one equally devastating. I went to war and I was unprepared. Just as you were."

Ten thousand tiny pinpricks jabbed his arm, causing him to flinch. With his stomach tied in knots, Rudy made a fist with his wounded hand, augmenting the sensation until his head lolled from creeping blackness.

"War is not uniforms and marching bands. The parades and the gilt sword handles are trappings of deceit and trickery. They are lies, disguising the blood and the gaping holes where bullets tear through cloth. I thought I knew all that. Just as you thought your time had come. Not until your innards turn to mush do you realize how deceived you were."

Steadying his breath, which came irregularly and in shallow gasps, he daubed at his face, wiping away the rivulets of perspiration.

"I had no uniform. I marched naked through the fields and across the mountains. The only band I heard played victory tunes for those who would surrender.... Inscribe their names in the *Book of the Defeated*. I cause death, gentlemen, and I saw death. Death on a scale you cannot imagine, for it is beyond the power of human ken to see what lies beyond the vale of distance. I wept; I soiled my pants and felt no shame. I howled to God and no one answered. I buried the living, knowing they were better off in graves then crawling on their bellies, entangled in their own guts."

Without volition, Rudy's feet began a slow shuffle, first one, then the other, as he paraded across the battlegrounds of hell.

"I saw rape and committed... atrocities no sane man could endure. I starved and withered and froze. I sweated and begged for water. I held my ground, then gave it up, littered with the bodies of men I should have died for. I found no glory, no reward. I never – not once – felt the thrill of victory, for there was no victory. The issues of winning and losing blurred with the endless days and the sleepless nights. I obeyed orders from fools while wearing the clothes of a dead man. I saw wilted flowers on bridegrooms. I... stood on the deck as the ship sunk around me. I was," he added softly, "not the last man off. There were no heroics. I went down with the ship. Without bravery, without honor."

His feet continued to march. Without understanding why, Canary reached out and placed a hand on Rudy's toes. The legs quivered, then ceased their restless inactivity.

"You were right to challenge me. I should have expected it." His face contorted. The hurt was great. "I am not what I was. The... king... has returned from the Holy Land, his crusade a failure. I have... described him to you. Now you know."

With the pain growing more acute, dominating his existence, Rudy worked his arm from the sling, letting the material hang loose; a noose, after the condemned has been cut down and left to rot. Grasping his bandaged wrist, he hoisted it up, a standard without a breeze. The moment was nearing its end. Panic, of a dull, muted ache, wracked his soul. They were waiting for him again. To sign his name.

In the *Book of the Defeated*.

The *Bible of the Damned*.

The chapter of revelations was not yet completed. He would have to hurry.

"Why, D'Artagnan. Why?"

He could not hang his head. Rudy had paid the penance for them.

"Because, sir, I had not seen what you saw. I should have gone to war."

"No... sir." The words were low, gentle. Forgiving. "It was mine."

Leaning forward, D'Artagnan crossed his hands. He rocked slowly, back and forth, assuming for Rudy, the power of mobility.

"I made a mistake. The greatest – sin – I have ever committed. You were right." He smiled, but it was sad and filled with resignation. "I wished to be you. I always have, you know."

"Yes. I did that to you."

"No, sir. I did it to myself, by wishing to be someone I was not." Placing his palms to the floor, D'Artagnan pushed himself up, so that he was standing. The height difference between the two men was strikingly apparent. To mitigate its effects, the youth stooped. "You have given me fear. In this room, before you, I have tasted death and felt... my stomach turn to mush. I am not Rudy Blake. I never could be. I am... D'Artagnan. No other."

"Rudy Blake," lisped the whispered confession, "is not god."

"I thought you were." The admission was given without malice, the disappointment issued with humility. He smiled and it was boyish and loving. "I still think you are. But now I know that 'god' is not what we thought he was. He feels. He has the capacity for fear. His confidence is not overwhelming. I... did not know, sir."

"I fooled you."

"Yes, sir. You did."

"I will never be that same – god – again."

"Not to worship like cabin boys," D'Artagnan agreed, his smile widening. "But to follow, as men. You know me. I am a musketeer. I don't want to be the – *roi of coupes.*" Brushing aside a stray lock of hair, he indicated the table. "Let me pick another card. Will you permit me?"

"I will. If that is what you want."

Closing his eyes, the man standing held his hand over the scattered deck. With lips moving in prayer, he made his selection.

"This one. Upon its divinatory meaning I will stand or fall."

When Rudy did not reach out to take it, D'Artagnan placed it gently in his hand, prying it between stiff fingers.

"The six of *coupes,*" Rudy identified. "It is reversed. Upside down."

The youth swallowed, then held back his head, eyes flashing. Inside him, his muscles tightened, stiffening his resolve.

"Tell us the meaning."

"It portends future events. Opportunities ahead. Coming events. New vistas." There was more to come. The four waited upon the man who was not god, but went by the moniker of Rudy Blake.

"Plans which may fail."

"May fail." D'Artagnan saluted. The three others rose to their feet, emulating his action. "Or may not fail. This, I accept. I am D'Artagnan, with new vistas ahead. This," he introduced, "is Canary. Before him lie new projects. This is Smartmouth. He faces the challenge of interesting endeavors. The fourth of your crew is BoBo. He has the prospect of attainment. Between us stands prosperity without happiness, uncertain council, difficult situations and corruption."

Maintaining his attitude of respect, D'Artagnan grinned. "Without demeaning your powers of interpretation, Captain Blake, I say you have gotten precisely what you bargained for. A crew of malleable boys, neither all good, nor all bad. Whether we stand upright or on our heads, you have signed us up for life. That, sir, was a stipulation of being recruited into your service."

"Then I –"

"No, sir, Captain Rudy Blake. Without realizing, you have reaffirmed our enlistment."

"As we, Captain Blake, have accepted," Smartmouth reciprocated.

"I am not your god."

"War, Rudy, has changed us all. Our battles came after yours," BoBo avowed, shaking his leg so that he might have been a soldier on parade. "It was called by a different name, but the battles have been bloody." Wiping his eyes, he sighed heavily. "We have wept. We have crawled in the dirt. We have signed our names in the *Book."*

"Which book is that?"

The answer was self-evident.

"The *Book of Blake."*

A sob of tortured resignation broke from Rudy's lips. As his body began to spasm, he lurched forward, consciousness slipping away into the realm of darkness. Six pair of hands grabbed him, righting the ship. Clutching his cold, damp head, they held it back, breathing on him with the breath of life. His eyes fluttered open. Peering down were those of his crew, taut and frightened and hopeful.

Rudy Blake had returned from war, only to discover another. But unlike that former contest, this one he survived.

A new chapter in the *Book of Blake* had begun. What it contained, only God alone knew.

CHAPTER 34

Her back was to him as he entered the room. She was seated at the kitchen table, a cup of coffee resting by her left side. He did not have to touch it to know it was cold.

"Rose Bud?"

A plaintive question. The sound of a man, soul-weary and travel tired.

"Yes, Rudy Bud?"

In one fluid motion, Rose stood and turned to face him. Like his, her face was ashen white, pinched and drawn at the corners. Unlike him, her eyes shone with the intensity of hot coals which hot breath had just uncovered.

"I wish to go for a ride."

He expected a flat denial. Protestations. An unending string of reasons why it was unsafe. He should have known better.

"The horses are harnessed. I have prepared a basket of food... and a flagon of rum, 'me hearty.'"

Holding out her hand, he accepted it. Together, they walked through the kitchen and out the back door. They would not go through the front, least it be guarded by abettis and redoubts, remnants of the Late, Great War.

A driver sat in position, hands to the reins. He touched his cap as they approached. Rudy thought he spoke, but could not be certain. If he did, the words were low, indistinguishable. Not for his ears.

Rose held back, allowing Rudy to open the door. This he did with accustomed flair. Being hatless, he doffed his head. She nodded and slid inside, reaching back to assist him as he followed. The moment the door shut, the carriage sprung away.

They followed the old route, avoiding the main highway. Two minutes ride took them out of sight of the Blake House. Ten minutes more and they had put behind them the sparsely settled environs of the neighborhood.

Adjusting the curtains so the slanted rays of the sun would not shine on his face, Rose retrieved the basket.

"Shall we eat now, or wait awhile?" He was not up to a reply. She had not expected one. Pulling back the lid, she retrieved a loaf of hard salami and a crockery jug. Setting the bottle between her legs, she cut the meat, two large chunks, irregularly shaped. Handing him both, Rose deftly popped the cork, spitting it aside. It bounced against the side of the carriage and bounced to the floor.

"Damn. Got away from me. Lively little bugger."

That was his cue and he took it.

"Guess that means we'll have to drink it all."

"We will; or have this conveyance smell like a distillery. Wouldn't want that."

Sniffing the hard sausage, Rudy shrugged.

"Why not?"

"Bad form." Hefting the bottle to her lips, Rose took a long swig, swallowing with the ease of one accustomed to hard drinking. "Wouldn't want people to think we're wasteful."

He grinned and they exchanged *material,* she taking the salami while he accepted the jug. Working his thumb through the handle, he hoisted it toward his face. With a wink and a sigh, he gulped two swallows before burping loudly. She was immediately offended.

"Is that the best you can do?"

Blushing like a schoolboy, Rudy drank again, this time belching with authority.

"Better," she approved. "But you'll have to work on the technique."

"I am out of practice."

"It will come back to you," she promised meaningfully, watching with satisfaction as his color deepened.

"Do you think so?"

"I know so."

Sighing thoughtfully, he turned his attention out the window to her side. What trees there were grew in the distance, making them appear pigmy-sized. A rough landscape of wild grasses filled the near spaces. With nothing better on which to concentrate, he became aware of his heart pounding. For a moment it panicked him until he identified the sensation.

"Rose. I am afraid."

It was an admission she was not yet ready to address.

"No fear; I have brought two jugs. If we finish one, we will start on the second."

"You know what I mean."

"Yes, Rudy. I know what you mean." Drinking again, she swallowed, then wiped her mouth on the sleeve of her blouse. He cringed and dropped his gaze.

"You need not do that for my sake. I know what I have lost."

"No, Rudy. I don't. Neither do you. We shall find out. On our journey."

"To London?" he asked, cringing at the idea of so short a time.

"We are not going to London. Our destination is Liverpool."

Shifting uncomfortably in the seat, he found no position suited the throbbing in his buttocks. Grimacing in annoyance, he finally leaned back, closing his eyes.

"So far?"

"I am afraid so."

"I thought to go...." What he thought, he abandoned. "For a short ride."

"And I thought to go for a long one. You are uncomfortable. I am sorry. When we stop for the night, I will put salve on your hemorrhoids." As he flinched at the word, she finally smiled. "Your piles. Does that make them hurt less?"

"It does," he admitted. "You and your words." Diverting his attention to the sausage, he bite off a taste, rolling it around on his tongue as though the flavor were unfamiliar. "What is in Liverpool?"

Ignoring the scare in his voice, Rose shook her head.

"That is for me to know and you to find out."

"I am a burden to you. You have made a bad bargain."

"The same might be said of you, sir, adopting into your crew a harlot with no seamanship to her credit. Although it might be fairly said, I had 'weathered a few storms.' But I hardly suppose that counts."

"Will you listen to me?" he demanded, reaching forward to grab her. His awkward act of wild gesticulations, augmented by a sudden lurch of the carriage, caused him to strike her, the back of his hand making violent contact with her cheekbone. Yet it was Rudy who cried. "Oh, my God. Rose, I'm sorry!"

Blinking back a dampness in her eyes elicited from the blow, Rose stiffened in shock, her entire body going rigid. Unable to determine if her action was an offensive or a defensive posture, Rudy slumped back, pressing himself against the side door. Without daring to breathe or meet her stare, he curled into a ball.

"Stop the carriage. Let me out. Leave me here, beside the road. I will walk. In a day or a week, you will forget I have been here. Put me out of your life, Rose. I died in the War."

"Yes," she agreed, still without moving, for her muscles would not respond. "I could easily do that. Forget you have returned. Forget you ever existed. 'Take the money and run.' Isn't that your expression?"

With forced determination, Rose raised a fist. He cringed, but the weapon was not directed toward him. Banging it against the top of the carriage, she signaled the driver stop. A hurried, "Woaha," then, "easy, boys," and the animals came to a halt. Without thinking, Rudy fumbled for the latch. It was only Rose's hand, falling with the force of an anvil on her own thigh, which prevented his departure.

Her words severed his strings, eliminating any further thought of escape.

"We have both known violence, have we not?"

"It was an accident —"

"Waiting to happen," she finished, discovering the mobility to retrieve the flagon of rum which had fallen to the floor. Up-righting the bottle, she shook it, determined a quantity had spilled, then spitefully opened the door on her side and flung it out. The crockery struck a rock and shattered. Both stared at the wanton destruction before Rudy placed a shaking hand to his heart.

"There sure are going to be a lot of drunken ants out there."

He had not meant to amuse, but Rose's sudden guffaw shook him more greatly than if she had struck him.

"I suppose there will be. At least we have given some creatures a good turn today."

"But think of them tomorrow – when they all wake with hangovers," he observed, patting himself on the chest to signify the beating of his auricles. "Without a potion or a tonic with which to dose themselves." Leaning forward but not close enough to touch, he tried to envision a legion of inebriated ants. "We should have thought to bring with us a bottle of 'Unkle Jack's Black Tar.'"

"That, sir, would only exacerbate the situation," she dryly remarked.

Quizzically raising an eyebrow, he attempted to divine her reasoning. "Why is that?"

"Because it is nearly one hundred percent proof."

"What are you saying?" he gasped, nearly as shocked by the revelation as his blow had been to her.

"Alcohol is the primary ingredient. Why do you think it 'strengthens the constitution'?"

Licking his lips from lost ago memories, Rudy shook his head.

"Because of the ingredients – the mixture of magic herbs," he tried, finding his imagination falling short of supplying the requisite combination. "I had never given it any thought."

"That is your problem, Rudy. You take too much on faith."

"I? On faith?" He was stunned. Shaking his head in denial, he refused to believe. "I am the greatest skeptic of them all."

"Were I to make my living preaching to the unconverted, you would be the first man I summoned to the front," she remarked in disdain. "You are as easy to read as an open book."

"I?" he repeated. "I?"

"Three times lucky."

"But I am a heretic."

"You are a sheep in atheist's clothing. Mark well I did not say a 'wolf.' No one of my acquaintance has a greater capacity for faith than you."

"But the gods," he groped, struggling vainly to prove his point.

"Yes. Your denizens of Mount Olympus. Ready to pounce at a moment's notice on your hapless lapses. Or the gewgaws you wear for luck. Or your propensity to cross yourself before breaching the threshold of a holy place. Or your reverence in placing coins in a seaman's chapel box. Or your order, requiring services to be read aboard ship."

"Those – those are a requisite of the British articles –"

"Always an excuse to pay homage to a higher power. Superstition is not heresy, Captain Blake. It is a perverted form of acknowledgment. A demonstration of love."

"How can you say that? To me?"

"Because I know you, Rudy. Better than you know yourself. Just as I know you did not mean to hit me. But the propensity is there."

"For violence?"

"We have both lived rough lives. Violence is a way of striking back; of claiming a superiority against an unknown opponent. Or of making a foe of a friend, merely for the sake of trying to control your destiny. But what you do not know is that you are playing into the hands of a lesser power, rather than the contrary. Of excusing your failures by placing them in the hands of another."

"You are not my foe," he tried, vainly clasping his wounded arm to his chest. Reaching out, Rose touched him, applying light pressure to the cloth of his sleeve, so that he barely felt the touch.

"No. I am not. But it is – less cumbersome – to fight than to believe. Easy for me to put you out and leave you here. Easy for you to curl up and die."

"I came to you...."

"Without a true awareness of the battles yet facing you. They will be the hardest you have ever encountered. You have made inroads, yet you are far from triumph. You have fought your crew and won." His expression displayed a horrific disbelief. "Yes. I heard you speak to them. I was outside the door. Waiting."

"Waiting... to do what?" he whispered, seized with a fit of trembling, so that his teeth chattered.

"To kill them."

Gasping in shock, Rudy gagged, then put a hand to his mouth, spitting into it the bitter contents of his stomach. She waited until he had finished, then handed him a pocket linen from her own wardrobe. When he was unable to adequately wipe his face, she did it for him, taking care to absorb the acidic taste from the tip of his tongue before proceeding.

"All their fates, so brilliantly expressed. You did me proud, Rudy."

"But the cards... they picked them, themselves. I had nothing to do with it."

"And so they did. But the interpretation was yours."

"From the book.... I did not make it up."

"Didn't you?"

"No," he protested, shaking his head, then curling the handkerchief and wiping his brow with an unsoiled end.

"It was a masterful display of dispensing God's warning to them all. In parable," she concluded, tilting her jaw backward, in an obverse meaning. "In the same manner Jesus spoke to his disciples."

"I am not Jesus."

"No," she concluded sadly. "No one is. But you have qualities."

"What qualities?"

"You are not what you seem," she answered, leaving the vagueness of the answer open for discussion.

"But Christ was exactly what he seemed; God, descended to Earth. Made Man, so as to set an example."

"Of what?" Rose demanded, suddenly angered by his evasion. "An example of what, exactly?"

"Benevolence. Love. Forgiveness of sin."

"This, from an atheist," she scorned, reaching into the basket. Withdrawing a deck of unopened cards from the hamper, Rose broke the seal, then extracted the pasteboards. While he watched, eyes small representatives of full moons, she shuffled, thoroughly mixing the cards. "Hold them."

"Why?" he demurred, withdrawing in suspicion.

"I wish to draw one. So you can tell my fortune."

"No, Rose. That – scene – you witnessed with the crew. It was not meant for you."

"I will not be the only one left out."

"There is Jack," he protested. "And Forty-Niner."

"Their fortunes I do not doubt," she dismissed, wiping their names from the slate with a cute chopping motion of her hand. "Jack is loyal to a fault, and Forty-Niner is a boy. He will soon leave us."

"Will he?" Rudy whined, saddened by the loss.

"He has saved his money. Unlike the 'men' who have squandered their cut, Forty-Niner has all of his – poke." She paused as he smiled at her forty-niner reference. "It is as well for him."

"I like him."

"As do I. Let him cut the strings, Rudy. Ours is a crew of –"

"Reprobates?"

"You were reading my mind. Spread the deck and let me choose."

Reluctantly, Rudy fondled the cards, running them through his one good hand before bringing them to his cheek. The scratching against his stubble made a low, rasping noise.

"I am sorry. I meant to shave; to surprise you. I could not. My eyes... stared back at me. I did not recognize them."

"It is enough that I do."

"But, what do you see?" he pleaded, dropping his head to concentrate on spreading the cards.

"The man I love. Will you have it so?"

"I will," he replied, crinkling his eyes to hide the tears. "But I would as not read your fortune with the cards. This is... crass."

"Choose another way."

"Hold out your hand," he decided, raising his head to meet her gaze. "I will read your palm, instead."

"Which hand?" Rose asked, extending both.

"The left, in that you are left-handed." Dropping back her right, Rose allowed him to pour over the lines of her palm, alternately observing his technique and scanning his face. "You are not afraid?"

"No."

"And you are aware this is an... inexact science?"

"As much as preparing Unkle Jake's Black Tar is for me. While the recipe may change, the results are similar. Read my fortune."

Squinting, because his eyes hurt, Rudy bent low, scrutinizing the indentations and cross-lines on her hand.

"Your life line is long and deep. That means you are strong and wise."

"Tell the truth," she warned, straightening her back as proof of her assertion. "I want no lies."

"Nor will I give you any. See here," he indicated, pointing to an intersecting branch. "This is a significant person entering your life."

"You," she identified.

"Yes. I cross through but do not separate."

"It is well."

"We go on together. And see here. Another, smaller branch."

She did not ask him the meaning, for she already knew. "And that line?"

Curling his palm, Rudy startled her by placing the flat of his hand upon her head. Probing the contours of her skull, he nodded.

"Wisdom. Great knowledge. And here," he continued, sliding it forward, "Adversity. Trouble. Stress."

"Phrenology."

"They go hand-in-hand. Do you object?"

"I object to your pun," she attempted before replying more sternly, "No. Go on."

Taking back her hand, he studied the flesh, probing, then watching as the skin rebounded from his pressure.

"Temperance. Journeys. Long travails. An uncertain outcome."

"How so?"

"It does not end. See here," he indicated, pointing out the area of interest. "I cannot say for certain. It fades."

"Yet this line continues," Rose protested, marking the place with a fingernail. In the ensuing silence, she frowned. "It is neither you, nor I."

"No," he acknowledged. Closing his eyes, he shook his head. "Yes."

"Which is it?"

"This line indicates happiness. And this one love. Both are strong."

"You did not answer my question."

"I do not know." The answer was hard won. "On your hand I can only read your fortune. Not that of another. That is... a history with which I am, as yet, unfamiliar."

"Someone I am to meet?"

"Perhaps. Another influence."

"Another love?"

"Most certainly."

"Where does it lead?"

"I tell you, I do not know."

"And this line," she pursued, curling her palm to emphasize the creases. "A final outcome."

"Which is?"

"Ask Jesus," he replied suddenly, shuddering with fear. "As you say, this is supposition."

"I did not say."

"Superstition, then."

Angered by his refused, Rose reached out, grabbing his hand. Before he could deny her, she twisted his wrist, revealing his own palm.

"I will read your fortune."

"Go ahead. I am listening."

"I see.... This is the life line?" Rudy nodded. "A long life. Journeys. Long travails."

"My words."

"Our courses are the same," she dismissed. "And this – your happiness. What does it say?"

"I cannot read for myself."

Making a disparaging noise, she leaned closer, the hotness of her breath warning his hand.

"I read happiness. Contentment."

"You are making that up."

She ignored him. "Much work to be done. Ceaseless. A returning home." He attempted to jerk his hand away, but she held fact. "A discovery of home and then an abandonment. Does that suit?"

Meeting her gaze, he shrugged. "I cannot say." She returned to her task.

"A great mistake. Or," came the correction, "a travesty of justice. Pain."

Attempting to pull away, Rudy cringed. "Rose, I do not want pain. I have suffered enough."

"In this life, suffering is the road to salvation," she retorted, but her words were tense, frightened, for the revelation was not a pleasing one.

"Upon whom is this injustice perpetrated?" he pleaded.

"The lines intersect."

"Oh, God," he wailed, shaking his foot in abject misery. "Why hast thou forsaken me?"

"You are not forsaken, Rudy. You are but an instrument of His hand."

"I do not wish to be," he argued, curling his lips, then turning to spit. "Tell me plainly."

Instead of replying, Rose copied his former action by placing a hand on his head. Feeling the contours of his bone, she nodded without joy.

"You and I against the world. Yet we are not alone. There are others who join the cause."

"What others?"

"Unknown to either of us. A friend. Many enemies. The reemergence of an old friend. Trial. Escape. Flight. Arrogance."

"You read all that?"

"And more. Impudence." She finally grinned. "A journey. Far-away places. Uncertainty."

"And the outcome?"

"That," she declared, finally releasing her hands so that he was free to pull away, "I am in ignorance of."

"Why?"

"Your skull and your hand are yet – uninformed."

"Make up an answer."

"All right," she decided, reaching for the second flagon of rum and uncorking it with a simple flick of her thumb and forefinger. "Happiness."

"You make that up," he asserted, daring to grin.

"You told me to."

Lifting the jug to her lips, Rose drank deeply, before handing the bottle to him. He hefted it to his lips, then paused, kissing the rim.

"So I did." Placing his lips where she had put hers, he drank, his Adam's apple bobbing as he swallowed. "To happiness, Rose Bud," he declared, offering back the jug.

"To happiness. And adventure."

"Good or bad?"

"That would be telling."

"Ask God," he demanded, suddenly grasping her by the shoulder. She shook her head.

"God has already told us more than we have a right to know."

"I want to know more."

"Then drink from the bottle of wisdom," Rose teased, offering back the rum.

"Will give me the answers?"

"No. But with a supply of Mammy's Best Boy 'aboard,' you will, at least, have a remedy for your hangover."

"Which places me one step above the ants!" he declared, a boyish happiness stealing over his countenance.

"Aye," she declared, rapping on the roof with the neck of the bottle. Immediately the carriage resumed its forward progression. Lurching with the motion, Rudy glanced outside before returning his stare to her face, which he beheld was reddened with anticipation.

"Here's to the future – whatever it may hold."

"Here's to love – and the strength to endure," she amended, drinking from the bottle. When she finished, Rose heaved it out the window, watching as the crockery shattered against the unyielding landscape. "And to those friends yet unmet. May they be equal to the challenges we present them with."

"I'd drink to that," he sighed, wiping his mouth with his hand, "if only you had not tossed the rum overboard."

"Have no fear." Reaching into her basket, Rose removed a small, brown bottle the size of a playing card. Biting off the string with her teeth, she pried away the paper covering, then popped the cork. "To Mammy's best boy."

"And to her best girl," he added, grinning with wild expectation.

Quaffing half the bottle, Rose offered him the remainder.

It would be a long ride to Liverpool. And even if it were not, neither would notice.

CHAPTER 35

The rain came down in a slow, steady drizzle. The earth, already waterlogged, refused further ingress, creating puddles the size of water buffalo. Although Rose had not anticipated the downpour, a remedy was within easy reach. Disembarking at a wharfside "Sailor's Emporium," she directed Rudy inside, instructing him to choose a "slicker."

One arm suspended by the sling, the other hand shoved inside his trouser pocket, the long-haired, scraggly waif no one would have recognized as Captain Blake, wandered the aisles, peering cautiously at the selection.

"Are you sure I must?" he asked, dwarfed by the prospect of making a decision.

"It is either that, or take shelter. I do not want you catching a cold. While the air is not chill," she further explained, holding out a rubber cape for his inspection, "walking around in wet clothes will do you no good."

Shying away from her offering, he sniffed and was about to wipe his nose. Second-guessing the action, Rose offered him a handkerchief before the deed was accomplished. Nodding gratefully, he used the linen, then offered it back.

"Keep it," she advised.

Gratefully acknowledging the gift, he admired the embroidered initials on the linen before tucking it away.

"R.B."

"As fine a set of letters as ever were put together," she grinned. "While the color pink might not suit a gentleman, you may consider it a – conquest. A present from a lady."

Because she had used the words "gentleman" and "lady" in the same context, he could not argue. Wrinkling his nose then turning away, he examined a series of fishing lines. Comprehending that his tactic was a delay in making a choice, she gently steered him back.

"Do you prefer yellow or black?"

"Which do you like?"

Running her fingers over the material and determining both were equally acceptable, she leaned back, envisioning him in buttercup. While the image was appealing, she did not imagine it would suit.

"Black."

"Because I am evil?" came the whispered interrogative, making her regret the choice.

"No. Because it is mysterious. You are the random element, Captain Blake. No one knows when you will appear or what you will do. Besides," she continued, removing the slicker, "black makes a figure appear taller. I have always believed in accentuating my height."

"Why is that?" he recoiled, eying her suspiciously. "You are already as tall as a giraffe."

"But not as tall as you," Rose declared, making a face so that he was forced to smile. "But almost. Were I to add an extra inch to my heel, I would be your equal, sir."

"Then why don't you? I think you should."

Patting him on the arm, for she had hoped for a stinging rebuke rather than an invitation, Rose swept the rain cape around his shoulders. Fastening it at the neck, she nodded in approval.

"Now a cap. And then a rain hat to go over it."

"Pick one for me," he pleaded. "Whatever you decide has my approval."

"Very well. I will be but a moment."

Leaving him to stare at the rods, she went in search of caps. From out of the rear, a middle-aged man appeared, wearing an apron strewn with lures, so that he might have been a fisherman's Christmas tree, and not the proprietor. Recognizing Miss Theodore, he raised a hand in friendly salutation before sidling next to Rudy, whom he did not recognize and suspected of pilfering. His close proximity caused the younger man discomfort.

"Master Fisherman," Rose hailed, immediately surmising the situation. "Your assistance here, if you please."

Reluctantly abandoning his position, the man hurried over toward her, but not before letting his guard dog out. Taking silent signals from its master, the animal wandered toward the door, setting itself down to guard the premises.

"It is all right," Rose explained, lowering her voice so as not to be overheard. "The gentleman is with me."

Bowing respectfully, the shop owner apologized.

"They come in out of the rain, Miss, looking to steal."

Glancing sideways at Rudy, Rose could not find it within herself to blame the man, yet her heart hardened. A year ago, Mr. Bixler would have recognized Rudy, had he come in wearing a barrel for a suit and a flour sack over his head. It would be a long, long time before Rudy's unquenchable spirit and sprightly manner announced his arrival as surely as his handsome features.

"What can I help you with?"

"I am looking for a blue Nelson cap. Have you any in stock?"

"Aye. Just one, as luck would have it. I ordered it fer Captain Blake the last time he was in, but he never came to collect it. I supposed he had given up the business, miss, and gone abroad."

"It is for –" she eagerly began, then bit off her words. To announce the purchase was for that self-same Captain Blake would only make the man take a closer look at Rudy. She did not want it known he had returned, nor was it her desire to bring attention to the fact he was "not what he was."

"I shall take it," she declared, instead, hurrying him over to the counter. "As well as the rain cape my – associate – is wearing. And one for myself, of the same size. And two rain caps."

"More than happy to oblige, miss. Shall I wrap them for you?"

"No. We shall wear them out. Filthy weather we're having."

"A bit unusual fer this time o' year," he agreed, scurrying around the aisles to retrieve two rain caps for her inspection. His journey did not require he pass by Rudy, but he took the extra steps to satisfy his curiosity. Returning with the merchandise, he shot Rose a quizzical look.

"I'll just be a moment. The Nelson is in the back."

While he was gone, Rose amused herself by walking up and down the glass-fronted counter, staring at the seaman's goods displayed behind it. With a sudden cry of joy, she beckoned her companion.

"Rudy! Come here! Look at this; an entire jar of peppermint sticks."

Too late she realized her error, for Bixler had returned at almost the same time. Overhearing her exclamation and the peculiar name, associated with only one man, he shifted his eyes to the oncoming stranger before quickly dropping them.

Silently cursing herself, then abandoning any further attempt at obfuscation, Rose pointed toward the candy.

"How long has it been since one of those protruded from your mouth?"

Unable to come up with an exact answer, Rudy frowned, helplessly shaking his head.

"I don't know. A long time." Then, unsure he had articulated the appropriate response, he shrugged. "Is that right?"

"Right as rain," she laughed, tapping on the glass. "We shall take your entire stock. Those," she added menacingly, "you may wrap."

"Yes, miss," Bixler mumbled, this time being certain he kept his eyes away from the customers. "I'll put 'em in fish paper to protect 'em."

Signifying her approval, Rose took the Nelson cap from the counter and affixed it over Rudy's head. Setting it at his accustomed slant, she eyed him critically.

"Just the ticket. Now the rain cap and you are set to weather a gale at sea."

"Are we going to sea?" he whispered, fearfully glancing out the door and beyond to the wharf where the waves crashed upon the pilings.

"We are not. It was just an expression."

"Oh." His head drooped, allowing the cap, which was a size too large, to slip forward. Straightening it for him, Rose grasped him by the arm, leading him away.

"Stand here. I will be right back."

"How long?" he plaintively inquired, but too low for her to hear. Left to his own devices, Rudy bent over to pet the dog. It bared his teeth and growled.

"Tell – tell 'em not to bother ta animal," Bixler warned, handing over the wrapped package, tied with string. "It don't like strangers."

"It is all right. We are leaving."

Tossing what she presumed to be a slight overpayment across the counter, Rose tucked the candy under her arm, then hurried to the aisle where the rain slickers hung. Grabbing one to match Rudy's, she flung it on, then rejoined him by the door without bothering to fasten it.

"All right. We can go, now."

The dog, recognizing Rose's familiar voice, wagged its tail as they left. When the tinkling of the bell had fully dissipated, the shopkeeper hurried to the window, wiping the glass from the condensation of his breath to stare after the couple.

"Peculiar thing," he droned, addressing the dog. "I didn't recognize him at first, an' then I did. And then I didn't. But you heard what the Miss called him, didn't you, boy? Were that Rudy Blake, or not?"

Left to the dog, it flattened its ears against its brown and white hair, scratching at the door. The action was not friendly, as though it suspected the man of thievery.

"That's what I think, too," the master agreed. "I guess it weren't. He could fool me but he couldn't fool you. Ain't nobody could fool your nose, Sharkstooth. You knew him as good as I, an' there weren't a time he come in, didn't have a treat fer you. Peculiar, though, ain't it?" He scratched his head in contemplation. "There bein' two men wid such a name as 'Rudy'? An' being wid Miss Theodore."

Only partially convinced, he wandered away, leaving the imprint of his nose against the glass and wondering what had happened to turn the world upside down.

Rose did not look back and Rudy had no thought of doing so. Not until they were well out of sight did she speak.

"I know you are tired, but it is not much further. Are you up to walking, or do you wish to rest?"

"What must we do?"

"Two things. The first is close at hand. There," she indicated, pointing toward a low, weather-beaten structure. "The sailor's chapel."

"Are we going to pray?"

"No, Rudy. We are going to pay our tribute to Neptune."

Perking up at the mention of so familiar a name, he quickened his steps, leading the way to the small building. Running his hand over the woodgrain of the slats, he sighed in satisfaction.

"I know this building."

"Indeed, you do. You took me here many months ago. You put a coin in the poor box. For the widows of the men lost at sea. Since that time, I have never failed to do the same every time I pass this way."

"Is that why we are here? To help the widows?"

"That," Rose admitted, drawing out her farmer's purse. "And to thank Neptune for returning you safe to me."

"Neptune," Rudy repeated, feeling an odd sensation of awe in pronouncing the word. Confused by the image, however, he turned to her, eyes wet with rail-like moisture. "Was I away on a long sea voyage?"

"Since I saw you last, you have crossed the Atlantic twice. Therefore, I am twice blessed. We will pay tribute for your voyages."

"That is a good thing. Never forget the gods, Rose," he remarked with sudden sharpness. "And never challenge them. They are more powerful than either you or I."

"So I have been led to believe," she responded, failing to hide the bitterness from her voice. After noting his expression of hurt, however, she softened her tone. "How much shall we leave?"

"How much have we?"

Opening the change purse, Rose deposited the contents into his palm. There were seven coins of various denominations, one button and five pound notes. Not surprisingly, it was the button which caught his eye.

"Why do you carry this?" Picking it up, Rudy scrutinized it carefully, narrowing his left eye as though the item were a precious stone and not a two-holed discard. Tilting her head so the rain poured down her side farthest from the building, she started off into the billowing ocean.

"As a reminder."

"Of what?" he asked, wrapping his fingers around the button, then shifting his weight so that he, too, could stare out into the vast beyond of crashing waves.

"Never to forget that little things matter as much as big ones."

"Explain," Rudy pleaded, forgetting, in his eagerness, the tribute they had come to pay. The purse fell from his hand, into a puddle. Neither noticed.

"When you went away from me the last time... to go to war... as I knew you would... I found myself worrying. Day and night I could not sleep for fear you were in danger. I worried about you being struck by bullets as the Union forces surrounded Atlanta; of a stray cannon ball bursting into the hotel room where you slept. Afterwards, as time went on," Rose continued, curling up the ends of her cap to keep the drizzle from her face, "I worried you did not have adequate funds with which to purchase the necessities of life."

"Thank you," he commiserated, making a tiny wave with his own wet hand.

"It came to me one day when I was in London. I had just come from the bank. Making a rather substantial deposit. I had no other business to transact, so I took a walk. Through the finer districts, out into the poorer quarters. Where the children gathered in groups like unwanted urchins as their fathers were out of work because the textile mills were shuttered."

Marching forward, Rose took three military-precision steps, turned, then high-stepped back.

"It made me feel sad. Responsible. I wanted to do something. It was then a small girl came up to me and held out her hand. Reaching into my pocket," Rose demonstrated, going through the motions, though she had no other coins in her pocket. "I offered her a sovereign. She looked at it and did not recognize it as money. To her, it had no value. It was nothing to put in the pot and eat for dinner. There was another child... a girl, wrapped in a blanket. It was very small; hardly covering her thin arms and legs against the cold. When she moved, it fell off. Trying to hold one end up, the other dragged."

Grasping her own rain coat, Rose placed her fingers between the fastenings.

"'Buttons,' I said. If only she had buttons, she could hold the blanket close. So simple a thing as a button would have made that child's life easier. But she had no buttons... and probably had never seen one in her life."

"So you gave her your coat," Rudy supplied, shivering, then clamping his teeth so as to hold them quiet.

"What I did is of no consequence. But I learned a great deal that day. My Rudy was out there," she continued, marching in place yet leaving no trace as the rising water obliterated her muddy footprints. "He was cold and he had no buttons with which to fasten his – blanket. What good was money to him? He could not eat it. He could not drop a pound note into his pot and gain relief from the cramps and the hunger pains. Money, I realized, is not such a precious thing."

Retracing her path a second time, Rose stretched her arms, engulfing him in her arms. Whispering into his ear, she finished the story.

"The button reminds me never to take anything for granted. To live life as it is happening. To hold dear what is precious. To say 'I love you,' at any and off times. To apologize when I have given offense; to forgive those who trespass against me. You," she concluded, kissing him on a cold ear, "carry your coins to pay the ferryman. I carry my button. Neither of us dare spend our treasure, yours for the afterlife, mine for the present. But we make a good pair, do we not?"

"The best," he avowed, fervently pressing his lips to her brow and inadvertently knocking the brim of her cap so that water rushed freely over their conjoined faces.

"Give it back to me."

He complied, placing the small object into the square of her palm. When he went for the farmer's purse, however, he could not find it. Wailing in despair, he searched his pockets, coming up empty.

"Rose, I have lost our money."

"But not our love."

"We have nothing to leave.... For Neptune."

Straightening her back, Rose stared at the pitiful collection box, its rusty lock a child could pick, hanging with desultory despair against the elements.

"Then it is not yet time to pay our tuppence. It is clear, is it not?" she demanded, drawing him away from the protection of the building, so that the sleet pelted against his rubberized cape. "Our gift was not appropriate. I have a better one."

"What?" The pleading in his voice was a verbal depiction of the lock box.

"You will see. Come. We have not far to go."

She began her trek but he did not follow. Turning back, she bit off her admonition to hurry when she saw his hand extended toward her. Flushing with emotion of the type reserved for precious moments, Rose remembered her button and her pledge. Stepping back, she grasped his hand, covering it with her own.

She had him and she would keep him. She would treasure the moment, more precious than gold or all the tea in China.

Looping her fingers in the air, Rose Theodore tied the tiny, insignificant button between them, so that only their own hands could undo the fastening and part them.

That, she prayed, was acceptable to Neptune.

CHAPTER 36

Lightning cracked over the horizon, briefly illuminating the white-capped waves. Like disembodied fingers, they rose, grasped, strained, then disappeared, only to reform a moment later and repeat the process.

Standing at the wharf, Rudy and Rose were alone. No mere mortal cared to brave the elements. Even the stray cats had abandoned the area, seeking shelter and perhaps a handout from friendlier hands.

Without the sun, the two human beings cast no shadows. Standing still, a passing observer, his cap pulled low and his tread hurried, might have mistaken them for abandoned pilings, remnants, perhaps, of a bygone era. It was August, and the storm-laden air hung heavy, making it difficult for the uninitiated to breathe.

Such could not be said of the wayfarers. They were of, and about the ocean, nearly as much at home looking, as they were asea.

"I am glad you brought me here, Rose," Rudy admitted, strangely refreshed and leaning forward in acknowledgment of the irresistible draw. "For as long as I can remember – for as long as I have lived – the waters have called me. Standing here, so close... makes me feel alive." He groped for the word. "Hopeful." Turning his gaze away from the hypnotic effect, he scanned her ruddy countenance. "Is that too much to ask?"

"For hope?" He nodded. "No, Rudy. Hope is what life is all about."

He considered her statement, then withered.

"Am I alive?"

"As alive as you ever were," she affirmed, raising a hand to her brow to shelter her face as she watched the waves.

"But I have changed."

"Yes."

"Too much?"

"No."

"The boys... the crew. I fooled them."

"I know."

"Into thinking I was the same Rudy Blake. It was an act."

"For a while, you even fooled yourself."

Shifting his weight, then moving so the breeze caught him in the face, he distended his nostrils, a dolphin coming up for air.

"Is that a good thing or a bad thing?"

"Both."

"Explain it to me," came the plea. Rose took a step away, then pointed toward where a flock of gulls had gathered beneath an outcropping of wood.

"You are like a bird, Rudy. Look there." He followed her direction, taking in the varying shades of white and grey feathers covering the large avians. "If you didn't know better – if you had never seen a bird – you could hardly guess those creatures could fly. Watching them there, you would imagine they traveled by foot, hopping around the shore, pecking at the carcasses of fish washed up."

"I might."

"Writing... in your journal, you would describe their feet, the way their toes spread, giving them balance. The curve of their beak; the peculiar way in which they squawked to one another. You would count them; search for nests. Returning another day, a fair and sunny afternoon, you would scan the heavens, seeing far off specks floating on the currents of the air. You would marvel at the way they moved their wings, adjusting for altitude, dipping and diving with the ease of flight. You would make a diary entry, describing a different sort of caw; jotting down their coloration of brightness and fluorescence as the sun's rays sparkled off their feathers."

Casting about, Rose stooped to pick up a piece of driftwood. Cradling it in her hand a moment, she balanced it, then tossed it forward, toward the gulls. Those nearest flapped their wings, some resettling, others taking flight.

"Not until your third trip would you be enabled to put it all together: birds walk and birds fly. The revelation would stagger you. It would be wondrous; a joyous thing."

Desperately trying to catch her drift, Rudy watched as the gulls circled overhead before settling back among their companions.

"Tell me," he pleaded, moving his eyes from the birds to Rose and back again, as though the polling of his vision would reel in the idea.

"You always were two men, Rudy. One which walked and one which flew. Some people see only your legs. They presume you to be a businessman; or a gambler. Or a pirate. How they base their judgment depends on circumstance. What you allow them to see. How you act."

Taking his hand, she guided him along the dock.

"Unlike a gull, you have the conscious ability to represent yourself the way you want people to view you. You project an image which suits the occasion. You let them believe money is your god. That you are impervious; a man with a devil-may-care attitude. That nothing can harm you. That you are... almost always right. And when they catch you in a mistake, you turn it around, so that they ultimately believe the flaw is in themselves and not you."

Spying a low-shrouded object in the distance, Rose picked up her pace, dragging him along. Their footsteps make loud splashing sounds as they traversed pools of water, squeaking the old and waterlogged boards of the pier.

"Then, there are others; those who see you only in flight. To them, you are a scholar and a gentleman. The Earl of Winchester and his family, for example. They have never seen... never imagined your dark side. There are others; Cora Sommers comes to mind. She loves you with the faithfulness of a disciple." Stopping suddenly, Rose indicated the distance. "What do you see?"

Squinting through the patchy layers of fog, he identified the tall masts of a clipper ship. His breath caught in wonder.

"A sailing vessel."

Nodding assent, Rose continued on, their bodies disrupting the low-lying clouds, so near to earth they teased the observer into believing the sky had abandoned them.

"Only when a person gets to know you, Rudy – really comprehends that you are not one man or the other, but both – like those birds – can he or she fully comprehend the true spirit residing with."

"You, Rose," he identified, holding up his left arm which had begun to throb.

"Me," she acknowledged. "John Paul. Waterbucket."

"Names from the past," he whispered, trying to negate her argument. She ignored him, crossing so near the gulls they all rose as one, flying up and away from their protection.

"There are times, Rudy Blake, when you do not know, yourself, which man you are: the man with legs or the creature with wings. You overlook the obvious for the moment; the image you wish to portray at any given time. That which *suits* you," she added, darkly grimacing.

To avoid her expression, Rudy craned back his head, letting the rain pelt his cheeks as he stared ahead. As his eyes widened, his tongue snaked out, absorbing the falling moisture as a sponge.

"I know that ship."

Losing impetus for the argument, Rose placed a hand on his shoulder. "Indeed, you do."

"Is this why you brought me here?"

"Yes."

"To see this ship?"

"To see it," she admitted. "Shall we go closer?"

Using his tongue to wipe the remainder of the water from his dripping mustache, Rudy assumed the incentive. Although his footsteps were uneven and irregular, he made his way unerringly across the remaining planking, finally halting when they were within a stone's throw of the ship.

"I had forgotten," he spoke, the fog gathering around his face so that his breath appeared to be emerging in a cloud of frozen condensation. "She is still here."

"As you said she would be. There never were any buyers."

Releasing a sigh from deep within his lungs, Rudy shivered. With the keen vision of a man born of sun and wind and wave, as he once stated, he took in the skeletal masts, stark and lonely against the grey backdrop. Without treading the decks, he knew them to be covered with green slime, slippery and treacherous. The ropes, once so carefully wrapped around cross-bars, would be rotten, the tar binding the ends together long worn off, so that scraggly shafts protruded.

Moving his hand, he felt the grip of the great steering wheel, long detached from the inner workings. Cabin roofs caved in, aft decking splintered, yard arms sagging, paint peeling, figurehead missing, barnacles growing in profusion up the sides.

"A ghost ship," he identified, feeling his spirit both drawn and repulsed by the wreck, so that he tottered unevenly, buffeted by the memory of those who had served and those who had lost.

"Shall we go aboard?" He did not ask why. Guiding him further down the pier, Rose indicated a row boat. Without the leverage of two good arms, his descent was awkward. She waited until he was settled before joining him.

A half dozen strong pulls brought them to the side. A rope ladder hung from the port side. It was new and smelled of fresh hemp.

"You have been here before."

"I have," she replied, meaning "many times." He did not inquire further. "You will have to climb one-handed. I had not expected that," she confessed, the apology unspoken. "Go before me; I will steady you."

Grasping the rope with his right hand, Rudy pulled himself up, feeling the strength of Rose's two strong hands around him. With a huff and a grunt, his feet met the first step.

"A second," he pleaded, catching his breath. This time when he panted, the tendrils of fog dissipated, clearing a space for his wet shape. A moment, thirty seconds, then he moved upward, one rung at a time. The process was laborious but steady. As his hand wrapped round the railing she gave him a boost, hurtling his body aboard deck. Before he had recovered his equilibrium, she had joined him.

"The name of the ship. I have forgotten." His request was low and sad, as though he dared not raise his voice. Responding in kind, she answered "The *Tea Biscuit.*"

"Ah. Yes. It comes back to me. She has soaked long, has she not, Rose? In elements as cruel as tea to a biscuit."

"Aye."

"She was a China merchant vessel, once, if I remember. But I do not know her history."

"Make it four years ago," Rose began, leading the way across the deck, "half her crew was lost at sea. 'By the mismanagement of her captain,'" she quoted, without saying so. "He was a foreigner; not British, but a man well-versed in the art of seamanship. Or so the owners thought. He had captained other ships but none so large."

"They handle differently," Rudy acknowledged, wandering away from her toward the wheel. Once he had reached that destination, he gripped the worm-eaten spokes, staring upward where no sails blew.

"They were caught in a storm; a bad one. Unprepared for the ferocity of the gale. Sleet made the decks torture to traverse; one of the masts snapped." Overhead, another, or possibly the same flock of gulls, flew overhead, the sound of their wings eerily approximating sheets flapping in the wind. "Some were washed overboard; others froze to death at their stations. By the time they reached port, the third mate was in charge."

Joining Rudy at the wheel, Rose ran her fingernail against an encrusted protrusion, scraping away the years of neglect. Catching his eye, she indicated the coin, nailed to the shaft.

"Not so lucky, was it?"

"No. God help them." Stooping over, he examined the misshapen gold. "No one thought to remove this."

"Do they?"

He hesitated, then shrugged. "Usually."

"Why?"

"As a token of remembrance. Because," he continued, looking away, "it is valuable."

Removing a pocketknife from her jacket, Rose pecked away at the wood, finally prying the coin from its long-standing guardianship. Scrutinizing it carefully, she rubbed it against the rain cap until a corner of it glistened.

"Rose. Why have we come here?"

"You know the answer."

"To put her to rest."

"To lay to rest the *Tea Biscuit* and all her lost souls. And to relive the past, if you will allow me. I missed my chance, once. I would have gone with you."

Reacting sharply, Rudy stared at Rose with bleak incomprehension. She was not fooled, however, for his intake of breath betrayed him. As emotion spread, working its way from inside to out, so that his skin prickled with remembrance, he sniffed, then wiped his eyes with the tenderness of a mother comforting her own child.

"The *Molly Fae?*"

He pronounced the name with dreaded hate, as though it were a curse he cast after long and harsh consideration. Although she had before never possessed the certain identification, Rose fully comprehended the significance. Her own lips curled in distaste.

"Josias Rutledge's slaver. The one you destroyed."

"With all souls aboard," he underscored, jerking his body to indicate the innocent as well as the guilty.

"Yes, Rudy. With all souls aboard."

Quivering like a winter leaf, he grasped Rose, shaking her for all he was worth. "You will do this with me?"

"I am prepared. Come."

Leading the way, Rose took him to the edge of a descending companionway. Pointing downward into the dark, murky depths, she indicated a cord.

"A fuse. It leads to a cache of gunpowder. Thirty barrels."

"That will blow her to Kingdom Come."

"That, sir," she avowed, wiping a loose strand of hair from her face, "is the idea."

He began to nod, then caught himself. Squinting to sharpen his eyesight, he pierced her own blue eyes.

"What gunpowder?"

"That which I purchased some time ago," she conceded, raising and lowering an eyebrow. "For transportation to that last bastion of human servitude. It never reached its destination. Here, I think, it will serve a better Cause."

A smile of understanding fleetingly passed across the indentations of Rudy's sunken cheeks.

"I presume you did *not* buy the ship."

"No," Rose conceded, tucking the package of candy sticks deeper into her coat packet. "I did not."

"We are here to perpetrate vandalism?" The question, lightly offered, carried with it an undertone of worry. Gone, for a time, was his eagerness to participate in illegal acts.

"The ship's legal owners long ago put the *Tea Biscuit* up for sale. Since that time, they have moved, changed addresses, dropped out of sight. No taxes have been paid in some while. The ship, as she sits, actually belongs to no one. She is a – blot – on humanity. A reminder of sins, past and present. We are here to consign her to the deep, where she belongs."

"Give a ship a bad name, you might as well scuttle her," Rudy offered, appeased and mollified.

"I have heard that said. In other contexts, I would disagree. But not here; not now."

Awkwardly lowering himself to his knees, Rudy penetrated the darkness of the ship's interior. Brushing aside a strand of rope, he pointed below.

"How have you stacked the barrels?"

Remembering his foray of a similar nature, she grinned. "In a closed space. No windows; no ingress of wind. The air is heavy with black powder. The absent striking of a match, the spark of an officer's saber, and – boom!"

Pausing to watch a spider scurry away from its broken trap, he contemplated her words.

"Rose, you are dangerous. You never forget a thing."

"The picture you sketched for me of the warehouse in Atlanta is as vivid as if I had been there, myself. The Anderson brothers, was it not?"

"John and Richard. I wonder what became of them?"

"They survived the Federal occupation and have turned their swords into plowshares. The factory now produces metal springs, screws, nuts and bolts. Their next project is the manufacture of railroad iron."

Clearly surprised, he captured the spider between his fingers, taking care not to damage the spindly legs. "How do you know this?"

"I received a letter from them; addressed to you, of course. Enclosing a draft for your share of the profits and outlining their plans. I deposited the money, then wrote to the bank in Atlanta, instructing them to grant your partners a full line of credit."

"You did? Really?"

"Assuming that was your wish," she gently answered. "To rebuild the South. Inasmuch as you retained control of the Southern Central Railroad, I felt it was a good way... for one hand to wash the other."

"Good God! And I thought never to go back," he cried, torn and exhilarated by the idea. "Rebuilding the South was the dream of that other Rudy Blake."

"It is my job to see both halves are soldered together to make a stronger whole. Are you ready? Shall we light the fuse?"

Carefully depositing the spider into the recesses of his pocket, where he hoped it would survive until released on land, Rudy shakily offered up his hand. Grasping it with firm determination, he was lifted to his feet.

"Yes."

"The honor, Rudy Blake, is yours." Handing him a packet of waterproof matches, Rose removed one Lucifer stick. Lifting up the end of the cord, she fingered it. "It will burn slowly. Time enough for us to get back to the rowboat and safely away."

"That," he remarked, scratching the match absently against his lightly stubbled cheek, "is what I thought last time. And nearly died regretting my rashness."

"You had better hope my calculations are accurate, for I cannot swim. If we are flung overboard, it is you to whom I shall cling."

"Hardly an appealing thought for a one-armed man. We shall count on your natural buoyancy to keep our heads above water."

"It was not 'heads' you were thinking of," she teased, satisfied to see the color rise to his cheeks. "And if my natural endowments hold us up, I will personally write of the exploit to the London *Times.*"

Groaning loudly, he backed her off. "I believe you would." Crossing himself hurriedly, then casting a final glance around the woe-begotten deck, he struck the match, bringing forth a piercing blue-orange flame. Addressing the ship, he spoke. "To the sea you were born and to the sea we return you."

"Amen."

Touching the fire to the fuse, he watched it catch, then tossed it down. A stark hissing tracked the progress before sound and sight were lost to the depths.

"Let us be gone."

Hand-in-hand they returned the way they had come, Rose descending first so the captain might be the last to abandon ship. As his feet slipped from the rope ladder to the boat, she hurriedly rowed them away, disregarding the overlapping of waves sloshing into the bottom.

She had pulled seven times before an explosion rocked the interior of the *Tea Biscuit.* Smoke bellowed from the hatch, followed closely by a second and third blast, which cascaded waves, the height of a whale, over their heads. Burning timbers rained about them, splashing close, the fire aboard them quenched in an instant.

His nose stinging from acrid smoke, Rudy coughed, spit, then lifted his rain cap from his head. Flinging it away from him, he added that personal touch to the drowning of the ghost ship.

As the rotten deck caved inward, ten billion sparks were vomited toward the heavens, lighting the sky with preternatural illumination. The lone mast swayed, its once proud footing crumbling beneath, so that it hovered a moment, caught between shadow and substance, before tottering madly, a wayward seaman on his final voyage. With a dip of its lofty top, the mast came crashing down, spanking the uneven surface of the water with a resounding slap.

As the waves grew higher, Rose rowed furiously, baring her teeth in vindictive retribution. Following Rudy's example, she removed her cap, rotating it madly over her head before setting it sail. When it dropped to the water, the ship let out a final breath, a gasping of released air, before exploding into pieces. The aft portion broke away, plowing several hundred yards into the sea before succumbing to gravity. As the quenching fires roared protest, it sunk, setting free the spirits, sacrificed by mismanagement and neglect.

"Hurrah!" Rudy cheered, voice already hoarse from the effects of the ash. "Hurrah!" and then a whoop of pure joy, the like of which she had never before heard.

With the oars in her hands and her hair soaked from the brine, Rose Theodore sat witness to the last Rebel yell.

CHAPTER 37

Noting the crowd of onlookers gathered on the wharf, Rose steered down the coast, finally pulling the boat to shore in a little cove, far from curious stares. Placing her soaked feet down into the pebbly sand, she dug herself in, then turned to give Rudy a hand. Lifting one leg over the side, he straddled, half in, half out, before regaining his equilibrium. Using her shoulder for balance, he maneuvered the other leg out and into the shallow water, before shoving the boat back. It rocked unsteadily, righted itself, spun so that its bow faced eastward, then drifted away.

Grinning sheepishly at her bemused expression, he splashed in the water before altering his position so that he could keep both Rose and the boat in view.

"For the rats?" she suggested.

"No. Whatever four-legged creatures once habituated the *Tea Biscuit* abandoned ship years ago. Most likely with the last of the cargo. Rats are sentient creatures, Rose: they can sense danger better than most men." His arm stiffened, then spasmed, pantomiming the action of a swimmer. "The expression 'rats deserting a sinking ship' is no exaggeration. I've seen them hurtle themselves overboard in droves and paddle like hell for safety, while men on deck loitered like fools."

Smiling at the image his words conveyed, she indicated the boat. "You have cast it away. To be rid of the evidence?" Rose suggested, grasping her wet hair and flinging it backward, off her face. "Surely two people were witnessed leaving the scene."

"Not for that reason," he scoffed in so old and familiar a tone her heart caught. Stamping his feet, his shoes made low, squishing noises as water expelled from the soggy leather.

"For what, then?" she prompted, holding her breath in expectation for what she prayed he would say.

"To give us an edge." Climbing up the sloping, rock-strewn shoreline, he slipped, straightened himself, then turned back, offering her a hand. She willingly accepted the offer, daring to steal a glance at his eyes. They were dark and focused, matching his tone. "Never forget that I am a gambler."

Suddenly awash with an inner glow, Rose found her fingers curled around the gold coin they had taken from the *Tea Biscuit*. Unknowingly, it had become their stake in this revision of a very old game.

"I am always looking for advantage," he continued, setting the pace. While it was a matter of no consequence to match him, stride for stride, she would not have done so, had she the power to sprout wings to do so. "I never sit down at a table without sizing up my opponents. Their strengths; weaknesses."

Pausing spontaneously, not from exhaustion, but from a desire to absorb the vista of the sea, his hand tapped absently against his thigh.

"Here, Rudy."

Undoing the fastenings of her rain cape, Rose dug into the recesses of her jacket, withdrawing a pipe and tobacco pouch. Accepting them as a boy of six might have held out his hands for buried treasure, his face lit with unmitigated joy. Being deprived of the use of his left hand, however, he could not pack it. This she did for him with the comfort of one long-practiced.

When the pipe was perched between his teeth, she struck another match. He bent, dipping the bowl over the flame, then inhaling deeply. Stray chards caught, then soon the outer rim glowed with red. He puffed contentedly before resuming the narrative.

"Which gambler knows the rules; which is easily bluffed. Who will lose gracefully; who can afford to lose."

"Who has friends in high places; which one might wear a concealed derringer," she encouraged, watching as the smoke curled from his lips.

"Exactly. In some quarters, gambling is considered a game between gentleman. Those who ply it for a living know better. It is a contest of strength. Endurance. Courage, if you will."

"I will."

Removing the pipe, Rudy picked a bit of tobacco from his tongue, then resettled the briar more comfortably in his mouth.

"A professional learns the tricks of the trade; how to amend the fickleness of fortune. He marks cards, subtly slices corners, makes burrs only his fingers can feel. He palms aces – depending, of course," he chuckled, remembering the late conversation with BoBo, "on whether the ace is played as the high or low card."

"Precisely so," Rose agreed, striking another Lucifer so that he could relight the tobacco. When it had burned to her fingers, she blew it out then dropped it down, lingering to listen to the low sizzle as the damp earth extinguished the glowing head.

"Whatever it takes to win, he summons to his command. That is the 'unwritten rule,' not found in Hoyle, yet accepted the world over."

"As long as he is not caught."

Winking at her, Rudy puckered his lips and blew a smoke ring.

"If you are not caught, then no crime has been committed. Where is it found in law that the loser may seek redress from the gods for his lack of luck?"

"Nowhere that I have ever read. Which never stopped anybody from trying."

Grumbling agreement in his throat, Rudy resumed their walk.

"The gods do not listen to plebeians," he snorted again. "They have their favorites. Which does not always equate to success," he added, glancing upward. "Their caprice is well known." They both shuddered and let it pass. "Nor, does it mean they are averse to a gift, or two. An... acknowledgment of their power. That, Rose," he continued, staring off into the distance where the small row boat was nearly, but not quite, out of sight. "is why I set her adrift."

"In case you might need her...." Rose's voice lowered. "In the past."

Nodding thoughtfully, he drew on the pipe before tamping it down with his thumb.

"Because something has happened is no guarantee it will stay that way. Who understands the eddies of time, Rose? Who can say a mighty hand might not go back and change what was?" Catching her eye, he sought approval. "Who can take a chance?" Sucking inward to burn the tobacco more hotly, he shivered. "I blew up the *Molly Fae* and swam for my life. I was struck by some of the debris and nearly drowned. The next time that scene is replayed, it might be that I flounder... lose strength."

"In which case, you will need that boat," Rose whispered, drawing nearer to shield his body against time. "I approve."

"I thought you would."

"And I also acknowledge," she vowed, "and state for any to hear, that I will be in that boat, pulling you to safety."

Rudy dropped his head so swiftly he nearly lost his pipe. Fumbling for the briar, he steadied it, then held it out. Taking it from his cold hands, Rose placed the mouthpiece between her own lips, struck a match and relit it. This time, she puffed on the deep, rich tobacco, rolling the smoke around on her tongue before returning it to the master.

Taking care to place his own lips where hers had lingered, he smoked in silence as they observed the fog-laden clouds descend over the unending horizon. When there was nothing left of either the rowboat or the *Tea Biscuit,* and the noises of the distant crowd had dissipated out to sea, they turned their backs, effectively closing one adventure, while leaving the door open to others, yet unwritten.

He was cold, hungry and tired. Rose sympathized with his plight, but she was not yet ready to turn her back on Liverpool. Not when there was one stone left unturned.

"Are you game?" she asked, gently placing a hand on his forehead. His flesh burned with fever, causing her to regret the action. If he were not up to one last trip, their journey would end unfulfilled.

"I am game for anything," he lied badly, forcing a smile to his pale, sunken lips. "What now? March on the Customs House, demanding a repeal of the import tax?"

"Not a bad idea," Rose conceded, drawing him into the shadows. The walk back to the city had been a long, tiring one, requiring frequent rest periods. Lingering in the outskirts now, they found themselves alone. Not wishing to take any chances, however, Rose scanned the area before addressing him.

"It has stopped raining. Let me take the rain cape from you. That is," she added, knowing his weaknesses, "if yours weighs as heavily on you as mine does on me."

"Gladly," came the confession.

Raising his one good arm, she grasped the rubber ends of the slicker, raising them over his head. Once free, he breathed a sigh of relief.

"Water logged," he explained. She was only too glad to agree.

"Weighed several hundred tons." Tossing both capes aside, Rose critically inspected his bandaged arm. The sling was damp but the underlying layers of shirt and gauze remained dry. "When we get back, I will change the sling. Otherwise, you are 'shipshape' and ready for duty."

"Aye, aye, sir," he responded, touching four fingers to his brow. "What, next?"

"Just one final reckoning and then we are free."

"Another adventure?"

Spoken lightly, there was in his tone the expectation of dread. She rapidly reassured him.

"Not so much an 'adventure' as..." Failing to discover the correct word, Rose shrugged. "As a good-bye for the present."

"To the ocean?"

"No, Rudy. We shall never say farewell to the sea. It is as much of us as air and food. A final acknowledgment to the gods."

Perking up, he sought explanation from her inscrutable countenance. "Where?"

"Back to the seaman's chapel."

"Is that where they hide?" he whispered, caught up in her deliberate obfuscation.

"It is as good a place as any."

Nodding in enthusiastic agreement, Rudy allowed himself to be guided ahead. Their journey would have been made easier by taking a carriage the short distance to the chapel, but Rose did not wish that. Although those who had been drawn to the wharf to witness the sinking of the *Tea Biscuit* had returned home, the spectacular scene over, she did not want to be identified as having been in the area. Too many questions with too few answers would undoubtedly point a finger in their direction.

Crisscrossing the narrow, one-way streets, cobbled from stone hewed by the dictates of long-forgotten architects, they made their way unerringly, finally coming out a block above the chapel. The wind had come up, blowing steadily from the south, carrying with it the prospect of a change in temperature.

Six months ago, on January 10th, 1865, Jack had delivered the belated news of Rudy's enlistment. The word, he said, came from a ship's captain out of New York. She had asked only one question: Which side? The answer had been preordained.

Rebel.

She did not inquire how such information had been obtained. It was enough to confirm her worst suspicions. Long the stalwart of proclaiming "the War is not my concern," Rudy Blake had enlisted in the Lost Cause, as she knew he would. What she had not known, and never held with any certainty, was that he would return. That fact accomplished, it was finally time to pay their tribute.

Earlier, the time had not been right. The sinking of a vessel out of time had altered the circumstances. Within her possession was the bribe.

Sidestepping puddles, then shooing away a curious cat, once considered to be a familiar to witches and demons, Rose guided him, the penitent on his way to the Holy Land. There was nothing else to say. When they arrived, he would know. And not a moment before.

The moon rose slowly in the sky, illuminating their way. Peering out from behind the clouds, it shone, a beckon of light from a hand mightier than any which walked abroad that night. In the distance, a bell tolled. She did not pause to count the chimes. No need. Time was no longer their enemy but their friend.

The building stood out in stark contrast to its surroundings, its weather-beaten sides a bastion of faith and the endurance of hope. Ushering him alongside the lee wall, Rose let him catch his breath before producing the gold coin she had taken from the doomed ship.

"Here, Rudy. Gold."

Plucking the treasure from her hand, he warmed it in his own, feeling the heat radiate from his life's force through the precious metal. When it was sufficiently hot, he held it out, peering through the nail hole into the dark heaven.

Closing one eye, he squinted through the aperture, observing the night sky.

"What do you see?" she asked, resting a hand on the poor box for support.

"I see time, swirling around me. Billowing waves. Dolphins leaping. I smell salt and tar."

"What else?" Rose encouraged, tensing her muscles.

"I hear the tolling of a bell. The lapping of water. My feet on solid earth. I see... anger."

"What else?"

The muscles in his neck grew taut, while the slivers of moon beams, filtering through the clouds, appeared to grey the hair at his temples.

"Great trial and tribulation." With a cry of frustration, Rudy dropped his arm, letting it sag to his side.

"Give it to me," Rose demanded, taking the ostensive crystal ball from his clenched fingers. Raising it to her own eye, she peered into the future.

"What do you see?" he demanded, leaning too near and thus obscuring her view. Annoyed, Rose stepped to her left, the side of the devil.

"I see the end of one life and the beginning of another. I see," she decided, forcing herself to bear down on the enshrouded vision, rather than relying on her wishes. "Love."

"Love? Give it back to me," Rudy demanded, impatiently shoving her aside in his haste to retrieve the coin. Shaking her head, Rose denied him. She did not listen for the cock to crow, for this was only the first and not the third time.

"Enough. The gods grow impatient. It is time to pay Neptune his tuppence. We were refused once this day. Now we have the proper offering. Give it," she demanded, "And be done."

The overpowering command of her sentiment overcame his own quest to know the future. Reluctantly accepting the coin which had brought no good luck to those who manned the ill-fated *Tea Biscuit,* Rudy rolled it around his palm.

"In the name of all which is holy: to those who have lived and died and are yet to be born, I offer this, our sacrifice, to that which watches over the fates of Men."

So saying, he dropped it through the narrow slot, listening to the dull thud made by the priceless coin with resignation, born of a gambler whose existence depended upon the caprices of the gods.

"It is done, Rose."

"It is done," she confirmed, making the sign of the cross between them. "As God has marked you with scars depicting the crucifixion, so now we have atoned for past sins. Let us put behind us the past, marching forward to face what we will with charity and resignation."

"And good will to men?" he asked, fingering the lock which would not have kept out a babe.

"Good will to all?" Rose questioned, a smile dancing over her face. Clucking her tongue, she rolled her eyes before winking at him. "Let us not promise too much, for we shall be held accountable for our vow. The gods on Olympus," she reminded him, pointing upward, "are listening. Let us say, instead, 'good will to those who stand on the side of –'"

"Right." he finished.

"As good an answer as any. Right," she repeated. "Let us pray we recognize them when we see them."

"And that they recognize us."

"Amen."

"Where to?"

"Wherever our feet take us, Rudy Blake."

Slipping her arm through his, Rose drew Rudy close, inadvertently catching sight of his reflection in the small brass bell, suspended from a bent hook over the poor box. They were not the same bright, devil-may-care orbs she had first encountered so many months ago, but neither were they the eyes of a corpse. All things considered, she had many blessings to count.

Neptune, she decided, had accepted their offering.

Momentarily disengaging herself, Rose delved into her pocket, withdrawing the package, wrapped in fish paper. Breaking the knot with her teeth, she extracted two peppermint candy sticks. Giving one to Rudy, she popped a second into her own mouth, so that they both held protruding candy sticks from between puckered lips.

Whistling a jaunty tune, the lyrics of which were either bawdy or sentimental, depending upon one's point of view, Rose Theodore and Rudy Blake left behind Neptune, the wreck of a ghost ship and the Atlantic Ocean.

There would come a time when they faced each in their turn, but that time was not the present. What lay ahead of them was healing, peace, adventure and adversity. In whatever order, and to what degree the gods ordained.

The End

GSFE

ALSO BY: S.L.KOTAR AND J.E.GESSLER

A character based historical 1950's courtroom based murder mystery entitled "**The Hugh Kerr Mystery Series**"..

- Book I   **The Conundrum of the Decapitated Detective**
- Book II   **The Conundrum of the Absconded Attorney**
- **Book III**   **The Conundrum of the Sins of the Fathers**
- **Book IV**   **The Conundrum of The Two-Sided Lawyer**
- **Book V**   **The Conundrum of the Clueless Counselor**
- **Book VI**   **The Conundrum of the Loveless Marriage**
- **Book VII**   **The Conundrum of the Executed Defendant**
- **Book VIII**   **The Conundrum of the Jettisoned Jury**
- **Book IX**   **The Conundrum of the Perjured Pigeon**
- **Book X**   **The Conundrum of the Haunting Halloween**
  - **Party**
- **Book XI**   **The Conundrum of the Tuneless Tunesmith**
- **Book XII**   **The Conundrum of the Meddling Motorcar**
- **Book XIII**   **The Conundrum of the Blundering Bear**
- **Book XIV**   **The Conundrum of Shooting Fish in a Barrel**
  -
  - **To Be Continued!**

Next a series is "New Beginnings" a 1950's medical drama.

- Book I   **The Believer**
- Book II   **The Heretic**
- Book III   **Arrow Song**
- Book IV   **Peas In A Pod**
-
  - **To Be Continued!**

"the ReproBate saga" is a character based series in the 1860 American Civil War

- **Book I**   **Beneath the Rose**
- Book II   **skull and cRossBones**
- Book III   **Redefining Bastions**
- Book IV   **thicker than Blood**
- Book V   **prioR Battles**
- Book VI   **Requited Blasphemy**
- Book VII   **The waR Between**
- Book VIII   **To Richmond or Bust**
- Book IX   **carrying Battlescars**
  - **To be Continued**

Stand-alone novels include:

- **Catman** *He was every man; he was no man*
-
- **ONE** Science Fiction space travel

- **Shepherd of the Kingdom** a modern-day horror classic

Non-Fiction

"The Kepi Magazine," A publication specialized in the Civil War and 19th century life. The complete set, updated with an comprehensive index, is available again in print and electronically as :

- **The Kepi Volume I and II**
- **The Kepi Volumes III and IV**